DEAD
SUBMARINER

DEAD
SUBMARINER

DONALD
McDONALD

BREWIN BOOKS

BREWIN BOOKS
19 Enfield Ind. Estate,
Redditch,
Worcestershire,
B97 6BY
www.brewinbooks.com

Published by Brewin Books 2022

A CIP catalogue record for this book is
available from the British Library.

ISBN: 978-1-85858-751-6

Printed and bound in Great Britain
by Severn

In memory of Bandido.
My friend… my mentor.

Donald McDonald. Drawing by Enrico Fornaini, Pisa, Italy.

ABOUT THE AUTHOR

Donald McDonald has been writing and telling stories all his life; his imagination being fired by Saturday morning cinema in Worthing and his first hero Black Bob in *The Dandy* during the fifties. After the Suez crisis his family moved to Malta where he attended the Royal Naval School in Verdala.

Donald became a schoolmaster after graduating from Birmingham University School of Education though he has had a variety of jobs including advertising copywriter, assistant cinema manager and scaffolder's mate.

While his novels *Ignatius-Tagg* and its sequel *Sunshine for the Righteous* were published by *The Daily Mail* as one, titled *Ignatius Tagg – Dark Horse* and critically acclaimed by Amazon book reviewers, his American novel – *9/12 Another Day* – was published by Harper Collins (New York) on their authonomy site.

He has a canon of work including screenplays, stage and radio plays and having written the definitive sequel to the original *The Italian Job* film, he hopes Columbia Pictures will consider it.

Dead Submariner is Donald's fifth novel published by Brewin Books, his previous four: *The Bridge, For the Glory of Stevenson, A Village Tale* and *9/12 Another Day* also garnered five star reviews on Amazon. He is currently penning *Someone.*

His passion for film, sport, books and art remains intact and he has travelled extensively in Europe and America; no trip to New York is complete without a visit to Madison Square Garden (and he still believes Stanley Ketchel was, pound for pound, the greatest fighter).

He now lives in Lincolnshire and supports Birmingham City FC and Widnes RLFC.

The Stars Move Still, Time Runs,
The Clock Will Strike.

CHAPTER 1

U-boat 116 is still on patrol.

The jeering was loud. The cheering was louder. The bet was on. Engine Room Artificer Willie Schultz had challenged everyone, he could walk the length of their new submarine type VII C and name everything he passed with accuracy. Of course he would wear a blindfold.

He had declared his invincibility on the penultimate night of shore leave when everyone, himself included, was blind drunk and the officers who'd got wind of this decided to have their fun a mile out of St Nazaire.

He was spun round, jostled, walked forwards and backwards and eventually stood alone at the external torpedo tube, "After Hydrophones behind me!" he shouted. Everyone was there, packed tight and under instruction not to breathe a word. The Officers, Chief and Petty Officers, Engine Room Artificers, Seamen and Communications, Engine Room all collectively took two steps back as the square-shouldered bruiser from Lubeck walked U-boat 116. His grin was that of a Cheshire cat, supremely confident that it has disguised the fact that it has licked a bowl of cream laid out next to strawberries for Mother Superior's 95th birthday in a convent.

"Steering Compartment, aft escape hatch, auxiliary machinery, stoker mechanics mess, fifth watertight bulkhead, main motors, diesel engines, external torpedo tube." He swivelled and waved his hands like a conductor. The crew were reluctantly impressed and interest began falling off.

"Kapitän's quarters, store, third watertight bulkhead, magazine, ward room, number two battery Engine room, Artificers' Mess, Petty Officers' Mess." Suddenly it was dawning on some of the crew that they really were back at sea, where a different kind of loneliness and separation had to be met and overcome once again, including what U-boat men referred to as 'sad, nervous and jumpy'.

By the time the immodest submariner reached the torpedo tube department only a couple of officers made up the audience and they were wracking their brains as to what form of practical joke they could play on him during the next thirty-seven days…

U116 continued to roam about the Atlantic with its cargo of death but after three weeks had still not engaged the enemy though its weight had been reduced by losing tons of oil. The crew had stood watch, eaten the best food, drank oceans of coffee and digested unhealthy smells. The inevitable rhythm had been found, the routine established. Everyone on board was familiar with every manometer, pipe, valve, handwheel, lever and the snake nest of cables and no one bumped their head from bow to stern; the correction of posture was instinctive or subconscious, even in complete darkness. On deck the howl of the wind, despite late summer, was depressing and the boat's constant bobbing up and down against the sea complemented perfectly the submariners' apathy.

They had little appetite for food not helped by youthful Rostock radioman, who for five days and nights had picked up nothing but position reports from other boats. Everyone craved action and "damn the consequences" remarked Franz Overath the First Watch Officer. He was a confirmed bachelor from Leipzig with an ever increasing bushy beard who'd had an altercation on the final night of shore leave with a bar owner in St Nazaire – a cold, stern little man with a heaviness of paunch which looked like it would buckle his spindly legs at any moment. It was all over his bullying manner with the young barmaid, "I should have walloped him," he muttered to himself when he thought about the incident and he'd already decided that would be his first destination when the patrol was over. Not even two days, resident, in the Sistine chapel would have changed his mind.

On the twenty-third day came the official announcement from a Seaman Officer, "09:30 practice dive, 10:30 instruction for Petty Officers, maintain course 'till noon." When asked by a German journalist what the difference between a civilian and a submariner was, the engine room had declared, "A civilian struggles to cope with change, a submariner struggles to cope with the 'same old thing'."

It suddenly changed. The radioman leapt out of his seat and handed a message to the relieving Watch Officer. The decoding machine was slammed on the table and he began tapping keys. A senior officer snatched the decoded message and rushed to his commanding officer in the control room, bent over a sea chart with dividers in his right hand and the Navigator stood to his right. The words "convoy sighted" were like manna from heaven. Quick calculations were made and agreed at full speed the enemy would be engaged within twenty hours. The U-boat's complement experienced a collective catharsis and now rushed the boat eagerly towards its quarry; fuel raced through the pipes.

The orders came in a rasping tone, "Watch Officer steer three hundred and twenty degrees..."

"Check dockyard repair to crankshaft Chief..."

"Give me last observed position of the enemy..."

When the second watch assembled in the control room to relieve the lookout, the Helmsman blurted out with barely restrained joy, "Course three hundred and twenty-five degrees, starboard diesel running full speed."

At last the crew could relax when the Chief announced, "Repair good the port diesel is honourable." Everyone knew the only scum that oozed out was nothing to get too excited about, for now.

The challenge to each submariner's endurance and seamanship was building by the hour and one thought concentrated all their minds – the outcome… Gone was the brooding about sacrifices or the cost in men, the suspended activity after the initial adrenaline rush, an anti-climax was a real test of patience. It was known that in these circumstances the submariner sharpened all his senses – it was possible to smell a ship by her funnel gases. In fog, acute hearing was developed and sometimes it was possible to pinpoint a destroyer by her wash, the thrash of her propellers, the pounding of diesels and the whine of boiler fans. Even shouted orders on deck could carry.

The watch felt they were standing in the jaws of wind and sea and despite the oilskins, sou' westers and layers of clothing, each aggressive wave soaked and chilled them but only physically… The engines throbbed incessantly until U116 was inside the killing zone. Then she submerged. The Hydrophone Operator, a picture of concentration, mumbled, "Sound bearing 49° very weak."

The Navigator again examined the charts. He was certain "Periscope depth." All eyes went to the manometer needle that slowly moved backwards over the scale. Only the silence of a tomb and burr of electric motors was heard. The waiting had begun. Every word was a whisper,

"Flood tube four."

"Open torpedo doors."

Another whispered voice, like that of a fallen woman in the confessional, barely audible,

"One and two ready to release."

The enemy's course, Bow, Direction and Range had been meticulously calculated by the Watch Officer. The Commander had his hand on the firing lever and when the ship moved into the crosshairs, two torpedoes exploded out of the tubes.

"Close torpedo doors, dive to 175 feet… both engines full ahead."

The hunter now became the hunted as destroyers broke in well-rehearsed drills, away from the merchant convoy. Below, silence was the order. All the cooling machinery stopped and streams of sweat ran off each man. "Post fifteen, steer two-three," said the Kapitän. Again unbreakable silence. By altering another fifteen degrees U116 continued to edge until yards off the destroyers' line of advance. It was the difference between life and death for any explosion twenty-five feet away would tear a hole in the side…

"She's coming in close again," the whispered voice croaked before a crack of thunder rocked U116; light bulbs exploded, gauge glasses shattered; and she lunged and whipped, spinning like a large metal drum. The officer's eyes went to the aneroid barometer – the air pressure had not increased therefore the skin had not been punctured. As a precaution checks were quickly carried out throughout, in case the aneroid had jammed.

Through earphones the revolutions of the destroyers' propellers creeping up, again the course was changed, "Starboard ten, steer two-six," the Kapitän said softly.

Another hour passed, more explosions, more changes of course, more toil and sweat, and then finally, relief. "Kapitän it's fading, the revs are the same but it's fading." U116 maintained her latest course at seven knots, one hundred and five degree track.

Finally periscope depth and nothing visible but sea and sky. "Surface. Equalize pressure." Compressed air hissed in followed by eagerly anticipated fresh air. "Prepare to blow tanks, clear for ventilation." The Skipper's voice, authoritative not harsh. As a precaution the Diesel room were told to stand ready to dive.

The experienced officers knew they had secured their target, they didn't need evidence… What they did need was strong coffee and Marlene Dietrich singing to them. It was the post-match tradition.

Before midnight fresh intelligence reached them. A second attack, then they could go home. A new rejuvenation snaked through the boat and even for those on watch, in heavy oilskins and polished binoculars in hand, an uninhabitable sky became just as entertaining as the frothy spray layer waves threw up. Suddenly the wretched trial of patience lost its vigour and sleep was easily reached from bow to stern as U116 reached fifteen knots on the surface of a relatively calm Atlantic Ocean.

At the first light, the submarine descended beneath the waves and final calculations made. Three hours passed before she rose to periscope depth; the Chief had the boat firmly in hand as there was no trace of excessive buoyancy.

"Up periscope," the information was relayed as though it was from a log journal.

"Destroyer bearing 80° range 550 yards... run silent." The Helmsman was ordered to steer 240°, while the Navigator plotted the information at the chart table. U116 ran deep for almost two hours and mugs of strong coffee were circulated before the torpedoes were reloaded bow and stern.

On the Commander's order she raced to periscope depth and he scanned every horizon like a vulture. The timing was impeccable. Four torpedoes released, two tankers blown to smithereens and black clouds billowing high into the sky above a scorching red inferno. Both Seamen Officers were invited to look and the jubilation of seeing lines of fire rising high into the sky was tempered by the thought of men dead or dying in prolonged unbelievable agony...

The Navigator wrote down that flames were visible at 240°. Shortly afterwards the Radioman, his face tighter than a drum, informed the officers that an SOS had been picked up from British Ships. Then one of the wolf pack messaged U116 that it had sunk two merchant ships followed by depth charge pursuit and altered course. No submariner ever gloated at naval men in the sea holding on to a thread of life, for each knew the likelihood was that one day it would be himself unless entombed on the sea bed. The orders were strict – no picking up survivors unless airmen as it was perceived they had vital intelligence.

A battle damaged tanker running at seven knots, course 130°, was worth the risk despite angry destroyers with their sleekness of manoeuvrability, hunting and blessed with the latest sonar equipment.

Direct hit amidships, followed by blazing oil and never ending flames. Two more torpedoes were fired at Merchant ships but the damage was only temporary and the Kapitän decided not to push his luck but ran deep and continued with the ongoing repairs necessary after the previous depth charging. He confided in his officers, despite radiograms coming in from other U-boats declaring tonnage sunk after engagement with the same enemy.

U116 set a course thirty-five degrees at the most economical speed that would get the boat back to St Nazaire with litres of oil to spare. Now everything depended on the Chief Engine Room Artificer and his mechanics. Fortunately they were considered the best, even among rival submariners, for they worked as though guided by some primitive minor force and while some of the crew listening to the noise of battle in their head and were too terrified to move, these men revelled in what their Kapitän referred to as 'stubborn pride'.

When darkness fell, U116 rose and took her place on the surface, bumping and rolling southwards at a pace that was another wretched trial of patience because all around them, above and below, the smell of death hadn't deceased. The temptation to increase speed was occasionally overwhelming and each of the officers knew it would be foolhardy. There was an atmosphere of such self-conviction and God-like authority that any rival opinion would be immediately shattered at first contact. Heroic.

Supposedly out of harm's way, yet that could change in an instant and a routine established for light hours and dark hours, depending. The single men's' thoughts turned to waitresses with bobbing breasts wearing white peekaboo blouses, permanent teasing smiles and carrying endless trays of beers. They couldn't care less if the sky became a hard blue, a soft blue or a ghostly black. A warm bath, a wet shave, a decent bed for two and a proper cooked breakfast would soon be the order of the day...

These thoughts sustained them, helped them feel they were clinging to the top of the world but all were savvy enough to know that the collective submariners' victories were always pyrrhic in nature... Now wasn't the time for sour faces or maudlin reflection; it was a time for raised spirits and who was going to make out the leave permits as land could be seen on the horizon and the aroma of air gradually changed.

Eight hours later the diesel was run at a speed enough to hold the boat against the tide and it didn't matter that most of the crew had mouths as colourless as old scars, they were home. A further attribute of charming manners completed the image of a king returning to his fiefdom with a lust for life; and for young single submariners that translated into wine, women and song...

CHAPTER 2

He wasn't the best but he was destined for greatness and that was probably why he wasn't the best. His name was Peter Werner, Kapitän U-boat 116 and he had that much sought after commodity – presence. The sky over the Atlantic took on the hue of custard on early October mornings and it was refreshing for those in the conning tower to be able to breathe in air they couldn't see. It was a welcome change, but, always only a respite…

Two hours earlier, following incessant rain, the sun had finally burned through cloud cover bringing St Nazaire docks to life. The crew of U116 stood erect, proud on the deck while a military band played popular tunes and service women, most resplendent in uniform threw flowers towards the submarine. Despite the seeming joie de vivre, it was a sombre moment, for every submariner was wondered if this might be his last mission; and for those with a soupçon of hangover it was worse…

The Kapitän stood with two Seamen Officers in the conning tower; he was strong yet sensitive, an experienced man and his voice was rich and clear like a deep sounding ship's bell. Little wonder his crew adored him, saw him only as a true naval man not a Nazi gangster or opportunist. When it came to the safety of his crew, Peter Werner revealed an eternal vigilance.

The trio were joined by First Lieutenant Dieter Hoffman whose gaze was taken by a seagull flying overhead. The quartet looked at the bird thoughtfully, before Werner retreated below having patted his First Lieutenant on the shoulder. All points of the compass were covered by three pairs of binoculars fixed to alert eyes which scanned every horizon. Above, the sky retained its secrets and God sat alone, waiting – every submariner was acutely aware there was no such thing as an atheist in a steel can, below being depth-charged by Destroyers above.

In his cramped spartan wardrobe, Kapitän Werner though divorced, looked fleetingly at the framed picture of himself and his wife before opening his logbook and writing in it 'October 6th 1942'. He continued writing in pencil before reading, softly, his entry – *The crew are in high spirits. They hide their melancholy even if some of them are beginning to believe in their own immortality. God permitting, we will be home for Christmas.'*

In their quarters, the crew were laughing and joking despite the air fetid with diesel fumes and the stifling claustrophobic atmosphere. Almost any movement involved a physical touch but they were used to it; some played cards while others looked at photographs of loved ones and the soft sound of music playing over the P.A. system offered a balm of sorts to these men one step from eternity; and whenever it came to battle stations their souls merged with the rhythm of the toil.

Mother Nature heaved her sigh as the sun began to set late afternoon and the three crew in the conning tower looking for evening aircraft could put their binoculars away. Dieter Hoffman glanced at his watch; his face was pale having leant against the chill wind for over an hour.

"Give it another half hour then get below," said Hoffman.

"Sir," was the immediate response.

He descended and stretched his six foot frame out as best he could before weaving his way to the Kapitän's quarters. A gentle knock on metal to the right of the curtain and Peter Werner greeted him, gesturing for him to look at the map of the Atlantic that covered his desk.

"Take your coat off… sling it on the bed," said the Kapitän as he began measuring distances on the map. Hoffman inhaled deeply and opened the U-boat's diary.

"We will rendezvous with the rest, four days from now," he tapped the map with his compass before continuing, "about here, Dieter, then we will wait." He smiled and his strong-featured face seemed in repose.

"This is the bit I dislike immensely, it is tiring and morale falls amongst the men. It is an unseen presence that taxes us all… different from the pressure of battle."

"I know what you mean Kapitän," replied Hoffman almost in a whisper.

"Hey!" boomed Peter Werner, "we win because we have fire in us and our fires never go out… We should not be so melancholic after all we have hardly started the trip." Both men smiled and it lit up their faces. Hoffman addressed his Commanding Officer,

"Let's hope everything is like the last three trips, the tub is in good shape and Friedrich has done us proud again with the engines."

He paused, "It is a small thing, Kapitän, but worth mentioning. The new fuel tanks beneath the engine aren't to Friedrich's liking… he said it is not an improvement, maybe in looks but he is worried whether it will take unrelenting pressure even though the design engineers insist it is stronger than ever."

Neither officer looked unduly concerned.

"No one knows submarines like Friedrich," said Werner. "I will talk to him, he is something special… always professional about his work but difficult to know… somewhere in his life there has been tragedy…"

"Forgive me Kapitän but you sometimes have that look but carry it differently…"

The Kapitän smiled and changed the subject. "Tell me Dieter how is Marlene, the two girls and young Dieter?"

There was no mistaking the pride in the First Lieutenant's voice when he responded and he almost threw his shoulders back, "Fine, Marlene says Gabi is already a proper little lady," both men laughed, "full of airs and graces and now won't let her sister into the bathroom while she occupies it!"

Werner's eyes were shining, "It is over four months since you saw them." He paused in conciliatory fashion, "it is a long time."

Hoffman was a man of substance, stoical and had a voice synonymous with a lifetime smoking cigars, "Such is war. I must be thankful to God they are well and their letters are a comfort... Some men I have served with hadn't been home for nearly a year – so many missions."

A wistful expression appeared on his Kapitän's face as he spoke, "It won't last forever. The allies know they cannot afford to lose merchant shipping at the current rate... Soon the bubble will burst. Unfortunately many of the men are thinking in terms of the war being over within a year..."

The First Lieutenant remained effervescent and made no apology for interrupting Peter Werner, "You must admit that our success rate is phenomenal and it would be crazy to let up now." He chuckled and continued with boyish enthusiasm, "We are feted as heroes back home, bigger than the Luftwaffe much to Goering's chagrin."

His Kapitän nodded slowly, "Yes, Goering's chance has come and gone."

Both officers' attention was taken by the map once more, but before they could scrutinise it in detail they were interrupted by Seaman Officer Wolfgang Emmerich.

"Kapitän."

"Come in."

Emmerich, a precise man, lean with piercing blue eyes, drew the curtain across the flimsy rail. "I have just come up from up the engine room and Friedrich wants to know if he can look again at the valves that were installed in the docks.

Obviously he tested all work carried out in the dockyard before we sailed and was satisfied in his own mind. I think he wants to reassure himself again."

Hoffman looked at the Seaman Officer, "Does he think there is something wrong?" There was no trace of anxiety when Emmerich replied, "No, but Friedrich doesn't leave anything to chance, which is just as well."

The two officers looked at the Kapitän who grinned then said, "Tell Friedrich we will give him two hours tomorrow."

Werner looked at the map and pointed with his index finger, "We should be about here by mid-afternoon and weather reports are still favourable."

"Thank you Kapitän," responded Emmerich vacating the area.

"He's a good man, Emmerich… The only one who ever has any enthusiasm left by the time we get back to Port."

The officers exchanged smiles and Hoffman quipped, "Maybe when he gets married it will be different."

Peter Werner drew the curtain back and looked to see if any crew were in earshot before addressing his Lieutenant in a quieter tone, "We have the problem of a missing crew member. Fortunately the men have kept it quiet and that's the way I want it until I have seen Gunter Kessler and listened to his side of it. I don't want one of my crew court-martialled over something that might be trivial… There is no excuse for missing departure but I know Kessler will have a heavy heart right now. He's a good seaman and besides, he has my lighter."

The arrival of chatter and laughter was heard beyond the curtain and Hoffman waited until it passed before he spoke, "How will you discipline him, Kapitän, and keep it from the authorities? After all," he sighed and tilted his head to the starboard, "he can't hide for two, three months. Someone is bound to report him."

There was no compromise in Werner's reply, "That's his problem."

CHAPTER 3

In the engine room two crew men, stripped to the waist, were checking components and making adjustments where necessary. The gleam of the steel was mightily impressive and both men knew as the mission progressed this lustre would fade and they would become wild-eyed because of the dust and weary from a lack of sleep but wouldn't change their lot for anything else for here they were kings.

Seaman Officer Wolfgang Emmerich looked about, shouting above the noise, "Friedrich... Friedrich!"

The chief Engine Room Artificer suddenly emerged from the torpedo bay. His hair was close-cropped, his eyes alert, his upper torso coated in sweat and he wore the obligatory smile on his face. After the Kapitän, his was the most difficult job and everyone admired him, loved him, for often their lives depended on his muddling through when everything seemed lost. He pulled the upper part of his soiled overalls back up, threading his arms under the shoulder straps, his name tag just about visible across his top pocket.

Emmerich approached, "Ah Friedrich, Kapitän says he will give you two hours tomorrow, weather permitting."

The Artificer nodded agreeably while rubbing his hands with a thick rag. Emmerich turned to leave then suddenly turned back, "By the way, Kapitän says don't worry about the new structure." His words elicited soft smiles from the crew members.

The Atlantic threw its own version of early evening, different to that of the mainland and the submarine type VIIC almost silhouetted against the sky moved smoothly at twelve knots, way below maximum.

In the men's quarters the crew including Jorgan Bahn, Karl Boeck, Horst Kruger, Herbert Rasch and Franz Seilerman were tucking into bread, sausages, cheese and drinking hot coffee; they were ravenous. Ernst Bortfeld, the affable Cook, a comical figure with chins and stomachs to spare and the butt of every crew member's jokes, but with steely eyes held court as he picked up his knife and slashed a melon in half, splitting the fruit across the small table. It was spectacularly ripe and his grin of pleasure contrasted perfectly with those crew who expected it to be rotten. He cut segments off and handed them around.

Peter Niester the boyish looking Steward coughed up, "Mmmm, not bad eh, my compliments to the Chef... everyone."

Horst Kruger chipped in with, "Hey, Cook, not bad, not bad," he belched before he continued, "but not as good as that restaurant in St Nazaire."

The men laughed and he continued, "But I will say one thing, you are prettier than that fat bag who served me, even if your tits are about the same size." Wolf Hechler, the Hydrophone Operator who recently joined the submarine, nearly fell over with laughter. He couldn't resist banging his mug on the table, "Come on, let's see them, come on." Like an impromptu kangaroo court the noise level rose out of control and filtered throughout the submarine. Hapless, the grinning Cook obliged and the men cheered before dropping to their knees all singing *Lilie Marleen*.

Horst Kruger yelled out, "A toast!" then raised his mug, "to absent friends – Gunter..." The men responded in unison, "Gunter!" Horst continued in a whimsical manner, "Who's getting the real thing, right now – Gunter – she must be some woman for you to miss ship." He raised his eyes then continued, "Don't worry Gunter, we'll do your work but when we get back..."

Suddenly all the men stood up and like a well-trained choir sang, "When we get back," they looked to Horst and he continued, "the drinks will be on you and I shall relieve you of your friend."

The men cheered and it was their voices that revealed the quality of the vessel's company – voices of the brave, capable of making any enemy tremble.

The Commanding Officer and his First Lieutenant were in his quarters; both smiled as they listened to the jollity whilst also eating sausage and cheese. Hoffman spoke,

"This crew is special… they know when to play and when to work."

Werner nodded his head, "Submariners are the same the world over, Dieter."

He paused, "But you are right, the crew have brought something special to this can. It is essential to get the right mix among officers and men, no prima donnas, just honest men prepared to do their job no matter what befalls them."

Both drank coffee before Hoffman changed the conversation, "Hans is hoping for a girl this time. Two boys is enough and his wife Angelika, wants a daughter so she can name her after her own mother."

Werner interrupted him, "Hans misses his wife, you know, I just don't mean…" He left his sentence dangling and his First Lieutenant responded,

"I know what you mean."

Werner continued with calm authority, "I sometimes watch him off duty looking at, rather gazing at, photographs and re-reading all his letters. I have seen how men can be affected by the absence of home life, Dieter. I wonder how he will react the next time we're under real pressure. He's been fine up to now."

Hoffman was quick in his response, strong and virile, "Hans will be OK. We are close, I know him perhaps better than you, don't be misled by his appearance. We both attended the same training school. You will not be disappointed."

Werner poured more coffee into their mugs, "I hope you're right." He resisted the old cliché about a chain only being as strong as its weakest link but knew as every submariner did that no other vessel presented poorer living conditions than that of a U-boat. Away for two or three months unable to bathe, shave or change clothes, even the Kolibri, a cologne used to control body odour was often ineffective.

Kapitän Werner had always insisted that the crew were as one whether they were specialists such as radiomen, torpedomen or machinemen responsible for the operation and maintenance of equipment. Even the ordinary seamen responsible for general duty tasks such as loading torpedoes, operating gun decks or standing watch on the bridge which was frowned on during stormy weather when waves swept over the conning tower submerging the crew for brief periods, even the issue of special foul weather coats did little to keep them dry.

Crew habitability ranked low on the priority list of the German High Command and was a constant source of friction between them and the admiralty. Fresh water was limited and strictly rationed whereas privacy was non-existent, often the crew resorted to 'hot-bunking' as soon as one man crawled out another crawled in to grab desperate sleep. In order to maximise space, the forward torpedo room also formed the crew quarters.

First Lieutenant Hoffman had watched the food being crammed into every nook and cranny available hours earlier, including the toilet and it brought a wry smile to his face as he looked at the last mouthful of coffee in his mug. He knew that those fresh loaves of bread would, very soon, sprout white fungi in the damp environment and everyone would have to be content with canned food supplemented by a soy based filler called Bratlingspulver. His Kapitän asked him what he was thinking about.

"Diesel Food, Kapitän," he grated and both men couldn't suppress their laughter and then they roared when the Kapitän remarked,

"At least forty men will be grateful the flush system has a new hand pump... no more emergencies, eh Dieter."

Before leaving the Kapitän's quarters the Lieutenant remarked,

"Seaman Officer Fiebig has devised an addition to the usual pastimes to keep the men occupied."

Werner tilted his head back, indicating for Hoffman to continue.

"A lying competition where everyman on board has to participate."

The Kapitän smiled, "Ah, maybe someone will show up as Goering?" and then he chuckled as did the other officer for there was no love lost between the Luftwaffe and the Navy.

Suddenly the Kapitän took on a serious demeanour, "It's important, away from the heat of battle, the crew don't paint a vision of emptiness... Even after all these years I find it a struggle not to see trees, hills, land where I can put my feet rather than the deck."

Hoffman nodded for he was hearing nothing new. He chortled then left the cramped space while the Kapitän pondered the idea of reducing the seamen working in three eight-hour shifts: one for sleeping, one for regular tasks and one for miscellaneous tasks. In the past he had tried to ease the specialist crew's workload such as two radiomen on three/four-hour shifts between 8am and 8pm and two six-hour shifts during the night but it wasn't feasible.

Once human noise died down only the rumbling and cranking of metal parts and the constant burr of the engine was heard, it was relatively soothing, not beach-bunny perfection but a buffer against more facial worry lines caused by inchoate inner struggles...

CHAPTER 4

Joachim Reiz held rosary beads in his hand and a smile of self-satisfaction, despite closed eyes, stitched on his face. It was a ritual he followed during the sober hours on board and the crew respected his religious affiliation even the atheists who always abandoned their religion once depth charging began. The twenty-four year old native of Berlin opened his eyes and hissed in the direction of his friend Uve Stührmann, opposite.

"Hey, Uve. Wake me in an hour and don't forget, I don't want Friedrich breathing down my neck because I've overslept."

Stührmann, a Hydrophone Operator, born and bred in the cultured city of Dresden to parents who had rejected the Nazi ideology as bestial, smiled then stretched his arms parallel with his body, "OK, Joachim. Don't worry." He paused and smiled staring at the bunk above him, "and I hope you said a prayer for me."

"Don't forget," Reiz retorted in his boyish accent then turned and closed his eyes.

Two steps away Conrad Meiner, a rabid follower of Hamburg football team the city of his birth, was spread-eagled on his thin mattress looking at a picture of his fiancée. He caressed her face with his index finger and noticing Franz Seilerman approaching attempted to put the photo back in his shirt pocket.

"No, let me see," said Seilerman in a genial and homely manner. The photo was passed and studied,

"She's a fine looking girl" he smiled, approvingly. "She reminds me a lot of my wife when she was twenty. The blonde hair cut in the same style too." Despite his rugged appearance and obvious physicality, Seilerman was a sentimental man at heart and he passed the photograph back,

"Do you think you will get married or am I being too personal?"

Meiner smiled, "No, Franz, we were engaged when I was last at home and we plan to marry in the New Year." He then whispered, "I haven't told the others. You know they say it is bad luck to talk of next year, especially under the waves."

Seilerman crackled with conviction, "Superstition, no more, superstition."

The younger man continued, "How long have you been married?"

Seilerman laughed, "Ten years, ten happy years that have produced two boys." He reached into his back trouser pocket, "Here." He took out his wallet and extracted a photograph of his family from it, "Take a look." His pride was obvious.

"They are healthy looking boys. I bet they are proud of their father. I can see what you mean about the likeness between your wife and Elsa."

"Ah, Elsa. So that is your fiancée's name?"

Meiner nodded and Seilerman continued, "The next extended leave we get I am going to make arrangements to move the family from Berlin, it is too industrial." He paused as though an ominous foreshadow had suddenly flared, "I want to bring them up in the country. You know that is where my wife and I were brought up. How we ended up living in Berlin is still a mystery to me," he faltered and threw up his hands and Meiner chuckled as Seilerman put his wallet, with photo, back in his pocket.

"Get some rest, you will be on for two hours at eight." He instinctively pulled the blanket up onto Meiner before walking away and the latter looked at his photograph once more before closing his eyes.

The quarters were still and those resting retreated into themselves, all sharing one hope that when they woke up their gallantry hadn't deserted them and their constitutions remained robust. In training school those selected to go forward as genuine candidates had been told repeatedly until it was inked into their soul that submariners were a breed apart that their mind and soul must be as certain as their body, that way they would have the potency of a hero without the callousness of a brute. The routine for the next two months had just begun.

Kapitän Werner sat at the cramped desk in his quarters, humming along with a song playing at low volume over the submarine's speaker. His logbook was open and he gazed at the black and white photograph of his submarine taped to the wall above. He could recite, in parrot fashion if necessary, that it was of type XC, once of the larger long range boats that the U-boat fleet Commander Karl Dönitz had intended to use on the periphery of the Atlantic. More than two hundred and fifty-two feet long and displacing one thousand two hundred and thirty-two tons, she was designed to operate most of the time on the surface, diving only when necessary for attack or escape. Her battery driven electric motors could propel her at seven knots while submerged, though her diesel engines offered eighteen knots on the surface. She was armed with a one hundred and five mm deck gun located forward of the conning tower and twenty-two torpedoes. Before returning to his logbook Werner spoke out loud, "And sixty crew including officers, there!" He couldn't resist a wry smile which wasn't the case with Lieutenant Hoffman who couldn't get himself comfortable in a seat as he wrote a letter and despite adjusting his position the pervading dampness still assaulted the rheumatism he was prone to.

No such problem for Seaman Officer Hans Fiebig, agile and self-assured, he cantered over the torpedoes he inspected using all his considerable experience. He winced in a theatrical manner when he thought of the two crewmen on watch in the conning tower with only a black sky and perishing cold for company.

CHAPTER 5

Waking from one's slumbers was often a blessing in disguise since the temperature inside the boat was considerably greater than the sea outside; moisture in the air condensed on the steel hull-plates and continuously dropped on sleeping faces. Added to this was the storage battery cells which were located under the living spaces and filled with acid and distilled water, they generated hydrogen gas on charge and discharge which was drawn off through the ventilation system. If this failed, an explosion was inevitable and if sea water got into the battery cells poisonous chlorine gas was generated. It all added up to make the sleeping arrangements extremely unhygienic. Little wonder submariners couldn't wait to clear excess mucus from their nostrils and shake off the effects of 'oil-head'.

Nevertheless, many men couldn't fathom why they dreamed of summer where Mother Nature heaved a waking sigh and let everything take its course – robins sang, woodpeckers knocked incessantly, peacocks strutted in visible glory and butterflies floated harmlessly above the scene below.

The crewmen getting up for their duty rota were unaware it was Friday though the rituals continued. Meiner yawned as he pulled his vest on, Eric Steven smiled at Horst Kruger as he twanged his braces over his shoulder and Karl Boeck with open-mouth looked in the small mirror picking at his teeth with a penknife he'd had since he was a boy. Each man was careful to avoid, not to intrude into another's space, despite the occasional jostling that happened in a confined area and no submariner ever expressed tears of hysterical relief related to avoidance…

Jorgan Bahn left his half-eaten sandwich between his front teeth as he buttoned up his trouser flies and still half asleep groggily made his way to the engine room where Friedrich Schreiber was adjusting tappets while two other crewmen worked in unison. One lay on his back adjusting the screws on an engine component while the other recorded the temperature gauge readings. Bahn heaved his chest up and down, "Everything is OK, yes?"

The Chief Engine Room Artificer nodded, "She is more graceful than any high-class whore in Hamburg." His sanguine remark caused the new arrival to laugh, "And she goes a lot faster too!"

Smiling through chipped teeth, Schreiber kept up the badinage, "And not so expensive… Jorgan, I want to go over with you the procedure for increasing speed suddenly, should the Kapitän ask for it in an emergency."

Bahn hesitated for a second, "I know…"

Schreiber interrupted him, "Not since we were modernised in the recent overhaul."

The heat in the engine room never ebbed away and both submariners mopped their faces with rags permanently kept in trouser pockets as they inspected different parts of the engine. Schreiber cursed when a valve loosened and oily liquid spurted out before the crew member lying on his back sat up and tightened it with a serene looking wrench before returning to his earlier position. When the submarine swayed slightly, the men in the engine room instinctively knew the Atlantic was throwing up a grey, rough day. It was wisdom borne from experience.

Not so fortunate were the latest off duty crew resting, trying to sleep in the cold clammy atmosphere. Suddenly an unfamiliar silence entered the U-boat and every sound from outside and inside was both startling and magnified. The steady drip of moisture off pipes and plates and the subdued voices of the skeleton watch in the control room checking the vessel's trim and air supply – even to the breathing of their fellow crewmen. Bernhart Frantz cried out with a vitality that couldn't be repeated, "It's Henry Morgan, the pirate come to haunt us, men!"

No one laughed, even his Kapitän thought some atavism had been at work in the making of him but the Kapitän was a shrewd man, he'd told his fellow officers that at sea, especially in battle, a person's rank and education wasn't a priority, "You care only about how well a man did his job, how he used his brains and skills to master perilous situations and keep the boat alive… so what if he has been in trouble with the law?"

Inside the control room Dieter Hoffman stood behind two Hydrophone Operators, Uve Stührmann and Wolf Hechler, also a native of Dresden. Both awaited instruction. The Kapitän stood observing.

"Pump ballast to Chief," said the officer with conviction and the boat began to rise.

"Fore planes hard a-rise… Aft planes up five…" The expression on each of the quartet's faces remained sharp and intense as the two Planesmen pushed the button controls and the depth gauge needles trembled and the rumbling of the motors got louder. Hoffman watched the depth gauge needles turning counter-clockwise while he carried the points of the compass in his head, "Boat rising two hundred… one hundred and sixty… one hundred…"

Kapitän Werner smiled and looked relaxed as the boat rose. At eighty he issued the next order, "Hydrophone search." Both Hydrophone Operators listened intently before Hechler turned to look at his Kapitän, shaking his head. Werner thought for a second, glanced at his First Lieutenant, then issued further instruction, "Continue." When the gauge reached forty-five Hoffman turned to his Kapitän, "Periscope depth, Kapitän." Tension entered the control room as Werner moved the periscope and looked through it swivelling, slowly. The Kapitän nodded approvingly and the periscope was lowered.

"Ready to surface, Kapitän."

All eyes were on him as he said assuredly, "Surface."

While he climbed onto the metal ladder leading from the control room through the lower hatch to the conning tower, Hoffman issued further orders,

"Blow all main ballast tanks."

The control room Petty Officer opened the main valves on the blowing panel and suddenly compressed air hissed into the tanks almost in angry fashion. Hoffman, while still bolt upright, relaxed his facial muscles,

"Surfaced."

The submarine rocked slightly with the motion of the sea and suddenly the noise of waves lapping away along the steel skins of the boat's exterior was heard. Kapitän Werner stood on the ladder also looking relaxed.

"Equalise pressure… Opening upper lid, NOW."

He gulped in the air and clambered up from the tower through the upper hatch to the bridge followed by the quickly assembled look-outs. He issued the final order,

"Blow to full buoyancy and stand by main engines."

When the engine room telegraph rang, the U-boat shuddered as the diesel engines were clutched in. Suddenly the rocking motion gave way to a forward surge which all the crew felt; and it brought a smile to Friedrich Schreiber's face as he mopped his brow and gazed lovingly as the rhythmical beat of the diesels grew to a roar.

The U-boat's bow nosed through the Atlantic drenching the watch in the conning tower with showers of spray. On the bridge, Peter Werner repeated his instruction to the Helmsman in the conning tower,

"Course two hundred and seventy degrees."

His flashing eyes told him they were seemingly alone in the ocean and this knowledge relaxed the slightly nervous ingathering of his eyebrows. He stayed for fifteen minutes before looking at his wristwatch and deciding it was time to return to his quarters for a scheduled get together with Seaman Officer Hans Fiebig. He hoped those men in the conning tower, besides carrying out their duty, would find time to revise their philosophy of life as he often did. Despite the harshness of the environment, it was ideal except, for any atrociously vulgar man.

Back in his quarters he threw on a cream-coloured polo neck sweater made from Scandinavian wool before pulling back the curtain when he heard clanking footsteps. He and Fiebig shared a glass of Schnapps and listened to music effortlessly coming through the P.A. system. Their conversation was relaxed and it was time to have a moan, which the Kapitän encouraged for he was shrewd enough to know anything bottled up that became a grudge might take a man's concentration away from his job and put lives in danger.

Fiebig grinned. "Sometimes the lead in my skull from those fumes drives me mad. I've never been able to get used to it," he said.

His superior smiled, knowingly and the Seaman Officer continued as more Schnapps was poured into the two glasses, "I must be growing old, Kapitän, even the heat, the cold or…"

Werner interrupted, his smile reminiscent of a sage, "The novelty has worn off Hans. It happens to those of us that were in at the start. I sometimes feel like Jonah inside some huge shellfish. The public think that it is all glamour and adventure. The training schools are full of young men; Dönitz has seen to that – he calls it the spirit of selflessness and readiness to serve."

Fiebig paused before responding, "You sound sceptical."

The Kapitän remained relaxed. "No, not really. The six month training schedule is rigorous enough. It is good that all potential submariners are familiar with U-boats under all conditions. Sixty-six mock attacks will keep men on their toes even if they haven't experienced the baptism of depth charges. But," Werner shook his head in solemn fashion and leaned towards his Seaman Officer. "The fleet is too small. Dönitz predicted the war will last seven years. Do you think the volunteers will be so enthusiastic once we start sustaining losses?"

Fiebig looked surprised and his eyes widened, "Seven years?"

His Kapitän nodded. "Yes, he remembered the mistakes of the last war when the submarine came close to breaking Britain. That's why he wanted three hundred U-boats but the Fuhrer disagreed. There were only fifty-seven when hostilities began. Not enough to wage total war and that's what is needed for mastery of the sea, Hans."

Both men shuffled in their seats to get as comfortable as possible before the younger man, whose family had lived for generations in Munich, spoke.

"But the fleet is growing." His words were full of optimism and whereas Werner didn't want to dampen any enthusiasm he was renowned for his honesty regardless of any situation.

"Is it too late… How long do you think the British will put up with these losses? They will find a way of stopping this runaway success of ours before long. They're not fools."

The sparkle remained in the Seaman Officer's eyes, "Since Prien sunk the Royal Oak at Scapa we have been the toast of Germany." His statement was full of genuine pride, nevertheless his Kapitän responded with what he regarded as the genuine truth.

"That was a propaganda exercise and the Bull of Scapa Flow knew it. Lady luck smiled at him during the mission. Something had to be done to continue the life of U-boats as part of Germany's fighting force after the sinking of the liner Athenia. Dönitz gambled and won. The longer this war goes on, the shorter will be a U-boat sailor's life expectancy. Prien himself is an example. We are not prepared for a long drawn out campaign." Werner shut his eyes and listened to the music, "I like this song, it reminds me of a weekend I spent in Bieber. Do you know where that is?"

"No Kapitän."

"It's not far from Marburg," he smiled then continued, "we had a lovely time. Sometimes I close my eyes and build up a picture." He opened his eyes and smiled at his officer, "Here," he looked around his cramped quarters, "sleep is a cobweb veil which the slightest sound will tear to shreds."

Fiebig stood up, "Thank you for the drink."

Werner smiled and as Fiebig drew back the curtain he returned to the map, laid out on his bed and studied it, thoughtfully.

CHAPTER 6

Early morning the following day in the tiny galley, the Cook Ernst Bortfeld, watched carefully as Peter Niester the Steward stirred a large pot of stew, Niester was a native of Dusseldorf before moving to Wiesbaden when he was eighteen months. With his trademark lugubrious expression the Cook enthused,

"Ah, more mould with a delicate hint of diesel methinks."

The Steward chuckled and laden with crockery, squeezed through a circular door towards the men's quarters. A couple of men helped set out places with plates touching one another on a drop leg table while others lay exhausted in their hammocks too tired to make any comment under the bright glare of a light.

Ribald laughter broke out when Wolf Hechler dressed in black shorts, dripping with water and a towel slung over his shoulders appeared. Immediately Horst Kruger and Ernst the Cook ridiculed him with whistles.

"Where did you get those whore's undies?" bellowed Ernst, without any degree of self-consciousness. Some of the crew smiled then laughed when they looked at their Cook. Horst Kruger gained everyone's attention before blurting out,

"Come on, Wolf, let's have it. Sshh! Quiet everyone... what did she say?"

The Hydrophone Operator indulged in feminine mannerisms before he offered a soliloquy,

"And now you have jumped off the devil's shovel I will make life sweet and rewarding. You brave submariners deserve every pleasure on your holiday from hell... Come here, you devil."

Everyone roared, as much for the fun as a brief respite from the numbing monotony. Even those crew members further down, playing cards, looked up as did a crewman assembling a model U-boat in the Bow compartment, on hearing the racket.

Ernst Bortfeld shook himself into a more wholesome frame of mind and threw his meaty, though strangely manicured, hands out in front of him.

"Wolf, you can give your talk on the grandeur of female attire," his wink was as subtle as a zombie stalking its prey through mist, "I'm sure you would win the Tall Story competition."

Horst looked surprised, "What are you talking about – competition?" He looked around for comment but none was forthcoming so he returned his gaze to the Cook who continued,

"Wolfgang, told me the Kapitän had decided to introduce something to keep our spirits high throughout the trip."

Horst interrupted, "Thirty allied ships a day?"

The men laughed and collectively leaned forward, their interest aroused.

Ernst Bortfeld spoke excitedly and rapidly,

"A Chess competition, Tall Story competition, a funny verse competition. First prize is…" he deliberately looked at Horst Kruger who responded,

"Don't tell me – Marlene Dietrich!" Again laughter filled the air.

The Cook attempted seriousness, "First prize – to be allowed off Watch duty. Second prize – to Skipper the submarine for an hour in place of the Kapitän."

Again Horst interrupted him with impeccable timing, "And third prize – get shot of the cook." Everyone cheered, more so at his next comment, "Roast him!"

Eric Steven pulled at the Cook's slab of gut while two crew members man handled him in horseplay fashion. The Steward cried out,

"Just think of all that crackling!"

Another crew member bellowed, "Yeah and all that grizzle."

Almost as a defence mechanism Ernst Bortfeld burped aggressively then broke wind ferociously for what seemed half a minute. The crew winced and stood back wearing disgusted masks before Heinz Stegemann, another Planesman, smirked then looked at the crew, "I think you've hurt his feelings."

The Cook deliberately broke wind again then tilted his head backward, "Ach, it's useless talking to you numbskulls… I get more sense out of my parsnips," he turned and ambled away as the Planesman and Steward exchanged winks.

To keep the mood jovial Peter Niester spoke with warmth, "Think just over seventy days to Christmas, tomorrow one less and the day after… We shall all be back in Germany."

Wolf Hechler cried out and his words rippled around the quarters, "And I shall be drunk…again!" Everyone laughed despite the shadows beginning to appear on the men's faces.

"Tell me when you're not, Wolf, other than here," flashed Peter Neister.

Planesman Max Frommer, not noted for his ebullience but considered the most reliable in a bar room brawl, of which he was a veteran practitioner, said in a flat tone, "If anything bit you it would die of alcoholic poisoning."

It almost killed the badinage before Karl Boeck, the latest recruit to the crew and not yet twenty-one, said in all innocence, "Do you know what I look forward to most?" before he could say anything else he was assailed with ribald comment and guttural laughter, nevertheless, he persevered and it took nerve, "A traditional Christmas dinner, nothing spared, a feast that lasts from midday until midnight."

Suddenly everyone went quiet and the silence was unnerving before the Steward extended the young seaman's sentiments,

"There's something special about Christmas being with your family and friends." His words planted a flickering wedge of sentiment beneath the threshold of the submariners' consciousness and more silence filled the space before he continued quietly, without any physical gesture, "Everyone seems so much happier – silly things like sitting by a roaring fire, eating nuts or dates," he chuckled to himself. Suddenly the quiet was broken by a sudden jolt and clanging noise that momentarily unsettled the men.

However any tension was alienated by Horst Kruger's cry, "Can we have a new driver?" Smiles re-appeared on some of the men's faces.

There was no such thing on Ernst Bortfeld's face as he scrutinised the long, long list of supplies taken in for the voyage and distributed in every available space on board. He started reading aloud making a mental note of where each item was stored. Following an inventory made with the boat's Steward he had given a list to the Kapitän and the First Lieutenant,

"Right 494 fresh and cooked meats, 238 lbs sausages, 4,810 tinned meats, 325 lbs preserved fish, 3,800 lbs potatoes, 3,400 lbs vegetables, 1,200 lbs of bread dough, 600 lbs fresh eggs, 900 lbs fresh lemons, 2,500 lbs other fruits, 400 lbs honey, 600 lbs butter, 300 lbs fresh preserved cheese, 1,800 lbs milk, 200 lbs coffee, 400 lbs sugar." He breathed in deeply and it was a moment of bliss when his pencil point made a mark on the list and he signed it off, dated it and then laughed.

"Oh yes, a 100 lbs of chocolate... Make sure I keep mentioning that to the Kapitän... some sweet tooth he has." Despite the ebullience, often he had a rather sad, quiet voice and ponderously he stood up, stretched and groaned as fibrositis reminded him of its presence.

"Peter can check on salt, soup ingredients, rice, dried potatoes and anything else that's left." He laughed out loud deliberately, then abruptly stopped as though laughter was a sin to be retracted and in this sudden introspection he built up, as he regularly did, the view from his bedroom window –

the clocktower in the park visible through the tree tops and the haunting cries of waterfowl in the shallows of the lake which was the main attraction in this municipal land and which he walked around every day he was on leave.

Towards the stern, Klaus Bonner and Franz Seilerman were playing gin rummy but paused when Seaman Officer Fiebig leaned across the collapsible table the cards rested on to take a folded up map off the shelf. He apologised for distracting their game and took a quick look at the map before muttering "good" and leaving. Suddenly the absence of his seamed face and ungainly figure seemed to free up additional space in the cramped area rather than excite the usual, considerable amusement.

Their game continued and Bonner noticed the colour in Seilerman's face was high; a raspberry tinge, as though he might have a winning hand nevertheless they continued with the conversation prior to Fiebig's appearance.

"Kapitän says with luck we will be back at base by nineteenth of December and depending on the success of this mission we all might get leave to go home for Christmas. Just think, Franz, Christmas Eve in the Fatherland."

Seilerman ran his front teeth along his lower lip, his face a picture of concentration before placing a card down,

"Don't get your hopes up too high Klaus, it doesn't do – don't expect anything that way… Everything that comes is a bonus."

Without taking his eyes of his cards Bonner responded, "I understand what you're saying but I don't agree, everyone needs something to grasp, to have to look forward to even if it is a pipedream, that way it gives you a purpose. How many of us do you think would survive in these things if we had nothing waiting for us?"

Seilerman broke from his concentration. "Not all men are married, several are…" He was interrupted and watched Bonner also play another card.

"No, you misinterpret I'm talking about the simple things, silly things that other people take for granted – a hot bath, a glass of ice-cold beer. Haven't you been cold, tired, totally deflated and thought what wouldn't I do for a hot bath, a heavy meal and long, long sleep in a comfortable bed?"

Seilerman was about to put a card down, changed his mind and selected another before looking directly at the seaman opposite, "You have a point Klaus but don't build your hopes up too high remember last Christmas, we weren't even on day leave."

His comment seemed to wrong foot Bonner who hesitated before playing a card. Seilerman smiled before scrutinising his deck; his teeth ground together as he weighed up his options.

Seilerman asked, "What was the Kapitän talking to you about earlier?" He paused, quietly observing that the other card player had a haircut like a used toothbrush. As an afterthought he offered, "If it is personal… that's alright."

Bonner lifted his gaze from his cards, "We were talking generally. You know on each trip he likes to discuss things with his crew, not just the officers but all the men. This is what makes him a good leader. He thinks nothing of sitting down with Ernst and listening to him rambling on while they both peel spuds."

Both men put their cards flat to give themselves a break from the game and their conversation became more earnest.

"You have the advantage of having served with another Kapitän?" Seilerman watched Bonner nod then asked him, "What was his name?"

"Mathes, he was a good man too, but I have seen a few on leave, their arrogance is insufferable, their overbearing attitude does a disservice to all submarine crews. Kapitän Werner is a likeable man and you cannot question his seamanship. More importantly he never underestimates his responsibility to his crew." He paused then continued again with an instinctive warrior spirit, "I think he is haunted by what happened to U-boats 122 and 102 under the command of Loof and Van Kloth."

"What happened?" asked Seilerman with alert eyes.

"You don't know?" Bonner looked surprised. "Both vanished without trace in the North Sea in the summer of last year – everything, crew, the lot."

Seilerman looked reflective, "You're right about Kapitän Werner's seamanship. There's many a time he has got us out of a jam where lesser men might have snapped. He is lucky he can be both attached yet detached."

Bonner was brisk in his response, "That is essential if a submarine is to function at its best." He picked his cards up and played one, "One thing he said was enlightening."

"What was that?"

Bonner looked at his cards again, "He talked of courage."

Seilerman put a card down before looking at Bonner.

"And…" Bonner inhaled deeply, "he said that on his third patrol he discovered what courage was. He told me a fighting man will allow everything to come to a crunch and accept the risks. Usually he's elated by the feeling – it won't happen to me. But once he has suffered and carried his wounds back into battle, barely recovered then things look different; he has experienced hurt and knows he can experience it again at any moment and death is not only a possibility but a probability. The Kapitän said that to then carry on regardless required great courage. He wasn't applauding himself, he was speaking on behalf of all the men."

Seilerman offered his own philosophy, the maturity of which surprised the older submariner, "It's a known fact, one of the assumptions of war, that a professional fighting man is ready to sacrifice himself. A crew is eternally grateful when they return alive."

Suddenly noticing the time on his watch, Frank Seilerman put his cards down and stood up, "Excuse me but I have to go to the engine room."

Bonner smiled, "Perhaps we'll finish a game one of these times?"

The younger man smiled, "Well we've got plenty of time, eh?" As he walked away he did the buttons up on his shirt while Bonner put his own cards down, counted to ten, then took a sneaky look at the other cards and this elicited a mischievous smile, followed quickly by a pious one in case anyone might be watching.

CHAPTER 7

There was a distinct air of agitation in the control room, the expression on Werner's face was blurred and shadowed with a shine of sweat lighting up his nose. He looked around uncomfortably, like civilians waiting for a delayed bus in winter. Seaman Officer Fiebig hesitated then spoke when he caught the Kapitän's eye, "What's the problem?"

"Can you smell anything?"

He winced as his nostrils were assailed by an acrid stink. The officer from Munich remained nonchalant, "Only the usual…"

Peter Werner looked around, "No I mean…"

The Second Seaman Officer Wolfgang Emmerich joined the conversation, "I know what you mean. At first I thought I could smell something in here before we left port."

The Skipper scratched his chin and everyone's attention was taken by the sudden presence of First Lieutenant Dieter Hoffman. He looked quizzical then laughed, "Has someone lost something?"

His Kapitän tried to remain cheerful, "Do you smell anything unusual Dieter?"

"Like what?"

Werner shrugged his shoulders, "Anything."

"I can't say I do… it's your imagination Kapitän." He smiled and the beginning of craggy wrinkles on his face were there to be observed.

Werner's concerned expression remained, "I hope so… no it's not. I just got a whiff then." He screwed his face up as though he'd been hit by some disgusting suppuration.

"Hans tell me again, what did we do to get rid of those infernal rats we seemed to attract?"

Fiebig responded immediately and his tone was matter-of-fact, "We just closed down the submarine in St Nazaire and set off gas pellets in each compartment. A lamp was placed in each one – the theory being that each rat would stagger out of its hideaway and make for the lights, lie down and die."

His Kapitän looked with conscious eyes, "And." The immediacy in his voice prompted a swift reply.

"Well it seemed to work."

Hoffman was careful not to sound theatrical, "Even I was surprised at the number this time."

Emmerich spoke in a measured way, "It's strange, not all U-boats seem to get the problem."

"No but we do!" The cheerfulness had returned to the Kapitän and everyone chuckled and the silence entered the control room broken only by Emmerich's reluctant expression, "You don't think we've still got them?"

He looked at the others and Fiebig spoke, "I damn well hope not. It's no laughing matter." All of them knew the energy to be whipped up for the task ahead, if their prognosis was right, it would be taxing and so would be the hate.

The Skipper looked up at the plating and pipes overhead, adjacent to the main periscope; everyone followed his gaze as though they were hoodlums about to hurl tears into their hankies… He spoke with a surge of reluctance, "I think one of our furry friends has decided to end its days in the channel plating."

He looked at the grey faces cursing the metal structure, "Don't worry, before long you will smell it," he said.

A dull stupor hit Lieutenant Hoffman, "If you're right, who's going up to get it out?"

It elicited a smile from the Kapitän, "Are you offering Wolfgang?"

Seaman Officer Fiebig was quick off the mark, "Yes, Wolfgang, it's just the job for a keen enthusiastic submariner."

38

He seemed to shed ten years with these words and the others managed to keep the imp in their hearts firmly anchored.

Emmerich stuttered, "If you want me, me to."

The Commanding Officer deliberately remained low key, "We don't know for sure yet, do we men?" The men feigned mock concern and the Seaman Officer remained oblivious. He began leaning against the pipes and sniffing at the same time looking up at the channel plating. Behind his back the assembled crew were doubled up with silent laughter and Werner knew it was the perfect antidote to the times of tension and weariness when everyone's eyes would be ruined with tiredness and which would surely come, as it always did.

He retained his composure, "Dieter."

"Kapitän," replied Hoffman making a valiant attempt to control his chortling.

Werner continued, "Tell the crew they are going to notice a difference in the air conditioning over the next few days." With everyone smiling, Emmerich began to realise the joke...

The Kapitän raised his voice to the level a successful comedian employs when he has an audience in his grip, "And from the day after next whoever is daft enough to brave it," he began laughing and it was infectious, "the fee is one mark, going up each day, thereafter."

Fiebig spoke to them all, "I once heard of such a thing."

Everyone waited for him to continue and Fiebig deliberately dropped his face, "A week's wages."

It sounded like murderous attention but the Kapitän grinned, "Then, gentlemen I hope you have nose plugs for you may just find yourselves feeling like the sweating end of a nightmare." No one said anything but it was easy to see their collective expression screamed, "Oh no!" while their scalps began to prickle.

CHAPTER 8

Before night fell in, robbing the day of natural light, Kapitän Werner ordered, "Up periscope." He looked intensely slowly, moving his feet in an anti-clockwork direction. He saw nothing – no lights, no aircraft not even a single smudge of smoke anywhere on the horizon. He was grateful when mugs of hot coffee arrived in the control room and everyone relaxed for a few minutes.

The Commanding Officer discussed with his First Lieutenant his decision to take the boat up to the surface within the hour following a last look through the periscope. He returned to his quarters to peer over the North Atlantic maps, pinpoint his exact position and make further calculations.

When the order was given, U-boat 116 began its ascent, wobbling then creaking like a broken weathercock until it bounced down on the sea before settling. The half-moon in the sky lit up the silhouette of the type 1XC submarine. Three crew immediately took up their positions in the conning tower and scrutinised the horizon intensely, through binoculars. Movement was minimal as the sea was calm and the process of recharging the boat's batteries commenced, this was always a vulnerable time for any submarine.

Below deck in the engine room the crew, under Shreiber's directions, looked distinctly edgy for recharging was always a wretched trial of patience. The Chief Engine Room Artificer carried out a series of maintenance checks as well as issuing instructions to the tightly knit crew who worked with him.

When the Kapitän walked into the engine room he immediately picked up on the cumulative tension of men working semi-naked. He attempted to diffuse the strain by laughing, showing off his dazzling sharp teeth.

"Relax men, all is well up above." His presence was immediately acknowledged and the crew breathed more easily.

Friedrich Schreiber wiped an oily rag through his hands and looked at him, "Who is on lookout duty, Kapitän?" The cords of his slender neck strained as he asked the question.

Werner's broad jaw hardly moved when he answered the question, "Heinz, Max and Bernhart."

Schreiber smiled, "Ah, Max has good eyesight, he sees better in the dark than he does in the light."

The Kapitän nodded nonchalantly knowing the men were watching, interpreting his every mannerism and he wanted them to think he had the hide of a rhinoceros and a solution to any problem.

Schreiber spoke again with increasing confidence, "Not long now, another hour then we can submerge."

Werner looked at the men, "Did you enjoy your meal tonight?"

In unison they replied, "Yes Kapitän."

The Commanding Officer paused for effect and a twinkle matured in his eye said, "So did I, perhaps we will send Ernst on a Cookery for Beginners course when we get back, eh?"

Everyone laughed and any previous anxiety evaporated, it prompted Herbert Rasch, a skinny young man with centre-parted black hair and a sunless complexion to speak.

"Kapitän."

"Yes."

"Heinz says he's ready to go up into the plating to get that thing out."

Werner tilted his head, "Has he been losing again at cards?"

The men grizzled their laughter before the usually quiet Rasch responded.

"Well, he keeps throwing in three kings when it's aces high."

Karl Boeck added to the hilarity, "He's making a name for himself now."

"What's that?" asked Werner, immediately.

"King Rat." Everyone chuckled.

Schreiber looking at his watch threw his head back, "Come on that's enough joking let's get the work finished."

Before their Kapitän left the engine room he turned and addressed the crew, "You're all doing a good job, men." The response was unanimous and followed by smiles.

"Thank you Kapitän."

Werner had that air of authority that would only ever be challenged by the conceited and everyone knew it.

Within an hour the submarine had dived and propelled itself smoothly. Only the occasional echo interrupted the calm. Above them now lay a barely distinguishable line of shadow on what had suddenly become a black moonless night. Strange. Before turning in for the night U116's Kapitän opened his logbook on the marked page '6th October 1942' and wrote – 'radiogram sent from 45.00N – 31.30W'. Experience had taught him that in severe storms sometimes the readings accuracy weren't always exact, nevertheless he smiled and closed his eyes for tomorrow was another day and soon the wolf pack would meet up.

The following morning Eric Steven was smacking himself with both hands similar to a football player 'geeing himself up' before leaving the changing room and running out onto the pitch where the opposition waited in brooding fashion. His face registered distress and he was sweating as though trapped in some noisy hell at the extreme limit of stress. Jorgan Bahn was alarmed and walked over to him, "What's up...? You look like you've seen a ghost."

The young submariner began rubbing his eyes and his breathing became laboured, "I don't know, I just felt very peculiar all of a sudden... My vision is blurred."

Bahn sought to comfort him and spoke without anxiety, "Maybe you are sickening for something."

"Maybe, but I had a full check-up with the service doctor in port and he said all systems were in perfect order."

The older man was at a loss so offered genial advice, "Lie down for half an hour, just close your eyes, Eric." He stretched over to get another blanket as Eric Steven reclined in the hammock complaining of the cold.

Bahn threw the blanket over the weary looking man and attempted to keep everything light-hearted, despite noticing the extremely pallid complexion of the sick man.

"Here you are," he took another blanket off a hammock. "I'm afraid I can't kiss you good night or good morning. It's against orders."

Both forced a smile, noticing Heinz Stegeman who suddenly appeared, looking for an explanation.

Bahn obliged, "Keep an eye on him Heinz, it's probably fatigue – it does this sometimes at the beginning – sneaks up on you like a cosh."

Stegeman gazed at him with a bovine expression on his leaden features.

"Funny, Max is slumped up against the torpedoes, complains of feeling ill. Maybe I should tell the Kapitän. The last thing we want is people dropping like flies!" The expression gave in to a smile revealing immaculate white teeth, not a known characteristic in the German Navy.

Bahn was hesitant and prodded his chin with his index finger, "No I shouldn't bother him, he's got enough on his plate. See how things are in an hour or so. There is no point alarming anyone unnecessarily."

Stegeman didn't want to be accused of paranoia. "OK, let's leave it for a while." He listened for a few seconds then stepped in the direction of the toilet.

In the control room Lieutenant Hoffman was slumped down on a wooden crate packed with fruit; he looked like a dejected animal, listless and perspiring. Werner appeared, stood behind the Planesman, then turned and looked at his First Lieutenant. His concern was tinged with humour, "Just seen your mother-in-law, Dieter?"

The hampered figure offered resilience, "I don't look that bad, do I?"

His Kapitän noticed that the crew in the control room were looking at the officer,

"Ask the men?"

When he looked at Seaman Officer Fiebig, he didn't notice Werner winking at the men. Fiebig did and Hoffman heard a sick thread of voice remark,

"You look ghastly, Dieter."

Everyone kept a straight, serious face and it elicited worry in the other officer's eyes who tried fatuous bravado.

"I don't feel so bad, just hot and then cold." He looked around for reassurance but none was forthcoming and Hans Fiebig kept his poker face when he spoke,

"Last time I saw a case of this…"

Hoffman blinked twice, rapidly "A case… a case…"

The officer altered his voice to cheerfulness, "Well it was in the tropics…"

Hoffman cocked his eyebrow, "But you've never been in the tropics!"

"I know that but it doesn't stop making it a good story." He could no longer keep a straight face, aware that his voice could no longer continue the satisfaction in his exploit.

Everyone laughed heartily, almost thunderously before it was interrupted by a loud echoing sound that became repetitive and excessively heavier with each beat as though a thousand years of sea faring superstition was fighting to express itself, with horrific consequences. Werner's heart struck like a clock and he felt the heat haze dancing internally along the iron boat.

Above the waves raged an unyielding storm, light followed by darkness, interchanging as though grappling with one another for supremacy. The sea was rolled over in a grip of pulsating fury – moments of fatal lucidity, fatal hallucination with intermittent yelps of hysteria.

Fortunately, the submerged boat felt only a fraction of this freak condition nevertheless a record of human agony shot up and down – Herbert, Heinz, Max and Peter were paralysed with fear. While Karl, Horst and Ernst were racked with physical pain. All around was an unseen, foreboding activity. The senior personnel Werner, Fiebig and Schreiber tried desperately not to convey their fear for maintaining morale was essential despite the limited light, suffocation and scorching emptiness.

Suddenly the glass instrument panels cracked and the hands started rotating clockwise then anti-clockwise. The whole interior of the submarine rattled and the echoing was deafening. Technical failure on the relief valve on diving tank number six stuck in the closed position and the resultant imbalance of weight caused U116 to float onto the surface with its stern sticking up in the air at a 30° angle.

The crew experienced further anxiety until Schreiber could get the boat on an even keel and dive. It would have been understandable if their Kapitän had been yelling his orders but there were no falsetto words of command which spoke volumes for Werner's self-control. His coolness, later garnered further respect from his terrified crew who had endured another three minutes of this insanity before everything suddenly resumed to normality.

The boat's lights flickered and then they were stable. All the men looked like they had awoken from some distant nightmare, several had wet themselves and all stood in a super-sensory trance as though the power of speech, movement and thought has been rendered impotent.

Nothing like this could have been imagined and now Kapitän Werner stood in a strange frame of mind, resting in a pronounced state of emotional regression as though indifferent to everything, like a new-born baby. He closed his eyes and everything still remained null and void as though his brain had gone to sleep. Only when he opened them and immediately recognised the surroundings, he attempted to break the silence, ameliorate the situation. He faltered, then tried again, "Is everyone alright?"

The control room crew responded unconvincingly.

"Dieter? Hans?"

The two men looked like an explosion had rocked their whole nervous systems, having been plunged into the thick of an experience without precedent. Werner raised his voice, again and only the First Lieutenant responded.

"Kapitän."

Werner left the control room and moved as quickly as he could towards the engine room, offering words of encouragement to those crew he passed, many of whom were too dazed to acknowledge him.

In the engine room Friedrich Schreiber was gripping a pipe with rare ferocity as he struggled to gain control over himself. Werner immediately put his arm around the Chief Engine Room Artificer's shoulder which alarmed him.

"It's OK… it's OK… it's over."

A stiff hysterical silence followed before Schreiber asked in a subdued voice, "Kapitän, what in God's name?"

Werner's lip curled faintly, "I don't know."

Schreiber relaxed his grip, "We have never experienced this before." His eyes were pleading for an explanation and his Kapitän increasingly gaining composure looked around the engine room before responding.

"We are learning every time we take this fish out, Friedrich."

Both men looked at each other and blew their cheeks out before inhaling deeply and exhaling any residue of fear.

"I'll be back later," Werner said croakily, smiled then left.

Siggi Maier, the radio operator looked puzzled. His skin was hot and dry and cramp still attacked his legs causing acute discomfort which the twenty-five year old chose to ignore. He took off his headphones and gave them to the First Lieutenant whispering, "I don't understand what it is we are picking up, it is unlike anything I have ever heard before... strange music, a band *Guns and Roses...*"

When Hoffman put the headphones to his ears a look of astonishment engulfed him and momentarily he trembled before regaining composure.

"You'd better get the Kapitän."

Maier heaved himself from his seat. Hoffman's instincts told him the best course of action was complete radio silence for two hours – everything still – utterly invisible in both sight and sound. It was the Kapitän's decision to make and the officer was grateful Werner was Skipper of 116, no one else.

Fortunately, Werner had shrugged off the pain and numbness each crew member had felt in various degrees of severity and from the wardroom shouted repeatedly, "Klaus! Klaus!"

Bonner swiftly appeared, "Yes, Kapitän." He watched the Commanding Officer making fists with both hands repeatedly, to loosen the stiffness then his words flashed out,

"Klaus, I've just come from the engine room. Friedrich is OK but will you check the engines are alright?" He hid his desperation and continued, "Whatever it is we have been through I don't think we could survive a second time. Check all the crew are OK and have everyone at battle stations." He paused, raised an enquiring eyebrow and his voice became blankly stubborn, "Something is not right Klaus, something extraordinary has happened. We are going to find out."

"Right away Kapitän," said Klaus urgently. As he turned he heard his final instructions.

"And Klaus, I want a full report on the state of batteries fore and aft ballast. Tell Friedrich right away."

"Yes, Sir."

Werner put his cap on and walked out only to be interrupted by Horst Kruger.

47

"Kapitän come quickly, Maier has picked up something strange in the headphones, he told me he had to tell you but I said I would do it."

Both men hurried towards the control room and on seeing them Maier handed the headphones to Werner who looked at Hoffman before holding them up to his ear. Silence entered the confined space broken only by some of the crew still in fear's grip shuffling towards their leader as he listened and praying internally they didn't face a horrifying, howling black future.

Half a minute became one minute and then another minute passed before the Kapitän looked up, his nostrils dilating faintly as his expression changed from concern to a trance-like state.

Hoffman sensing something was wrong took the headphones from him and spoke in a slightly nasal, flat almost mournful voice, "Kapitän are you alright?"

Werner's response was barely audible as he looked at the crew who begged some sort of explanation. "Yes, Dieter."

The crew knew their Kapitän was a born storyteller – a natural with a poker face who could make people laugh but always kept politics and religion to himself to save conversation from turning from sweet to sour. All they wanted now was something plausible.

Werner's face gave a sort of spasm as he spoke, "What I have to say is barely believable, I am not sure I believe it myself. Perhaps it is a trick." He looked intently at the men. "I hope so for all our sakes." There was a terrible sadness about him like that of a creature in a zoo – irremediably displaced.

The First Lieutenant almost choked on his question, "What is it Kapitän, you look terrible?"

Werner's response was glum, "How else does an old man look, Dieter?"

Everyone looked puzzled. The Commanding Officer looked once again at the men huddled around him and spoke in sober fashion allowing a faint smile to offset complete gloom.

"Men, I have something to say. What we have experienced is no freak storm but something that defies explanation, even logic." He deliberately paused to allow his words to be digested. "If what is coming over the radio is true and I can't, no one can verify that it is true, then we have just entered into a dimension or void that has propelled us through time. According to the radio it is no longer 1941 but," he hoped his voice now sounded normal, humane not robotic, "it is 1988."

Stunned silence made the quietude seem louder than any murmuring would have done. Werner waited until the men put their gaze back on him.

"I know it is hard to comprehend, so many things come to mind: what happened in the war, where are our families? I am as staggered as you but we must continue as though nothing has changed. Later on we will find out the truth. I ask for your loyalty more than ever now."

The two officers wended their way back to the Kapitän's quarters leaving behind more, though this time acute, stunned silence. Both officers needed a drink and Werner poured large sized measures of whisky into two glasses and they were immediately drunk in one go without the glasses being chinked and then he poured another generous measure into the glasses.

After moments of silence Hoffman spoke, "Do you think it's a trap?"

His question was tinged with optimism and sounded like a prayer for the living. Werner pondered the question and how he wished for the comforting sounds of rooks in sycamores that had played a vital part in his adolescent years.

"I don't know Dieter but we must be on our guard. Tell Maier I want everything concerned with the news written down, I don't care what and he is to listen all night."

He snapped the last sentence out, then relaxed, "Thank goodness his English is passable."

Dieter Hoffman had always shown firmness of purpose and a glad confidence in life now he was flummoxed as though he stood outside himself looking at himself fingering the lapels of his uniform.

"I was thinking, if what you say is true then my son Dieter is older than me if he has survived till now and Marlene is older than my mother." He began to feel like an automaton with a variety of sensory impressions yet choking with fatigue. "I just can't take it in – how can forty plus years go by in less than an hour?" He raised his head and looked his Kapitän in the eyes. "One thing all of us will want to know is, what happened in the war?"

His Commanding Officer sighed rather helplessly, "What indeed and what kind of world is it to live in, in 1988?" He ached but was determined not to let the men see him groan.

His First Lieutenant empathised, "Kapitän you need to rest, it will be a trial of strength for all of us, you in particular."

Werner uttered a faint snort of laughter and lay down on his bunk, "Dieter wake me if anything alarming comes over the wireless, anything Dieter."

His subordinate officer left and Werner closed his eyes, listening to his breathing.

CHAPTER 9

U116 was stationary on top of the Atlantic and the midday sun seemed to have calmed the sea down. Two crew members in the conning tower were joined by Dieter Hoffman and the three submariners looked at the ocean as though it had just been discovered. Karl Boeck was the first to speak, though he still looked through his binoculars.

"Sir, what does Kapitän Werner intend to do?"

The formality of his question seemed strange yet understandable and Hoffman was quick off the mark with his response.

"Never mind what the Skipper intends, you keep your eyes peeled and remember no matter what you see or think you see, I want to know immediately."

"Sir," was their dual response.

The First Lieutenant continued while surveying the horizon occasionally squinting, "Horst will join you and the three of you will be relieved in one hour and then you will alternate every two hours." He returned to the control room and sat next to Siggi Maier.

"Siggi, remember the Kapitän wants you to take down everything to do with the world, anything that might be called news. It will be another long day, I know and tomorrow will be even longer."

The Radio Operator indicated to a writing pad already a quarter full with his scribbling partly in English and partly in German. Hoffman smiled and suddenly realised what he'd just done and felt good about himself as he walked through 116 observing the crew working and checking respective equipment despite an air of unreality having overtaken everyone.

He was relieved to find Friedrich Schreiber listening eagerly to the engines. "Thank heaven for one constant," he said quietly to himself before engaging the Chief Engine Room Artificer in light conversation which was sorely needed.

A snarl of throat clearing forced Werner to sit up and throw the blanket off himself. He spat as much phlegm as he could into the tiny metal sink adjacent to the bottom of his bed. He put his cap on then his boots before stretching both arms and making for the conning tower.

The spotters were about to stand to attention at his arrival but Werner gestured not to and he offered a philosophical smile.

"How does it feel to be over sixty then?"

The men laughed which was a distinct relief to him and he continued in similar vein.

"When we get home you can collect your pensions."

He pulled his own binoculars to his eyes and thought how beautiful the combination of blue sky and calm sea was.

"Remember, anything and I want it reported."

"Yes Sir," was the lively reply.

Before retreating and designed to keep their spirits up Kapitän Werner laughed out his last statement, "Even our furry mascot hasn't budged."

Below he was approached by Seaman Officer Fiebig, "All the checks including electrical installation have been thoroughly completed. There doesn't appear to be any damage Kapitän." He smiled self-consciously as though he'd just learned this gesture. "Everything is as before the storm, some of the men are still affected though."

Werner warmed to Fiebig's professionalism and wondered if the rumour he'd heard about the Seaman Officer's bullying gallantry with the ladies was true or merely content for an anecdotal story. Nevertheless he responded.

"I'm not surprised, Hans. I have checked our position and we are only four miles off course." He paused to consider and

Fiebig awaited instructions, "You had better make sure once again the instruments panels are giving the correct reading. We will either make the rendezvous on time or…"

Fiebig waited a second then repeated Peter Werner's last word, "Or… Kapitän?"

The latter's face couldn't disguise sudden morbidity and he gazed into the distance. "Or, we will be over forty years too late."

Fiebig did not hesitate to give his opinion for this Kapitän had always encouraged the crew to speak freely, knowing it was a sign of strength not weakness.

"I think it is a trap. All night Maier has listened to the wireless and most of the time he has heard strange electric music and shipping forecasts." He dropped his considerable shoulders, "All right, the forecasts are not like usual but it could be a ploy the allies are using to try and disrupt us. They know the war in the Atlantic is all but lost and it is only a matter of months before their supply routes are completely severed. No one could sustain the loss of shipping that the allies have, even with help from the Americans."

Werner listened intently, now he concluded their conversation, "We'll see, Hans. After you've looked at the other instrument panels again, I want you to look over some charts with me." He left Fiebig to carry out his instructions while he walked to the main operations area and everyone could see the characteristic spring in his step was gone. All hoped it was temporary…

In the conning tower Karl Boeck, Eric Steven and Horst Kruger remained cold and vigilant. Looking at the sky lessened the prevailing tension those below were enveloped in, nevertheless it was exhausting and the three submariners had a volley of curses stored up for when the ocean sprung up fifteen foot waves. Ten minutes passed before conversation joined the three crew.

Karl cleared his throat, "I don't know what it is we are supposed to be looking for, not that there's anything out there.

Oh, for one of those French girls now." He whistled loudly, then continued, "Horst, what I could do to her."

Horst laughed scornfully, "Remember you might be seventy something so don't get too excited."

Boeck took a deep breath and expelled it abruptly, "I feel one hundred having been up this long, so much for relief. Does the Kapitän know we haven't even had a hot drink?"

The sympathy he was looking for was denied him.

"I'm sure he has more important things on his mind than worrying if you have had a drink," said Horst, his youth still strong in him.

Eric Steven, who'd always considered he'd had a dreary past before naval life and who'd searched inside himself for the return of forgotten confidence since the incident snapped, "Shut up you two!"

Suddenly the young man had an air of exultation, he took his binoculars away from his eyes yet still looked intensely at the sky, "I thought I heard something." He repeated his words eagerly but was dismissed.

"Your imagination Eric, you'd be seeing Santa Claus if this was December," offered Kruger still looking through his binoculars.

Karl Boeck cocked his head to one side as though he was listening for the sound of planes, he smiled before giving his face another expression, "Don't talk of Christmas, Horst, it just depresses me to think we might not be home for it."

Kruger shuffled from leg to leg still with the binoculars firmly gripped, "When was the last time you saw your family, Karl?" It was a question most submariners thought about during normal night-time silence.

"Nine months ago, that's what happens with being a good submariner – the better you are the more the Navy want you!"

Only a hint of chuckle was heard before Eric Steven spoke without lowering his binoculars, "Some men have not seen Germany for over a year and may have only had perhaps two weeks shore leave in that time, but because of operations have not been allowed more than forty miles away from their base."

The other two thought quietly about what they'd just heard before Horst spoke with a smile wrinkled in the corners of his eyes, "I am lucky, I was home four months ago and met someone very special. I never thought I would say I hope this war finishes but now it is different."

Only the waves lapping against U116's steel skin could be heard as the temperature began to fall and the three men struggling to fight fatigue remained tuned up and on edge, ready and waiting to engage whatever lay ahead.

Below deck, those men off duty were trying to get some sleep; their young faces still revealing a strained, unsure anxiety while their bodies moved uncomfortably to find a restful position.

CHAPTER 10

Two Phantom jets had taken off after lunch on reconnaissance – UR is what the pilots in Lossiemouth referred to it as – Uneventful Reconnaissance. They had often joked about taking a decent walk "especially if you've had a hot pud" before getting airborne less indigestion entered the cramped cockpit. Today it was a recently qualified pilot and his Squadron Leader to take the monsters into the sky.

The Phantoms roared over vast expanses of ocean; nothing seemed out of the ordinary until John Fogarty, the senior pilot, noticed a small bleep on his radar screen. He looked twice before engaging his colleague, "Red leader to Fox one, over."

His communication was acknowledged.

"Something on the screen, may as well have a peep, over." Within seconds both Phantoms veered to the right and roared through the clouds.

Above the U-boat was a clear blue sky. In the conning tower the three submariners, still scrutinising everything through their binoculars, were becoming impatient for their relief. Horst Kruger moistened his lips repeatedly and knew his face was probably as grey looking with tiredness as the duo stood either side of him; and his tongue fought for articulation.

"We're an open target staying up so long, particularly on such a clear day." He bobbled up and down, bending both knees simultaneously in the hope of speeding up his circulation.

It elicited a chuckle which might have developed into a laugh had Karl Boeck not spoken, "Can you hear anything?"

"Not again," sighed Kruger still continuing his exercise.

"No, shhh… listen," said Boeck.

Suddenly two sleek metal monsters broke through the colour of the sky and screamed over U116. The submariners ducked and cried out in panic but their yelling was mute for it was trapped in their throat by fear. All three tumbled to the internal ladder amid chaos and the two jets flew with blistering speed merely feet above the submarine as Eric finally closed the hatch. The roar of engines had been heard in every corner of the boat and immediately battle stations was sounded.

Werner remained composed as First Lieutenant Hoffman awaited further orders.

"Take her down further." The officer looked at Franz Seilerman, "Continue the dive."

Everywhere the crew were leaning against objects for support and gradually continuous creaking echoed as the pressure mounted on the submarine.

Most of the crew had a look of restrained anxiety about them, a few had a death rattle in their throat; and all tried desperately to mask their emotions. In the control room the two officers watched the panels.

"Release, Dieter." The order was conveyed and carried out.

Karl Boeck continued to breathe stertorously and in his throat were the gasping noises of someone overwrought. His Kapitän looked at him.

"I've never seen anything like it, it just appeared… the speed… it was just…." Boeck's words were almost too rapid for translation, nevertheless Werner adopted a relaxed expression.

"Gather yourself Karl," then he looked at Horst Kruger, "tell me what you saw. Take your time, Horst."

While everyone listened intently, Seaman Officer Fiebig shouldered his way to the officers' quarters to retrieve the aircraft identification book. He returned immediately to the control room, reassuring those crew he passed that everything was OK even if he wasn't convinced himself.

Werner took hold of the book and opened it, "OK, Horst, again."

Horst's body stiffened at the words and any rational gleam was absent in his eyes, "It was like a fish, the wings were built at a strange angle to the cockpit. But there were no propellers."

His Kapitän scratched his chin as he digested the description.

"Something like a rocket. There is talk in Germany of developing such things but it is talk about space adventure." The tension was relieved by a couple of crew chuckling.

"Maybe it is not so funny. Siggi keeps reporting strange music or sounds coming from the wireless. It is like nothing we hear in Germany." Again a couple of the assembled men laughed.

Karl Boeck looked diligently through the aircraft identification book before shaking his head, "No it is nothing like this."

His jaw dropped and Werner looked at Kruger, "Horst?"

He too shook his head, conscious that all eyes were fixed on him hoping for some explanation, some crumb of comfort.

Their Kapitän refused to be dismayed, "Hans, what do you think?"

The native of Munich paused then looked around the crew, "Jorgan, get your sketch pad and pencil."

As he left, the Seaman Officer addressed Boeck, "Karl, when Jorgan returns describe as near as you can what this aircraft looks like while he draws. Then we will find out if what you said, Kapitän, might after all be true."

A state of limbo continued in the control room. The engine room was suddenly beset with problems an hour later while the Kapitän, Seaman Officer and spotter Karl Boeck were in attendance there. Water was trickling in and suddenly a loud clanging noise followed by a gargle sound heralded flooding. Everyone was immediately drenched. The lights flickered which didn't help the pandemonium that had broken out.

Fiebig looked for the source and bellowed, "The inner exhaust valve is fractured!"

Dieter Hoffman appeared holding a screw as thick as a thumb in the corner of the conning water chamber and yelling, "Kapitän!"

When the commanding officer looked in his direction the First Lieutenant spoke abrasively, "The cover can't shut!"

Werner immediately shouted, "Get Friedrich up here quickly, we'll need caulking to make everything watertight!" He looked around desperately aware the lights continued to dim as more water poured in.

Hoffman was near Homeric anger, "It's going to take hours. Those bloody dockyard workers... saboteurs."

Joachim Reiz, who wondered if he would ever walk in Berlin again, all but dragged the Chief Engine Room Artificer out of his hammock. Both ran towards the engine room, past perplexed faces, some of whom believed they had arrived at their first date with destiny; and this was something submariners accepted as natural like a hangover.

Above the waves the Phantoms scoured the empty spaces, like vultures scanning the horizon, in dramatic fashion. The Squadron Leader flashed, surprisingly, fine teeth in his leathery face that seemed worn and battered after two years of exhaustive flying; and he was only too aware of service pranks.

He spoke slowly, deliberately to the young pilot, "Someone must be putting us on, what else would a U-boat be doing here in the Atlantic?"

The response was more excitable than curious, "Did you notice the way it dived?"

John Fogarty chuckled, "Suspended slow motion... did you manage to get some shots?" he said as an after-thought.

The younger pilot remained eager, "Yes, Sir... Whoever set this one up went to a lot of trouble."

Red Leader retained his geniality, "Can you imagine reporting this one if you'd been on your own? Seeing King Canute would have been more believable."

Blue Fox smiled and turned his head to look at Red Leader whom he discovered was laughing silently, "All the same, we're going to have some interesting snaps."

Caution entered the conversation when the Squadron Leader spoke, "Let's just keep this to ourselves until we've seen the prints, no point rising to the bait until we have them... How long will developing take?"

His question was answered immediately, "I'll get it done straightaway and call you."

Inside U116 and in the control room, despite being soaked, the crew had worked feverishly to rectify the damage and Kapitän Werner was convinced the worst was over though not everyone shared his optimism...

He sought out Jorgan who produced his sketches showing an overall impression of the aircraft and some rough drawings of the Phantom from various angles. Some crew gathered round their Kapitän as he examined them.

"Interesting, Dieter, isn't it? I wonder what armoury she carries." He paused and looked at the men before squinting his eyes much the same as a mathematician does when confronted with a formula. "Why didn't she attack? We were like sitting ducks."

Officer Fiebig offered the obvious explanation, "Maybe the pilots were as surprised as we were." He looked at his fellow officer to elaborate and Wolfgang Emmerich nodded, sagely.

"Especially if the war has been over twenty or thirty or even forty years."

Everyone digested his suggestion and it was left to Peter Werner to break the silence, "Let's go to periscope depth."

Hoffman repeated the order while his Kapitän moved to the periscope. All he saw was a perfect, pale blue sky and calm sea and he was aware that in an hour's time complete darkness would cocoon everything for in this Atlantic, change came rapidly and often sinistrously.

Werner released the periscope, "Maintain speed, Dieter, we will plot a different course but will rendezvous as planned. That is the only way we will know what is really happening." He tried to ignore his rheumatic pinchings as he made his way back to his quarters, conscious that his movement didn't resemble that of some relic from an ex Sailors' Refuge.

CHAPTER 11

Inside the laboratory the young almost foppish Blue Fox pilot waited anxiously as the negatives were developed. Such was his urgency, he hadn't bothered to change his flying attire. To offset his anxiety he hummed the chorus to the biggest selling single to date *Do They Know It's Christmas?*, much to the amusement of the young technician. As the prints were hung up to dry he stepped closer and as the images sharpened up he could see the unmistakeable insignia on German uniforms, especially the headwear.

Red Leader pilot John Fogarty was sat in his functional office writing out a report. A filter cigarette dangled from his lips and he had resisted lighting it several times as he was determined to pack in what even he described as a "filthy habit". The shrill ring tone on his telephone was alarming and he snatched the handpiece off the base angrily.

"Yes," he snapped then visibly calmed down when he realised who was on the other end. "OK… As soon as they are dry bring them to my office and by the way, keep it under your hat."

Beneath the waves, jollity, one of the hallmarks of U116's crew had seemingly re-appeared. The crew were eating a meal of very hot soup and stew and despite intense tiredness the obligatory sounds of slurping and burping bounced between several men. Eric Steven threw his shoulders back in an upright position unaware that even he looked a tad green around the gills – unusual for one so young.

"Do you know that I could be seventy-six?" He began impersonating an old man and some crew laughed, others didn't.

"This is not so funny for the married men on board," said Uve Stührmann in a flat voice.

Not everyone heard him, including the self-appointed court jester, "Just fancy being married to an eighty year old woman."

Franz Seilerman looked up, unamused and left the table.

Karl Boeck looked up, "Eric." he said quietly.

The latter looked annoyed, "What did I do wrong… Don't you think that maybe I am as frightened inside but we've always said humour is the best way to dispel fear. Or have you forgotten when we were depth charged that first trip we made Wolf and Ernst fart, in unison, for every salvo dropped, kept us all from shitting ourselves in fear…"

Joachim Reiz responded, "You're right, Eric, but Franz…"

He was interrupted almost immediately by Eric, "Franz nothing, there are other men married. Meiner has just got engaged. Monier what about him? They haven't or didn't get the chance to raise a family."

Silence entered the confined space and with it a strange atmosphere broken by Horst Kruger, "Come on, let's eat our meal, we are all going to need every ounce of courage, whatever the outcome."

The last vestiges of light had finely disappeared over the Scottish mountains and now the whole of Great Britain was plunged into near winter darkness – a four month period when most adults went to work in the dark and felt they were hibernating. For many, Christmas only exacerbated the situation and the ever increasing number of self-help books evident on bookshelves did little to alleviate the predicament those prone to melancholy endured, including the Squadron Leader happily drawing on his lit cigarette.

He was excited as he held a large magnifying glass over the photos with the younger man stood by him. He kept staring at the insignia.

"It's remarkably authentic whoever it is, Tom."

"But who on earth, Sir, would go to the trouble to pull…"
He was interrupted.

"Look, I'm going to get on to the Ops boys and find out in a roundabout way what it's all about. Someone is bound to know, there will be some explanation. All right, leave the photographs with me."

Pilot Officer Spurr turned to leave, but held back inviting a comment from his superior, "What is it?"

The concentration of blood running into his face suddenly gave him a rosy rustic some would say almost virile appearance.

"I was thinking whom do I know, a real practical joker among the boys who'd go to this length." He shook his head, "No, Sir, we do have a couple who like to play devil's advocate but no, this is way out of their league." He laughed and said "No" to himself which aroused Fogarty's interest who encouraged him with a raised head.

"I was thinking of Officer Alan Inglesby, a contemporary… we're still in touch; had he been around in the last war probably would have been flogging nylons during the blitz and flogging Messerschmitts during the day. The type that might win a medal out of sheer stupidity not a brave act!"

Both men laughed and the younger pilot drew an unctuous face and spoke piously, "Always a rumour that he cheated in his exams to get into Cranwell. Shhh…" He raised his index finger to his lip and winked. Fogarty reacted with a belly laugh – a roar almost as loud as his plane on take-off; he threw his shoulders back and almost toppled out of his uncomfortable Ikea chair before lighting up another cigarette.

Alone, he studied the photographs forensically and couldn't get the image of the three startled faces looking at him out of his mind even when he retired to bed, exhausted.

"Nobody would offer an elementary parlour trick as outlandish as this to justify his existence, surely, unless he thinks he's God," he muttered before turning off his bedside light having checked the time on his watch.

CHAPTER 12

U116 powered its way underwater at an acceptable rate of knots following emergency repairs. Conversation centred on one topic throughout the submarine and in the wardroom three officers bent their ear forward as though granting the semblance of a deferential hearing.

Hoffman pursed his lips, "I'll be more settled when we reach our supposed rendezvous. This not knowing is getting me down… Marlene, Dieter, what has become of them if the worst is true?"

Werner put a friendly hand on his Lieutenant's shoulder, "Courage, Dieter, we will all be relieved by noon tomorrow. It isn't easy for any of us, particularly those of us with families."

The glum looked heavy on Hans Fiebig's face, "Kapitän, do you think it is an ally ploy of some sort or can it be possible that we are, indeed, in a different age?"

Both junior officers looked intensely at Kapitän Werner and he was only too aware that tough days lay ahead and hoped he was in shape for it; and he knew he had to eschew melancholia.

"I don't know, Hans, I don't know," he paused, "all of us have our own internal struggles but morale must not be allowed to sink. Have you ever been in a boat where morale is rock bottom?"

Fiebig's reply was immediate, "No Kapitän." A hint of defiance had crept into his voice which pleased Werner.

"It's not pleasant, fear and mistrust is everywhere, you feel it but can't do anything about it."

There was a pause before Hoffman broke the silence, "Kapitän."

If the Commanding Officer was tempted to tell the officers about horrible heroic exploits in a world of ghosts and abstract densities he checked himself for their current situation was extraordinarily demanding.

"Tomorrow when we reach our position I want all the crew together. It will be important to talk to them, to dispel everyone's sense of isolation. We are in this together, all of us." He refrained from further vocal effort to let his words sink in, and they did. He continued, "I know underneath the banter the concern is there. Past, present, future I don't want anyone to feel twisted, gripped like locked snakes."

Fiebig rallied again, "Sir, the men are with you, they hold you dear and would be willing..." He was interrupted.

"Thank you, Hans." Werner repeated the words slowly before continuing, "It's good to know I can rely on both of you, this will be a good example to the men. They don't always show it but I know they regard you as friends, besides, being their officers. It isn't always so."

Buoyed, both officers left and their Kapitän began poring over the map stretched across the table top having been lowered from the wall by a chain. Within a minute he was utterly absorbed, plotting possible positions on route, talking to himself though the words had no sharp point of bitterness.

The building that housed the British Air Ministry was establishment through and through. Everyone in the R.A.F. was acquainted with the anecdotal story concerning the Wing Commander who commented that the architect's heart couldn't have been in the right place and was subsequently overlooked for further promotion.

Personnel walking some corridors were assaulted by severe looking former high ranking officers photographed in black and white and sturdily framed questioning their every step, from head height.

One of the more civilised rooms, housed oak shelves weighed down with hundreds of books featuring biographies, commentaries, post humorous volumes and a recently added fiction section concerned with warfare. Tea was served on silver trays at precisely 4.15pm each day and there sat two former pilots now relegated to desk jobs courtesy of age; both had faces as creased as the leather armchairs that tucked around them.

Sellars and Larky had been added to the team 'flirting' with recent events and were quite happy to do so provided it didn't encroach on their Tuesday afternoon/Friday morning game of golf. Both wore reading glasses and both had eyes almost hidden in the folds of near collapsing lids. Sellars, a Yorkshireman, his face as creased as a windfall walnut but surprisingly not dour, waited for the waiter to leave before pouring tea into two china cups.

"Will you get someone in archives or if that's no good, someone at the war museum, naval records, that sort of thing to follow up anything about a U-boat 116. Hold on," he checked some notes in his worn folder, "Yes, 116."

Larky, a Fen man, unfairly thought of as having a heart of rusted nail-heads by former girlfriends, responded airily, "U116, any particular…"

He was interrupted by a fetching smile, "Yes, one of our reconnaissance flights reported what looked like a U-boat."

He noted his colleague's playful expression, "Yes, hard to believe, anyway, the chaps think it's another practical joke of some sort. Remember last year some naval bods dumped a twenty foot capsule with distinctive Russian markings on it on the surface knowing full well our boys would spot it later that day. Well the Minister wasn't pleased, apparently he was the only one who didn't find it funny… What a black shovel he must be. It went to the PM, you know the usual mess."

Both men lit their pipes almost in unison then each gulped a large mouthful of tea. Larky smacked his lips, "Why the need to bother with the supposedly U116?" He looked at

Sellars who suddenly produced a disdainful expression before he spoke.

"Whoever's gone to this great length and I can't for the life of me think why – let's find out about one U116 so that the joke ends up being on them." The expression changed to a coy grin. "Do you follow my drift?" he said, ignoring the pain accumulated from a disastrous foray into amateur boxing during his youth...

"I think so," replied Larky while stretching over to another seat to retrieve a discarded copy of *The Daily Telegraph*. "Hope no bugger's done this crossword." He tore through the pages until he found what he was looking for, "Oh, good."

Sellars smiled. Had the 'Fen man' looked at the weather prediction he would have seen that fierce storms over much of Britain stretching out to sea, were predicted for the early hours with possible warnings going out to vessels in the Atlantic. U116 was already tucked in beneath the sea, closer to her rendezvous.

The musty aroma that circulated the austere Naval Warfare Records room hadn't changed for over sixty years; it belonged to every decade of the twentieth century and the lack of sufficient natural light made it oppressive. Here, the elderly curator, white faced with a loose slobbering mouth gave the spinsterish librarian a sheet with hand-written instructions and left abruptly. Miss Fish, attired in black skirt, cream blouse and wearing sensible shoes made muted application as she read the notes. Heck, she was efficient. Within minutes she had located the ageing cardboard boxes and despite dust shaking everywhere when she removed them from shelves for the first time in years, she began checking references and cross references making some scrawled notes of her own on a piece of white card. She sauntered to another metal frame laughingly called shelves and brought a large volume, resting at head height and placed it on the solid oak table positioned half way along the aisle.

She used a ruler to run down the list of U-boats, having looked through several papers and stopped appropriately at U116. She read aloud to herself the description, class, armaments, measurement and "action in the Atlantic during 1940/1942".

Obviously pleased with her own efficiency she allowed herself a mouse-like smile, quickly returned the papers to the box and placed it back on the same shelf she'd retrieved it from. The lights were quickly turned off and the door slammed shut and locked.

In a cramped office, desperately in need of two spring cleans her chain smoking, morose superior Geoffrey Heath, who prided himself on his tie pins, sat gnawing at a sandwich oblivious to the crumbs falling onto sheaves of legal documents. He was startled by the young woman's brisk entrance; he didn't have time to nod in recognition. Also present was the recently retired Francis Southall, a life-long friend of Heath's and known to have a penchant for attending strip clubs two lunchtimes a week… To anyone who would listen he loved relating the tale of one stripper who removed his glasses, while he was sat in the front row, breathed slowly over the lens then 'cleaned' them with her nipples before returning them to his face; and he salivated with each memory…

Miss Fish was immediately dialling the Air Ministry and turned her back not wishing to witness the revolting spectacle of their eating habits. Within a minute she was through to the appropriate office, "Hello, yes, nothing much I'm afraid. Just the usual information – anything more and you'll have to contact the German Nord museum in Munich."

There was a pause, "Yes, we can, but you will have to authorise it," there was another pause and she grimaced for hearing them eating was just as bad as watching them eating, "OK, I'll deal with it today. May I phone you tomorrow, probably get the information by Telex… Goodbye, goodbye."

She put the phone down and hurriedly left the office... Along the corridor she winced and couldn't wait to splash some 4711 perfume over her to dispel the memory of two inspirationless men happy to be Government officials; and yet it never occurred to her that the latter thought she could never be involved in a private dance with sin!

CHAPTER 13

At the same time a bustling bar in Munich was catering for its pre-evening trade. The atmosphere was convivial and all ages were represented but while the older patrons drank beer, the younger set were tossing down shots of vodka because of a special promotion. One white-haired man with grizzled features but soft eyes, sat alone; his shirt was immaculate, his suit shabby and his shoes highly polished and he was absorbed with the crossword that challenged him daily.

He failed to notice his two friends until they were almost sat down and the waiter knowing their tipple arrived promptly with three glasses of beer carried on a very shiny silver tray. With a vaguely smiling mouth he said "Hello," put the three glasses down then spun on his heels and breezed back to the bar. The trio gazed in a generalized, benign manner as they quaffed the heads off their drink before commencing conversation. Within two hours they had departed, each going his separate way as the temperatures fell rapidly.

That night Squadron Leader Fogarty slept uneasily in his Holborn flat for an unusual atmosphere had been generated in his office. Each time he woke up he scurried to the fridge and drank milk hoping it would neutralise the acid causing his prolonged indigestion. Eventually he showered at 7.00am and when he looked at himself in the mirror, a dull gaze and doglike jowls were looking back and he contented himself with the hope that Spurr would look worse when he was that age. He looked at his teeth and said two words, "Good God!"

He had been in his office almost two hours when the telephone rang. He tore the receiver off its stand, "Yes, yes, I see OK. I'll come round." He dialled using his internal phone and while he waited drew a swastika and the words *'Heil Hitler'* before smiling effortlessly. His call was answered.

"Tom, I'm good. I'm glad I caught up with you. Listen, records have been on to Munich and turned up some interesting information. I'm going round, may as well pick you up," he paused, "good OK. About fifteen minutes then."

After the pleasantries the Squadron Leader was driving his pale blue Triumph Herald the quick way across London. Both men made small talk but were itching to get to the bottom of this quest and possibly the reason. He parked his car in a reserved place eschewing the public car park, this amused the Pilot Officer though he said nothing.

Miss Fish was alarmed at the speed with which they had arrived but soon composed herself though her complexion remained as pale at the white blouse she was wearing with the same black skirt and same sensible shoes. She gave the senior officer the telex and he began reading it half to himself and half aloud. Miss Fish was unnecessarily apologetic, "I'm afraid that's all Munich could come up with."

Fogarty looked at the telex again, cleared his throat and inhaled deeply, "Sounds interesting... After a successful series of campaigns in the Atlantic during 1941, U116 went into St Nazaire for a complete overhaul and refit. She left Nazaire on October 6th 1942, destination rendezvous with pack of U-boats in Mid-Atlantic. Following campaign highly successful, no U-boats lost, thirteen merchant vessels sunk."

The Squadron Leader screwed his face up and Spurr waited expectantly as he saw Fogarty's expression change, "This is interesting, in the logbook of Kapitän Hoettges is the following *'U-boat 116 failed to make the rendezvous, radio silence never broken'*."

Pilot Officer Spurr fiddled with his spectacles, a cheap brand which now gave his face a suggestion of professional austerity.

"Hmm... if this is some joke, someone's going to a hell of a lot of trouble, done their homework..."

Fogarty interrupted, "Yes," he pondered and turned to the librarian. "Look, I don't want to cause you too much trouble, but could you get back to Munich and ask them to send everything they can on U116 – you know pictures, press cuttings, details of crew. They must have something."

He turned to the Pilot Officer, "Will you drop these pictures off in the morning?"

"Aren't you taking this a bit far, Sir?" whispered Spurr.

The imp in the Squadron Leader's heart jumped, "I'm just intrigued as to why anyone, anyone should go to such great lengths. Anyway, if the joke ends up on them it will have been worth it."

He smiled and then turned to address the librarian, "Will you get Munich to send it directly to me, it will save time." He then smiled warmly at the librarian who felt emboldened enough to enquire.

"Certainly, can you tell me what it's about?"

Despite limited sleep Fogarty suddenly looked refreshed, "Probably nothing... wait till it's sorted out then I'll put you in the picture."

"OK," was the polite response.

Out in the Atlantic there was a slight mist as U116 surfaced. Once the hatch was released Werner, Hoffman and Emmerich stood back as sea water splashed around them. All three climbed into the conning tower and fixed determined gazes through their binoculars.

In the engine room Friedrich Schreiber watched the pistons slow down as the engines decreased in speed. The earlier incidents had left his voice as indistinct as a

disembodied spirit and he was determined that wouldn't happen again; he shouldered his responsibility to the crew long before he ever thought of himself and felt he'd let some down, though Kapitän Werner had assured him this wasn't the case and he had responded better than most. Probably everyone during the crisis and his officer had echoed the same words.

"Karl, check all the main batteries, I want to know the levels."

Karl looked up, "OK Friedrich."

The Chief Engine Room Artificer continued wiping his hands with a stained cloth, "I'm going to find the reason we're burning up oil."

Karl Boeck asked him a direct question, "Is it serious?"

Schreiber was reassuring. "Not yet but it could be if the Kapitän demands the optimum from her... but we'll cope won't we," and he smiled a boy's Christmas Eve smile.

The three officers in the conning tower Werner, Hoffman and Emmerich remained apprehensive. They had coped, albeit in a manner that reflected their different personalities, though each retained a large measure of grace and chastened sympathy for the situation, unprecedented, they found themselves in.

Below it was no different; some men reminisced about the luxuries the naval high command ensured U-boat crews enjoyed. They pictured the band there to greet their return and the soldiers' theatre where they could watch German films followed by bread, sausages and genuine German beer and, of course, the well-appointed brothels where the girls were inspected regularly... After dicing with death in the Bay of Biscay regularly patrolled by bombers to such an extent it became known as the graveyard, shore leave was never underrated. Now they were confused.

Kapitän Werner's eyes were busy picking out the accumulation of clouds that would shortly signal more treacherous, thundery weather. Nevertheless his face broke into a broad smile which contrasted with the sober expressions of the other two.

"Not long now, eh Dieter, we shall know."

The First Lieutenant stood erect like a piece of well-tried oak despite the increasing strength of the wind. If he felt disenchanted internally he was full of zest on the outside, "Yes, Kapitän," he spat the words out.

Seaman Officer Emmerich also stood resolute and glanced at his watch, "Just under four hours Kapitän," he said in an upright manner which pleased his Commanding Officer.

"Four hours," Werner paused, "before we submerge I want Friedrich to check everything again in the engine room. Dieter will you see to it and any malfunctions even if Friedrich says it's nothing, I want you to tell me."

Hoffman rapidly cleared his throat, "Do you want me to see him now?"

The Kapitän remained looking through his binoculars. "Yes, Wolfgang can stay up here awhile with me."

"Very well." Noiselessly, he departed for the engine room leaving the duo scanning the horizon despite the greyness stretching itself over the ocean like a large eiderdown being pulled over a single bed.

"Dieter seems more than preoccupied, Wolfgang?"

He was about to reply when his Kapitän asked him the obvious question, "What has he said about our dilemma?" Werner's tone was light, which was an invitation for the other officer to speak freely without any recrimination.

"He is as concerned as everyone but if we are now in a different era he says he would rather die out here than go home."

Werner dropped his binoculars to his chest and looked at the Seaman Officer, "Why? He has a son who would only be nine or ten years older than him."

As Emmerich replied a strange copper colour was leaving the sky and spreading over the dark water. Undeterred he spoke, "He is frightened, Kapitän, not of that but..." he hesitated and was interrupted by a sympathetic voice.

"But what?" Both men had started to resemble silhouettes.

Emmerich's voice remained light, "Finding out that his family perished during the war, that he might have been living a lie."

Suddenly, Werner looked dumbfounded, the easy affectionate manner cut off as he inhaled the different scents still lingering in the Atlantic despite the cold. He spoke with a vulnerable uncertain smile, "I see, poor Dieter, maybe this affair has taken more out of him than even I realised. He's been with me since the beginning of the Atlantic campaign and he has coped well under very difficult conditions. Maybe I should have realised what effect this might have on him, the fact that he is a thoughtful man, intensely thoughtful."

Emmerich looked impassively and turned to look as best he could towards the horizon, "I hope, that this is just a bad dream."

A few hours later in Britain, torrential rain had blanketed the island and this didn't help Squadron Leader Fogarty's mood as he paced around his office like a convict in solitary trying to maintain fitness. He was alarmed by a sudden sharp knock on his door.

"Come in!" he rasped and a young officer entered carrying an envelope.

"This has just arrived, Sir."

"Thank you," was the brusque reply as the enveloped was handed over and the pilot left. Fogarty sat down at his desk and ripped open the envelope with a paper knife. He eagerly poured the contents onto his large blotting pad before separating photocopied press cuttings and the only surviving photograph of U116's crew.

He was absorbed by the material unaware of condensation pouring down both windows and onto the wall. He held a magnifying glass over the pictures of the submarine crew before examining his own photographs and his facial expression completely altered.

"Good God," the words were cries of exultation and Fogarty leaned back still holding the magnifying glass and staring as though in an induced trance.

In Munich, where the weather was also inclement and contributed to making dingy buildings forbidding, a lonely old man drawing an audible quick breath uneasily climbed a flight of stairs pausing at several intervals. All the landings were dimly lit and it took an effort of will for him to unlock the door of his apartment on the fourth floor.

Inside he peeled his coat off and hung it on the wooden clothes stand before removing his Trilby and placing it on the middle peg. His cat came to greet him, purring while he talked about the rain and cold. Both moved slowly into the sitting room and he removed an L.P. from a small collection and put it on his turntable before retreating to the kitchen to make himself a sandwich and cup of coffee; he smiled when he saw the cat's empty bowl.

He winced with arthritic pain when he lowered himself into his armchair but his mood was lightened when his cat settled on his lap and responded to his gentle caresses to her head. He looked at the framed photograph of himself and another young man taken just before Germany invaded Poland. "Fritz and you, Peter Werner were young men with the world at our feet." He closed his eyes and hummed along with the melody singing out of his record player before taking a drink and falling sound asleep in gradual stages, while his cat warmly ensconced on his lap didn't flinch.

CHAPTER 14

Squadron Leader Fogarty and Pilot Officer Tom Spurr relaxed in the Officers' Mess which always enjoyed an aroma of beeswax polish regardless what season of the year was present. No sooner had they finished their whisky, a waiter carried over two more in crystal glasses resting on a silver tray. Both men politely thanked the waiter.

"I'm glad you managed to get down, Tom. I feel as though I'm bursting inside," said the senior officer excitedly. He eased the contents of the A4 envelope onto the table making sure it was empty. "Take a look, not at the blurb but at the photograph and then look at the press photocopy."

The Pilot Officer obeyed but looked vacant.

"No, look closer," insisted the Squadron Leader.

Suddenly the expression on Tom Spurr's face changed, "It looks the same!" His eyes looked for an explanation but all he heard was a desperate voice.

"I know but it's impossible."

Both men sat perplexed and both took a drink before the Pilot Officer spoke, "What are you going to do? If it is a stunt it's a bloody good one, the best, in fact."

A grimace twisted Fogarty's mouth, "Have you ever heard of things like this? I don't mean supernatural or poltergeist, but transportation through time?"

Spurr was taken aback and stuttered, "W-w-well... I suppose... Yes, but it's always been something you've read about in science fiction."

Both RAF men wanted to laugh, wanted it to be an elaborate hoax.

"The kind of ruse the old firm Hickaday and Lang were famed for?" suggested Spurr.

Fogarty sprang to life, "Those two are legends in the RAF – the Scottish Presbyterian and the Welsh Baptist up to every dodge, skive and scam ever invented and some… Lang used to take a week off – Madrid, Rome, Edinburgh, London even New York… The blighter had a supply of civvy sick notes and as for Hickaday," he shook his head in utter disgust before continuing, "spent the last few years out on the golf course trying to improve high ranking officers' swing AND claiming overtime, expenses." Fogarty gritted his teeth before calming down.

He continued, "Suppose he eventually had enough of trying to make silk purses out of sows ears or something to that effect and handed his papers in at the same time as Lang. Maybe they saw something like this as their crowning glory… no can't be… surely?" He paused, squinted then spoke, "Mind you Hickaday could convince the Principality that it was him in the number nine red shirt feeding David Watkins at the Arms Park in the mid-sixties while the other culprit could persuade the Loch Ness monster himself, into believing that he actually existed!"

They wanted to tell fellow officers at the next official dinner but a haunting reality had gripped them. The Squadron Leader spoke in hushed tones as he looked at the photograph once more, "This isn't science fiction. It's real, no matter which way you look at it." The finality in his words drew no response. A minute later he lit a cigarette and talked about the aerial reconnaissance he planned to undertake the following day, flying a new course that anticipated how far a U-boat could travel from the original sighting.

U116 had been below the waves for many hours before Werner gave the order to go to periscope depth. He took his cap off and eagle-eyed scrutinised everything he saw. At first he thought there was nothing but a slight hesitation caused him to pull back his head, wipe his eyes with a clean linen handkerchief before resuming his original position. Again he stepped back.

"Dieter take a look."

Hoffman obliged and held the periscope handles firmly, "I can't quite make it out Kapitän, but, there is something."

"Good." Werner turned to Hans Fiebig, "Set course ten degrees full throttle. I want to have a closer look."

The Seaman Officer looked puzzled. "But Kapitän it is off course for the rendezvous."

Werner was reassuring, "Hans, this may answer all our questions."

Fiebig remained reluctant, "Yes Kapitän." He repeated his superior's instructions for a change of course as Werner walked towards the wardroom. Despite the cavalier nature inherent in him, the Skipper pinpointed approximately the time of rendezvous with the just sighted vessel. He measured the difference from the arranged rendezvous with the wolf pack and calculated the additional time; methodically.

Fogarty and Spurr greeted the new day, overflowing with anticipation; they couldn't wait to get airborne, eschewing a traditional breakfast for strong coffee followed by a smoke.

The Phantoms flew low over the Atlantic.

"Two minutes, Sir, and we should be at the same spot."

"We'd better spread our wings, nothing stays in the same place very long."

"Will do, Sir," was the brisk reply.

The roar from the Phantoms' engines as they turned away accelerating in opposite directions would have induced icily sweating palms and lungs paralysed from terror in anyone on surveillance duty in U116's conning tower; it was unimaginable.

Hamburg retained much from its elegant past despite the notion it had been a sheer industrial city for most of the twentieth century. The modernising had been a carefully thought-out process even if some purists railed against the carbuncle of post-war buildings they considered an assault on civic pride. This backlash was common in most Western Europe's rebuilding of city centres, where money took precedence over artistry, nevertheless suburbs and parks abounded in parts of Germany's second city. Inside a pretty detached house, Dieter Hoffman Jnr, his elegant wife and children awaited the arrival of his mother, Marlene. Despite the teenage girls' growing interest in fashion, music and boys they were excited about their grandmother's visit.

When a battered Mercedes pulled up outside fifteen minutes late, the occupants in the front room cheered and watched as the elderly woman's driver helped her out of the back seat and escorted her to the front door where Heidi, Dieter's wife, waited smiling with arms outstretched.

While Dieter paid the driver and walked him back to the car, the woman indulged in an all-consuming embrace, the imp rose in the elderly woman's heart.

"Where are the children?" she enquired. They arrived as though on cue and made a fuss before their mother instructed the girls to take Grandma through to the sitting room. They obliged and Dieter, back on the front step, kissed his wife spontaneously.

"You know she loves coming to see you, Dieter," she said.

He smiled. "Not just me but you and the children. We must persuade her to stay the night. It seems such a pity that she leaves just when we're all comfortable."

He sighed, "You know how independent she is, she's been like that all her life according to Uncle Karl." His wife smiled before ushering her husband into the front room where Grandma was giving each of the girls a small meticulously wrapped present. They received them graciously and both shrieked when Angelika opened hers to reveal a box of chocolates.

"My favourite, look!" the younger, slimmer sister was also the recipient of a box of chocolates which she opened immediately and offered around. Only her father declined patting his waistline and making reference to his weight.

Grandma was having none of it. "Dieter, life is too short to worry about silly things like that." She frowned but her son resisted, much to the chagrin of his wife who was enjoying her second soft centre.

Even sat down, Marlene Hoffman with her poise and charming smile presented an image of romance, despite the near lifetime loss of vernal intimacy. The married couple in a spirit of abstract contemplation knew she was going to stay the night and that would delight their daughters.

There was no time nor any appetite for chocolate in the Operation rooms where Squadron Leader Fogarty paced up and down like a mechanical soldier occasionally looking at a large-scale map crudely stuck against a wall with Blu Tack. When Pilot Officer Spurr arrived, his Commanding Officer stuck a disc against where U116 was sighted. He spoke with passive urgency, "Right, that's where she was and this is the area of observation we've covered."

He ran two fingers over the map, "I know it's very much hit and miss," he concluded reluctantly.

The younger officer looked at the map without confidence and said, "Ludicrous as it is, I think it should be reported if only to keep in line with procedure."

The Squadron Leader looked dismayed because he'd become absorbed by the whole episode, had taken his life out of the mundane and even saw himself entertaining the German Officers in the Mess. Though he kept this fantasy to himself should it turn out to be as Spurr believed, despite the evidence, the 'daddy of all hoaxes' that anyone was duped by would be their own cross to bear while they remained in the Armed Forces. In his imagination he could see the "old firm" taking a bow. Almost in desperation Fogarty was scraping the barrel – anyone, anything but this!

"Inglesby, a stunt like this?" His eyes pleaded. Spurr's face dropped, he looked at the Senior Officer as though he was a nincompoop.

"Has the brains and guts of three mice," he said. "Wouldn't have the imagination… could enter Pharaoh's Tomb, Sir, and think he was at a church fete! Besides he has all the ease of a man suffering with dysentery frequenting the toilet." A beaming smirk wrote itself in bold letters across his face and even the senior man chuckled before running his tongue over a loose filling and wincing.

Spurr noticed this, offered a civilised smile then said, "The Welshman?"

His C.O. nodded as pain thickened his features, "The last time he removed a filling, felt like he was clearing out a ruck for Pontypridd's fourth fifteen!"

The Pilot Officers always enjoyed seeing Senior Officers in discomfort or better pain.

"Simon means well," he said laughing inwardly before adding, "you could confine him alongside Pilot Officer Inglesby to a padded cell, straight jacket with a voodoo ventriloquist to keep 'em company."

Fogarty couldn't resist a smile which encouraged Tom Spurr, who added, "Saying in the Mess that if you have an appointment during the Five Nations and England have managed to beat Wales," he paused deliberately, "cancel it!"

The subject was changed. "How's your friend, the one you said had the appearance of a rather heavy-jowled Roman emperor?" he struggled for a name, "The bastard who keeps two steps ahead of the Inland Revenue?"

"No change there, Sir… When cornered by those jobsworths Frank just looks down at them condescendingly and sniffily asks, 'You know I'm a Marlborough man?'."

With utter disdain came Fogarty's reply, "Yes, I've met the type. He'll end up patronising God and expect Him to get used to it… mind you beating the tax man?"

Both men smirked. "Has a simple strategy, coined it off a 'Johnny Machine' in the local pub bogs." The pause was deliberate, "Buy two and keep one jump ahead!"

Spurr was in his element, "Pity about his brother, called him 'dad' and no one knew why but when he lied he was more interesting than many men telling a true story... sad though – Lieutenant Colonel retired, couldn't cope with civvy life, reduced to playing bingo three mornings a week in the community hall."

He shook his head releasing specs of dandruff, "Army arranged for him to see their shrink but after three sessions the shrink had to see a psychiatrist himself!"

Hearty laughter was heard before Fogarty paused, as though in thought, before asking Spurr, "Can you say anything pleasant about Inglesby?"

The retort was immediate, "He has a face like unactivated syphilis!"

Spurr left the room with the imp rising in his heart and offered the starchy harridan in the corridor an ingratiating "morning". There was no reply from the universally acclaimed 'dragon' whose face resembled a slab of bacon on which mould grew, which brought a grin to the Pilot Officer's ruddy complexion.

In the grey uninviting Atlantic wilderness U-boat 116 suddenly surfaced like a proud warrior. The hatch was opening and two crew members, Bonner and Seilerman, went up into the conning tower; both breathed in the air as though it was a drug before lifting their binoculars to their eyes. Despite being wrapped up in warm clothing including scarves round their neck and lower faces they were soon aware of the persisting cold but neither released the gleam of curiosity that events had thrust upon them for while this plus humour remained intact so did morale.

"Franz want a bet on what we might see today?" Bonner asked.

His question was bracing and answered with wry amusement, "Klaus, you haven't enough money to cover your bets, you're still in a shit over those three Aces that Horst sprang on you the other night. How much is it you owe him?"

The question was shrugged off. "Don't worry, I'm due a lucky streak. I'll take it all back before the end of this week, you'll see." Despite the conversation both men concentrated intensely as they looked for anything through their binoculars.

"Klaus, you have a true submariner's optimism."

Bonner chuckled, "Well, someone's got to look on the bright side, no point walking around with a long face like old bloody Peter." Now it was a moment for the other crew member to laugh as he took the binoculars away from his eyes.

Suddenly he tilted his head towards starboard and nudged Bonner, "Can you hear something?" There was no mistaking the seriousness in his voice, even if the other crew member remained unimpressed.

"Is this another joke?" he asked feigning exasperation.

Franz Seilerman was deadly serious, "No listen… listen, Klaus." Both listened, one keen, one reluctant before Bonner spoke with sudden impetus.

"I heard something," he put his binoculars back to his eyes.

"I'd better call the Kapitän," said an alarmed Franz Seilerman.

Less than thirty seconds elapsed before Werner, in the engine room with Friedrich, was suddenly interrupted by Emmerich bellowing.

"Kapitän! Kapitän! Franz has heard something, quickly!"

Within three quarters of a minute Werner and Emmerich were in the conning tower where Franz gave his binoculars to the Skipper.

Werner cursed, "These damn clouds!" There was an atmosphere of brooding silence broken only by Bonner's high pitched exclamation,

"It's coming from that direction!" He pointed and Peter Werner adjusted his position accordingly,

"Yes, I can hear it."

Emmerich spoke, instinctively, "Shall I give the order to dive Kapitän?"

Werner didn't respond immediately and the wait was nearly unbearable for the men in this exposed position.

"No," he said with firmness, "not until I've seen whatever it is."

Though none would admit it, each man, Werner included was seized with such petrifying apprehension that four hearts missed four beats while four men grappled to reassume control of their emotions.

From the cockpit of a Cessna aircraft, the pilot Bill Cole, who occasionally looked moth-eaten due to his drinking habits, whistled gaily, looking at the surrounding cumulus nimbus clouds through pale oddly sleepy eyes. His expression changed when through a large break in the cloud formation he saw U116.

Immediately, he descended to take a clear look as the officers in the conning tower savagely scrambled below with the sound of 'battle stations' ringing in their ears as the submarine began to dive.

First Lieutenant Hoffman the last down and responsible for closing the hatch looked very wet and worried. Kapitän Werner stood, impassively, next to him acknowledging the depths being reported to him; his eyes never left the instrument panel until a depth of "one hundred and twenty" was reached and then he darted one splinter of a glance at his Lieutenant.

"OK, Dieter, set course for rendezvous, we will proceed as planned." Hoffman repeated the Kapitän's orders, his mind racing like a ferret in a cage.

Above them, the Cessna's pilot had made contact with his base, "You aren't going to believe this. I've just seen a U-boat; it's submerged now position ten degrees north of Delta, on chart reference A... will be able to give you exact bearing on larger map. Is this some kind of leg pull?" A grimace twisted his mouth and he gasped, "No I haven't been drinking!"

News travelled rapidly especially that which, on the surface, seemed sensational... Squadron Leader Fogarty felt his face working alternative expressions as he hurried along the corridor of the fifth floor to Wing Commander Johnston's door. He knocked and entered to a rasping voice, "Come in." The Wing Commander hauled his bulky frame out of the seat offering a convulsive sigh.

"Look old boy, sorry to get you off your arse and all that but I've had an extraordinary call from the Ministry... claims some Johnny saw a..." he deliberately paused before frowning, "look I want you to..."

He was interrupted by a question spoken sharply, "Saw what, Sir?" The dullard might have outranked him, had a superior golf handicap and frequented church more often but he was nondescript, stumbled over his words as though in the grip of suffocation.

"Er, a... a submarine, er a... German U-boat." He then tried to look at the Squadron Leader with lively curiosity.

Fogarty's question threw him off balance, "Did he give the position?"

The senior officer tried to laugh but settled for sarcasm for that was what he excelled at or so he thought, "You don't think... oh... come on..."

The other officer straightened up unaware of his imperfect profile, "Sir, I haven't reported this yet, but now is as good as any. This pilot did see a U-boat – the same one as I saw and photographed."

The Wing Commander looked bewildered and Fogarty waited for him to assimilate the information before continuing, "I was out with a Pilot Officer doing the usual recce – you know."

Johnston nodded scarcely believing what he was hearing but suddenly very attentive.

"And well, Sir, not only did we see the mysterious U-boat but also photographed her with two or three crew." He shook his head almost in disbelief at his own words, "in the conning tower. You are aware of the practical jokes we tend to play on the Navy and vice versa but this time I don't think it's a joke." He waited but there was no reaction and when Wing Commander Johnston did speak it sounded like a person coming round from unconsciousness.

"You're serious, Squadron Leader?"

Both officers moved towards two dusty armchairs in the corner of the Spartan room. The Wing Commander continued to look feeble and piggish as he listened to Fogarty looking extraordinarily dignified as he spoke in an undramatic voice.

"Sir, if I may continue. U116 was lost in the Atlantic in October 1942. She was last seen leaving St Nazaire to rendezvous with a wolf pack. I don't know the exact coordinates but it's somewhere, maybe in some faded logbook…"

He was interrupted, "Where did you find all this out?"

He waited for the Wing Commander to finish rubbing his eyes with both palms before giving a detailed explanation to this man he knew attended 'Battle of Britain' reunions and stood beside a group of men who had walked so modestly with Death, would resemble an oafish figure. Already, events were proceeding at an alarming pace beyond the control of Her Majesty's Armed Forces.

A story appeared in the afternoon edition of a regional paper about a tanker exploding in the Atlantic and though the crew were rescued no cause had yet been given to the tragedy despite speculation. A smaller article on the next page under the heading 'Pilot spots U-boat in the Atlantic' was given two column inches; and it was brief with a footnote 'pilot insists he hadn't been drinking.' What it didn't mention was the same pilot had previously lost his driving license following a rowdy night out…

CHAPTER 15

The Berlin wall when looked at day or night was grotesque. The Eastern section of the city looked quarantined and no one, it seemed, ever woke up in a rapture of happiness that those who smell the sweetness of wild thyme at daybreak do.

In one dimly lit road with squalid houses there appeared no sign of life despite a splinter of light occasionally escaping through drawn over curtains. The whole atmosphere was barbarous more so when a jeep with four soldiers, heavily armed, stopped and its occupants got out, lit cigarettes and spoke in sullen tones knowing that a couple of residents might be daring enough to peer through a hole in the curtain to observe them.

Inside one of these near derelict dwelling an old man, downtrodden, sat alone with only a radio playing melodic music, at low volume, for comfort. Occasionally he coughed and his relief was palpable when he heard the military vehicle drive away. He sauntered over to the window and gingerly drew back part of the curtain; he wanted to be certain. His gaze from behind old glasses was dull for his eyes betrayed withdrawal and worry and his jowls were drooping.

Before dropping back into his battered leather seat, which tucked like a shroud around him, he lifted a newspaper and a couple of letter off a small side-table. He looked briefly at the newspaper held close to his head before putting it down, utterly disinterested before holding one of the letters up to his eyes and reading loudly the name of the addressee, Gunter Schreiber. Then he opened it.

The sea shone with the cold in the North Atlantic where U116 was still submerged and racing, on its new course, to the rendezvous. Hoffman and Fiebig were sitting at the mess table drinking coffee when Emmerich suddenly appeared, mug in hand.

"Not long now, an hour or so and the Kapitän says we will have reached our destination just within the time limit set out." His eyes looked pinched and the arid smell didn't help his mood.

Fiebig responded disparagingly, "You really think they're going to be there, don't you?"

Emmerich's smile resembled a snort. Hoffman left the table without saying a word, leaving both Seaman Officers to pursue their conversation despite the fatigue that assailed them and had already caused two ratings' bodies to crumple.

Emmerich now spoke in a voice from which everything had disappeared save a sober humility, "Let me ask you, if you had a choice what would you want to see out there?"

Fiebig remained motionless thinking about the question then replied in a compressed voice, "My dear Wolfgang you are in for a mighty shock. Haven't you looked at any of the latest reports the radio is picking up?"

Emmerich drew a long breath, "No, why should..." before he could finish he was interrupted.

"Then I suggest you do." Fiebig finished his coffee and put the mug back down on the table, "it makes very interesting reading." He smiled reluctantly and left. The other officer stood alone in his thoughts, conscious of his heart beating and sweaty palms.

No one cocooned in U116 was aware that a nuclear armed Frigate was on patrol in the Atlantic and moving swiftly across the surface with the grace of a gazelle. In the radar room, Number One had instructed the rating to contact him the moment anything appeared on the screen; their clean shaven faces, bright eyes and pristine uniforms contrasted perfectly with the Germans as did the computer fed control panels.

On the bridge the Captain and his First Lieutenant resembled heroic figures of Naval myth. Both wore obligatory Duffle coats and both slurped tea from large white mugs and both had large binoculars suspended by straps resting on their chest.

"Do you think there's anything in those reports, Sir?" asked the younger officer.

His Skipper smiled in mature fashion, "Well, someone wants to find out what it is out there, if anything. Our orders came straight from the Admiralty so it's obviously something at ministerial level."

The Lieutenant looked at the grey, sunless gloom in front of them before stating the obvious, "I think everyone is intrigued." The wind had begun to freshen, from the south and the occasional wave-slap against the bows was increasing the swell and lifting gently the ship. The Captain wondered if his Lieutenant was aware of this but said nothing.

In Germany speculation was spreading like a forest fire. On the front page of *Bild* to the right of the main story was a column headed 'U116 a mystery?' The report continued that a reliable source at the German Naval Museum in Munich had revealed that the British R.A.F. had made extensive enquiries concerning the missing U-boat. The article continued with the suggestion that there was a cloak of secrecy shrouding these matters and speculation had been fuelled by a reported sighting in the Atlantic. At the bottom of the report was the Factfile of U-boat 116 and a small photograph of her leaving St Nazaire on an earlier mission. The editorial team had been unanimous in their decision to make this a front page scoop even if a couple of senior journalists kept tongues firmly in cheek.

CHAPTER 16

Parliament as ever was awash with rumour, conjecture and intrigue despite the evidence and clamour from the press for clarification. Inside a private members study against a background of framed political cartoons and two watercolours depicting views in the Cotswolds – all on the South facing wall – three senior, overweight politicians were in frenetic conversation, a characteristic of all politicians when no longer in control of a situation. The youngest of the three stared out across the river and spoke with his back facing the others.

"The press are hounding us all and sundry for a story on this presumed sighting," he said.

His colleague, himself a product of public school and Oxbridge, responded with a sudden sardonic dryness, "The P.M. wants to know why the information wasn't relayed straight to Downing Street."

The right honourable gentleman facing the windows turned and pursed his lips, "Something about a joke within the services – they're forever indulging in one-upmanship."

The third politician smiled as if he had been caught off guard, "And they call us boy scouts," he rasped.

The second politician's face was a portrait of dismay when he said, "It seems leaks aren't the sole property of Her Majesty's government."

The youngest strove to assert himself, "Cold comfort if you ask me. Anyway we've got to issue a statement soon or we're going to look pretty stupid. The European press are beginning to go overboard on this," he deliberately paused as though he was practising for Prime Minister's question time one day, when he would be sat directly opposite the leader of the opposition.

"Why can't the bloody Yanks cock something up, give us a bit of breathing space."

His colleague chipped in, "Or the Russians mobilise somewhere," raising his eye brows as he spoke.

"What exactly," said the quietest of the three, "is the score with this missing U-boat; rumours are rife within the house with so-called unimpeachable sources?"

All three murmured their disapproval on hearing that banal phrase before the youngest man walked over to examine one of the political cartoons, at the same time trying to loosen his rigid spine. Once again he spoke with his back to his colleagues which didn't go unnoticed for it was appalling bad manners mixed with smug arrogance.

"The RAF have sighted and photographed a U-boat with crew in the conning tower. The U-boat 116 was reported missing in the Atlantic in October 1942."

The other two listened with increasing interest despite their obvious irritation looking at his back. He must have sensed this because suddenly his legs spun round and he continued.

"Now the photographs, our chaps match or at any rate bear a resemblance if not exact resemblance to the original press pictures from Forty Two. Incredible though this is, a further sighting has been reported and we cannot discount the explosion, as yet unexplained of a French Oil Tanker in the Atlantic, being the work of this submarine."

His intensity had increased as he informed the other politicians who remained open mouthed, "I know it's fantastic but it's the sort of *Boys Own* stuff the press have a field day with."

The eldest cabinet member gritted his discoloured teeth before coughing and his colleagues waited.

"Supposing, and I mean exactly that, there is a U-boat out in the Atlantic continuing its own private war, what does the

P.M. propose to do? Surely with all the latest gadgetry the submarine can be located?"

His question was greeted with dismay.

"Where does one start looking?" the aspiring party leader asked shrugging his shoulders, "the RAF have worked out the possible range U116 could have travelled to since the first sighting but it's still a large area…"

The quietest MP interrupted, "Have any of the RAF boys tried to find out what U116 was up to before it disappeared, it surely can't have been going into the Atlantic for a picnic?"

The rosy cheeked politician who seemed to have most information spoke again with a quiver of revived excitement, "Yes, that is in hand. There are one of three rendezvous points she may have been ordered to but not many records, detailed records exist or if they do, no one knows exactly where to lay their fingers on them. Our German friends are trying to contact former U-boat Skippers who were operative in the Atlantic in the Autumn of Forty Two but it's a question of narrowing down through a process of elimination. Very few survived the whole war."

He paused once more for effect, before continuing, "Many had their moment and then were gone."

Immediately the senior of the trio spoke. "Sure if," he paused and shook his head, "God, I don't believe what I'm saying, their wireless is still intact they can be contacted?"

Then he answered his own question, "Not if they are maintaining radio silence. Remember if these poor bastards still think it is 1942 well…"

The potential for disaster suddenly dawned on the eldest cabinet minister, "Good Lord, anything in the shipping lanes could be a potential target then… I don't believe I'm saying that."

The obviously most ambitious and knowledgeable on this matter gained the other two's attention, "I'm due at Downing Street at 2.00pm with Naval and Air Force people. I hope by then we will have a clearer picture. Surely the scientists can come up with something to give this whole business credibility?"

All three nodded their heads in mutual agreement before leaving the office.

Out in the Atlantic Peter Werner was looking through the periscope and experience told him that a storm was imminent. He released the periscope and as it went down he turned to Hans Fiebig.

"Hans we had better maintain radio silence from now just in case this is all an elaborate plan." His whole demeanour was becoming luminous and soft and he preferred that to the monotonous and chilling he felt he had become during recent events and for which he had berated himself, in private, for no Kapitän who lost the complete confidence of his crew could lead with conviction. Foulness was an unmoveable stain.

His instruction surprised the Seaman Officer.

"But Kapitän surely we have evidence enough from what we have picked up?"

The Skipper smiled, staring into the faithfulness of the crew surrounding him.

"Maybe, but what is the worst thing we or any submariner can do?" He looked with inquisitive eyes then continued, "It is to give away our exact position. We not only give our adversary the upper hand, we give him us on a plate." He was warmed by the response he saw in their eyes.

Fiebig straightened himself, "As you wish, Kapitän."

Above them, the storm was gaining ground – rain fell out of the sky so heavy that visibility was sorely restricted and the bitter wind howled its own lament. No one cast into the ocean would have survived longer than three minutes.

On a housing estate in Dresden, clean and well-cared for by Communist standard, an old woman with an angelic smile on her face sat in her favourite chair with her feet not far from a two bar electric fire. She dozed in that serene matter associated with nuns and wasn't paying particular attention to the news programme flashing out of her television. The television anchor man paused as a picture of U116 was flashed up behind him and he began relating the story. There was a sense of restlessness in the room as the elderly lady dozed despite the swollen joints of locked rheumatism. Suddenly a big picture of U116 flashed up on the screen and the narrator's voice gathered momentum as the story unfolded about a sighting of the missing boat. The monotonous piling up of hours which occupied most of her day, like some ancient burden lost its weight as she sat up, throwing off her tiredness. Something began to stir in her as individual images of the crew appeared on the screen.

There was a pause before she heard the name 'Klaus Bonner' which activated her memory banks... Her eyes flickered and she looked astounded, then frightened, then mesmerised by the television before pulling herself out of the chair and shuffling uneasy to a chest of drawers and rummaging about with unsteady fingers before extracting an envelope and emptying the contents out; her breathing continuously laboured. The shock was harsh as she picked up a creased black and white photograph of a young, energetic couple on their wedding day. She continued gazing at it through moist eyes, as though it was a young girl's picture dream. In the background, the weather forecast for Europe was bleak and the tone in the reader's voice reflected this.

Out in the Atlantic it was far worse and despite the latest improved design in Royal Navy warships they appeared to be hopelessly tossed about by the waves. In the radar room of one of two Frigates on duty, a rating with a florid face and a long Roman nose looked bored as he watched a screen that revealed nothing.

CHAPTER 17

Like some primordial creature U116 surfaced and Werner, Emmerich and Hoffman appeared in the conning tower. The Kapitän had the blank look of obsession, the fixed eyes, the voice without emotion and a pulse hammering in his wrist while the waves bashed all three officers as they struggled with their binoculars. Above the fury his voice, surprisingly, carried.

"It's impossible."

The first Seaman Officer braced himself against another wave and responded, "It's no good, Kapitän."

Peter Werner hoped it was sea water not tears of sorrow, pain and fatigue rolling down his Officer's cheeks, unchecked. The other Seaman Officer spoke with driving energy.

"Are you going to take her down, Kapitän?"

Both waited for his answer which came with a nod of his head.

The crew gathered round, anxiously as the trio, utterly soaked, descended. Hoffman addressed the men.

"I don't know if anything could be there but visibility is in feet not even yards!"

The crew turned away puzzled, dejected and homesick. Werner had been the last to come down the steps and alone in the conning tower had said to himself, "Where are you friend or foe?" He couldn't allow himself to appear weighed down by the loneliness of leadership and offered reassuring smiles to those he caught the eye of, even if he suspected some now believed in the possibility of ghosts.

Above the waves a young Lieutenant eagerly stepped on to the bridge carrying a sheet of paper.

"Sir."

The Captain, athletically built and highly thought of by his crew, smiled as he took the sheet while listening to his junior officer gabble his words.

"Something came up on the screen… I've pinpointed the exact location."

He waited anxiously as the information was examined by his Commanding Officer.

"Number One set course," the Captain gave the sheet to his fellow officer, "The hunt is really on," he announced to everyone on the bridge, briskly.

The international media were issuing bulletins, hourly, in different languages on different frequencies all pursuing the theme – U116 surfaces after forty-six years.

All that was heard in the submarine, now at its pre-optimum depth, was a cheer when the lights flicking at first finally came on after she had been plunged into darkness for half an hour. The crew were instantly relieved despite the fact that water was trickling in from several leaks.

In the engine room Friedrich, splattered with oil, climbed out from where the batteries were housed; he looked wild with fatigue and utterly spent as he spoke to his leader.

"I don't know, Kapitän. I will try again later. Give me a few moments." Fiebig waited for a response, still keeping his emotions in check.

"Thank you, Friedrich, if we have to we will take her up."

The Chief Engine Room Artificer's response was swift, determined, "Not before I have tried again."

Werner knew he was at the extreme limit of strain and tiredness and running on his nerves so he smiled softly, "Thank you Friedrich."

The two officers left for the control room and approaching them was the Steward, Peter Niester, carrying a tray of coffee "Kapitän" he said with a smile, completely incongruous with the situation and it warmed both officers. Werner took one mug and gave it to the Munich man before taking one for himself.

"Thank you Peter."

Fiebig took a sip and deliberately widened his eyes, "Thank you."

Both watched as the Steward walked on to serve the rest of the crew.

Werner took a drink then spoke, "It's important to have the right caterers on board as well as the best engineer in Dönitz's Navy."

Both men smiled and Fiebig gave his superior a knowing look for that was all that was necessary. What no one in U116 was aware of was the presence of several ships – part of Nato's fleet in the Atlantic furiously signalling to each other and pursuing different courses with one aim in mind.

CHAPTER 18

Nearer Frankfurt's busy city centre people were going about their business grateful for the warmer than usual temperatures and blinking when they caught the view of the low winter sun. Everything was relatively peaceful despite the hustle and bustle of city life.

The contrast with what it had been four decades earlier when the unique medieval city centre universally acclaimed for its timber-frame buildings was almost completely destroyed by allied bombing, was hard to reconcile as was the persecution of the Jews who witnessed their synagogues destroyed during the Nazi era. Despite fierce urban combat in March 1945 the city was eventually captured by the 5th infantry Division and the 6th Armoured Division of the United States army and became part of the American Zone of Occupation of Germany. It eventually lost out to Bonn, preferred by Konrad Adenauer, the first post-war Chancellor. Post-war reconstruction had largely been a simple modern style thus changing the architectural face of Frankfurt though some landmark buildings were reconstructed historically including St Paul's Church, though in a simplified manner. A newspaper vendor was busier than usual as customers swiftly bought their copy of *Frankfurter Allgemeine Zeitung*, all eager to read about the latest instalment in the saga of U116 which was now the main story of the day.

One of those quietly waiting was an elderly, yet still sprightly, priest who looked heartbreakingly poignant, his face pinched white and woeful. He walked away from the stand engrossed in the front page coverage. Before hastily crossing a main road he folded the newspaper and put it in his coat pocket.

He walked towards his parish church Heilig-Kreuz-Kirche, in the Bornheim district and was greeted by two middle-aged ladies, persecuted with worries, who attended morning mass each day, "Good morning Father Reiz... lovely day." His polite response was automatic but he didn't stop. He felt perspiration beading his upper lip as he walked up the aisle towards the front pew; his hand trembled as he brushed it across his mouth before sitting down.

The shadow of a cross was thrown across the altar as the sun moved and Father Reiz's face had taken on that terrible look of strain and fear; gone was the sheen of humble sophistication that had endeared him to countless parishioners down the years. The church was empty save for two sisters deep in silent prayer midway down the side aisle, and a middle-aged mother with her daughter who was instantly challenging and piquant but chaste though it was obvious would bloom into something more sensual because of her teasing blue eyes and yet to be discovered, blasts of blood shaking emotion. The aromas of stale incense sharpened the still air as the priest knelt down, closed his eyes and joined his hands in silent meditation.

The solemnity was shaken by a small man, haggard, with lank hair and a bulbous nose far too big for his furtive face who was coughing and spluttering; perhaps he was carrying some taint – bankruptcy, an unfaithful wife, alcohol abuse or just shot nerves. Whatever it was he left as quickly as he entered the church; and only Father Reiz remained – unaware.

He was joined by the middle-aged woman, who'd noticed his demeanour earlier, leaving her bored daughter to gaze at all the religious artefacts, "Father, forgive me but I couldn't help noting how worried you looked when you walked into the church," her smile was saintly as she waited for the priest's response.

"Come," he moved along the pew, "come kneel down with me."

The matronly woman obeyed immediately, letting her rosary beads dangle through her fingers. A silence followed before he spoke with a prickling of uncertainty that ran through his body like warm schnapps, "I have had something of a shock today."

The woman looked alarmed, "What is it, Father, is there anything I can do?"

Joachin Reiz's brother took her hands, gently, to reassure her, "There is nothing you can do, nothing any of us can do."

"Tell me, Father."

Both sat back in the polished oak pew.

"A German U-boat from the last war has mysteriously appeared in the Atlantic. At first it was considered a hoax but now there is indisputable evidence." The priest paused gauging the woman's response, "You must have heard it on the news or read about it?"

The mother nodded her head, twice, slowly.

"It is the same U-boat my brother was in when it went missing all those years ago." There was the beginning of a smile on the elderly man's face, which buoyed the parishioner.

"But, Father, if it is true then surely it is a miracle and evidence that God exists today and that centuries of faith and hope have not been in vain." A larger smile enveloped her face and she listened to his emotional response.

"Perhaps you are right." He looked at the altar before continuing, "These men will find great difficulty resuming their lives after forty years or more, particularly if time has stood still for them. The world is such a different place," he looked at the woman who remained motionless.

"Remember men from all over Germany fought then, now the country is partitioned. How could any man return to the East sector and hope to find any recognisable way of life or for that matter in the West?"

"You forget, Father, that the tyranny of Nazism was the worst thing that happened to Germany. My family and relatives were victims, you know. That beast with his heady and hypnotic ideas of making the Fatherland great, his rhetoric whipped German society out of its torpor then came the scapegoats."

Father Reiz had remained motionless while the woman spoke for he found any movement might stop the flow of words. Now he took hold of her hands, "You are strong I can tell that. I should rejoice that my brother might be alive and that we will possibly meet up again. Maybe there is a way that God will help all those men to find a meaning in life."

He stood up and smiled in the direction of the daughter who returned the gesture, "Come let us light some candles."

What had transpired between the priest and the woman was nothing compared to the ongoing drama in U116. In the engine room Friedrich lay exhausted on his back covered in oil, wet through. Kapitän Werner climbed into the diesel room fearing the worse as water was spraying everywhere. His Chief Engine Room Artificer looked bowed but not beaten.

"I'm sorry, Kapitän, I'm sorry. The pressure…"

He was interrupted, "It's alright, Friedrich, you have done your best," he smiled and hoped it conveyed reassurance.

"We will take her up." His words were greeted with a reluctant smile.

It seemed a lonely walk to the control room and he reflected on his years and training and experience the navy had prepared him for critical moments but this was not in the mapped out programme. Gauging chances, foreseeing the next eventuality, avoiding it were part and parcel and familiar to U-boat commanders but this was freakish and both Werner and his crew had to fit into the evolving picture which was not of a familiar pattern. Seaman Officer Fiebig was biting his lip when he acknowledged his Kapitän's presence.

"We will have to surface, Hans, there's too much water in the boat; diving tanks are waterlogged except for number one."

"Yes Sir," was the Munich man's abrupt response. He repeated the order.

Werner continued to hide his anxiety, "Hydroplanes hard a-rise, motors full ahead." There was a gradual, if painful, moment as U116 struggled to the surface. Her crew remained silent, drenched in sweat and breathing in jerks as the oxygen supply was very low.

The relief was palpable when she bobbled on the surface and the hatch to the conning tower was opened to reveal a storm, arguably over its worst, but visibility very poor.

On the bridge of an R.N. warship the Hampshire born Captain was looking at the latest report from the radar room; his Number One was looking impatient.

"Number One."

"Sir."

"Set course. Range is four miles. Signal positions to the others and we may as well get the RAF to recce." There was no mistaking the origins of his creamy burr even if on this occasion there was a deliberate sharpness to his words.

"Yes, Sir," his Number One replied.

In the conning tower five submariners were only too aware of a turbulent sea lashed by a tempest and more unruly than an excited crowd as distilled waves ran into them repeatedly. Werner, Fiebig, Emmerich, Hoffman and Bonner held binoculars in different directions uttering thunderous shouts of defiance. It was enough to make the Kapitän laugh and his gradual build-up was infectious and increased the energy of the sodden men and their genuine camaraderie. Below, Stührmann lay on his bed breathing in fresh air in a theatrical manner before grabbing his groin.

"I hope some air going in there!"

Horst, Wolf, Ernst, Jorgen and Karl also prostrate on their beds looked at each other and began to smile. Joachim Reiz turned to the small wooden crucifix fixed to the plating beside him and gently ran his index finger over it – his religious connection was the only safeguard he ever needed and some of the crew were envious but never said anything.

Unknown to U-boat 116, two Phantoms were screaming through the sky.

"OK, Johnnie, should be there in less than two minutes, better go down and get a closer look," the younger pilot said.

Suddenly the noise was ear-splitting and Emmerich screamed, "Kapitän!" Everyone turned to face Emmerich and two dark shapes raced over the top of them leaving agonised expressions on the Germans' faces.

Despite fatigue, the submariner crew dragged themselves towards the conning tower wanting to know what all the commotion was about. Werner delivered his verdict to the other officers.

"Whatever armaments these craft carry, if any, are beyond me. We cannot risk going under again."

No sooner had the roar died down, it returned with a vengeance as Fiebig shouted, "Sir!" A sudden parting of the dark clouds gave a clearer view of the aircraft. Peter Werner watched the Phantom roar over and kept his gaze over the sky.

"Hans, I think you have your answer." A mournful silence emptied over the whole of U116's sailors.

On the horizon a British warship was approaching and the advances in design, capability and technology over nearly half a century were blindingly obvious. Some more crew had squeezed into the conning tower and watched in awe as the nuclear powered warship loomed within sight as the sky cleared. Several submariners began pointing out features to one another that they had never seen before.

A bland, somewhat sad, smile arched the U-boat Kapitän's expressive mouth as the realisation dawned on him that they had been made captive.

"Hans, I don't think our guns will be a match for theirs."

Fiebig forced a smile which was severed by Emmerich's interruption, "Kapitän, a signal."

Werner's response was swift, "Get a signal up immediately." The signal from the warship was replayed. Emmerich retained his professionalism but it took an effort of will.

"She wants identification immediately. I am trying to translate the rest of the message but hold on, I think it's something like part – a N.A.T.O. force… spotted, no sighted, some days ago."

Werner sucked his teeth, "Just give our class."

"Yes, Kapitän," acknowledged Emmerich.

A signal was flashed from U116 and within half a minute came the response, "She says our signal is not enough, wants full identification and the name of Captain."

The mellow tone in his voice vibrated with his inner feelings when Peter Werner gave further instruction, "OK give it," he paused "and ask what the date is."

The signal was sent and there was a long wait, which seemed like an eternity for the submariners before any response was flashed back. Emmerich tried to contain the worrying excitement in his voice.

"She is replying – thank you for identification – information you requested is as follows it is October 11th 19…" there was an agonising pause which caused many of the German men to close their eyes, "…88. Am coming alongside, would like to meet officers and crew – boat will be sent across."

"Everyone below!" rattled the U-boat Skipper.

The men responded leaving Werner alone on the bridge looking at the approaching warship. When he retired below he left the hatch open.

"Crew assembled?" he asked Hoffman who'd already anticipated his Kapitän's next move.

"Yes Kapitän."

Werner looked with admiration as the crew rapidly assembled in the control room. There was an uneasy silence which Werner immediately punctured, "I think you could say that we've grown old, overnight."

Most tittered at the remark and it was significant all the officers laughed boldly but without exaggeration.

Their leader continued, "I cannot explain what has happened but it has happened. We are no longer in 1942, the year is 1988." He deliberately paused to let this sink in but the men remained silent; he drew a deep breath, blinked then continued, "I know what must be going through some of your minds at the moment. I understand but I am your Kapitän and whatever has happened we will stick together," he paused, "stick together eh?"

He smiled and the crew responded with mixed applause, "Yes, Kapitän."

He began to feel like a drunk person knowing that each movement, each word had to be performed with exactitude and concentration less everything slipped into a blurred fog. He cleared his throat then spoke, "A ship is coming alongside soon, I and two officers will join the Captain of this vessel. Hans, you will assume command in my absence."

He had already turned his gaze towards the Seaman Officer before giving him the authority.

"Yes Kapitän," the words were said with reluctance.

Peter Werner looked over his crew, before straightening up; it was a subtle movement barely noticed, "Your loyalty to me must be transferred in my absence. Before going to board the ship I want assurance that nothing will befall my crew of U-boat 116."

He noticed the relief expressed in many of the young faces staring back at him, "It will be a testing time for us all but let's not forget who we are."

He hoped his words might be similar to early morning sunshine melting the stiffness in his crew's cramped bodies and minds. He wondered if he should say more but was concerned he might begin to sound theatrical, given the circumstances – better to leave it as a challenge to their endurance and seamanship.

"Dismissed."

Kapitän Werner felt no sense of anti-climax when he turned to face Hans Fiebig, "We had better go back into the conning tower."

The warship was less than half a mile away and clearly visible for the sky had cleared and what a majestic sight, thought Peter Werner, as she appeared to glide over the waves. Hans Fiebig looked with reluctant admiration and the warm mist that earlier dimmed his eyes was gone for here in front of him was one of life's current facts.

Werner chose his words deliberately, "It is important we don't lose our heads no matter what."

A few seconds passed before Fiebig responded, "We are helpless, Kapitän."

"I know but we are independent as well. I want the men occupied while I'm away – there is plenty of work that can be carried out. I want as much water cleared as possible."

Their conversation dried up but neither let their outward confidence wane as they became aware of British sailors, starboard, getting their first glimpse of U-boat submariners; time and reality had blissfully mingled and there was no going back.

CHAPTER 19

Dusseldorf had enjoyed a chequered history from being guardian of the Rhine to hostilities with Cologne which culminated with its elevation to city status, it was no stranger to bloodletting though most of its citizens were aware of two events – the custom of cartwheels was credited to its children to the extent that each year there was a cartwheeling contest and following the General Strike in 1920, forty-five members of the German Miners Union were murdered by Freikorps.

What no one wanted to remember was the city had also been the target for strategic bombing by the Allies culminating with 700 bombers bringing death and destruction in one night in 1943 as part of their campaign against the Ruhr industry. Large areas were devastated in Rostock and Lübeck but this was minimised compared to the industrial damage done to the city where 400 acres were obliterated and evacuation hampered because of damage done to the main railway station. This was something those crew members who came from the city could never envisage; to them Düsseldorf produced the best beer in Germany – Altbier, a hoppy beer where Brewers used pale malts and the old method of using warm fermenting yeasts. Even Peter Werner had remarked about it having stayed in the city on a couple of occasions.

By April 1945 resistance was negligible as US forces had overrun the city and in the post-war years it had recovered much of its former grandeur, particularly in terms of its most significant historic buildings. Peter Neister's face would have filled with anguish had he known but then so would all of U116's crew.

In one of the more prosperous suburbs and in the kitchen of a large detached home an elderly lady, with traces of youthful attraction, was ironing clothes. The classical music playing out of the radio offered her a balm of sorts as well as producing a scattering of energy to get her through the chore.

Suddenly the program was interrupted with a news bulletin, *"We apologise for interrupting the program but have confirmed reports that German submarine U116 lost in the Atlantic in 1942 has been sighted and reports coming in suggest captain and crew are safe."* The suddenness and content paralysed her and the iron dropped from her hand; and the broadcast continued, *"the scientific world has been completely thrown over as searches for an explanation not since…"* She turned the radio off and struggled to her seat, having picked up the iron; all her actions were a blur.

For over forty years she had put her fears away as unworthy, though it was often impossible to cure the melancholy that haunted her because love was an indestructible rock no sea could devour. She'd turned to religion as many bereaved had even if their faith often faltered and now the sudden announcement was at odds with most of the sermons she listened to. Her seat was vacated and the gentle lady shouldered her way to the sitting room and picked up a framed photograph reading aloud the handwritten message – "To Grandma, with love from Switzerland, your favourite grandson Conrad (Meiner) 1986".

Elsa looked exhausted and missed the first ring on her doorbell. She heard the second, a more prolonged shrill and struggled to the front door where she was greeted by a woman of similar age, conservatively dressed and with conservative manners.

"Come on, Elsa, we will be late," her friend offered with vigorous enthusiasm, she heard Elsa's reply.

"No, I'm afraid not today. I'm not feeling too well."

Suddenly her friend's expression dropped and she put her gloved hand on Elsa's shoulders.

"What's the matter? Do you want me to call a doctor?"

Elsa took a deep intake of air, "No that's alright. I think I will lie down besides Helmut will be back soon."

Her friend remained genuinely concerned, "Are you sure, I can stay with you."

Elsa perked up, "No, you go. I will phone you later."

"Are you sure?"

"Yes go now," and she ushered her friend out of the doorway, smiling before closing the door.

Hours earlier in the North Atlantic a navy boat propelled by an outboard motor had drawn up alongside the warship; the German Kapitän, his First Lieutenant and Seaman Officer had climbed up a rope ladder lowered from the port side.

The trio were escorted to the Officers' Mess. They looked about trying to familiarise themselves with what they saw but were gripped with such a petrifying apprehension their hearts missed beats though they managed to disguise it; Hoffman in particular felt he was teetering on the edge, frightened he might not survive the greatest dramatic moment in his life. He struggled with his Commanding Officer's, seemingly, calm attitude but he used it to steady himself; and he also noticed Emmerich blinking, not fully in control.

Captain Shaw and Lieutenant Commander Herd both in their forties, both with advancing girths due to insufficient exercise, invited them to sit down. A Steward passed large whiskeys for each man and dutifully left. Each man simultaneously drank the whiskey in one go, more to relieve self-consciousness from a situation that had no precedent. The Captain filled the glasses once more smiling at his opposite number, acutely aware of the contrast in the state of the uniforms. He cleared his throat in a subdued rather than raucous manner that suggested an Independent School education and was about to address his guests when, to everyone's surprise, Peter Werner interrupted, speaking in a quiet yet authoritative voice.

"You said it was 1988?"

Shaw responded immediately, "Yes, that's right." He looked inquisitively at the Kapitän whose fellow Germans swallowed as they knew the next question was inevitable and might be a "cartload to hell" but they were astute enough to know it was essential. The German's face did not change expression, "Then what happened in the war?"

The British Officers looked at each other in near disbelief as their former enemy took a mouthful of whisky suddenly aware he hadn't tasted such a good single malt for over forty years and if given one final request it would be to have a bottle; and he noticed the rouge like touches of colour in the Lieutenant Commander's cheekbones as well as the tidy English head as the son of Lyme Regis hoteliers moved forward in his seat.

"The war, Captain?"

Werner relaxed his shoulders, "Yes, the war between our two countries."

Shaw's interruption was immediate as it was awkward, like a lifelong subscriber to *Reader's Digest* informing the magazine's editor that he wasn't renewing his membership.

"The war you're talking about ended in 1945," he paused to allow this information to be digested by the Germans, "Forty-three years ago."

Dieter Hoffman, about to pick his glass up, knocked it over then stood it up ignoring the puddle of whisky before looking at Captain Shaw.

"What happened Captain?" He looked confused and was holding his breath in a morbid sense; then the English Captain answered without any trace of emotion.

"Germany was defeated."

None of the submariners showed any indignation and waited for their own Commanding Officer to continue the conversation. He paused as a self-conscious Steward resplendent in a brilliant white tunic, knocked and entered the room carrying a tray holding a coffee pot, mugs and a large plate of sandwiches generously filled with honey roast ham with a tube of Colman's mustard resting on a saucer. Shaw began filling up the mugs and the aroma soothed the atmosphere in the mess.

"And then what?" asked Werner.

Shaw adopted an Old World mood, conciliatory, for he knew his former enemy would be devastated by what he had to tell them and he was determined to hold on to the notion they were all sailors first and foremost; religion and politics if necessary could come later.

"Well, the allies pushed across Europe having invaded in June 1944 and pushed west while the Russians mobilised everything they had and moved from the east." Again there was a lull which gave Herd the opportunity to leave his seat unobtrusively and turn down the heat.

Emmerich from looking a little ragged became smoother, "Did the Fuhrer surrender?" he asked almost innocently.

Captain Shaw's voice remained even, nearly toneless, "Hitler committed suicide in the final days." He looked at Peter Werner, "Captain this is as much a shock to us as it is to you. I can only but try to understand how you must feel…"

Werner could see the sympathy in the Englishman's eyes for, while he respected him as well as a complete lack of raffish qualities in his character, unusual for a naval officer or so he thought.

"Please Captain go on."

Shaw looked perplexed.

"Go on."

The men drank from their mugs and the Germans declined cigarettes offered to them. Peter Werner quickly looked at the décor again before smiling at the English Captain.

"The war, you see for days my crew have lived on a knife edge not knowing our fate. We picked up strange music and reports on the wireless and then we sighted two aircraft, the like of which we have never known and now this, the…"

The younger Englishman spoke up, "Captain if I may be permitted. In 1945 the world had had enough as a result of the victory over Germany, your country was divided into the east and west."

Emmerich interrupted, "How do you mean, East and West?"

Herd continued in a voice he hoped sounded authentic, not triumphant, "East Germany because Russian controlled and the West – allowed to continue under Allied guidance."

"Were there new boundaries drawn?" asked Emmerich cautiously.

"Yes, except Berlin, which has a western section operating there also."

The German responded immediately though this time with a larger degree of emotion, "How do you mean a western section operating there?"

Throughout the conversation both English officers had been relieved that the Germans spoke English better than tourists and that most of what had been said by both parties was understood.

Captain Shaw stood up as did everyone else, out of courtesy.

"Captain, may I suggest you rest, get some sleep and food and that goes, of course, for your crew and then we can start again. I have one officer on board who speaks German pretty well and he will be briefed. My orders are to escort you to the nearest port and God knows what we do from there." He smiled and the earlier apprehension everyone had felt was dissipating, certainly his stomach was no longer churning in queasy turmoil.

"Obviously you will want to report back to your crew. Is there anything we can get you right away? Medical supplies, water…"

Kapitän Werner spoke, "We have taken in water – do you have some pumping equipment or engineers who can help my engineer?"

Herd looked at his Captain, "I can see to that."

"Thank you."

"Captain, if you would excuse me I will arrange for a party to come across to give you a hand once you have briefed your own men."

Werner nodded his head appreciatively, "Thank you Lieutenant Commander."

Captain Shaw departed and the men sat down; Herd poured himself another whisky and was disappointed the Germans declined but said nothing.

Within fifteen minutes the submariners were back in the outbound powered boat exchanging waves with Hans Fiebig stood in the conning tower.

"The Kapitän's returning!" he yelled down the hatch.

It was a short ride and gave Werner time to reminisce about his life as a submariner for he knew now he faced the biggest challenge of his life. He recounted submarine school and crews trained to deal with every combat situation including the grim task of escaping from a sunken submarine which was rare.

The instructors sought to weed out those having second thoughts by emphasising the horror of a boat plunged out of control into the depths and unable to rise again; of the pressure hull creaking and exploding under the force and waiting to die one by one as the air supply ran out. Surprisingly, Werner thought to himself looking towards the horizon it never put anyone off and no one quit the programme. The immortality of youth he smiled to himself before looking at each of his men and wondering...

All three officers were deliberately expressionless as they boarded U116 and made their way to the control room where an extremely impatient crew waited for their Kapitän to address them. For his own part Peter Werner's own confidence was steady, upheld by faith and strengthened by the conviction that before him stood the finest crew any Kapitän could ask for.

"I have just been speaking with the British Captain of a warship which is part of a force called NATO of which Germany is a part."

A mumble emanated from the assembled men and he paused before continuing.

"The war has been over for forty-three years." The silence, immersed in superstition, was deafening and the Kapitän scratched his chin then spoke without altering his tone.

"Yes, my friends, we are now all old men." He nodded slowly releasing a smile but could feel his eyes watering, "I have to tell you Germany is a divided country. When the war finished in defeat in nineteen forty-five, the Russians took over the east and the British and Americans the west. Berlin is like an island in the east; it has two sectors one Russian and the other British and American."

A few of the crew looked towards Joachin Reiz to see the Berliner's reaction but he remained steadfast.

"This, I know, is hard for us to understand. We need all our strength and fortitude. I asked you many times before in the heat of battle and not one of you let me down. I am asking another time. Only God can decide our fate now but we are not helpless. The world we inhabited may have passed but in time I'm sure all of us will adapt. We have to…" Immediately each man's thoughts turned to his respective family; it was suffocating, burning throats with a thirst never before felt.

"Sir, what has happened to our families?" shouted Conrad Meiner, roused from his mournful reflection.

"Conrad, I can't answer that. Who is dead? No one can explain what happened to us… some freak of nature the British Captain says. Even scientists today can't agree," he paused to smile to himself, "so not everything has changed."

Some of the crew returned faint smiles and this buoyed the officers.

"The world is astounded by the news of our U-boat-116, so perhaps in time we will be re-united with our families and I know that will frighten many of you."

Hans Fiebig who hadn't spoken much but had conducted himself with an air of great dignity and reserve during the crisis turned from looking at the crew and towards his Commanding Officer, "Kapitän, what are our immediate plans?"

It was what the crew wanted to know and he'd anticipated it.

Werner spoke with renewed confidence, "We will assemble on the deck and be taken to the British ship. I want a skeleton crew to remain – there is work still to be done. The Captain has offered his assistance and I have accepted."

He looked at his crew, proudly, discouraging any reticence.

Friedrich Schreiber who'd been cleaning his hands of oil with a rag throughout the meeting spoke, "I don't want to leave the submarine, Kapitän."

The crew watched their commanding officer who responded immediately, concisely.

"OK Friedrich."

He turned to his Seaman Officer, "Hans, find out which men want to stay with the Chief Engine Room Artificer."

The crew were left talking amongst themselves as Werner left for the wardroom. He was watched by Wolfgang Emmerich who recognised the enormous courage of his Kapitän.

Had anyone been in the conning tower they would have been aware of a trick of light, a feature in the Atlantic Ocean that allowed a copper colour to spread over the sky, the dark water before racing inland and covering smouldering autumn leaves. For centuries naval men had marvelled at what they termed nature at its finest – that season before winter and when it was over the cycle continued as it had done since creation and seasons rotated crawling like cripples with no hope but heaven…

CHAPTER 20

The outboard powered boat moved swiftly towards U116, watched by the submariners lined up on deck. The two British ratings, charged with bringing the German crew over, decided there was something almost mystical about this image. When the boat moved into position parallel with U116, self-conscious smiles were exchanged; the mood was friendly but muted.

All this was observed by Friedrich in the conning tower who remained there until his crewmates were boarding the ship before descending below.

U116's crew were led into the wardroom where they were greeted by Captain Shaw and his officers in pristine uniforms obviously pressed with starch. It wasn't lost on the submariners who relaxed, undoubtedly recalling to themselves images of English men they had gleaned through books, films and hearsay. All were impressed by the lavish hospitality – a table in the centre laden with plates of sandwiches and large mugs into which two stewards were pouring piping hot coffee. The two captains stood shoulder to shoulder and the German crew waited.

"Go on, it is alright," said Peter Werner moving his eyes in the direction of the spread.

"Smoke if you want," offered the English captain airily.

The crew moved hastily, some pausing to look at the portrait of Elizabeth II which hung in prime position and higher than other photographs.

Emmerich brought a plate of sandwiches and mug to his Kapitän before returning to serve himself. Captain Shaw settled for a mug of coffee flanked by one of his officers who noticed that their counterparts were scrutinising the ribbon on his uniform trying not to make it obvious.

"Thank you," Werner took in the aroma, "This looks good."

"I hope you enjoy it, there is plenty more," said Shaw affably watching the German take a sip.

"It is good."

Both men smiled, particularly Werner, who noticed his men devouring the sandwiches but not abandoning their manners in the presence of the British. The atmosphere was friendly without being jovial and this suited both parties for many questions remained and some answers everyone knew would cause anguish and sorrow and heartache among the submariners. The two captains moved to a corner leaving the other officers to make small talk.

"Captain, I have made Lieutenant Williams available to your crew and yourself, he is an expert on Germany and I know, obviously, there will be many questions to ask. God knows in your position I would be exactly the same."

Werner pondered, "One thing I would like to know, Captain."

"Yes, fire away."

"Fire away, Captain, what does that mean?"

Shaw chuckled in an engaging manner, "I'm sorry, it's just an English expression. What did you want to know?" He noticed Werner smile.

"Is there a war at the moment?"

Shaw sucked in his breath before he responded, "No, not on the scale of '39 to '45 but we have gone into a nuclear age."

The German looked puzzled, "Nuclear age?"

"Yes weapons, nuclear weapons so much more destructive than anything you could imagine, Captain, have surprisingly kept the peace between the east and the west for Russia and her allies and America and her allies – since 1945."

Peter Werner thought for a moment then responded, "But British and Russians all fought Germany and your officer told me that America joined their side in December 1941 declaring war on Japan following the attack on Pearl Harbour and that we were allies with Japan?"

Shaw thought for a few seconds, "Yes Captain but I can't explain what happened so easily. There have been wars all over the world despite the fact that everything has advanced so rapidly in the last forty years, that is, except human nature. Let me give you an example, Captain. Nearly twenty years ago man landed on the moon."

The U-boat Skipper was taken aback and it showed all over his face, "On the moon, that was the stuff of H.G. Wells was it not?"

Captain Shaw sucked in more breath and nodded his head in agreement, "Yes, Captain you're right but despite that scientists still have not found a cure for the common cold," he laughed hoping the shock of what he'd added would relax his guest whom he knew, under the surface, was in turmoil.

Werner added hastily, "I see Captain that the English sense of humour has not changed."

Both men moved towards the food and the host insisted that his guest helped himself to the new batch of sandwiches that had just arrived. His crew stood back as he helped himself. This example of protocol and etiquette was not lost on the British Captain or his officers.

Shaw turned to the submariners, "Please, gentlemen, don't stand on ceremony… help yourselves."

"Thank you Captain," was the collective response which impressed the Englishman.

It was obvious to the assembled group that both Captains had high regard for each other; a tacit understanding that naval men possess regardless of whether they are friend or foe. Captain Shaw noticed that his opposite number had almost finished his coffee and instinctively picked the coffee pot up and refilled his guest's mug, then his own.

Both men's eyes flashed warmly and with wisdom borne of experience the Englishman felt this was the right moment to draw up a delicate subject, "I would like your crew to watch a film we have on board. It will help clarify the situation, somewhat sketchily, I might add but it shows how the world has moved on in every sphere of life since nineteen forty five. It may give your men something to think about."

Werner listened intently and Shaw continued in a genial manner, "Would you mind if the ship's doctor examined your men? It's usual procedure."

The Kapitän nodded in the affirmative then spoke. His words were clear cut like the lash of a whip.

"What are your orders concerning us Captain?"

Shaw strove to avoid any sense of pragmatism, "Depending on your fuel, we are to escort you and your crew back to Portsmouth where you will be met by a delegation from the West German Embassy."

Werner calmly received this news then asked the obvious question, "What about East, some of my crew lived in that part of Germany."

The question had been anticipated and the response was frank, "Well, I'm not sure what the East plans to do. You see there is a constant veil of secrecy. I think that after you have seen this film you will understand a bit more. Come, let's take the weight off our feet."

It was a relief for Shaw to sit down for in his late forties he'd been plagued by occasional bouts of sciatica which he knew made him 'crusty' but was loathed to have spinal surgery for he'd heard so many horror stories. Werner too, was surprised at how comfortable the easy chairs were. They watched the fraternisation between the men as Captain Shaw adroitly pulled his chair into a position so that he was closer to the submariner who was eavesdropping on the conversation Wolfgang Emmerich and Lieutenant Commander Herd were enjoying. Both were pointing out features of a modern warship, the design of which was framed and fastened to a metal structure. Herd's eyes were sparkling but not mischievously as he explained how the war in the Atlantic began to turn in the Allies favour from late nineteen forty-two and both Captains could see a cordial friendship had sprung up between them; it was visible despite the crowded room thick with tobacco smoke.

"Actually it went into nineteen forty-three. In fact we were just about on our knees. In the latter half of forty-two, three million tons of allied shipping had been sunk with minimal loss to your U-boat fleet."

Emmerich absorbed this but showed no emotional reaction and the Lieutenant Commander continued, "Historians have argued ever since how long we could have held out and the popular notion is probably three to four months, certainly no more."

Shaw could see that Werner was listening intently and didn't want to distract him.

Herd paused, "What changed it was the allied escort system being completely revamped."

Emmerich listened, fascinated but queried the word "revamped".

Shaw explained, "Support groups were attached to the convoys with a brief to hunt out and pursue U-boats before they could reach the convoys and this allied to greater surveillance, the result was the number of U-boats sunk, increased."

"Please continue," said Emmerich and because his words had the geniality of common comradeship it encouraged Herd though the latter was conscious of neither sounding triumphant nor resembling a pub bore.

"We had new depth charges that could be set to shallow depths, a newer more accurate homing torpedo and an anti-submarine rocket."

Emmerich expressed surprise but allowed the English officer to continue. Any questions, he thought, could wait.

"In Germany it was thought that this continued lack of success was due to the inexperience of young commanders but the fact was U-boat effectiveness began to wane, as well as her being inferior to the then rapidly improving defensive techniques."

Emmerich, like many German officers, understood and spoke reasonable English and because the Englishman had been articulate with his intonation, translation was unnecessary. The German again looked at the display board and began pointing, drawing the Lieutenant Commander in.

"The lines are so fine it is hard to imagine that this ship carries more destructive power than the Bismarck, Gnaisenau and Tirpitz added together." He gestured with his hands, "and much, much more." He turned to look at Kapitän Werner aware that he'd been listening to their conversations and he could see a warm overplas of blood in his cheeks which enhanced his universally acknowledged good looks; more appealing though the mellow fire in his eyes was still there.

Herd addressed Emmerich, "When we get to Portsmouth I'd like to show you around. In fact I'll clear it with the Skipper, Captain, to take you around the old girl sometime."

"Please," was the smiling German's response.

The gathering broke up within forty-five minutes and arrangements were confirmed for the crew to return to U116 with large bottles of mineral water and boxes of fruit and then return early evening to watch the documentary film in the projection room.

Naturally the submariners discussed this amongst themselves and an air of anxiety ran throughout the boat and it was left to the Kapitän and his officers to re-assure the crew despite acknowledging that what they were going to see would be painful and involve much soul searching.

"How else could it be?" Peter Werner asked them. Again he pointed out their strength lay in their commitment and loyalty to each other. He insisted it was a chain that could never be broken. He always spoke with the correct tone for each occasion, the officers remarked afterwards and it was decided each submariner would wear full uniform if possible following a wash and shave. There were no dissenters.

When word came from the conning tower that the boat was speeding towards them with a powerful light fitted on the bow.

Werner issued one more instruction, "Men, we watch in silence there will be days, weeks for any discussion." He looked at his crew, could see the primitive, strong in them despite everything and it warmed his heart and strengthened his manhood.

The Seaman Officers took charge and ushered everyone onto the deck while the commanding officer went to the engine room to the handful who were staying in the submarine to carry out more repairs and light duties.

Though transportation only took twenty minutes in the relatively calm sea, Peter Werner's thoughts just like the previous occasion turned to his early days in the submarine service. He remembered a survivor from a doomed submarine coming to talk to the aspiring trainees and explaining in fine detail that it was impossible to open the escape hatch underwater; as the sea pressure would have jammed tight the hatch and controls. The only method of escape was to flood the interior with sea water equalizing the interior and exterior pressure of the boat before the hatch could be opened. Peter Werner remembered the palpable relief on the faces of the audience before the veteran U-boat sailor talked about the hazard of the boats batteries exposed to sea water, emitting poisonous chlorine gas.

All submariners were aware of incidents of U-boats forced to the surface and abandoned when salt water had seeped into the battery casings which had cracked under a depth charge attack. Once again he looked with discernible pride at his men despite the concern writ large on their manly faces...

The submarine crew were greeted, again, cordially by the British and were led to the kitchen where hot chocolate and biscuits were provided. Twenty minutes later they were escorted to the projection room and seated in rows on collapsible chairs already in place. At the back, resting on a table, was a projector with a large spool of film and two ratings ready to operate it. No formal announcement was necessary as the men had been briefed by their Kapitän who sat at the back alongside Captain Shaw and two officers including Lieutenant Commander Herd. The atmosphere was tense as occasional flashes hit a blank screen already lowered from the ceiling and the familiar sound of a film spool rolling punctuated the air. The title appeared in large letters 'War 1939-45'. It was in newsreel form with footage including the Atlantic campaign, Germany's early conquests, the invasion of Russia and the turning point in North Africa that eventually turned to defeat and a bomb ruined Germany. The commentary was sharp, concise and occasionally damning especially when an American voice took over from his British colleague.

The Germans watched with little more than agonised expressions and some eyes brimmed with tears. Captain Shaw felt self-conscious but was resolute that this was the correct thing to do and his officers agreed even if those present also felt uncomfortable particularly during the brief section devoted to the liberation of concentration camps which drew gasps of disbelief among the submariners including Peter Werner.

The second half of the film concentrated on the post-war years including the Berlin blockade, Korea, Elizabeth II's Coronation, Bay of Pigs, Kennedy's assassination, invasion of Czechoslovakia, space exploration, Middle East conflict and nuclear accidents. It was a relief for the audience when the film depicted changing fashions, design technology and the pursuit of excellence in sport before returning to the disasters of famine and earthquakes.

When the screen went blank and the projector was turned off a forbidding silence entered the room. Captain Shaw stopped one of the ratings from switching the lights back on and felt it was his duty to address everyone. He whispered something into Peter Werner's ear before standing and walking in sober fashion to the front. Only the night lights were on giving him the near appearance of a silhouette figure.

"Gentlemen, I know what a shock this has been and I know all of you will have retreated into yourselves… understandable. We have arranged to take you straight back to U-boat 116. If anyone has any questions please…"

The walls of silence as Shaw would later reflect, "Were bomb proof and growing taller by the minute." Lieutenant Commander Herd told the submariners there was hot tea and biscuits for anyone before boarding but his voice was lame and fell on deaf ears.

The projection room emptied until both Captains were the only occupants. Peter Werner knew his host was uneasy but being the professional he was found the right words.

"Captain Shaw all of us had to know… you did right… now it is up to me and my officers…" No more words were necessary and Shaw offered his hand before escorting his guest to the boat where his men sat in continued stunned silence. Only Emmerich spoke when helping his Kapitän with a seat.

The ride back to U116 seemed longer despite the calmness in both sky and sea. The moon was as big as it could get and Werner looked at it; he could sense its restless power and a driving energy that lit up vast areas of the ocean. Within himself he felt an urgency to address his men but didn't want to disturb the quietness and was happy to let the burr coming from the outboard motor act as a balm. He was pleased both British ratings remained silent and wondered if that instruction had come from Captain Shaw or despite their lowly rank they had integrity.

That night the crew of U116 officially listed as missing until now, ached with guilt heavy enough to break the back of a donkey, more than tiredness and sleep was a precious commodity only a few took possession off. In the morning Werner gathered his officers together and told them exactly what he was going to say to the crew – that we were and are proud German sailors – we fought for the Fatherland – we were not complicit in the atrocities perpetrated by Nazi ideology. He mentioned briefly to the officers that they had witnessed the rise of Hitler, National Socialism, but they were men pursuing naval careers and it would be unnatural for anyone on board to carry the burden for those appalling acts of crimes against humanity.

The officers were impressed especially when he remarked, "We are all dissatisfied, unhappy because our dreams have been shattered, now we have to rebuild as best we can or we are finished… it is our duty to lead the men… I want everyone assembled at 11.00am." As an afterthought he said, "We can't deny what happened but we won't grow sullen in a quiet or resigned way. We have to learn to sleep again easily and deeply." They might not have been able to articulate to each other but these German officer class knew that the man stood before them could never resemble an orphan devoid of friends, inner strength or mercy from the world.

CHAPTER 21

What many thought was the final journey of U-boat 116 began with a deafening roar; jags of lightning darting, zig-zagging up and down barely dampened by torrential rain and atmospheric disturbances and then as though by divine intervention change was complete. The sky cleared to a pale blue and the sun insinuated itself subtly everywhere. It was a deceptive almost early winter sun and had with it a buzzing sleepiness that relaxed all sailors, extinguishing unnecessary anguish.

The changing waves were a feature as the warship escorted U116 towards the English Channel. In the conning tower Werner, Fiebig and Emmerich scrutinised a helicopter that flew overhead and mumbled at its ability to remain motionless above them; all three were in awe and the trio looked cleaner and more relaxed having taken advantage of the hot water bath, haircut, shave and laundry facilities offered by their escort. Almost gone was the gauntness attributed to food rationing and lack of proper nutrition, as well as exercise.

This comparative state of sublime grace lasted until nearly 2.00pm when it started to get chilly. The men could feel a gradual unpleasant sinking of elations as reality began to niggle again. The Commanding Officer told his officers to bring back the uplifting sensations, possess them with a vengeance if necessary and be grateful they are there and he told himself to take his own advice, too.

He invited more personnel into the conning tower when through his binoculars he could see a flotilla of small boats coming out to greet the lost submarine. The officers were aghast and Emmerich arranged for the U116's company to dress in uniform and line up on the deck when they approached harbour.

Captain Shaw signalled to U116 that he wanted them to enter harbour first and they would pick up the rear. He finished with – 'Welcome to dry land'.

The submarine crew were taken aback at the fanfare they could see. Many thought they would be treated like lepers and not allowed to set foot in England, that all negotiation for any future would be done on board the submarine moored in the harbour with armed destroyers circling them. Jorgen Bahn whispered in Eric Steven's ears, "Hundreds."

He was corrected, "No, thousands."

Kapitän Werner, Seaman Officers Hans Fiebig and Wolfgang Emmerich were still ensconced in the conning tower watching their men's reaction to the large crowds that had gathered to see this momentous event. They were completely taken aback by the carnival atmosphere and Peter Werner nudged his officer, "Hans, Goering would turn in his grave if he saw this."

Fiebig smiled.

"It's all so puzzling," said Emmerich with an expression of awed reverence.

Werner spoke thoughtfully, "This isn't a show of false daintiness, it's human nature. That is the puzzle. Look the sons and daughters of men and women who wanted our heads now fete us, like gods."

The trio were interrupted by Friedrich Schreiber joining them, "Kapitän, everything is as it should be. With more fuel there is no reason why we can't return to Germany. Those British engineers have done a thorough job." The Chief Engine Room Artificer was particularly deaf so wasn't aware of the cheering but when he looked away from his Kapitän and saw the spectacle in the distance his mouth fell open and his eyes looked in disbelief, like a hypnotised lamb.

Werner waited for the shock to recede and then spoke, "Friedrich, all talk of going back to Germany must wait until we have met with some of our own people. Don't despair, Friedrich," he smiled, "you will be fine."

He looked again at the crowds in further bewilderment as the submarine moved effortlessly ahead of the warship, at twelve knots.

U-boat 116 was a mile out from the harbour and Schreiber turned to the officers, "I think I will go back below." He started to climb down when Werner called to him, "Friedrich, don't worry... everything will be alright." Both men exchanged smiles as half a dozen seagulls flew over the stern.

The nearer both vessels got to the quayside the more muted the assembled crowd became. The realisation that approaching was a U-boat with authentic German submariners whom were fighting in the Second World War less than a week ago jarred them into silence. It was unnerving for the crew lined on the deck in uniform for naval men, especially submariners, were superstitious many believed in signs and the unnatural in nature as well as convictions about black cats, lucky numbers and weather predictions and symbols; and most avoided palmistry. When U116's engines shut down only the breeze made some semblance of sound and this unnerved some.

Klaus Bonner became aware of Bernhart Frantze for whom this was his maiden voyage having graduated from intensive training, breathing hard like a horse whose saddle has just been removed. He flicked his arm and whispered words of encouragement that allayed some of the tension the twenty year old was feeling. Ernst Bortfeld's remark about whether the Queen of England was coming to see them as most of her country had, elicited a warm smile from those who heard it.

While a launch parading the flag of West Germany and the Union Jack, carried a delegation from West Germany's embassy to the warship now at anchor, an outboard powered boat approached U116 for the purpose of taking Werner, Fiebig, Hoffman and Emmerich to meet the delegation with Captain Shaw in attendance. The array of boats that had manoeuvred their way out of the harbour to meet the submarine, kept a discreet distance away though some on board occasionally waved to the submariners whom were under orders not to "fraternise" with civilians at "this point in time".

In the officers' wardroom the delegation of six men, all career civil servants and expensively dressed in bespoke overcoats and suits, greeted the officers enthusiastically with prolonged handshakes.

It wasn't lost on Captain Shaw that the submariners' enthusiasm didn't match the civilians'. Maybe, he surmised, they thought they were being viewed as exhibits rather than naval personnel. Despite initial reticence the Englishman had enjoyed the Germans' company, marvelled at their command and ability to converse in his language and their overall countenance. He caught Peter Werner's eye and smiled two words – "I know".

Everyone's attention was taken by a Steward wheeling in a trolley holding plates of honey roast ham, cheese and tuna sandwiches plus a large metal teapot and large jug of milk. Werner instinctively walked over to the trolley, watched by everyone, and picking up a tube of Colemans mustard and a jar of Branston Pickle announced, "Branston Pickle... now I know I am in England." Everyone laughed, whimsically and any air of seriousness vanished. Captain Shaw insisted that the civilians join the naval men for a snorter of Oban whisky. He rattled on about it being twelve years old and one of Scotland's best kept secrets. Again laughter filled the air and Kapitän Werner appreciated what his opposite number was doing but said nothing, for words would have been superfluous.

The party enjoyed the ship's hospitality before sitting down at a beautifully polished oak table which still carried a faint aroma of beeswax. The submariners graciously accepted another tot while the other guests declined; the ship's photographer took some pictures for posterity then slipped out the wardroom just as effortlessly as he'd slipped in, as did the Steward.

The senior official sat opposite the officers of U116.

"Whatever has happened, no one can explain yet, but you are regarded as true heroes in Germany. The world is astounded at what has transpired. As a West German I am filled with immense pride and obvious amazement." He smiled but it wasn't characterised by smugness or conceit. Humble, thought Peter Werner who responded in a measured tone.

"You are very gracious, Sir, but my crew is from all Germany – a Germany we have been informed no longer exists?"

There was a pause but it wasn't awkward and the representative still looking in awe at his fellow countrymen replied, "Yes that is true Kapitän; it is also true that despite Germany being partitioned, Europe has enjoyed forty years and more of relative peace." He smiled and waited for a response.

"That is little compensation for some of my crew. You see my men are thinking about their future, if one exists for them. They are going to be foreigners in an alien country whenever they try to rebuild their lives. At the moment everyone seems euphoric but I don't see any of that in my men."

Another official, of similar age to his superior but with an athletic build; high forehead and broad mouth joined the conversation, "We understand the problem you face…" He attempted to say more but was interrupted by Dieter Hoffman, deliberately.

"Do you? Can you imagine what it feels like to know your family, if they are still alive, have lived their life? Your son or daughter, the little one you cherished is suddenly older, much older than you are?"

Captain Shaw admired the First Lieutenant's restraint for he was neither histrionic in voice or movement and he remembered after their first meeting when he and Lieutenant Commander Herd had shuddered at the prospect of "What if Admiral Dönitz's request for twenty more submarines and crew per month had been granted by Hitler." Both Englishmen had winced at this idea. "What if Hitler had been a naval man not army and hadn't listened to his Luftwaffe supremo?"

The warship Skipper listened while the younger official spoke with cool precision.

"Herr Hoffman, extensive searches are being made to locate friends, relatives and families. The shock is immense for them also, but we hope that when you arrive back in Germany there will be a reunion for all those."

He paused, waiting for what he'd said to sink in before he was beckoned to continue.

"We are hoping that the east will adopt the same policy of ours in offering generously to help resettle the men of U116 with their families and offspring. I know it will be difficult and some even will find acute difficulty in readjusting. There just is no precedent to act upon."

Werner thought this man oozed sincerity not the type associated with mendacious politicians and he spoke with honesty.

"You are sympathetic and have somehow grasped the situation better than your colleagues."

The senior official looked embarrassed but said nothing.

Werner continued, "My men will respond to you."

The second official looked relieved, "I should like to meet your crew, as soon as possible."

Captain Shaw sprang to life and spoke as clear as a steel engraving, "As soon as you are ready, Kapitän, I would welcome your men aboard. They must be all in."

Werner turned to face the Englishman, "I would like them to stay in the submarine. We will work out the schedule among ourselves."

Shaw raised his hands in an agreeable gesture, "Of course, Captain. Lieutenant Commander Herd will see that your men are well looked after."

The German officers nodded their gratitude. Already Herd was planning in his head to cordon off an area that had washing facilities and bunk beds without putting any of his own crew to disadvantage.

When the launch returned to the quayside, the German officers at Captain Shaw's request, remained on board. Tea was served over discussions about sport and reminisces about their respective teenage years. Each found the others absorbing and the Englishmen were mightily impressed with Hans Fiebig's recollection of attending the Olympic Games in Berlin with his father whom, having caught a glimpse of the Fuhrer taking his seat in the main stand had whispered to his son, "That man may take this country to hell."

The Seaman Officer looked at the English officers, "I never replied, I was so absorbed in my career in the navy and if politics was ever mentioned, which was rare, the common enemy was only ever Communism." He had been unaware that, politically, Berlin was seen as a left wing stronghold with the Nazis calling it "the reddest city in Europe after Moscow," which probably accounted for propagandist Joseph Goebbels engineering a march through the capital in 1926 which devolved into a vicious brawl in the communist stronghold of Wedding.

Fiebig paused, "I remember the final of the hundred metres was the next race… Jesse Owens." Everyone looked amazed and then Fiebig forced a smile, "I still remember it vividly fifty-two years later." No one laughed out loud despite everyone feeling amiable in present company.

Before the submariners were escorted to their boat Werner confided in Shaw that he would speak again to his men at length.

The ride back to U116 was filled with a curious air of unreality as though the current situation had been built by somebody else for somebody else and the German submariners had unwittingly sailed into it from another world, more astonished than creatures from another planet.

For inner peace Peter Werner again retraced his training in submarine school and recounted to himself a couple of anecdotal stories the senior instructors used to tell the aspiring men chosen for officer training; he was determined the first hiss of the scythe of depression would not be for him.

CHAPTER 22

"Remain vigilant," Kapitän Werner had told his crew amongst the up-to-date information he had for them and now they waited on deck for the boat to arrive, their grips stuffed to capacity with laundry.

Earlier, the sea had been as still as a milk pond now it was hostile and grey with waves snarling and splashing. The two ratings in charge looked curious, the submariners didn't and no one noticed Portsmouth's skyline fading under the darkness.

The officers disembarked and were escorted by a young Lieutenant to the wardroom while Lieutenant Commander Herd welcomed the scruffy looking Germans and, together with four ratings and a German speaking Sub Lieutenant, walked them to their quarters.

The laundry facilities were explained to them in a manner it was easy to understand and the Sub Lieutenant took Max Fromer's clothes, put them in the cylinder, added washing powder then pressed the on button. He explained that the programme settings were already in place and the whole cycle would take up to an hour. The submariners watched, listened intently, marvelling at the technology. It was explained that after the spin dry, the clothes should be removed and placed in one of the hot tumble dryers. Four ratings had been dispatched to iron their clothes or show them what setting to use to avoid any burning.

Siggie Maier, the mid-twenties Radio Operator, asked the Sub Lieutenant if he would thank the British sailors for their assistance and said that if the roles were reversed he hoped the same hospitality would have been reciprocated.

"Yes," agreed the men in unison and when the translation was complete, it brought a warm smile from the British sailors.

While the washing machines built up white bubbly suds, hot tea and biscuits were provided, cigarettes exchanged and personal photographs were shown; it was a very relaxed atmosphere. Captain Shaw had emphasised, and had managed to keep a straight face to the warships personnel, that he didn't want to hear and neither did the Officers, "any rendition of *Colonel Bogey's March.*" He knew that in some quarters raucous laughter would have broken out as his instruction went over the PA system.

The submariners were impressed by the bathroom facilities of showers, baths, large wash basins and couldn't wait to stand under hot water which showed no sign of getting cold. Most shaved with razors and shaving gel provided, then dressed in sweatshirts and overalls provided which caused great hilarity.

The warmth in the quarters and the provision of hot steak sandwiches and large mugs of tea, relaxed the men further as did a dozen or so copies of *Playboy* and *Men Only* discreetly left by ratings, following the ironing of the men's clothes.

Horst Kruger and Wolf Hechler emerged from the steam filled shower room with outsized white towels wrapped round them. Steam was pouring off them when Eric Steven flipping through one of the magazines called to them, "Hey, at least some things haven't changed." He laughed and held up the centre page spread of the model for them to see.

Wolf, full of German vigour and ideas about women which had never quite materialised, knelt down in front of the picture and began kissing it; his eyes were still vital and the others roared their approval as they gathered round, each man thawing out if not in mind certainly in body. The humorous remarks were designed, sub-consciously, to leaven anxiety and give respite and they were succeeding for now; and some still remained in a trance of enjoyment having had a hot soak.

The German cook took another large gulp of tea and belched deliberately to get everyone's attention, "I hope the Kapitän has arranged shore leave now that we are celebrities."

Karl Boeck, quiet, well-built but with a humorous, deep voice usually associated with the best cigars looked at several of his colleagues, "Forty years, that's the longest I've ever gone without it." He waited for the outburst of laughter then continued, "And it's a long time to wait for a shit." The response was bellowing and the laughter remained hearty when the submariners' Steward remarked, "Not being ashore for forty years must be some record."

Jorgen Bahn turned the PA on and fiddled with the dials until music was heard – New Romantics singing in heartfelt rhythm about love and disappointment and it was as tasty to the submariners as food wrapped in cellophane so he switched off. The skylarking continued as did the jovial badinage and it shielded the vein of anxiety about what the future held potentially for those family men.

The atmosphere by contrast in the Officers' mess was relatively subdued; it could almost be described as formal, which the Officer class preferred unless written on the official agenda were the words – get drunk, let your hair down! Feibig, Emmerich and Werner were sipping Marston's Pedigree beer from pint glasses with Captain Shaw and his Officers. In the corner was a buffet laid out with the ship's best silver on display.

The two Captains shouldered over to look at the cold meats and vast array of salad meticulously placed on salvers. Werner was smoking a Havana cigar he kept for special occasions and was relieved that he had enough in the wooden box he took with him on every mission to offer them around. Though two in the gathering had declined he was pleased Captain Shaw ran one along his nostrils in that time old tradition before lighting Peter Werner's with his personal cigarette lighter. Both men blew smoke rings and smiled warmly at each other as Werner opened the conversation.

"Captain, it is amusing that here we are about to eat with you and your men and yet a week ago we were trying to sink you."

The Englishman swallowed some beer then remarked quietly, "Forty years ago."

The German made light of the remark, "Oh yes, I forgot forty years ago. Tell me, Captain, your father must have fought during the war?"

"Yes he did, he was lost at sea in 1944. He was First Officer on board a destroyer that was sunk by a U-boat."

Werner was visibly shaken. "Forgive me Captain I ought not to have asked."

Shaw immediately put his guest at ease, something he had become a master at through instinct and breeding, "All right, Captain, it's such a long time. From what I remember of my father he was a good man but my mother never got over it. I don't think women ever do. Still it didn't deter me from joining," he laughed warmly, "it must be in the family blood."

Kapitän Werner gave him a direct searching look and his heart quickened, "The sea is contagious all right, most of my crew had fathers who served in earlier submarines, atrocious environments – who knows maybe even sons."

The other officers found their Captains and Herd was sent to bring U116's crew to join them. Most had changed back into their own clothes but all looked scrubbed clean, particularly finger nails and this pleased their Kapitän who invited his host to speak to them before he did.

"Gentlemen, please, the bar is open to you." He directed their gaze with his hand and they saw a Steward in a brilliant white tunic beginning to line up pints of beer on the counter.

"Thank you Kapitän," the men responded, collectively.

The atmosphere was pleasant, helped by Captain Shaw's invitation to those ratings who'd shown the men to their quarters to socialise with them. It wasn't lost on Peter Werner how the Captain eased the ratings self-consciousness by directing them to the bar, joking he wasn't going to make a habit of this. One of the officers moved behind the bar to help the steward and soon everyone had a drink in his hand and something to say. At 9.30pm Captain Shaw announced 'last orders' and fifteen minutes later a trolley with mugs of hot chocolate, biscuits and cake was wheeled in.

Ernst Bortfeld always guaranteed to have the right quip for the right occasion despite occasional crippling melancholy gazed at the latest offering and shook his hand before walking a few paces in determined fashion, watched by the others until he stood in front of both commanding officers holding three biscuits and his mug of chocolate.

"Kapitän I have a request," his voice was like an echo of many moods and the officers waited, "may I transfer to the English navy?"

The Captains burst into laughter like an engine at the first pull of the starting string. Herd, who'd moved from behind the bar, also laughed with pleasure, as the long suffering Cook rejoined his crew some of whom were laughing with abandon having heard what he'd said.

By 10.15pm two stewards were clearing everything away and stacking glasses on the bar ready to go in the washer. Most of the Germans were in their bunks as tiredness caught up with them. Some were asleep, some were snoring and some were awake thinking and nobody had a dark scowl on their face.

Conrad Meiner was staring at a picture of his fiancée. Opposite him Franz Seilerman watched and when he detected a sense of unrest started up quiet conversation.

"Are you trying to imagine what she looks like now?" His eyes and teeth flashed whenever he bestowed his frequent smiles and his chin was at a new angle as he waited for a response.

Conrad turned to him, "Yes, it's so hard to comprehend how I will react when or if we meet – she is older than my mother." His eyes changed from shining brown to dull and his mood wasn't helped when the Berliner said in a compressed, serious croaking voice.

"And perhaps you are younger than her son." The words fell into silence like a boulder in a pool and it alarmed the younger man. Both seemed in a trance.

"Face it, Conrad, she is probably married with a family of sons, daughters and grandchildren. See it in that light, she has at least lived for forty or more years. That is something, eh?"

Conrad looked again at the photograph and felt a shaking spasm flood through his body and his words were relevant, "Yes, I suppose you're right Franz…. There isn't any future." He shook his head and the movement had an odd wistfulness.

"Nonsense," said Seilerman, regaining Meiner's attention. "There is a future for all of us. I wonder if my wife and sons are alright. I hope so. My sons, yes, they will be older than me. I am excited not dismayed at meeting them and maybe their grandchildren, who knows. Each of us will have to take one day at a time as though we were starting our life from scratch, Conrad, not some abyss from which you can't get out. We are submariners, we have the pride of endurance few possess."

Meiner felt a splash of hope had been dropped into his eyes, "You're helpful Franz… I feel a bit better having talked."

"We have to help one another but I also sense there is going to be heartaches. No man should have to treat it like cancerous pain because there are no drugs to hand." He stretched his frame into a more comfortable position before rolling over onto his side.

Meiner reminisced contentedly. He built up pictures of the Swing Dance movement he and his friends subscribed to in their early teens eschewing the Hitler youth as unexciting much to the chagrin of Party leaders. He remembered the Café Heinze and wearing his homburg hat even while dancing; he, like his friends even had Union Jack pins on the lapels of their jackets. It was where he met his fiancée whom like the other girls wore short skirts, applied lipstick and fingernail polish and wore their hair long and down instead of German style rolls.

The authorities called them 'Swing-Heinis' and the movement was huge in Hamburg and Conrad Meiner was smack in the middle of it unwittingly in direct opposition to its National Socialist elite because this music was performed by negroes and several Jewish musicians and the song texts defied Nazi ideology and encouraged moral depravity with their use of coarse jargon mostly made of Anglicisms.

Only later would the native of Hamburg find out that many 'Swing Kids', having been accused of anarchist propaganda and sabotage of the armed services, were tried by the Volks-gerichtshof and sentenced to death or concentration camps.

Close to the dormitory's steel door entrance, Hydrophone Operator Wolf Hechler lay on his bunk lighting a cigarette; he took a pull on it before tossing it over to Horst Kruger and lighting another for himself.

Horst took a very long pull and the tip took on a rich red glow, "Not bad these."

Wolf responded, "Yeah, they're OK, Horst, so was that beer we drank tonight. It seemed fizzy at first but the more I had the more I got used to it." He chuckled and was surprised when his friend didn't.

Horst inhaled before speaking, "Do you think that our families have been contacted yet?" His words sounded like those of a self-contained inward looking submariner adjusting to new surroundings.

Wolf replied in quiet voice, nonchalant even, out the corner of his mouth, "Who knows? I only have a sister besides my parents; let's see my father would now be ninety-one, my mother younger. That's if they are still alive. My sister she would be sixty-eight."

The two submariners continued the conversation in an expanse of warmth and comradeship despite events.

Horst took another long pull on his cigarette, "Only my mother and brother are alive or were alive. My father and sister were killed in a car crash in 1937."

Wolf adjusted his upper body to ease the thudding ache in his right hip, "It's not so bad meeting your parents because they have always been old."

Horst nodded and watched Wolf blow smoke rings into the air which quickly dissolved them.

Wolf continued, "But the men who were married, I'm not so sure." He quietened his voice, "One leave a provocative, sensual young woman, the next an old woman both physically and mentally."

Horst delayed his response until he'd chewed over what he'd just heard.

"What do you think will happen?"

Wolf opened his eyes wide and sucked his teeth, "God only knows. All of us were shaken by what has happened to Germany. Those concentration camps – how could Germans let that happen?" His voice was barely audible now for he only wanted an audience of one, "It made me feel bitter and yes, Horst, ashamed. I don't want any part of Germany now. Look at these Englanders... proud in their merits and memories – Dunkirk for example."

Horst cleared his throat, almost apologetically, "I know what you mean," he said quietly, slowly. "I felt it, but war if only because it dehumanises you, eventually permits such things to happen... I bet these people, too, have skeletons in their wardrobes."

Wolf gave Horst a long look which prompted him to continue.

"I know it's no excuse, Wolf, but what can you say? Our people just let it happen; there must have been a reason why it couldn't be stopped. Us submariners are true seamen, Germans, proud of our allegiance to the fatherland. This National Socialism and the political factions did not mean much to us..."

The rugged looking young man born and brought up in Dresden and highly regarded by his crew remained sceptical, "Or if we were aware, we just turned a blind eye." He didn't talk about the utter destruction of his home city for that too was a painful conversation and one he only wanted to share with his fellow Hydrophone Operator Uve Stührman, also from Dresden. The sequence in the documentary footage U116's crew had watched, related to nighttime bombing by both sides had left them aghast…

CHAPTER 23

During the day an onslaught of rain had never weakened; enough had fallen to swell a paradise of fruit but this was one of the characteristics of Munich and one the locals had learnt to laugh about down the centuries and ridicule the vigilant eyesight of self-styled amateur weather forecasters.

The 6pm church bells had strangely announced the death knell of this month's storm though many drains in the city centre had failed to cope and those in the immediate suburbs less so, nevertheless the air cleared of pollution and dust was savoured by people often breathing in theatrical manner often unaware of their actions. Mid evening and most of the bars in the city centre were getting into full swing and one in particular was a regular haunt of old men who carried their ailments stoically but daren't look beyond the end of the month. The most elderly still alive could remember Hitler and his supporters staging the Bier Hall Putsch in 1923 in an attempt to seize power from the Weimar Republic. Many thought it was the end of the Nazi party, virtually unknown outside Munich.

However, the city became a Nazi stronghold when power was seized in 1933 and those in their seventies living peaceful lives didn't like to talk about Dachau, the first concentration camp built only ten miles north west, or remember Prime Minister Chamberlain being duped by the Munich Agreement in 1938 – an appeasement he thought would bring peace.

Hans Fiebig, brought up in the city, would later find out that it had suffered extensive bombing causing over forty per cent of the population to leave before peace was declared in

April 1945. Following American occupation Munich had been completely rebuilt, preserving its pre-war street grid and the population had grown as did its prosperity and with most of the older generation living in relative comfort preferring to keep any skeletons firmly locked in the cupboard. Events of the last week had changed much of the cosiness.

Suddenly Fritz Werner appeared like an apparition and shuffled towards his friends with an immeasurable smile on his face and tears in his eyes and his friends responded when he opened out his newspaper to show them a picture of his brother. A lean waiter with greased back hair arrived with a tray of drinks and patted the elderly man on his shoulder, glimpsing the picture and story before he spoke with heartfelt warmth, "I am very happy for you, Fritz. Please these drinks are on the house." Not wanting to intrude further he swiftly collected the empty glasses on the group's table having placed the new round of drinks down and circled his way back to the bar collecting one or two empty glasses on route.

The newest arrival was choking with emotion, "Thank you, thank you."

His friend lifted his hand, smiled with brightness in his eyes and offered advice, "Now you mustn't get too excited, Fritz. Remember the old ticker." He patted his hand on his chest, "is not quite what it was."

Everyone smiled while the submariner's brother scoffed, "That doctor has been saying I could drop dead any time, for over five years. Just a few months more," he remarked humbly, "and I couldn't ask for much more."

Another octogenarian piped up, "You take it easy, Fritz. Tell us when do you expect to meet your brother?"

While they waited for a response everyone took a drink including Fritz who then threw his hands in the air, "I don't know, officialdom has gone berserk. At the moment they are in England. No plans have been decided whether to fly them home or what."

As he finished his sentence Bavarian music began playing over the music system and brought smiles to older customers.

Another friend looked at the men, "Some of them won't be able to go home, at least not to what they left even taking in allowances for the modern world."

His suggestion was quickly followed up by another member of their party whose right hand badly deformed by arthritis had resulted in amputation of two fingers, "Do they know how many crew come from the Democratic Republic?" he said with genuine concern.

Fritz shrugged his shoulders, "Who knows" he whispered defiantly taking another drink of beer.

He was asked by the comparatively scruffily dressed man to his left, "Do you think your brother will recognise you?"

His question was dismissed by the others with facial gestures before Fritz's closest friend in the group spoke, "Don't be silly, of course he will, years cannot erase the bond between two close brothers. He may not recognise him at first but what's important is he'll know."

"Maybe," offered the man softly who'd asked the question, then he took a drink.

Everyone looked at Fritz and he smiled, "I wonder what Peter is thinking right now or for that matter all the others who are going to meet again for the first time after all these years."

He looked wistful and the friend to his right put his hand on the brother's knee, "It will be a wonderful moment you'll see." He smiled and so did Fritz deliberately offering a degree of levity, "I know one thing, he'll be better looking than me."

The men cheered, all with waxen wizened faces and raised their glasses.

CHAPTER 24

In Portsmouth harbour the crew of U116 were carrying out maintenance and an air of relaxation permeated proceedings particularly among those polishing the internal piping. The submariners had been given shore leave the previous evening and most had taken the opportunity to experience modern life with ratings from the warships who had volunteered to take the U-boat men in small groups of three and four. The highlight for the cook and steward, both football fanatics had been a late afternoon rendezvous at Fratton Park, home of Portsmouth F.C. and holders of the F.A. Cup during the Second World War, having beaten Wolverhampton Wanderers at Wembley in 1939.

One of the ratings had a relation on the staff who had managed to pull a few strings. For both Germans it was a wonderful memory and thoughtful gesture to be allowed onto the pitch where the ghosts of Jimmy Dickinson and Duggie Reid still held sway.

"A terrible weakness struck me... and the wonderful joy to juggle a football in the centre circle," the cook later told the submariners.

Both were given letters, on official paper with the Pompey Crest, rewarding the visit and the hope that if they returned to England in the future one of their destinations would be Fratton Park. The Club Secretary had gone out of his way to accommodate them with a complete tour of the ground including the dressing rooms and boardroom where the trophy cabinet gleamed with silverware.

When both men were presented with the club's football jersey, Ernst Bortfeld declared he would lose weight so as not to embarrass Pompey when he pulled the shirt on. Everyone laughed even the *Portsmouth News* photographer who recorded the event. As a parting gift, each received a small clock with the Pompey Chimes playing at each hour. Little wonder, as more darkness fell, that the next stop was Southsea and a walk along the front to South Parade Pier followed by another treat – a traditional English pub that had, fortunately, escaped marketing trends.

"It's called Brickies," said the rating, placing four pints of Brickwoods Ales on the table where its quartet were sat, close to an open fire. The submariners were overwhelmed by the geniality of their hosts; men a fortnight earlier they would have regarded with acute hostility. Of course the ratings were as much intrigued and for them a wonderful experience to tell their own children, maybe grandchildren. The fact that the Admiralty, in an understated way, were footing the bill was not lost on the hosts who offered their own cigarettes and a wry smile followed by the word "Cheers!" when the third round arrived.

The officers on U-boat 116 were getting to grips with the new routine completely alien to them and the pressing sense of the future being shaped in a way they didn't necessarily want it shaped. Each submariner had lived through an extraordinary few days and Kapitän Peter Werner was very conscious of keeping everyone, as he told his officers, "intact".

His watch revealed 11.00am and he was sat on his bed reading *World War III* by Richard Nixon. He had been absorbed from the first page and was half way through it; occasionally he put the book down and pondered its content.

He recognised Wolfgang Emmerich's footsteps, "Come in, Wolfgang."

The Seaman Officer drew back the curtain, "Excuse me, Kapitän."

"What is it?" replied a smiling Werner.

"Captain Shaw has asked if you will join him for lunch."

The response was enthusiastic, "I accept his invitation."

Emmerich looked at the cover of his Kapitän's book which provoked a remark, "Very interesting… you should read it."

The junior officer smiled, "There is something else, Kapitän." There was nothing in his tone that gave cause for concern and Werner tilted his head, "some of the men went drinking last night with some of the English crew and there was trouble."

Both officers were aware that Naval men from time immemorial let their hair down when shore leave beckoned; it was a fact of life and Peter Werner wasn't overly concerned.

"What sort of trouble, Wolfgang?"

Emmerich smiled and Werner thought it really lit up his face and perhaps he should do it more often.

"Oh not serious, Kapitän, there was a brawl."

"With the English sailors?"

"No, Kapitän, a couple of groups met up as arranged by the Englishmen and some civilians started joking about Weber and Krantz. Ernst and Peter just laughed it off but the sailors didn't, I think they wanted to show us what's past is past… that we are all seamen and share a common bond."

Werner shook his head shortly before responding, "A month ago, less, we were sinking their fathers, uncles." He pursed his lips and exhaled through his nose, "OK, leave it with me."

As Emmerich left Werner called to him, "Did anyone get hurt?"

Emmerich turned, "No, not really just damage to tables and chairs." Once again he looked to the cover of the book.

"One of the delegation gave it to me. It's really interesting; it seems nobody ever really learns anything."

Emmerich looked puzzled, "Kapitän?"

Werner picked the book up, "It doesn't matter."

Emmerich walked towards the hatch and was soon standing on deck breathing in fresh air bemused at the number of small vessels stationed outside the ropes that cordoned off the submarine, and their occupants waving at every submariner on deck or in the conning tower as well as taking photographs. Overhead a film crew in a helicopter recorded events.

Peter Werner resplendent in laundered uniform, scrubbed, shaved and meticulously polished boots was escorted to the Captain's quarters. He was barely recognisable from the U-boat Skipper who'd boarded the warship a few days earlier. Immediately he entered, he saluted in earnest, and it was reciprocated. Both men removed their caps and shook hands in manly fashion.

Shaw turned to the drinks cabinet and retrieved a twelve year old bottle of Oban Whisky which he showed to his German guest.

"Been to the distillery when I was up in Scotland touring... thought I might have to be carried out the place."

Both men now more at ease in each other's company laughed and it wasn't just polite laughter. He poured generous measures into two traditional whisky glasses, so clean they almost shone. Peter Werner declined ice and as an afterthought his counterpart did similar. They chinked glasses.

"Captain I'd like to apologise for last night." Werner said.

Before he could expand, Shaw raised his left hand, "Your men were exemplary. Unfortunately my crew have a few hot heads in it." He smiled, "We were all young once Captain."

"Yes, but from what I've heard your men showed great restraint in the face of provocation." The submariner knew that Krantz was fiery and had been on disciplinary charges before joining U-boat 116 and thought how magnanimous it was for this Captain to assume all responsibility, nevertheless he offered some mitigation.

"Maybe they don't understand this modern world of yours, Captain Shaw. My crew on shore leave..." He left the sentence, dangling deliberately.

Shaw laughed. "Yes, but I'm impressed with the self-discipline. I hope some of my crew learnt something."

Peter Werner had a twinkle in his eye as he spoke, "Maybe they will concentrate on drinking next time."

Both men took a drink and Shaw invited the submariner to sit down, "I have asked Lieutenant Commander Herd to join us. He has some news about getting you home, or at any rate some proposed plans."

Werner pondered, admiring the whisky glass. "I see."

They were interrupted by the Lieutenant Commander knocking on the door and entering. Both men stood up.

"Sir, good day, Kapitän Werner."

The German responded, politely repeating the greeting.

Captain Shaw pointed to the drinks cabinet, "Help yourself to a drink then come and join us. I've told Kapitän Werner you have been dealing with travel arrangements and trying to cut across red tape."

Herd hurriedly joined them having poured himself a conservative measure of whisky while Shaw having finished his, indicated for Werner to do likewise so he could replenish both glasses. 'He loves the navy and loves his whisky,' Peter Werner thought to himself and he speculated whether, despite the conservative affability, underneath it all he was passionate, exuberant in a world that now too often contained dull, safe people who might need a war to bring them alive, to appreciate the preciousness of life, before Herd gained his attention.

"Kapitän Werner, HM Government have arranged in conjunction with the West German Embassy to fly your crew to Berlin within the next few days. As far as we can make out several relatives and families of the men have been contacted and provision is being made to bring them to Berlin. The Eastern Section has been most cooperative, surprising when one considers their usual politics, concerning movement."

The German Kapitän digested the information as Captain Shaw placed the whisky glasses on the small mahogany table adjacent to the armchairs.

"Thank you, Captain."

The Senior Officers exchanged smiles before Shaw eased himself into a chair and spoke to both men, "I suppose the Russians have become sensitive to world opinion, especially during the last decade. They've wanted to be seen in a very attractive light; had they pursued anything other than a reunion well…" He raised his eyebrows.

Werner responded, "I will put it to the crew. You must understand that some are not as keen as others to return, to return home. We are one big family," he smiled luxuriously and both English officers acknowledged his gesture, "and U116 is our home." He threw back his broad shoulders which suddenly had the strange effect of highlighting his high cheekbones, "What is going to happen to our submarine?"

Captain Shaw was almost apologetic, "That is out of my hands. I, personally, would like to see her presented to a Naval museum," he deliberately paused, "certainly not scuppered."

Lieutenant Commander Herd rattled out, "Hear, hear!" as a polite knock was heard on the door.

"Come in," the Captain's voice was magnetic and a rating peered in.

"Lunch is ready, Sir."

"Thank you, we'll be there in a minute."

Both British officers smiled at each other and their guest noticing their exchange quizzed them not with words but with an impish tilt of his head.

Shaw inhaled deeply, "Roast beef and Yorkshire pudding, Kapitän, and if you have any room left, spotted dick for pud." He laughed and so did his subordinate and before Werner could say anything Herd chipped in, "I'll explain spotted dick later."

He began laughing, more so when his captain said, "You see some of us never leave school!"

The German shook his head, "We always hear about you English and your strange humour."

The dining table was covered with spotless Irish linen and the cutlery was shining as were the wine glasses. All three were mightily impressed as one of the stewards in a high quavering voice spoke to the officers before showing them to their seats and pouring wine.

Back in the submarine Fredrich Schreiber stood back from the pistons, mopping his sweating brow with his customary orange woollen cloth. His skin would have had to resemble a blackout curtain to stop the light shining through from his heart when he gazed around the engine room. If he'd occasionally been unable to reach the meaning behind words this wasn't the case behind the sound of music and because no other crew member was present he began to sing in a hoarse voice yet his singing was like that of a bird in appalling weather singing for a grief so old the world had forgotten about it.

CHAPTER 25

The conversation buffeted across the table having commenced with Captain Shaw, as an afterthought, apologising for not also inviting one of the U-boat 116's officers to lunch.

Lieutenant Commander Herd, who'd never lost his passion for twentieth century history having studied it extensively at Dartmouth College during officer training, couldn't wait for the U-boat captain to fill the blanks in his knowledge and the guest was only too happy to oblige when Captain Shaw asked about his training. The hosts were informed that all U-boat recruits commenced their training as infantrymen, where they learnt basic combat and survival skills. After graduating, the recruits attended basic naval training aboard a sail training ship and modern cruiser after which those who opted for submarine service had to attend submarine school.

Both British men were entranced and when the main course arrived, following complimentary remarks to be conveyed to the chef, the stewards were dismissed by their Skipper. Kapitän Werner remarked on how succulent the beef was, while Herd poured more wine; the conversation now ran parallel with the eating; and the whole atmosphere was extremely cosy.

Peter Werner talked about the phase of training when recruits would learn about the inner working of the submarine and sit for specialized exams which, if they passed, were appointed as officers, radiomen, torpedo mechanic et al.

He stated that all would visit shipyards and familiarise themselves with their boat while undergoing construction –

once completed it would become their platform for "hands on" training where the entire crew practised diving, manoeuvring and combat procedures, "It took five years of training before men reported for their first tour of duty."

There was immense pride in his voice and deportment and it wasn't dispelled when the Lieutenant Commander spoke authoritatively, "You were in the golden period, Kapitän. By 1943, however, U-boat losses were so great that in an effort to rush crewmen into combat, the training time was shortened and standards probably lowered resulting in a less qualified crew."

Captain Shaw offered sympathetically, "In the end the young men paid the price by needless operational errors and a high rate of combat casualty."

His guest was pragmatic. "That is war."

Their conversation briefly moved to the quality of the vegetables and Kapitän Werner remarked about the way the English hid their food under a blanket of gravy; it elicited laughter before the subject of survival underwater was brought up.

"Kapitän," said Herd eagerly, "your Dräger apparatus, if you don't mind me saying was, is, really primitive by today's standards."

Shaw, despite the wine, remained alert, "The Dräger apparatus?" He looked at both men and the junior officer responded.

"It was a simple device, Sir, which functioned as an artificial lung. It consisted of a tube attached to a face mask, an oxygen canister, a canister filled with carbon dioxide absorbent materials, a control valve. Everything fitted into a special vest, like a life jacket."

Werner joined in the explanation and turned to the Captain to explain how air was obtained when the oxygen valve was opened then exhaled through a small vent in the face mask – air was recycled so it functioned as a re breather. He also explained about the special valve which had to be manually opened to expel used air when carbon dioxide had accumulated to high levels.

Werner broke into a chuckle, "It's supposed to be used for underwater repairs and escapes up to 400 feet though none have survived at that depth as far as I know... Captain, come on board, you too Lieutenant Commander and I will give you one."

Both responded eagerly, "Yes."

"Good," said Werner, "but sensible advice, don't wear full uniform once you've been."

He was interrupted by his avuncular host, "Kapitän, all aboard have overalls, I regularly spend time in the engine room."

Everyone laughed and their smiles hovered over their faces as they were interrupted by a Steward who, having knocked, just poked his head round the door and enquired whether they were ready for dessert.

"Ten minutes thank you." The Captain's words sounded like lavish praise as he poured the remains of the house red into half-filled wine glasses.

"Kapitän if I may," Herd wrestled in his inside pocket and produced a card with what looked like shorthand written on it – utterly illegible, "I researched miraculous escapes."

Both captains indicated for him to continue and he informed them of a remarkable escape that took place in January 1945 when U1199 plunged to the bottom of the ocean, unable to surface.

"At 73 metres a Petty Officer managed to open the conning tower and reached the surface using Dräger apparatus."

Werner looked stunned, "Please Lieutenant Commander go on."

Herd again looked at his notes, "October 1942, U512 sunk to the bottom at 43 metres. When seawater reached the batteries, the crew collapsed after inhaling chlorine gas but three managed to escape using Dräger. One survived."

Both captains were intrigued.

Herd continued, "There are others but luck played its part… U413 in August 1944 sank in the English Channel, approximately 30 feet. The leading engineer went forward to investigate the damage when an air bubble blew him out of the boat and safely onto the surface."

"Remarkable," stated Shaw.

The three officers tucked into spotted dick and the German's assessment was, "Recommended."

Swift arrangements were made for the Warship Captain, Lieutenant Commander and the Lieutenant who spoke German to be brought over to U116 the following morning where they would be given an in-depth tour and meet the crew, informally. Both naval officers eagerly talked about the proposed visit like schoolboys presented with tickets for the Calcutta cup game at Twickenham.

"Make sure we take our plaque to give to the U-boat Skipper and his crew as well as a couple of crates of fruit and ham hocks and, oh yes, make sure the ship's emblem and surrounding wood is highly polished."

"Sir," Herd's response was immediate and he left the wardroom thinking about the German's request that he bring as much information as he had about the U-boat war which he wanted his own officers to be aware of. The sincerity with which Werner had complimented him about his knowledge was not lost on the Lieutenant and he intended to immerse himself in the ship's library after hours.

CHAPTER 26

At 10.00am Captain, Lieutenant Commander and Lieutenant resplendent in navy blue overalls with rank press-studded on the shoulders made the short trip, across the harbour; their vessel was weighed down with boxes of food supplies and two ratings also on board for purposes of protocol.

Werner had most of his crew lined up on deck, in uniform, which impressed Captain Shaw who was helped onto the deck by Wolfgang Emmerich followed by the other two British officers before the ratings transported the supplies and motored back to their own ship.

Everyone enjoyed the sensation of being totally relaxed in the Autumn sun and the Kapitän introduced members of U116's crew formally to Captain Shaw who saluted each submariner before shaking his hand.

The British officers were nearly overcome with the pungency immediately they went below deck and were put at ease by their host quipping, "No one gets completely used to it," followed by a smile.

They were escorted to the engine room and for a few seconds the compartment seemed to swim in a blur of faces and German voices. Shaw marvelled at the layout and the antiquated panels, though his Lieutenant Commander was eager to parade his knowledge.

"Sir, this was the latest Type VII C developed from the Finnish Vetehinen design."

"Very good, Lieutenant Commander," interrupted Werner who followed up with, "what else can you tell us?"

"Correct me if I'm wrong, Kapitän, but I believe the boat displaced around 770 tons on the surface, had saddle tanks, four bow tubes and two stern tubes."

Emmerich and Werner smiled to each other, both nodding their heads which encouraged their guest.

"Diesel engine gives you a top speed of 17 knots on the surface and eight knots underwater…. the only drawback was the limited range of operation 6,500 miles at an average speed of 12 knots but because of the simplicity of design repairs at sea are relatively simple and these boats are reliable."

"Christ," interrupted Shaw, his eyes startled. "When you leave the navy maybe you'll work as a curator in a naval museum."

Everyone laughed and the submariners on duty chuckled once the elicited interpretation by the younger British Officer had been complete.

A tray of coffee was brought into the engine room by Peter Niester who offered it first to the British trio then his own officers. It looked and tasted stronger than Camp coffee, thought Herd though he kept that to himself and was pleased the mugs weren't large.

"Captain Shaw, maybe you will come to my quarters while Wolfgang gives your men a guided tour and then I will take you to meet the best Chief Engine Room Artificer in the German navy." He spoke with such an encouraging smile and the two captains departed as though they had shared many years of friendship.

"Lieutenant Commander, if you'd like to follow me." Herd marvelled at the Seaman Officer's command of English and remarked that very few Englishmen spoke a second language with anything near the fluency of his host.

Emmerich led them to the area where food was stored explaining the three principles every U-boat adopted – secure so as not to become loose during an attack, "That's obvious," he said with a smile. He spoke about the importance of the stores being evenly distributed in order that the trim of the boat wasn't disturbed, "This is ongoing as we eat every day and consumption is weighed daily and the trim adjusted, accordingly." He paused and pointed, "Of course there has to be free access to all hatches and valves."

Emmerich introduced the Quartermaster to the German speaking officer and conversation between the two was rapid. A menu was introduced and the officer explained to Herd that menus were strictly followed to promote diet and nutrition. The Quartermaster spoke enthusiastically and his confidence grew as he sensed his own officer's approval. There was a pause and the translation was immediate.

"Sir, breakfast consists of coffee, buttermilk soup, biscuits, hardbread with butter or honey and eggs." Herd nodded his head approvingly while looking at Emmerich. Further conversation and translation continued.

"Lunch would be soup, potatoes, cooked meat and vegetables and fruit, the dinner sausages or canned fish, cheese, bread and coffee or chocolate."

"Crikey, not exactly bread and water then," the Lieutenant offered with a smile.

The party moved forth into the starboard sink where the galley was located between the chief's quarters and the wardroom. The hotplates and two small electric ovens were pointed out as well as a refrigerator, self-heating soup kettle and an enamel sink with fresh water and salt water.

The Quartermaster walked them to the forward torpedo tubes where hams, sausages and other preserved meats were stored then explained that bread was kept in the forward torpedo room and electric motor room. Fresh meat was in a small refrigerator and pantry as these were the coolest places but had to be eaten quickly. Emmerich turned to his guests, "Needless to say a good cook is worth his weight in gold especially if he has imagination." Everyone laughed and the British officers shook the Quartermaster's hand, who offered a clown's grin, obviously pleased with himself.

In the Kapitän's quarters, both Skippers were immersed in conversation. Werner informed Shaw that everyone knew Germany could not produce enough U-boats fast enough because the Kriegsmarine had developed its requirement strategy around the war being over quickly.

"Sixty U-boats were launched in 1940 but in the same year thirty-two had been lost in action." He paused to let the English Captain digest the information before continuing in a less melodramatic voice but one tinged with melancholy. "At any one time during the so called 'Happy Times' there were only ever a maximum of thirty submarines at sea. For an area the size of the North Atlantic…"

He left the sentence suspended inviting his guest to remark, "Yes with more wolf packs who knows what the Battle of the Atlantic might have thrown up."

"What happened?"

Shaw cleared his throat. "The sinking of merchant ships peaked in 1942 and night attacks became the norm because ASDIC was designed for underwater detection and of course at night the silhouette of a surfaced U-boat was barely visible…"

Werner interrupted, "Kapitän Kretschmer had suggested this at a conference for U-boat Kapitäns."

Shaw continued, "The allies were developing a large array of anti-submarine weapons including more modern depth charges 'hedgehogs', 'squids' and more sophisticated radar equipment including radar designed to see U-boats on the surface at night."

Werner thought then looked at the Captain perched on a collapsible chair, "We were becoming more vulnerable…. Obviously."

The Steward interrupted them with two mugs of coffee which were greatly received and the two captains resumed their conversation. Werner was informed that U-boat development resulted with 'homing' torpedoes which travelled slowly but with greater accuracy. He also informed his host that Cryptanalysts in Germany had cracked the British cypher and the largest wolf pack of thirty-nine U-boats was sent by Dönitz to attack allied shipping, "and that resulted in twenty-one merchant ships lost to only three U-boats."

"And then the tide turned Captain," said the submariner in a matter-of-fact way.

"Yes it did," was Shaw's immediate response. "Radar was the biggest influence, allied planes with Air to Surface Vessel radar could attack U-boats on the surface without them knowing they were about to be attacked because U-boats couldn't pick up ASV on its own radar, the Metox receiver."

Their conversation was devoid of any competitiveness or animosity even when Captain Shaw relayed to his host what Lieutenant Commander Herd had assessed, which was Dönitz making the mistake of ordering all U-boats to be fitted with more anti-aircraft guns – the planes stayed out of range and relayed the position to the nearest escort ship and when the U-boat dived putting its guns out of use the aircraft would attack.

Werner wanted to hear it all and Shaw obliged, "109 U-boats were lost between April and July 1943 and Dönitz withdrew the boats as a temporary measure while scientists worked on methods to boost their defences, increase speed, endurance but steel that priceless commodity was in great demand but bombing reduced its output and the navy came third in the pecking order way behind the Luftwaffe and army."

His words were spoken almost reluctantly and he was slightly relieved when Emmerich made his presence known. Just before though, Captain Shaw said quietly, "Dönitz ordered all U-boats to cease hostilities on May 7th 1945."

"Thank you Captain," said Peter Werner, quietly.

Though the five men cramped the quarters, there was still room for handshakes as Captain Shaw took possession of his warship's plaque from his Lieutenant Commander and presented it to – "Kapitän Werner and the crew of U-boat 116". He put on his private school debating voice, as clear as footprints in wet mud and said the right words but they weren't politicians' utterances for they were shot through with humble sincerity. The German officers present were taken aback and Captain Shaw knew this was the Navy way, no showy fanfare and he knew that Kapitän Werner, at the appropriate time would inform his crew.

Both Commanders were unaware that Emmerich and Herd had also talked at length during the tour about the early days of the Second World War. Both agreed that the collapse of France in 1940 did a great deal to change submarine warfare because the U-boat now had open access to the Atlantic from bases on the Western coast following occupation. Previously, the German Officer had pointed out energetically, that submarines had to move either through the North Sea or the English Channel to get to the Atlantic.

"Both journeys are fraught with danger," he had said in a knowing way.

Herd agreed and added the advantage was now with Germany as twelve U-boat flotillas were based along the coast including St Nazaire which gave the type VII more time at sea, "We couldn't have sustained the losses, Wolfgang." It was the first time he had used Emmerich's name and this pleasantry wasn't lost on the submariner who was aware the British officer outranked him.

"Gentlemen, may I suggest we retreat to the deck or the bridge and suck in more of this harbour's clean air." His words had the desired effect for though the hatches were open the English officers still found the confinement oppressive and each knew his overalls would have to be laundered.

"Wolfgang, would you arrange for coffee and German biscuits to be brought from the galley in say twenty minutes?"

"Consider it done Kapitän." His reply had mettle and he excused himself.

"Captain Shaw, later I will introduce you to Friedrich Shreiber," Werner said ushering the English officers towards the deck before adding, "perhaps the Lieutenant would like to acquaint himself with my men – I know they have a thirst for knowledge and he will be warmly received."

Before Shaw could respond, the young Lieutenant piped up, "I was going to suggest that Sir."

As an afterthought, the Kapitän turned to the linguist and the faint curves in his face hardened, "Don't get drawn into a card game... they all cheat."

The men broke into raucous laughter and laughed even louder when the Lieutenant following a pause announced, "So do I."

The breeze up on deck had all the qualities of ecstasy and as they passed submariners smoking or huddled in small groups, the officers were immediately saluted. Werner informed them that the German speaking officer was below and would field any questions as best he could.

"Thank you Kapitän," was the universal response.

Captain Shaw said, "It's true, Kapitän... hardship binds men, particularly service men in a way most civilians couldn't understand." He added, "I can sense their loyalty to you before anything else..."

Werner changed the subject. "This harbour of yours, Portsmouth, has a long history together with Plymouth. We learnt about it during training – the history of Navies." His voice was milder and he turned slowly on deck to savour the view, "Who'd have thought it."

He leaned his face towards his visitors, "As you know each Navy is riddled with rituals and superstition and I want to tell you a ghost story unless you already know about it." The English men shook their heads and Werner continued, "The World War One boat U-65... Every German submariner is acquainted with it but let's wait until the coffee comes."

Below deck the warship's Lieutenant was almost subject to an inquisition and the majority of questions were about the war, despite the crew having seen the documentary earlier. He felt the overriding endorsement was that Britain and Germany should have united to fight the Russians and he remained tactful in what he said just as his own Captain had suggested.

Emmerich had joined the other officers and had walked with the traditional naval gait along the deck. His smile was disarming and he suggested that they made their way "upstairs."

Peter Niester, carrying the tray with large mugs of steaming coffee and two varieties of biscuits, was a welcome sight.

"Thank you," was Captain Shaw's almost blustery acknowledgement as he unwittingly studied the burnt edges of the biscuits. Peter Werner smiled to himself before commencing his story.

"You know Captain, submariners aboard U-boat 65 were as terrified of the ghosts on their vessels as they were of allied attacks. Let me put it in context – after the mayhem of trench warfare the only breakthrough it seemed might come from the sea as the Kaiser's navy led by wolf packs were taking a heavy toll on British shipping."

The two English officers listened intently and Werner continued, "Anyway, U65 came off the production line in 1916 and immediately became infamous before launching when a worker was crushed by an iron girder – of course an enquiry found there had been no faults in the chain used to hoist the girder. Then two months later another tragedy…"

"Crikey," intervened Herd.

Werner looked at him, "Yes, three engineers were assigned to the engine room to test the dry cell batteries and were overcome by chloride fumes."

"Did they die?" asked Captain Shaw, slightly alarmed.

"Unfortunately yes, and no one ever determined why the batteries leaked toxic fumes. Fortunately there were no more incidents until she set sail for sea trials. She ran into a fierce storm in the Channel and one hapless sailor was swept overboard when the vessel came up to test her stability on the surface during rough seas."

Herd was about to interrupt but the Kapitän held his hand up to check him.

"The Kapitän ordered the U-boat to dive and as she did a ballast tank sprang a leak, flooding the dry cell batteries in sea water and filling the engine room with the same deadly gas that had accounted for three lives. After a dozen nerve-wracking hours the crew finally managed to get the 'Iron Coffin', as she was nicknamed, to the surface. Amazingly no-one was killed and the craft limped back to Germany for repairs."

Shaw drank from his mug before speaking, "Things like that spread like wildfire in the service."

"But that wasn't the end Captain."

Both officers looked bemused.

"Go on Kapitän," offered the English Lieutenant Commander.

"After repairs she was readied for sea and her first on-line patrol but as a battery of torpedoes was being placed on board, a warhead suddenly exploded killing the Second Officer and badly wounding some of the crew. Yet again an enquiry was conducted but no explanation could be found. You could imagine how her crew felt?"

"Of course Kapitän," said Shaw directly, before continuing, "she should have been scrapped and her number withdrawn if only to alleviate the mention of a cursed vessel."

Kapitän Werner nodded, "My sentiments exactly, but no, her crew were given extended shore leave then reported back. Again tragedy, she had to return to port and this as she was about to leave, a bizarre incident occurred."

The English men were transfixed so Werner continued, "A member of crew swore that he'd seen an apparition of the dead officer but the Kapitän dismissed it. Later the dead officer was seen casually strolling up to the bow before vanishing into thin air."

Shaw intervened, "I don't know how I'd react if I'd been Skipper." He looked uneasy.

"Despite some success the crew felt their boat was haunted," Werner paused then raised his voice. "There was panic just after she recorded her second kill when startled sailors in the engine room saw the dead officer observing the instrument panel as he'd done previously. Now the whole fleet knew, despite the Kapitän trying to dispel the rumours."

"What happened?" said an eager Lieutenant Commander, possibly more intrigued than his Commanding Officer.

"Well, in January 1918 as the war dragged closer to its inevitable conclusion, its Kapitän, too, saw the apparition as U65 was prowling off Portland Bill. Because of the harsh conditions he ordered the boat to the surface. A lookout stationed on the starboard side was scanning the horizon and when he turned to port he saw an officer on deck. At first he thought it was a foolhardy risk but then realised all the hatches were still battened down except the one he had climbed out of onto the deck. When he got a full look at him his face drained of blood."

"The dead officer?" interrupted Shaw.

"Yes, the Kapitän raced up the ladder and saw the dead officer himself before the ghost vanished through raging winds."

The subordinate officer pondered for a moment and turned to his Captain, "Surely Sir, the authorities would have been forced to act?"

Shaw was matter of fact, "I imagine each crewman was interviewed separately by officers?"

He turned to Peter Werner who said, "Everyone knew that U-boat crews were among the hardiest and most reliable in the navy and life expectancy was little more than fifty, fifty so they couldn't dismiss the stories as idle ranting, especially not from innately, fearless men."

"And, of course, the question of morale," chipped in Shaw.

"That's right, Captain Shaw, the sea lords couldn't admit to having a haunted ship or worse a mutinous crew so overwrought by what they were convinced had happened that the crew were broken up and sent to other submarines and destroyers."

"Was that the end then?" asked Herd innocently.

"No," Peter Werner took another drink of coffee, "an exorcism was completed and a stern Kapitän known for his rigour took charge and a new crew. Everything appeared calm but in May 1918 the ghost appeared again, three times in fact, seen walking through a solid iron bulkhead into the engine room and visiting a torpedo handler at night. The man was so terrified that when the vessel surfaced to recharge her batteries, he leapt into the sea and certain death. Finally in July 1918 U-boat 65 was spotted by an American submarine floating on the surface – an easy target – then mysteriously exploded spewing metal and crew into the ocean. All that remained was a heavy oil slick, yet no-one in the American submarine gave the order to fire."

The men looked aghast before Captain Shaw offered tamely, "Not something any navy would want to publicise…"

All the men drew breath like the onset of a gale. The three naval men retired to the engine room where they were greeted by crew members inviting the English Lieutenant, who informed Shaw that he hadn't spoken so much German in a long time and had answered questions as honestly and as knowledgeably as possible; his slow nod told his Captain that he had also been tactful.

"Captain Shaw, I'd like you to meet Friedrich Schreiber the best Chief Engine Room Artificer the German Navy has to offer." He sounded very eloquent and Shaw remained impressive and enthusiastic.

"Lead the way, Kapitän," he said with a smile and bidding crew members below deck a hearty "good morning" he was finally introduced to Shreiber who carried a dirty oil covered rag in hand yet it didn't deter the warship's Captain from poaching a strong, affectionate handshake. Rapid words passed between the two Germans and Shreiber, gaining in confidence, showed the Captain and his Junior Officer who'd caught up with them the nuts and bolts including the gyro compass and depth rudder hand-operating gear which kept the boat at the required level. The gnarled features of Shreiber came to life as he spoke in German, barely pausing for his Kapitän to translate. He showed them the bilge pumps, blowers for clearing and fitting the diving tanks – both electronically driven – as well as the air compressors.

Werner joked about not showing them the toilet screened by a curtain, "unless you've taken some opium this morning." The guests roared their approval and were fascinated by the engines that could be coupled in tandem and the electric motors for submerged cruising.

Shaw and Herd shook their heads in near disbelief. Wolfgang Emmerich had already described the conning tower and the use of periscopes, a platform for the Helmsman and the levers used to control the valves for releasing air from the tanks. Captain Shaw had been very inquisitive about the electrical controlling gear for depth steering, a depth indicator, voice pipes and the electrical firing device for the torpedo tubes.

Finally, both Captains retired to Peter Werner's quarters for a last coffee before the scheduled return to the warship; he was pleased his crew had taken up the questioning with a certain relish in their voices as they responded.

The Kapitän informed his guest of his early days having to work hard to gain his 'sea legs' and the need for adjustment on his first mission in heavy weather, "No matter how sick someone was, he had to do his duty without mistakes in the control room... even if everything was rolling at 30 degrees from side to side he had to be perfect or the boat could sink. I was lucky the weather was that bad because if you start the hard way, it's easier later. Some men never adjusted though to the motions of a submarine and returned to duty on destroyers. My first Kapitän knew I was a mechanic first class but assigned me to the Control Room... that's how it was."

Captain Shaw looked at his host with admiration, "When we meet again I will relate some of my stories at naval college, though I know they will pale by comparison."

Both men laughed and the U-boat Kapitän had the last word, having looked at his watch, "We'd better get back on deck... You can ask Lieutenant Commander Herd how he got on with the Drager apparatus... Friedrich would have enjoyed that!"

They exchanged smiles and moved towards the second hatch; once again the air looked and felt transparent. Both were joined by Emmerich and Herd, the latter sheepishly carrying his souvenir – the Draper apparatus – nevertheless he was also relieved to be breathing in the milk mild air. Everywhere on deck the hum of chatter and controlled laughter rose higher than the water lapping the metal sides. Within minutes the warship sent over its own boat to bring back the two Officers; handshakes were offered and Kapitän Werner watch the Englishmen in animated conversation as soon as their vessel left U116 behind.

"Kapitän Werner asked me about Karl Dönitz again," said Shaw. "He was highly decorated, Sir, Iron Cross first and Second Class during the Great War then Knights Cross with Oak during the Second World War."

"The Kapitän informed me that after a few months as Watch Officer he took his first command in 1918 but later that year lost his boat and six crew during a dive with an unstabilised boat... Had a great effect on him." Captain Shaw looked at the smiling sea then pushed his face upwards into the constant wind.

"I didn't know he spent nine months in British captivity, Sir." Shaw heard his Officer then pondered for a few seconds.

"Kapitän Werner couldn't understand why the Admiral was accused of war crimes... he has a point, maybe he was punished for being efficient at his job, still eleven years..."

Herd interrupted, "Did you tell him there was a turnout for his funeral?"

"Oh yes and also that Officers from the Bundesmarine were forbidden to wear uniform because the German Government felt Dönitz was deeply involved in politics during the Third Reich."

"How did he take it?" asked the Lieutenant Commander.

"All right but his face dropped when I told him about the Admiral's sons."

Herd looked quizzical as their boat slowed on approach to the warship.

"The younger was killed serving as Watch Officer when U954 was sunk with all hands in the North Atlantic in May 1943 and though the other brother Klaus was withdrawn from combat duties and trained as a naval doctor he went down after he convinced friends to take him along on a fast boat for an attack on the Selsey on the English coast." There was not one iota of creamy satisfaction in the Englishman's voice, quite the opposite.

The Officers were piped on board and Shaw suggested Herd might like to spread out a map of the Atlantic and explain what the German First Lieutenant had told him about their Naval Grid System, "About an hour or so?"

"I will come to your quarters, Sir."

If they hadn't known before, they certainly knew now that despite the spectre of death for U-boat personnel theirs was an honest web of life for all its brutish strands. "No wonder their limbs ache for as far back as memory goes," the Englishman said to himself before widening his gazelle's eyes.

CHAPTER 27

In the Engine Room of U116 Friedrich Schreiber with drooping shoulders and black locks of hair resembled a small bear roused from his cave, sniffing the air but there was no hunting to be done so he vigorously finished polishing down a piston until it shone like metal caught in the midday sun. When he paused he caught sight of Wolfgang Emmerich carrying two mugs of coffee. He smiled as he approached and both men sat down on metal structures.

The Seaman Officer adjusted his legs. "You really love this girl, Friedrich?"

The Chief Engine Room Artificer raised his mug and took a drink before responding, "The Kapitän would have something to say if she didn't go as well as she does, eh?"

A long smile descended on his face and it had the effect of adjusting his Officer's expression, though sub-consciously, "Yes Friedrich, the Kapitän thinks you were the best engine man in the German Navy."

He looked surprised, "Were, Wolfgang?"

There was a minor pause. "You've forty years to catch up, Friedrich, technology is all different." There was an impish tune to the Officer's voice which Schreiber responded to bluntly.

"A submarine is a submarine, the principals won't change, you know that."

The Seaman Officer detected a challenge – it was all part of the sparring that characterised submariners' conversation and the secret was to remain nonchalant, like a sound poker player. He smiled, "Friedrich, sure you can adapt much easier than the rest of us." He took a drink from his mug and relaxed his back against solid metal, "Tell me Friedrich are you looking forward to going back to Germany?" He knew it was an obvious question but one, perhaps the Artificer would respond to truthfully when in the company of one officer rather than several crew.

"I only have a brother, that's if he is still alive. We were both put into an orphanage when we were four and six."

The Seaman Officer straightened up, "I don't want to pry, Friedrich."

The latter still returned a stance of understated joy despite what he was about to reveal.

"That's alright, I've never told anyone that before, not that you will be interested anyway." There was an uneven edge in his voice and Emmerich immediately put his hand on his shoulder.

"No, go on, Friedrich." He removed his hand and allowed the other man all the freedom he might need to remove the monotonous lumber cluttering up his head before confronting what he had long buried; and it took courage.

"My father was a drunk and used to beat my mother," he paused as though the unsavoury event was being played on film in his mind. He grumbled, "I still remember it visibly, the suffering, yet she still loved him as much as she loved Gunter, that's my brother, and me. When he wasn't drunk, he was reasonably kind to us but it was seldom."

The Seaman Officer could feel the spirit being sucked out of him and the potentially suffocating iron-sodden atmosphere didn't help but he was determined to let the Chief Engine Room Artificer open up for probably the first time in his life, one of tragic poignancy which had an unbearably moving quality.

"Then, one day he never came home and we never saw him again. The next few months were very happy. One day my mother went out and we never saw her again. Someone came to tell us she had been killed, run over by a car." He paused for he looked very lonely, "The authorities put us into an institution full of bullies, thieves, sodomites. The God my mother prayed to every night had abandoned us... I escaped to the Navy."

Emmerich, his face pinched white, threw an arm around Schreiber, "Friedrich you have made something of yourself. You are a very respected and much-loved submariner. The Kapitän often sings your praises. After him, I think you may be the most indispensable man here."

He smiled to himself before responding, as Emmerich removed his arm, "We are all indispensable once out in the sea. That's what makes us all special."

Emmerich returned the smile but was only too aware the knife turning pain the man sat beside him had endured, maybe still did if a berating conscience was at work.

The atmosphere in the Officers' Mess on board the warship was in stark contrast. Captain Shaw had decided to invite a few Officers to listen to Lieutenant Commander's explanation of the German Grid System instead of using the navigational standard of latitude and longitude to denote global location. Though Navy history was part of Dartmouth College's officer training course he doubted this had been one of the subjects and besides he was intrigued.

Resplendent in uniform they had arrived promptly at 3.30pm where two large pots of tea and ginger snaps (the Captain's favourite biscuit) had been left by the Steward. The Captain spoke briefly about the purpose of the gathering and the tone of his voice suggested he wasn't in the mood for frivolity.

Herd rolled out a map of the Atlantic that also included Britain and Northern France; he had drawn large square sectors, with each sector given a two letter designation; and because he was a competent speaker those present were immediately immersed.

"Each sector was further divided into a 3 x 3 matrix so that there were nine medium squares." He explained that these were immediately divided into nine smaller squares pausing only to have a mouthful of tea, "There were now 81 total grid squares within a sector, each given a two digit designation so the Grid System would now have two alphabets and two digits."

When asked to give an example he responded immediately, confidently pointing with a ruler, "For example the Grid AN79 would cover the area of Dover and parts of the Channel."

A murmur of understanding only encouraged him to continue.

"Each of these Grids were again divided in the same manner so that a further 81 squares were formed, again given a two digit designation. The complete Grid would now read as two alphabets with four digits…"

The Captain interrupted, "And operational manoeuvres?"

"Referred to as the patrol zone, each one covered an area of six nautical mile areas. This way, Sir, the Germans could pinpoint any location on the globe using only six characters – two alphabets for the large sector and four digits to fix the location within six nautical miles within the sector."

"So obvious… so simple." Said one of the officers shaking his head.

Herd explained that generating the first matrix would contain squares numbered 11-19, the second 21-29, the third 31-39 and so on, "Even the large sectors were not divided equally for tactical reasons." He gave an example and fielded questions referring to what he had garnered from the German officers.

The officers retracted from the map and one of them poured more tea while the last ginger snap on the china plate was, tactfully, left for the Skipper.

Commander Whitehill, non-descript, in decay and a recent addition to the ship's complement as a temporary secondment and whom the other officers had mixed feelings about, jutted out his skinny jaw and asked loftily, "What about the allies deciphering the patrol reports?"

"Good question," said Herd before continuing, "Admiral Dönitz wrestled with the problem and as a precautionary measure patrol zones were transmitted using coded sectors – instead of transmitting the actual patrol zone, an offset would be used so that any zone that was transmitted over the waves would be an offset of a secret location. This secret location was changed at random intervals and the U-boat Captain would calculate the new patrol zone based on the offset."

The Commander nodded sagely but it was as convincing as semi-skimmed milk being passed off as the full cream variety and Captain Shaw allowed himself a wide smile for he disliked his self-serving manner: fairground barker one day, the next a whining voice like a worn-out, gap-toothed saw! At the same time life in all its simplicity, absurdity and incongruity was happening throughout all Europe especially in Germany a country still divided after forty-three years by political ideologies.

CHAPTER 28

The spinning wheels of a West German train speeding towards Hanover produced a tantalising rhythm and instant sound that often acted as a balm to travellers. Inside the last carriage a middle-aged couple, a young woman and an elderly woman sat in a blot of silence.

While the young woman flipped through a glossy magazine, the elderly woman stared out of the window and though the view was picturesque she was deep in thought for age had not withered her mental faculties nor her ability to think visually as she often indulged in when travelling in comfort. She went back to 1928 and blossomed at the reminiscence of family life – lying about squawking with laughter under the warmth of the sun, stationary over a municipal park. This passenger, conservatively dressed and still possessing hints of youthful beauty smiled when she conjured up the enjoyment everyone, children and adults alike, displayed in this serene setting with its multitude of plants, aged trees and what most enjoyed, the heady aroma of freshly cut grass.

She remembered a girl talking to a masterful looking neuter cat, smooth coated, black with white paws and imperial in its movement, without the slightest trace of apprehension, before she recalled her own conversation with a boy, almost word for word, "Come on, Uve, throw the ball to me." She chuckled at the imagined sight of herself holding up both hands and despite the ball being thrown high, catching it to loud applause from her mother and brother before walking towards a bandstand where middle-aged people swayed in their seats, listening to a German ballad.

The technicolour pictures in her mind speeded up while the train slowed as it approached its destination; a carousel of images appeared as brother and sister matured until, minutes before the train stopped, she settled on one of him in his naval uniform. Ruth Stührmann could see the tears of pride in her mother's eyes and it brought a lump to her own throat. Suddenly the middle-aged man stirred her from daydreaming, politely asking if he could lift her small case down from the luggage rack. Miss Stührmann smiled her answer and three minutes later passengers were thronging their way to the metal barrier where two sullen employees checked travel warrants or clipped passenger tickets.

In the distance an official looking man wearing a dark grey suit, crisp white shirt and undistinguished tie was trying to catch her attention, waving his hands aloft. When Ruth caught sight of him, she smiled and he relaxed his excitable pose making him much more masculine in appearance.

"Miss Stührmann?"

Her heart gave a lurch. "Yes, that's right."

"Allow me." He took hold of her suitcases confidently and she didn't protest for she was intrigued.

"I trust you had a pleasant journey… it certainly is a fine day." He said looking up at the blue sky dotted with small white clouds, like ink pellets on blotting paper. They walked outside the main terminus.

"Ah here's our car… Let me introduce myself. I am Reinhard Mauser, a junior partner in the solicitor's firm." Ruth climbed into the front seat without hesitation and thought how well-mannered the young man was if only because he walked round the back of the vehicle, not the front, to get into the driver's seat having put the suitcase on the floor behind the driver's seat.

Once they had cleared chattering traffic which bedevils the immaculate vicinity of most city railway stations the solicitor visibly relaxed.

"I was a bit nervous of meeting you in view of what has happened. It has come as a shock to everyone." He shot her a quick look which she was aware of despite her taking in the sights.

"Anyway, I have booked us a table in a restaurant, which is quiet but serves delicious food. There we can, perhaps, discuss your mother's will." He could see the change in her expression to sadness and it caused self-consciousness, so he spoke rapidly.

"My father was very fond of your mother, he thought her such a warm person and felt he had lost a friend when she passed away… not a client." He hoped his words might sound compassionate and she knew he wasn't used to this type of conversation, despite his profession, so sought to put him at ease.

As she spoke she turned her head towards him, shaking off a whisper of Eau de Cologne, "That is very kind of you to say. It is ten years now since she died but she never gave up hope of Uve still being alive. You see the reports surrounding his disappearance were vague. My mother never stopped hounding officials for information but there was a veil of secrecy surrounding the disappearance."

She noticed Herr Mauser nodding sympathetically and the elderly passenger continued without raising her voice, "I know the submarine service operated independently but she was never convinced; it was a feeling she said she sometimes got. After the war she would look out of the house and hope to see Uve."

There was a deafening silence before Ruth spoke in a quieter tone, "We were very close, my father died when I was ten and although my mother was comfortable, she was lonely."

The solicitor listened in a spirit of passivity tinged with mild grief and was relieved that his passenger suddenly perked up.

"Oh she didn't have an unhappy life but she treasured the time the three of us spent together, particularly holidays." She smiled at the memory and the junior partner decided that was the ideal moment to offer his input to the conversation.

"I can understand why she declared her will in the manner she did. Such faith, she must have been very strong and yet vulnerable to cling to such a faint hope." He shook his head and sucked back spittle from his front teeth, "It's a pity she can't be here today."

He smiled warmly and Ruth spoke. "Yes, but maybe Uve will see his mother when we meet again. They say I look very much like her. I wonder what his reaction will be…"

Mauser glanced at her. "Probably uncomfortable but at least they know what to expect. There will be much excitement tainted with a little, or maybe a lot, of fear."

He slowed to take a minor road off the autobahn, "Not long now," he said too loud.

"I'm ready for something," and as an afterthought she added, "I'm sure I'm going to need all my strength these coming weeks."

What stoicism, thought the young man and it was easy to understand how his father had held Ruth Stührmann's mother in such high esteem. As he said these words to himself he could feel his muscles slacken and his mouth falling slightly open nevertheless he offered the lady sat next to him a gracious smile and was eager to continue their conversation.

"You know they have traced many friends, relatives, families of these men but I have a hunch not everyone has come forward. Surely these people must have heard but perhaps some never survived. I have tried to put myself in these men's position and don't know what I would prefer. The old Nazi movement have tried to turn the discovery into a propaganda exercise. There have been a number of rallies and clashes with anti-fascists."

He looked again at Ruth Stührmann and she looked extraordinarily dignified, dramatic, "My brother was never a Nazi."

She pondered her remark, raised her head and smiled into his eyes and he noticed just how thick the iron-grey hair that thatched the dome of her forehead really was and he listened without interruption as she spoke softly, eloquently.

"I don't think many seamen were. Uve never talked politics, only about being at sea and the comradeship he found there. You would think these submariners would have been sick of the sight of each other after being cooped up together for so many weeks. But no, when they returned to port many went off, together, to the rest camps near Brest. I think they enjoyed the idolatry and the feeling they were special. The hardships were just part of their working life."

She paused and tickled her cheek with her finger before reflecting on what she had said before sighing, "I suppose there must have been some fanatics but Uve never talked about them I think he, like others, spent much time getting to grips with the pains and occasional lifts of solitude."

She looked to the younger man for a response but he said nothing as his concentration, as he steered the car, was in finding a suitable parking place close to the restaurant, now in view. Nevertheless, he shot her a sincere smile and marvelled at her unsuppressible spontaneity and selflessness.

Back in England Kapitän Werner and his crew were assembled below deck in the warship. Captain Shaw was the only British Officer present and he allowed his guest to take centre stage with a polite gesture which was, as ever, understated. Before he addressed his fellow submariners Werner noticed Lieutenant Commander Herd, in full uniform, slip into the back of the Wardroom exchanging smirks with members of the crew he recognised. The Kapitän thought about making a light-hearted remark about naval drycleaners but could feel the anxiety reaching out to him from those crew members who stood out the front; and he didn't want to appear flippant; altruistic was more appropriate.

"Men I know you are anxious to find out what is going to happen." He waited until the murmur had stopped before continuing, "We are going back to Germany… back home.

The government in our country have agreed. I know for some of you that prospect seems an ordeal but we are Germans."

He paused and Captain Shaw continued assimilating the reaction of the submariners to their Kapitän's words.

"You are brave men who were caught up in some freak of nature. The British have offered to fly us but on your behalf I have said that we will travel home the only way we know."

The crew suddenly marched on the spot for seven seconds then suddenly stopped, taking the two Englishmen by surprise, leaving them baffled until they recognised the significance prompted by cries of, "Thank you Kapitän!"

"We will refuel and carry out any necessary repairs, not that much is needed thanks to the help of Captain Shaw."

Both Skippers exchanged smiles.

"We will have an escort for most of the way. It will give you a couple more days to gather your thoughts. This evening some of you will speak with your families and relatives – Seaman Officer Emmerich has a list of those who have been contacted. I have instructed him to talk with each of you. A committee has been set up on shore. I'm afraid not everyone will get the chance."

Werner could see the drop in some facial expressions and inhaled deeply, "Things have happened in the last forty-five years. I think you understand my friends."

There was a mournful silence and the Kapitän resembled a man full of compassion yet abject loneliness and his opposite number immediately attempted to relieve him, momentarily, of the burden.

"Please, gentlemen, be my guests for dinner tonight."

There was little response and Shaw continued as best he could, "I cannot appreciate what is going on in some of your minds but I am sympathetic to your predicament. Please for any assistance see my Officers or me."

His words were roughly translated for those who had no command of the English language.

Kapitän Werner then responded, "Thank you, Captain, I accept on behalf of my crew... naval men together." Both Captains shook hands and marching on the spot suddenly erupted though louder this time and like last time suddenly stopped as if on cue.

While the crew walked about the deck of the warship discussing the armaments, the Captains retired to Shaw's quarters where both worked out that the voyage would be just over five hundred nautical miles and surface speed at an average of twelve knots would take about two days if the weather didn't turn and reduce the speed to ten knots.

"I know the crew will want to dive as if we were still on patrol," remarked Werner with a rattling grin, "a symbolic gesture, I suppose."

"Of course," replied Shaw, "of course."

Their conversation was interrupted by a Steward knocking and entering carrying a jug of coffee, two large mugs bearing the ship's crest and a square plate with three large slices of fruit cake. It elicited a smile from the German who said "Thank you" to the Steward who hurriedly put the tray down on his Captain's desk and left. Shaw poured the steaming coffee into the mugs and Werner spoke again.

"Captain Shaw, I've come to the conclusion that a submariner's brain works better and clearer amidst noise and jumble but wilts when presented with yawning space maybe even shrinks?"

Shaw laughed but it wasn't loud and he went on to tell Werner that two submarine Captains were close friends of his and all three often exchanged ideas about being on patrol when they met up three, four times a year. He quickly conceded that patrol was not war and made a joke about the next batch of submariners probably having an indoor pool as well as squash courts. Both chuckled at his remark and drank their coffee before talking, once more, about their respective service life, comparing and contrasting their early years and

Werner was tickled when Captain Shaw said with a wry smile, "My grandfather once said when he joined the navy they had wooden ships and iron men... now it's iron ships and wooden men."

There was a pause before the Englishman erupted in laughter; it could be heard in other quarters but not in a residential street in Stuttgart where silence had returned following a fifteen minute thunderstorm.

CHAPTER 29

In the kitchen of her home Elsa waited for her husband Helmut, a respectable business man approaching the sanctuary of full retirement. Her home help had left after three hours work and it was time for the lady, now approaching her seventh decade, to make coffee. She thought how marvellous the blue cloudless sky now looked but once sat down couldn't resist looking once again at the national newspaper her cleaner had brought in. Blazoned on the front page was a picture of U-boat 116 and the banner headline – *'Sea Wolves Coming Home'*. She was transfixed and only half-heard her husband call out as he closed the front door behind him. Helmut dropped his briefcase and whistling walked to the bathroom to wash his hands and face; it was a ritual he'd carried out ever since his working life had begun. There was a spring in his step as he hurried into the kitchen.

"Elsa, didn't you hear me call?" His enormous smirk was encouraging.

"I'm sorry, Helmut, I was absorbed in something," she said innocently.

His eyes were diverted to the newspaper. "Ah you've been reading the news? Everyone at work is talking about it. In fact you can't get away from it – television, magazines, radio even the church has said it's the Lord's doing."

He paused and moved to pour himself a mug of coffee, "It's certainly exciting."

Elsa couldn't betray the turmoil she was in but knew sooner rather than later she would have to tell her husband that the baby she had when they met and whom they had both brought up as their son was the son of Conrad Meiner, the returning sea-wolf. Helmut had always believed that the boy, Conrad, was the result of a brief liaison and that perhaps Elsa, being young and impressionable was unfairly taken advantage of. They were married shortly after Conrad was born and the boy always believed that Helmut was his father – they saw no need to tell him otherwise. Though Elsa loved her husband dearly and despite receiving a telegram in October 1942 which read *'Missing in action, presumed dead'* she had never stopped loving Conrad Senior. Her inner conflict was beginning to get blurry, not helped by her loyal husband's observation.

"These men will get a shock when they return to Germany… it's barely recognisable."

He took a drink then put his mug down, "Conrad phoned me today, asked would we go round and see him and the children sometime next week. I think it will do us good."

He touched Elsa's hand and smiled into her eyes. "It must be two months since we last went. What do you think?"

She had only half heard his words yet instinctively replied, "Oh yes, fine."

Helmut threw his frame into the tall backed chair that was a feature of their kitchen before stretching in the manner of someone waking up early morning, "Good… I think I will take you out tonight to dine… let's treat ourselves to a decent bottle of wine."

He gathered up the paper and his mug and didn't need to say he was going to return to the sitting room for half-an-hour. Elsa, confused, stood up kissed her husband on the cheek and forced a smile.

"Right, let me read for a while then I will telephone the restaurant, wash and change etcetera."

He looked so fit and behaved with aplomb, unaware that he often wrinkled his nose like a rabbit and certainly unaware of his wife's melancholy. She stood alone in the kitchen as though at fate's mercy and looked at the clear blue sky for some semblance of comfort.

A similar solemn mood could be felt in Portsmouth harbour as crowds gathered to watch the departure of U 116. Her arrival had heralded a fanfare, now her crew stood to attention on deck and no submariner looked up at the clear blue sky, as the wind sighed and sucked like a malignant spirit for they knew shortly they would be slipping into a dusk worse than the grey ghost of winter.

CHAPTER 30

A NATO warship had been detailed to escort the submarine into the open sea and the Officers in the conning tower were only too aware of the sense of hopelessness that engulfed many of the crew. Below deck the men went about their work and though they looked cleaner, healthier and many wore recently laundered uniforms there was little jollification with Friedrich who saw his life's work, his life, coming to an end. It showed in his face. Agony.

In his cramped accommodation Kapitän Peter Werner was looking over the North Atlantic charts even though the course had been plotted. He checked them thoroughly and as he did he was joined by Wolfgang Emmerich.

"Kapitän."

"Yes, Wolfgang."

"The latest update."

Werner didn't look up from the charts.

"Twelve of the crew have contacted some family or relatives." The Seaman Officer waited for a response.

"And the rest?" His tone was distinctively quieter.

"Nothing."

There was a thoughtful pause before Werner looked at his Officer, desperate not to convey any sense of morbidity.

"What was the response of the men?"

Emmerich swallowed but quietly regained composure, "Shock, Kapitän. They knew but it still came as a shock. I have a list here." He offered it to his Kapitän and both men returned eye contact. Werner didn't take the sheet and Emmerich withdrew his hand summarising that this perhaps wasn't the correct time.

He continued in resolute fashion, "Kapitän, some of the men felt rejected. Fortunately there are more single than married men. Two wives told the men not to try and contact them."

Werner nodded slowly, his eyes looked dull. "It is understandable if regrettable."

"Forgive me, Kapitän, but I heard you mention once your brother. I'm sorry you have had no…"

Werner brought a calm smile to his face, "And what about your family Wolfgang?"

He tried to mask his disappointment, "Nothing, Kapitän, yet."

There was something admirable in the way he said the last word and Peter Werner thought, as he'd often done, how lucky he was to have the man stood next to him, his Seaman Officer.

"Didn't you have a sister?"

"Yes," said Emmerich nodding.

"Don't despair, maybe there will be good news for both of us when we reach the Fatherland." Werner patted him on the shoulder before adding, "Leave the list with me. I will speak individually with each of the men before we reach our destination."

For the first time Peter Werner noticed how clear and delicate the other man's hands were, an observation he'd missed until now and was prompted to ask him if he played the violin. Emmerich looked baffled and laughed quietly but his Kapitän didn't elaborate.

Their conversation continued.

"Kapitän."

"Yes."

"What do you think Germany is like?"

Werner pulled up the Cavalier in him for it always dissolved tension, "I think everyone will be more experienced than the last time we were there."

It had the desired effect and both men were able to exchange warm smiles even though both knew they could never press the spring of a magic watch and recover lost time… As evening approached and darkness had already swamped the ocean, strict orders were issued that no submariner was to go up on deck no matter what – suicide would crack the fragile morale that held the majority of the crew together. The Atlantic was unusually calm that first night and average speed of between ten and twelve knots was maintained which impressed the Officers. If ever a seagull was seen at night it was considered a good omen by submariners for they didn't have anything to lose from the sea; they were the guardians of the human dead lying below the surface listening to their echo; and anyone in the conning tower catching a glimpse would shout 'downstairs,' joyously.

The crew lying on their bunks didn't hear any voice, breaking away from the watch, to assail their attention. Nevertheless many were occupied. Ernst Bortfeld was reading a 'lads mag' from the eighties while Jorgan Bahn was sketching a nuclear powered submarine using *Navy News* as his source of reference; he had been given a set of pencils and a larger sketchpad than his own by the British Ratings he'd mingled with days earlier.

Conrad Meiner dug into his back pocket, extracted his wallet and took out the picture of Elsa. Franz Seilerman smiled and it was returned.

"Remember when I showed this picture," he held it up for Franz to see, "some days ago."

"Yes, it's your fiancée… I'm sorry, Conrad, you have heard nothing."

Word about the outcomes of each man's search for family had spread like wildfire through the crew for Kapitän Werner had instructed his Officers to let each man's predicament be known to everyone so any conversation could be conducted cautiously.

Conrad's response surprised the older man, "No, it's me who should have sympathy for you." He began his explanation before any quizzical look could come his way, "You have a family yet no one has come forward. You must be feeling wretched yet you have it in you to consider me. That makes me feel very humble, Franz."

There was a deafening silence before he continued in a lowered voice, "No one apart from Elsa has ever given me true friendship. I know we all love one another inside this metal tube but whatever happens I won't forget your kindness."

The Cook who'd heard their conversation couldn't resist interrupting, "Conrad, you'll be able to get work on the stage or something… I'm nearly crying."

The men, close by, knew his remark was not intended to be hurtful more Ernst trying to regain his previous status of devil's advocate even if he wasn't convincing and besides Conrad hadn't really heard his mumble. Despite his affability and self-depreciation Ernst Bortfeld, Cook, had all the child's weapons of nasty retaliation, with all the cruel time in the world. This temperamental liberty had cost him a pasting, once, so he kept it locked up until he was on shore leave… a disconsolate clown with his mask slipped sideways.

Franz brought his knees up to his chest to alleviate the pull on his back muscles which often became inflamed if he lay spread-eagled for too long; he groaned, "That's better" and gritted his teeth. Conrad watched him before instinctively, altering his position to assume more comfort. Franz was determined not to let the spirit be sucked out of him and was grateful for the flow of pure air rushing through; it was in stark contrast to often being barely able to breathe in the suffocating iron-sodden atmosphere that accompanied submergence for long periods, making conditions deplorable.

All submariners quickly learnt that suffering in numbers was not nearly as agonizing as suffering singly. The keenly piercing night air and chill was never so welcome particularly to those covered by a large blanket and racing towards sleep. Conrad waited for Franz to continue their conversation; on patrol he'd gotten used to his touching blend of melancholic maturity coupled with his previous youth's bubbling up of spontaneous fun. Outwardly he seemed unperturbed.

"I just hope Helga and the boys have had a happy life. I don't despair because when we get back all of us can find out for ourselves what happened over these last forty-six years."

The young man from Hamburg admired his fortitude as always, "You're a very sensible man Franz… we should all take our lead from you." He felt his own spirit rise and looked over towards the Cook, "Ernst, anything good in that magazine?"

He didn't move but answered the question. "I don't understand some of the political stories but the advertisements are quite cute if you don't pay much attention to the price of everything."

There was a chuckle among those eavesdropping submariners looking at him.

"And the girls?"

"Not enough meat on them for me… some look ill with malnutrition."

A few ribald comments travelled to and fro before Ernst continued, "Now and again though there is a woman trying to persuade a man to buy Russian vodka who could persuade me to do anything if you follow my meaning." He immediately let off an orchestra of flatulence which heralded meaty laughter and cries to open all the hatches. Then everything went quiet again, not a sinister silence, more of a pause.

Conrad turned his attention to Jorgen who was propped up opposite him, "What are you sketching Jorgen?"

"It's what's called a nuclear submarine."

"And the magazine?"

"It's the British *Navy News*, one of Captain Shaw's Officers and a Rating gave me a copy." He put his sketchpad down before continuing, "I don't understand the text but the ships are interesting to look at. Everything seems to go fast today. To think we thought we were modern."

Those listening laughed in subdued fashion.

"Our armaments are like bows and arrows."

Ernst Bortfeld having passed the magazine to another crew member joined the discussion, "I wonder what reception we will get from the German people of 1988. Will they welcome us back like gods or lepers?"

Jorgen stated, with a twinkle in his eye, "In your case, Ernst, the latter."

Only Conrad heard and he smiled, loudly.

Ernst continued, "Half of them will never have seen a U-boat before – strange that."

His point was taken up by Meiner, "Maybe we will look as different to them as the British sailors did to us. We all have national characteristics but these sometimes change as the years roll on."

Ernst dismissed his remark with the word, "Rubbish."

"No, it's not rubbish. You take a German born in 1800 and one born in 1900, each will have characteristics of that era he was born into. It's hard to define but you only have to look at paintings of famous Germans through the ages to see what I mean."

"Yeah like women – tits get bigger or arses get rounder." He laughed at his own comment while Jurgen shook his head before commenting.

"God knows how the Fatherland is going to accommodate you, Ernst… God only knows."

The Cook winked at him and the men chuckled through dry throats and continued doing so when his jaw dropped with theatrical imbecility as if he couldn't believe the last remark and a surge of blood suffused his neck and face.

Those submariners asleep had told one another before closing their eyes that when they stirred they hoped it would be to wake from a trance and the trembling would be no more. All would be disappointed… and they knew it.

At least those crew members on watch in the conning tower had a vast bowl of ink blue sky to absorb them and their hopes for the future; and fortified with hot chocolate both Peter Niester and Eric Steven could feel a warm overplus of blood in their cheeks.

"God it's something," said Eric Steven as he looked up with a certain mellow fire in his eyes. The Steward was about to reply when Kapitän Werner climbed up unnoticed. Both crew stood to attention.

"That's OK, men" said Peter Werner with an effervescent smile. He breathed in deeply, admired the view and his healthful optimistic spirit warmed his men too.

"Do you, either of you, know anything about astronomy?" His tone was so even he could have been talking about a legal transaction.

"Only what we were taught at school, Kapitän," said Eric Steven, innocently.

"It's a very interesting phenomena," offered Werner continuing to look at the stars, engrossed.

"Do you know about such things?" asked Peter Niester whose charm and vulnerability were inseparable, making him almost impossible to dislike.

Their Kapitän turned his eyes towards them, "A whole lifetime wouldn't be enough to even scratch the surface."

He waited for them to digest his words then continued enthusiastically, "But this is the best time of year." He turned his gaze towards the stars, "When Autumn comes there is something special in the sky to see. There are tiny groups of stars in the East called Pleiades. At first it seems only a bit of mist then it begins to sparkle. On a clear night you may see six or seven stars in the shape of a plough."

He smiled and this prompted his Steward to ask, "Where did you learn that, Kapitän?"

Peter Werner could feel the prickling of excitement run through his body like warm Punch as he spoke, "My grandfather used to spend many nights gazing at the stars. He was considered eccentric but he was fascinated by it all and hardly a week went by without him reading something new. My brother and I would sometimes keep him company when he visited us."

The trio were interrupted by Dieter Hoffman passing up a cardboard shoebox holding three mugs of steaming chocolate. The submariners received this gratefully and lit cigarettes before the Kapitän continued.

"At first it gave us a chance to stay up but gradually his enthusiasm rubbed off on me. I still recall the excitement I felt the first time I saw Orion, the great hunter."

The men took a drink from their mugs before Eric Steven asked almost with frantic excitement, "What is that, Kapitän?"

The latter's love and knowledge of the subject and the infectious manner in which he spoke would have been capable of waking any submariner in his deepest moment of sleep.

"The first thing you see in Orion is three beautiful stars. They make up his belt. A sword hangs from his belt."

They looked back up at the stars before he continued, "His two biggest stars are in his right shoulder and his left knee. His right arm is high above his head." He demonstrated the poses as he spoke.

"His left arm carries a shield and at his heels is Sirius, his dog. You can see Orion in November though the best months are December, January and February." He paused to look at both crew men, "It sounds complicated but it's not really once you get hooked."

Again he returned his gaze to the sky. "So peaceful."

A blot of silence was everywhere and the sea lapping at the side of U-boat 116 as she marched evenly through the Atlantic contributed to that silence. The escort that had accompanied her in the early part of her voyage home was now a memory; and at last the submariners felt they were inhabiting their own environment and a request from the crew filtered through to First Lieutenant Dieter Hoffman who took it to his Kapitän now relaxing in his quarters.

"Kapitän, the men have requested that we dive, once more for old time's sake."

It elicited a smile from Peter Werner, "How sentimental our crew really is Dieter?"

"I think there are several aching hearts, full of emptiness… the joy of doing something familiar from the past."

The officer and his Kapitän smiled and nodded their heads in unison as Peter Werner put his cap on, "Prepare for battle stations."

Their movement to the engine room was swift and on hearing the siren the crew swept into action; and it was almost balletic as everyone knew exactly his role. U-boat 116 stayed submerged for an hour carrying out familiar manoeuvres before rising to periscope depth. She dived again amidst loud cheering that echoed throughout the submarine and even the officers were tempted to join in but just managed to retain their decorum, by the skin of their teeth. Fifteen more minutes passed before the internal silence of these living souls matched the eternal silence of the dead. Bliss.

Half an hour later U116 broke the skin of the Atlantic, rising like some primordial beast before slapping down and stabilising on the ocean. Werner ordered the engines to be cut while Emmerich climbed into the conning tower to be greeted by a magical view – romantic, he said to himself before allowing a thought of his family to enter his conscious mind.

He was followed by Peter Werner as U116 became stationary on an extraordinarily calm sea.

"We'll take full advantage of the conditions Emmerich… get the men up on deck as quick as possible and ask Hans to bring that crate of Scotch lying on the table in my quarters."

Before the officer turned his Kapitän spoke again, "And bring the plastic cups jammed on my bookshelf."

Within minutes the whole crew of U-boat 116 were standing on deck, sufficiently wrapped up against the stark coldness of the night. They gathered as near to the bridge and waited for their Kapitän to address them.

"Men, a parting gift from Captain Shaw and his crew."

Seaman Officers Fiebig and Emmerich held up four very large bottles of whisky and because the full moon was operating at maximum the crew could see more than silhouettes and cheered.

Peter Werner smiled. "Captain Shaw suggested that once we were on our own it might be a good idea to toast this iron tub one more time with what he described as a," he deliberately paused trying to keep a straight face, "a delightful single malt."

The crew cheered and Werner wasn't finished, "He even provided plastic cups… apologising at the same time."

Now everyone chuckled, a few roared their approval and the officers circulated handing out the cups and pouring out generous measures. When the Kapitän was satisfied everyone had a drink he raised his cup.

"To U-boat 116 and the greatest crew any man could command."

The submariners barked out their response then drank the whisky in one go. Again the officers circulated pouring smaller measures so everyone got a second whisky.

"Your First Lieutenant Dieter Hoffman came up with a wonderful suggestion."

Werner deliberately paused to listen to the ribald comments before continuing.

"He suggested we put a message in each bottle saying when and where and by whom the whisky was drunk… I think he deserves a round of applause."

Bellicose cheering filled the air and Peter Werner was laughing as loud as anyone, as though the tumult of the previous week had been forgotten. Another fifteen minutes elapsed before the crew returned to their stations via the hatches and jugs of hot chocolate were rapidly prepared.

In the Control Room the Kapitän decided to increase the average speed to twelve knots and no one had to remind him that in good conditions he had eighteen knots at his disposal for they accepted he always had a sound reason for his actions and their trust was absolute; and regardless of rank each submariner always felt a zest in his company.

Before turning in for the night, Dieter Hoffman made a spur of the moment decision to thank, again, his Kapitän for a splendid get together. He approached Werner's quarters slowly hoping to establish first whether his Kapitän was asleep. He was reading, in a commanding voice, entries from his logbook.

"Kapitän."

"Come in, Dieter." Werner indicated for the Lieutenant to sit down on his bunk and he read, again, some more extracts; and both men's faces swelled with pride.

"August 1st 1942 0630 Dived in position 05°07' south for submerged passage through known shipping lanes – Noon Position 03°50' south 102°45' east. Wind E, sky b.c., vis.7, sea 11. 14.15 Sighted merchant ship approaching from astern. Went to 90'. Enemy passed close but detected nothing. 14.35 Went to periscope depth. 14.40 Torpedoes prepared. 14.42 Enemy position relayed. 14.43 Torpedoes one and two fired. 14.50 Merchant ship listing, crew scrambling into life boats."

Both men smiled for sinking an enemy ship with minimum loss of life never disturbed sleep patterns which were fragile, at best. Emmerich noted a hand-written inscription on the Kapitän's book mark, half of which stuck out above the next page. Seeing his officer's quizzical expression he informed him it was written by a U-boat Skipper when his boat sank to the sea bed and he thought they could never surface again because of depth charge damage. It was supposed to be the final entry.

He read it slowly, "The hours turned to ages of eternity the minutes dallied, holding on to life as if the heartbeat of Time himself had slowed in the agony of a lingering death."

The crew woke at various intervals on what they knew was their last day at sea and understandably there would be a collective nervousness on the last leg of their journey. Werner made a point of walking the length of U116 mid-morning and shaking everyone by the hand and offering his individual, engaging smile; little wonder the crew held him in such high regard. To them he was nonpareil. He told each man he would address them through the P.A. System, before they reached Hamburg.

Unknown to anyone, he had written a speech but he'd worked on it because he wanted everyone to know he was speaking from his heart – a naval man's heart not a politician's heart.

He'd decided to cut all engines at 10.00am and instructed Friedrich Schreiber his Chief Engine Room Artificer accordingly. The men heard the drone slowly die away and their U-boat suddenly seemed lighter. The Kapitän and First Lieutenant were smoking as the former looked again at his notes aware of the encouraging look Dieter Hoffman gestured with before looking at his watch and announcing over the P.A. system that the Kapitän would address the crew in fifteen seconds. Werner removed his cap, not knowing why, before he spoke.

"Soon our journey will be over or should I say odyssey… Every one of us will be starting afresh. I'm sure all of you have thought at length about the future, your own future. Don't let uncertainty become a nagging fear in this old tub – fear is only fear whatever disguise it takes."

He paused for he hoped the crew would reflect on his words and they did for some were already in tears, "Some of you are in for a nerve racking time, others will surely strain their nerve ends searching for any semblance of their family, particularly in the East. None of us can be happy at Germany's outcome from the war. Some of you, I know, cannot believe the atrocities that were committed by our own people. But the war is over, long gone – you my friends must get used to that if you are to survive and adjust. I hope you will. One month from tomorrow I hope you will attend with me a final reunion. I will be interested to know what has happened to each one of you during the month. I will be staying in Hamburg and the government have granted you every access and free passes to travel for one month."

This buoyed the crew but there was no flamboyant response as they listened intently.

"There isn't much left for me to say except again thank you for your loyalty; it was unswerving from start to finish. No Kapitän could have asked for a better crew. Thank you and good luck."

Dieter Hoffman quickly turned off the P.A. system for he could see his Commanding Officer's eyes mist up and he looked spent having spoken intently without any choppy and disconnected fragments.

"Pure genius and so much heart," he whispered to himself before offering his Kapitän a cigarette and the promise of a coffee topped with Captain Shaw's favourite drink for the First Lieutenant hadn't drained the final bottle up on deck the previous night; he wanted Peter Werner to have the final measure and no one would query that. No one.

CHAPTER 31

Of the fifty two crew in U-boat 116, five were sons of Hamburg and though they had sketchy information about the final days of the war they knew their city was involved in one of the last battles of World War Two when troops of the German 1st Parachute Army fought the British 8th Corps for control between April 18th and May 3rd 1945.

The prelude to this was inevitable – after the Western allies crossed the river Rhine the German armies in the west began to fall apart. Army Group B under the command of Walter Model was the last effective defence in the west. However the Army Group consisting of three armies was encircled and captured by the 1st and 9th American armies.

Communications between German forces organizing resistance in a few cities had broken down and with Berlin also under siege by the Russians no reinforcements were sent to Hamburg, on orders of the German High Command. The British advance to Hamburg was spearheaded by the 7th Armoured Division attacking the city and advancing to the River Elbe across from Hamburg. The German resistance began to disintegrate and a sense of the inevitable dawned on the citizens despite ferocious house to house combat provided by the 1st Parachute Army – a mix of SS, paratroopers, Volkssturm along with regular Wehrmacht soldiers and Hitler youth.

Following Hitler's suicide on April 30th Grand Admiral Karl Dönitz, who was commanding forces in the north, ordered General Alwin Wolz to open discussions about surrendering the city to the British. It was completed on 3rd May, nevertheless survivors of the 1st Parachute along with

Army Group Northwest retreated into the Jutland peninsular. Most of them met ailing soldiers from the Army Group Vistula fleeing from the Russians on the Eastern Front.

Like most German cities Hamburg had been subject to mass bombing particularly later in the war and the intensity and frequency increased because of its location and strategic importance. Civilian casualties were immense but within fifteen years it had been rebuilt, was a symbol of modern Europe and a thriving economy made it a desirable place to live by the mid-1980s.

Max Frommer, Planesman and Conrad Meiner stood side by side on the deck struggling to recognise the port as they remembered it; only the sea was familiar, the old outline had vanished and both felt dismayed despite the noise from the quay where cheering crowds had gathered being faint as U-boat 116 slowed and prepared to approach.

"At least the water looks the same," said Max Frommer in a voice that concealed passion in its quietness yet revealed a smouldering volcano, far from extinct, within him. Meiner put his hand on the Planesman's shoulder – a gesture of solidarity that didn't require words.

Police were trying to control the crowds for it seemed the whole of Hamburg wanted to be part of this historic occasion and everywhere was engulfed in an all-embracing excitement for all they saw as a few more crew appeared on deck was bunched up submariners, not one of them broken, frayed or frazzled; little did they know…

The U116 officers on the bridge and in the conning tower were silent; it was as if it had suddenly dawned on them, collectively, that the picture of a torpedoed ship which had been tucked away in the brain for years after becoming a reality was extinct and they had nothing to replace it with…

The harbour was rapidly approaching as Werner gave orders to decrease the speed and several small vessels provided an escort. These weekend sailors could see the blurred, shadowed expressions on many of the submariners' faces which didn't change when one of its escort crew played the German National Anthem loudly over its P.A.

Peter Werner had no intention of taking the tub right up to the jetty; he had informed the crew early that morning with the rider, "We're not exhibits but submariners finally coming home." To try and add a degree of levity he had also told them, "Some of you have shaved these last few days, some of you haven't and that includes me." His tone had been easy without any clipped intensity lest the crew thought his spirit had finally been exhausted. It hadn't but in his heart he knew all the crew, himself included, had embraced traditional values: stoicism, endurance, courage but in this new world could they deal with the dreadful loss of patriotism, selflessness and honour?

In a hastily erected stand an aged group of men, distinguished by their naval headgear, sat together; part of a dwindling number of submariners who'd survived the war. One of the group wore a vague impression of pain and clenched something tight in his right hand and the nearer the submarine came the more tears rolled out of his eyes though he remained self-contained.

Final preparations completed, most of the crew came up on deck, through the hatches. They shook hands and it appeared few words passed between them despite the roar of the crowd, reminiscent of a night time football cup replay.

Like something from an ancient past U116 moved closer and slowly turned starboard, almost within grasp of the crowd who were reduced to near silence made that way by the unbelievable sight, motionless, before their eyes. There was no more sea for U116's bow to part.

Kapitän Werner, on the bridge, again looked towards his crew with compassion then at the crowd, civic dignitaries and the Film and television camera crews. When the crew looked at him and suddenly stood to attention, he saluted them; it seemed mystical and some by product of heart coupled with instinct took over the crowd who suddenly erupted into wild cheering with total abandon and none of them could imagine that the upright men they currently adored might one day be crumpled bodies staring blindly into a morbid sky already peopled by their spirits. Some of the crew smiled and some remained calm; and everyone knew the final U-boat had come home; and half of Germany now saw Peter Werner as the gleaming pennant of achievement.

CHAPTER 32

The first object anyone noticed in the sumptuous lounge of Hamburg's city centre four star hotel was the brightly lit chandelier; it was the perfect accompaniment to the Strauss Waltz that could be heard early evening as guests arrived for dinner.

Former Kapitän Peter Werner had been given a suite with everything he required just a phone call away. After seven days he sensed he'd put on a few pounds despite using the hotel pool every morning and a couple of forays into the multi-gym where a fitness instructor had explained biomechanics to the bemused guest.

He'd enjoyed a long drawn out shave each morning and the hotel barber had trimmed his hair. Having enjoyed a long hot bubble bath he'd strolled into the lounge resplendent in grey suit, pale blue shirt and dark tie. No sooner had he sat down than young waiters were eager to take his order which was always cold beer and Schnapps. He couldn't quite come to terms with how comfortable his Italian shoes were and chuckled at the fact his new wardrobe was courtesy of the government as was his accommodation; and yet a part of him found it all as blank and bare as a fridge full of ice.

Each evening he had chatted with former seamen; he looked relaxed, faintly amused at his celebrity status which included women of all ages and degrees of attraction smiling his way and wishing him luck. His response had always been cheery; even the hotel's doctor, not known for his flexibility, had laughed after Peter Werner having undergone a stringent medical declared him exceptionally fit, for a man in his seventh decade.

"Well, Kapitän, what do you think of the new Germany?" asked a former weather-beaten seaman, never considering how banal his question was.

Werner remained faultless, "I have only seen Hamburg. I was last here in 1940 when I was stationed at Kiel. I remember some of the older buildings, those left standing but these shopping precincts, without traffic… well they take some getting used to."

It was obvious that the ex-serviceman would laugh.

"Fortunately I'm not in a position to spend much but I doubt if I could afford many Schnapps on my wages."

It had the desired effect – everyone laughed even louder and some other guests turned their heads. Another of the group who appeared to have a sluggish motion with his hands spoke quietly.

"Many of us hope that one day the Fatherland will be united and live as one."

His remark was dismissed by his friend, "Fine chance of that happening. The Russians will never concede to that."

There was a brief lull broken by the youngest member of the party, "Come now, the Kapitän doesn't want to hear politics. We've been through this a hundred times."

Werner smiled and the group's obvious leader caught his eye.

"Tell me, Kapitän, have you heard from your crew?"

Werner's eyes lit up. "Yes, I have received four letters already but that is a private matter between my crew and myself."

"Of course, Kapitän," was the immediate response.

"May I be permitted to ask you if you have heard from your brother… I believe you did have a brother?"

Werner crinkled his face and addressed the quartet, "Yes, I have a brother but no word so far. It is in the hands of God and the department that has been put to work retracing family relatives."

Everyone took a drink from their beer glasses and another of the former seamen offered words of comfort, "I'm sure they will turn up trumps, Kapitän."

His words met with approval and were appreciated by Werner who spoke honestly.

"Maybe, but tracing is one thing, whether or not a reunion will take place is another. Not in my case. I am thinking of my men. How does a man cope with the knowledge that his wife is nearly fifty or so years older than he and maybe married to someone else, living a satisfactory, happy life. What can be gained by such a reunion? I think in some cases the old saying – let sleeping dogs lie – is very apt. That is why I must try to safeguard my crews' privacy in their most soulful moments."

He let his words sink in and watched four men nod affirmatively before continuing.

"I do not wish to see them as the players in some sort of human circus."

"You have great regard for your men, Kapitän, and I think in the circumstances I, we, would be exactly the same."

The conversation was interrupted by a middle-aged waiter bringing another round of drinks, "Gentlemen, dinner will be served in twenty minutes." He placed the drinks on the table and effortlessly disappeared to the kitchen. The naval men toasted, "friends and absent friends."

Over dinner Werner was eager to hear each of the men's own naval experience, anecdotal stories as well and he wasn't disappointed. When the party left the dining room he was ready for his bed though he did force himself to walk a couple of hundred yards outside to aid digestion and help clear the muzziness in his head the Schnapps had provided. He decided against going upstairs to get his coat lest he changed his mind. All around him was neon lighting and a continual buzz and traffic and conversation. The rain, without warning, started to pelt down and he quickly turned back and made for the smaller lounge in the hotel which boasted an open fire; it was pleasant to think of the wind and rain outside while flames danced continuously up the chimney. After ten minutes he returned to his room.

Finally he locked his bedroom door behind him, removed his jacket and tie and walked over to the polished mahogany table next to the window on which rested a side light. Before pressing the switch he stood looking out over Hamburg and the never ending lights, then he looked up at the lights in the sky and smiled to himself at the vibrancy of everything. He picked up the telephone on a smaller table beside the large bed and dialled for room service; immediately a voice was heard and Werner spoke, "Will you send some coffee and a small bottle of Brandy up to room 17… Thank you."

He kicked his new shoes off and lay spread-eagled on the bed having adjusted the brightness of the ceiling lighting. Motionless, he thought about the statement one of the elderly men had said downstairs, about fascism being a lie told by bullies and immediately erased the discomfort he felt by thinking, again, of his crew. The images came quickly and he glowed as if in the fire of Hades then he yawned and whispered, "Even if I sleep for a month, I shall never overtake all the sleep I have lost."

CHAPTER 33

Within five minutes he heard polite knocking on his door and sprang agilely off the bed and opened the door to be greeted by night service wearing a smile. He took the tray from the young waiter and bade him goodnight before putting it on the table beside the window; the aroma was intoxicating and induced immediate memories of Berlin's coffee-houses pre-war.

Werner stood looking out the window, coffee cup in hand when a gentle knock on his door turned his head. The night porter, in his sixties with a lived-in face and soft eyes, apologised for the intrusion before speaking, "Excuse me, Kapitän, there is a man downstairs in the lobby says he would like to see you. He asked me to give you this."

The porter gave him a small package and waited for his response. Werner looked baffled as he opened it; suddenly he was transfixed at the content and looked at the porter.

"Ask the man to come up to my room," he said in a measured tone.

"Certainly, Kapitän."

The porter closed the door and U116's commanding officer looked giddy as he shuffled to his bed where he sat down and tipped the lighter, his own lighter from the envelope into his hand. He stared at it before flicking it alight and gazing at the flame. For the third time since coming upstairs there was another gentle knock on the door to his suite. He remained seated, making no attempt to get to his feet, for what seemed an eternity before another knock, slightly harder than the first penetrated the room. The Kapitän inhaled deeply, rose forward and walked upright to the door but paused before opening it.

In front of him stood Gunter Kessler, rather unkempt, with a curved nose and a halo of grey hair yet he had the self-contained, inward look of a man feeling his way in unfamiliar surroundings. The submariner who failed to turn up for U-boat 116's last mission, choked with emotion and sadness, "Hello, Kapitän."

These words took an effort of will. Peter Werner was hypnotised and said nothing because sadness engulfed him as he recalled to himself the old days when Gunter Kessler had been joyous company, the unpromotable buffoon – a reputation he revelled in. Also someone whom the officers always knew, in a tight corner, would do over and above the call of duty just as well, probably better, than dull dependable types.

He looked beaten and his second-hand clothing included a cap worn at a jaunty angle which framed the right side of a grey, lined face. Both men were tired but in incomparable ways; Werner ushered his crew member in, walked him to the table where he poured two large glasses of brandy after switching on the table light. Gunter Kessler broke down and his Kapitän put both glasses back down on the table before cradling him; and he could feel the shaking storm of grief that had plagued the former submariner for over forty years.

"It's OK, Gunter, it's OK – it's OK." His words reigned in some of the distress, the burden of shame which Kessler had lived with but it needed a couple of large brandies, drunk swiftly, for any balance to return and reduce the entrancement both men were in. Fortunately the bottle of brandy was three quarter size and now Werner poured another measure and both men managed to chink glasses and the Kapitän tried not to see Kessler's life, written in bold, all over his face, for he could feel the other man's agonizing soreness in his heart; and that was enough.

He decided on levity, "You've certainly looked after my lighter," and he lit both their cigarettes.

"Yes, Kapitän."

Smiling, Werner responded, "I wonder how much it is worth today?"

Kessler replied eagerly, "I have treasured it all these years, Kapitän."

He smiled and reasoned to himself that after U116's reported disappearance with all hands lost, Gunter Kessler's sense of guilt must have driven him near to the conclusion that the only anaesthetic was suicide.

"It hasn't been very easy has it?" The compassion in Werner's tone was immeasurable.

"No," replied Kessler in a whisper.

The pragmatism in the Kapitän's character took charge, "Come on it's over – drink up, take your coat off make yourself comfortable… there is much to talk about."

Kessler's tatty coat was slumped over the upright chair and both men shouldered their way to the settee, carrying their glasses after Werner had replenished them. The alcohol was having a soothing effect and Werner encouraged his guest to speak.

"That night before we were due to leave St Nazaire, I was travelling with my girl to Redon. We had talked of marriage." Kessler looked into the distance while Werner waited determined not to interrupt.

"Her family were against me from the start. We were very much in love, Kapitän – and her family thought she was going alone. Petrol for civilians was scarce but her father always managed to get some."

Both men exchanged knowing looks.

"However, she picked me up outside the town and off we went. It was our last night, we had both had a drink, not like we drank as a crew, but we were merry. We were going over a hill and the car just seemed to veer out of control. Francois panicked and that was it. The next minute we had hit a wall and the car somersaulted. When I came round Francois was lying across me still. Her neck was broken."

Werner felt his stomach turn over in a spasm but his face didn't betray anything and he continued to listen, intently.

"I was in a state of shock and must have staggered for a couple of miles then blacked out. When I finally came round I couldn't remember anything." Kessler, unable to control nervous breathing, looked at his Kapitän and saw nothing judgemental in his expression which encouraged him to continue relaying events.

"I had no identity on me and the shock had left me dumb. I was finally found by a farmer and taken to hospital. Gradually I began remembering things, pictures would come into mind about the crew, of Germany – eventually six months later I had recovered enough to be allowed out with someone. One day we went to the port and I saw a U-boat returning. It was as though everything came back, everything except the power of speech. When I found out what had happened to Francois and the fate of my boat missing, unable to speak, life did not seem worth continuing. I knew I would be branded a deserter. I could never go back to my family – they would have already been informed that I was missing presumed dead. I lived with some nuns in a nunnery and in return for working for them I was given food and lodgings. They were kind to me; when I eventually plucked up the courage to, to speak one day I was staggered that they did not turn me out."

Werner looked quizzical and Kessler knew why.

"It had taken a long time for speech to return. The war had changed course and I resolved to live in the nunnery where no one asked about my past. Sometimes seeing these soft angelic women only made my conscience turn more at me. The blame for not driving that night has never left me. Sometimes… and believing my crew members were all dead while I lived, well existed, that made me hate myself even more."

There was a deep humanity about him; his weariness beyond suffering and an inner strength that had somehow defeated this weariness. He explained that eventually the nuns found him a job as a hospital porter and gradually he mastered the French language. He had a room in the grounds of the hospital but still visited the nunnery once a month.

"I could speak German as two nuns, maybe an act of reconciliation, transferred from a convent in Bonn."

Werner was full of admiration, had always been for those who had crossed the frontiers of courage while pursuing self-destruction. More tears filled Kessler's eyes.

"As years went by, gradually I was able to look at your lighter but the torment would still come. I felt I owed it to you to…"

Werner broke his silence and put both hands on his friend's shoulders in a solid embrace, "Gunter, you have no need to suffer one more minute – enough, I will not let you suffer again." His words were defiant, deliberate and much, much more than well intentioned. He could also feel himself welling-up but was able to retain that decorum that all good commanders exercised in perilous or extreme moments.

"You never went home even long after the war then?"

"No," said Kessler quietly, then he returned the smile on his Kapitän's face.

"Your friends will be coming back to Hamburg, I hope, three weeks tomorrow. They will want to see you. I know that it will be good for you to meet them just like old times, eh? You're still one of us Gunter… still with us."

Werner said it with absolutely no pinch of irony and disregarded the fact that he'd been in conversation with Gunter Kessler merely two months previously. In one way age hadn't dulled his fellow submariner; his smile was still like a ray of sun through a low cloud and a heart still strong enough to give a butterfly 'backbone', thought Werner.

That night Kessler stayed, sleeping on the settee and in the morning soaked in a hot bath before tucking into a full breakfast sent up to the Kapitän's room. Throughout the morning Kessler related tales about his home city, the sixth largest in Germany, between rounds of coffee and assorted biscuits brought up by the catering staff.

Kapitän Werner was fascinated by how much knowledge the former submariner had accumulated without being returned and he was ashamed of the persecution of the Jews.

"It was mob rule and decent Germans, like us, just stood by…"

Now Peter Werner could see traces of nobility in the ageing man's face despite a near lifetime of suffering and he knew 'the final solution' still nagged him for it had pierced the sense of justice in the submariner's heart.

Both men enjoyed a light lunch in the private suite and the Kapitän was happy to let Gunter Kessler talk, even more.

"Under the Nazi regime Stuttgart began deporting its Jewish inhabitants as early as 1939, mind you around sixty percent had fled by the time restriction on their movement was imposed. That was exactly a year before our tub went out for the last time."

He paused and his voice trembled when he told his commander that those Jews living in Wurtemberg who'd been moved to 'Jewish apartments' before being concentrated on Trade Fair grounds Killesberg were shipped off to Riga in cattle trucks, "This began in December 1942." His voice tailed off to a whisper, "Only 180 held in concentration camps survived."

Silence entered their conversation until Werner broke it asking Kessler how Stuttgart faired after 1942.

"The centre was completely destroyed by air raids. The worst was in September 1944 over 180,000 bombs." He shook his head, "I found out seventy percent of the buildings were destroyed and there were over 4,500 deaths."

"What happened during the last month of the war?" asked Werner, crossing his left leg over his right and adjusting his back into a more upright position.

Kessler waited for him to take a sip of coffee before responding, "The US 7th army and French 5th Armoured Division captured Stuttgart on April 21st. There was little resistance – the French occupied the city until it was transferred to the American military occupation zone in 1946." Kessler nodded his head and adjusted his position before taking a drink of coffee.

His Kapitän pondered before asking whether the old city became Americanised but not before saying he knew it was where the first prototypes of the VW Beetle were manufactured. This elicited a small smile between them before Gunter Kessler continued.

"In the fifties and sixties, 45,000 Americans were stationed in and around the city… I suppose it brought much needed jobs but numbers decreased as the Americans and Russians aren't at each other's throats so much now… Yeah American bars, diners they're a feature of modern Stuttgart and of course the rock music…"

Werner interrupted, "Yes, that's something we are trying to get used to but it is a shock." He chuckled at his own words and Kessler smiled making the creases around his eyes obvious.

"You should go back Gunter… now that we've met and after you've met with the crew."

Kessler thought about his Kapitän's suggestion, he didn't dismiss it out of hand as he would have done two days earlier, "Maybe… if I did it would be to go, one last time, to the Christmas market; it was a special moment in childhood, the largest anywhere wonderful lights." Then he looked directly at his Kapitän with suddenly acquired rosy cheeks, "I would also go to the Karlspatz side of the old castle for there is a museum dedicated to the memory of Claus Von Stauffenberg."

Neither man needed to elaborate.

When Kessler left, having written down the time and date of U-boat 116's final reunion, his Kapitän hoped a substantial weight had been lifted off his crew member. Certainly he left the suite with greater elasticity in his movement and the memory of this buoyed Peter Werner as he stood under a hot shower before wrapping the hotel's thick towelling dressing gown around himself. He felt exhausted, understandably so and before he lay down on his bed and closed his eyes he moved to the window acknowledging the darkness dropping from the sky. "I wonder how the crew are coping?" he said aloud before reflecting on his meeting with his former crewman hoping his genial and homely manner had struck the right note. He knew it had, for he had a style characterised by clarity and force and his own brand of compassion, an extremely rare commodity.

CHAPTER 34

Hamburg, perhaps the most vibrant city in Germany, especially at night where generations of visitors made for one location. A place which made other capitals' red light district pale with comparison. In one particular bar a loud commotion was going on which could be heard on the pavement outside where inquisitive passers-by paused. Suddenly a man, worse for drink, was thrown out by two burly doormen who probably enjoyed brutalising the living. As he staggered to his feet, unkempt, snarling, it was hard to reconcile the pitiful figure with Eric Steven the quintessential sober and ever reliable submariner. He took a bottle of whisky from his coat pocket, stumbled, before unscrewing the cap and taking a gulp before tightening the cap and putting the near empty bottle back inside his pocket. Obscenities were yelled before he staggered away, aimlessly.

A blonde prostitute appeared from nowhere, ridiculously overdressed in an underdressed manner, but seeing his drunken state quickly veered away as he staggered towards her, "Fifty years ago your kind were queuing up to screw us. We didn't have to pay a thing. If anyone paid it was you." He slurred his words, "Do you hear me? All Germany was proud then. I was a hero." The cold air was contributing to his headiness and he shouted, "A hero!"

Other revellers looked at him with disdain which only powered further forcefulness, "Go on take a look. What's the matter then?" The fact that no one recognised the lost submariner hurt Eric Steven's sense of dignity. Perhaps the novelty value had worn off. He looked exhausted when he slumped on a bench a few streets away and having drained the last of the whisky threw the bottle over his shoulder. When he buried his face in his large hands it created an image of a wretched lost soul who couldn't cry his troubles away. Nature was less blind – a sudden torrent of rain coated Hamburg and drops of water hit hard surfaces then climbed six inches back up. Within minutes the pedestrian ways were empty of people with one exception.

In a more optimistic mood earlier that day, yet nevertheless pensive, Horst Kruger looked out of the taxi window in which he was a passenger. Unlike Eric Steven his face didn't manifest an exalted state of terror for he was readily absorbed with life in 1980s Germany: the cars, people, shops and buildings. If the taxi-driver recognised him he remained tactfully silent until he saw through his front mirror the submariner taking a piece of paper from his coat pocket and examining it.

"We will soon be there, Sir," the driver remarked casually when slowing to take a corner before accelerating, noting the smile on his passenger's face. Eventually the Mercedes turned into a grand suburban street and Horst Kruger could feel the tension in his chest rising as the car slowed to a halt. He looked motionless at the house while the youthful looking driver got out and opened the passenger door. The naval man got out very slowly looking for signs of life coming from the house.

"No fare, Sir, I wish you luck." The driver smiled for he knew his passenger had only half heard him.

Horst Kruger didn't notice the Mercedes drive off, his eyes remained on the property and a small suitcase stood by his feet. Three doors away a neighbour looked at him sharply from her upstairs window – taking in his broad shoulders, big hands yet oddly gentle face. He inhaled deeply and walked slowly towards the front door observing how well cared for the front garden was. He stopped when he noticed the front door open and framed in perfect alignment stood an elderly man with a walking stick and a very frail small woman with white hair.

He choked for he knew less than ten yards away stood his mother and brother and Horst Kruger made no attempt to conceal his emotion. The brothers hugged each other with tender ferocity and his mother trembled before her son relinquishing his grip looked at her before putting his arms around her frame, gently.

Inside the home they shuffled to the sitting room and Siegfried indicated for his brother to get close to their mother, "Horst, let mother touch your face, she is nearly blind... go on."

Horst took hold of his mother's hands and guided them towards his face and tears, far from rehearsed, ran down his cheeks, "It's wonderful to be here with you, mother."

Two invisible hearts were pulling at one another and the men's mother spoke; stuttering her words, "Oh son, this is the happiest day of my life... I have prayed every day but never did I think that this would ever happen. All these years..." She had nothing more to say for she was utterly spent, utterly exhausted as her returning son guided her into a comfortable armchair before embracing his brother again. Siegfried tried to control his trembling as he poured a generous measure of Schnapps into two glasses. In this room it seemed all the petty irritations of the previous forty-six years had vanished.

"I think we could do with these." He gave one to his brother now kneeling down beside his mother holding her hand, occasionally squeezing it as words were superfluous for the sense of strength, endurance, suffering and indomitable courage was evident as well as remarkable.

Only after the men had drunk and the older brother had replenished the empty glasses did the conversation resume. Siegfried smiled, "The years have been good to me, yes?"

"You're looking fine." Horst slowly stroked his head.

"It is hard to believe..." Siegfried was immediately inter-rupted.

"I know…" The pause allowed his mother to look at her two sons while pulling higher onto her shoulders an embroidered shawl.

"You both must be hungry?" she said innocently.

Siegfried pushed his best smile forward, "Mother, tonight I am taking you both out, we will celebrate in fine style."

He laughed to himself as his mother responded, "Thank you, it is a long time since we went out."

The submariner had been aware that his mother's and brother's eyes had rarely been off him since he'd arrived and he wanted to lesson any strain so offered a jocular remark, "I suppose it's not every day someone turns up from the past."

It was enough to reduce his mother, once again, to tears.

"Horst, my Horst," she said fondling his face when he knelt down beside her once again. It was also difficult for the older brother to contain himself, once more.

Back in Hamburg, that following midday, hotel reception were experiencing frantic activity: guests arriving, guests leaving, taxis being ordered, the extension for room service ringing continuously yet the staff remaining as unflappable as ever. Perhaps that was why the hotel in the city centre was so popular with an enviable reputation.

Just off from reception in the lobby, stood Kapitän Peter Werner looking about, anxiously. He didn't see an officious middle-aged man with sharp aquiline features shoulder his way to reception where he made enquiries, "I am supposed to meet Kapitän Peter Werner here at 12.30pm." Before the uniformed receptionist could respond, her colleague a middle manager and possessor of an engaging smile stated that the Kapitän was in the lobby and he would take the new arrival to meet him.

The introductions were brief, both men shook hands and the hotel employee suggested they might want to take the two leather armchairs in the corner where they wouldn't be disturbed, before departing. No sooner had the two men sat down, Werner stiffened his shoulders like he'd done every time U116 went to periscope depth.

"Have you any news?" His words were rushed.

"Yes, it took quite a bit of unravelling – records you know."

The Kapitän nodded impatiently, waiting for the next instalment.

"Anyway we have traced your brother, at least we have traced him to a bar he frequents, in Munich. The owners informed me that he has not been seen for a few days. They were under the impression that he was coming to Hamburg to see you."

Werner rapidly digested the information before responding, "To meet me?"

"Yes, apparently, since the story broke he was telling everyone about you and I believe got someone, or did it himself, to find out when you would arrive. He even had a celebration drink with his cronies."

Momentarily Werner feared the worst, "He can't have disappeared, have you contacted…"

Before he could finish his sentence he was interrupted, "Hospitals yes, police and church. Remember, Kapitän, Munich is a vast city. There are numerous hostels, old people's homes, private nursing residences. We know that your brother has a flat but the cleaning lady who comes in once a week says he wasn't there and that was yesterday."

Noting the sudden increased alarm registering in the submariner's face he tried to put him at ease, "Don't worry, Kapitän, we will find him even if we have to turn the whole city upside down. I understand your anxiety – so near, yet so far."

Werner weighed up his options, something he excelled at, "I will go to Munich immediately."

The smiling bureaucrat nodded his head, "That's what I thought. I've reserved a seat for you on the next plane." He looked at his watch, "Take off two and a half hours… time for you to pack and get a bite to eat?"

The men stood up and shook hands and though the bureaucrat appeared to have little poetry in his life at least he appeared valiant, thought Werner.

"Thank you for your help, it is kind of you to go to all this trouble." His words were sincere and the recipient knew it.

"Don't mention it. Remember to be at the airport an hour before take-off and when you arrive in Munich I want you to telephone this number." He took a card from his inside pocket and handed it to Werner, "Mr Hertz – he will be expecting you and everything will be laid on transport, accommodation."

"Thank you," said Werner, again offering his hand.

The bureaucrat returned the optimism he'd arrived at the hotel with, "Perhaps by the time you arrive we will have located your brother. I hope so and hope it is a happy reunion. Kapitän, I would like to stay longer. I'm sure we could have enjoyed a long conversation but unfortunately my schedule is hectic. We are all too busy these days. No one has time any more to stop and," he gestured with his arms before continuing, "just think. The pace of life you may struggle to come to terms with but I wish you every success and happiness." Both parted in different directions.

As punctual as most servicemen are, Kapitän Werner arrived before the allotted time at Hamburg airport and waited in the departures lounge fascinated by the aircraft screaming down the runway and coming into land while other passengers merely took it for granted. He was excited at the prospect of flying at 28,000 feet and couldn't wait for the thrill of taking off and landing. He also convinced himself that meeting his brother wasn't that far off and the bright sunshine low in the sky, he took as a portent of things to come; his face was no longer shaped by earlier disappointment and his heart no longer bare of hope. Then he thought of some of his crew – what had happened to their dreams? Was God asleep and the Devil awake?

CHAPTER 35

Kapitän Werner was given VIP status on arrival at Munich airport; he was whisked through passport control and customs before being met by a Mr Hertz who guided him to a waiting car.

The submariner looked impatient as the Mercedes accelerated away from the airport, before Mr Hertz a middle-aged career civil servant put him at ease.

"Kapitän, I have good news. Your brother is OK. Apparently he had a minor stroke; he has a history of heart trouble but the doctor assures me he has the constitution of an ox and with plenty of rest will be allowed home. Perhaps the excitement had caught up with him. It happens." His tone was that of a familiar aunt, liked by all the family and it provided Werner with a degree of comfort.

"As far as we've been able to put it together your brother went to see a friend outside Munich prior to his intended trip to Hamburg. He was taken ill but wouldn't let the friend call even a doctor. Apparently he was frightened that if he went to hospital, he wouldn't see you and according to the friend, worse, that you would have thought he wasn't bothered with meeting you after all these years."

Finally, the Kapitän was able to relax and he chuckled as he remembered their competitiveness as boys.

Mr Hertz also smiled, "He's some man, very stubborn by all accounts."

Werner could feel the weight dropping off his shoulders and he chuckled, "Yes, he always was, my mother used to say that his determination could well be his undoing. When can I see him?"

Hertz assumed an attitude of benevolent authority, only too aware whom he was travelling with, "Not until tomorrow I'm afraid. You see it was only after he lapsed into semi-consciousness did the friend call a doctor who sent for an ambulance, immediately. We were looking for admissions for a week ago or thereabouts. Your brother has only been in three days." He sighed but remained forthright, "The doctors have insisted it be a short visit tomorrow as too much excitement might cause another relapse."

Werner thought for a few seconds before responding, "I understand."

Hertz shuffled in his seat to get more comfortable and he appeared at his most relaxed since introducing himself to the Kapitän. In fact he had loosened all over like a punctured air-sack, "Please stay in Munich a few days, my wife and I would be glad to entertain you for dinner each evening."

His offer was genuine, thought Werner, and had none of the whipped cream of flattery.

"Thank you I shall not forget your hospitality."

Both men smiled before Hertz sensing they were near their destination remarked,

"It's the least we can do in the circumstances."

The driver turned left, then immediate right and began to slow.

"Ah, here we are, your hotel."

Werner opened his eyes in exaggerated fashion.

"I will see that your reservation is kept over till you wish to return to Hamburg where I do believe you are meeting your crew, once more?"

Werner nodded. "Yes, but not for a couple of weeks. Right now Fritz is my main concern, everything else will have to take a back seat."

The duo walked into the hotel lobby and Peter Werner looked about the trappings of another elegant four star establishment, smiling to himself for he could never have afforded this pampering three months ago. The atmosphere was calm yet invigorating and he knew that on this evening, at least, he would dine like a king.

Mr Hertz returned from reception with another encouraging smile, "Everything is fine." He gave Werner his card, "Phone me tomorrow morning and I will arrange for a car to take you to the hospital and in the evening I will come personally to the hotel and take you to my home. Angelika will cook something traditional."

The men shook hands and Werner picked up his suitcase and walked to reception to collect his room key while Mr Hertz swiftly made for the exit.

Before taking a shower the Kapitän returned his thoughts to the crew of U116. He could recite their names and he would have been pleased if had he known that earlier Horst Kruger had been reunited with his brother and mother and the trio had enjoyed a slap-up meal with wine helping the conversation flow and Horst in his element, never needing to come up for air, "It was unbelievable. I don't think I would like to experience anything like it again."

Horst looked to his brother who responded, "You make it sound like the special effects of some horror film." The smiles were gregarious.

"No, it was real all right, as though all of us were being taken outside ourselves before being put back."

Siegfried realised, despite the bonhomie, that talking of the 'incident' made his brother uneasy so offered a warm hand on his shoulder for reassurance. Fortunately the coffee and Cognac arrived together with two Cuban cigars.

"On the house," said the burly waiter before collecting their empty dishes.

The brothers immediately gestured to the owner talking with an employee behind the bar and smiles were exchanged, which the brothers found strangely comforting. Horst suddenly felt a tad ebullient; it seemed his emotions could race up and down like mercury in a test tube exposed to hot and cold.

"Siegfried you're spoiling me. That's the second meal you've treated me to in as many days and I never thought I would be smoking anything like this." He drew slowly on the cigar and his action was replicated by his brother. Both grinned when the younger Kruger asked his brother in a whisper whether it was true Cuban ladies rubbed the leaves with their thighs; fortunately their mother didn't hear this but she did tell her son that smoking was bad for everyone's health… it was scientific fact.

Horst replied, "This will be my last, I promise you. It would be too easy to get used to them." He smiled at his brother who turned the conversation in a different direction.

"I know it's a bit early to start talking about what you are going to do but eventually you will have to think about the future, Horst." His voice slightly louder than usual and strained, communicated its concern.

The submariner reasoned that, like the others must know, they couldn't become part of an etching of modern Germany. That would be cruel, yet it was essential that they remained stoic – that was the word their Kapitän had used once they'd realised their fate.

"I know. Before we left Hamburg Kapitän Werner and First Lieutenant Hoffman told us that the Navy would do everything in its power to accommodate us… obviously technical skills will have to be relearnt." He paused and his brother drew his seat closer.

"All of us were surprised at the technological advancements. It seems buttons are pushed and everything happens." He smiled, then continued, "The mechanisms of the modern age, the Kapitän and I find a bit complex but I hope in time and with the right tuition I will master it all."

He leaned towards his brother with a steely glint in his eye, "I remember how frightened I was when I arrived at the Naval college and that after a week I nearly came home."

Siegfried was relieved to hear his brother speak in this manner for he had deliberately avoided talking about the future until now.

He felt good, "Yes, Horst I remember us laughing about it one night after you had completed your first Part 1 of training."

Horst raised his eyes to the ceiling, "The Navigation… it all seemed beyond me but gradually, like a jigsaw, it began to fit. Like so many things, once you know how, it's easy."

He looked at his mother who had smiled throughout the whole evening because she was in the presence of her two sons and she couldn't ask God for more. She said, "I remember how proud your father and I were when you eventually passed out. I wish he could have been here today."

Silence circled their talk, broken only when the brothers chinked their glasses one last time before finishing their spirits. Both looked at their mother and Horst spoke.

"I think it's time to go or you will be getting over-tired you know." With those words ringing in Mrs Kruger's ears, her son leaned over and kissed her on the forehead.

Siegfried patted his stomach with both hands, "Right then, I will get the bill." He looked across the room and signalled to the waiter who'd attended to them for most of the evening who promptly brought the bill over on a small silver tray. Siegfried turned to his brother.

"It's been a long day and I've a bit of catching up to do, with work, tomorrow."

The reply was immediate, almost determined, "You're retired Siegfried, why don't you enjoy it like other men?"

"Then I would be asking you for pocket money." Both laughed heartily and it caught the attention of other diners.

"No, I find part-time work keeps me contented. It's good."

Siegfried took the bill over to the counter to settle up while Horst retrieved his mother's coat from the small cloakroom, helped her on with it and took her arm guiding her to the front door. Siegfried, having paid and thanked the staff for a pleasant evening, ambled his way to the door. As the trio emerged into chill air Siegfried pulled his collar up.

"When we get home we will have a final nightcap… The owner says our taxi will be here in less than a minute."

Horst nudged his brother, "Next time we go out, I will pay."

Their mother remained staring at the silver stars shining in the ink blue sky convincing herself again, not that she needed to do, that there really was a God and he was paying her back for years of devotion.

CHAPTER 36

For Berliners such as Franz Seilerman, Heinz Stegemann, Jorgen Bahn and Joachim Reiz the Battle of Berlin had made grim reading. Following U116's entrance into Portsmouth harbour they had visited the city's library and gorged as much information as they could about the events in their capital from January 1945 onwards. Each submariner researched a different aspect and then they had huddled together to exchange their findings using a large map of Berlin as a point of reference. They had little left to sustain their spirit and much to make it bleed away.

Seilerman informed them that the Battle of Berlin was the final major offensive of the war in Europe. He had made copious notes and the others, with barely disguised blind rage, listened.

"On the 12th January the Russians breach the German Front and advanced westwards as much as twenty-five miles a day following the Vistula-Oder Offensive." He pointed out on a second map that showed most of Europe. He continued, noting that the crew members scanned both maps as he did so, "East Prussia, Lower Silesia, East Pomerania and Upper Silesia temporarily halting thirty-seven miles east of Berlin."

"Go on," said Heinz Stegemann softly.

Notes were carefully checked before Seilerman continued, "Two Soviet fronts attacked Berlin from the east and south while a third overran German forces positioned north of Berlin. The battle within the city lasted from the 20th April to the 2nd of May."

The submariners looked pickled for they were building up their own grotesque images having encountered black and white images from newsreel footage they had been shown by the British navy. The annexe they had sat in had a peculiar cheerlessness with what resembled canteen furniture and featureless lighting; and it added to the men's dismay.

Joachim Reiz took over as narrator for he too had written a few hundred words, nevertheless he gave an edited account, "The Soviets had managed to encircle the city as a result of their success in the battles of the Seelow Heights and Halbe."

Seilerman placed his finger on the map, at the correct location.

Reiz went back to his notes then spoke once again, "On the 20th April, led by a Marshal Georgy Zhukov, the shelling of the city began. The German defences were badly equipped and disorganised despite having Waffen – SS divisions alongside the Wehrmacht as well as poorly trained Volkssturm and Hitler Youth."

He was reluctant to continue but the other submariners looked at him silently.

"Within days the Russians rapidly advanced and reached the city centre where brutal close-quarter combat raged." Inevitably, disappointment was written all through his face and Seilerman concluded in an emotionless tone.

"Before it was all over the Fuhrer and a number of his followers committed suicide." He had let the silence in the room sink in before adding, "The city finally surrendered on May 2nd though German units fought westward so that they could surrender to the British and Americans rather than the Soviets."

Jorgen Bahn looked for approbation from the other submariners before commencing his narrative though he couldn't be sure he was able to penetrate the numbness that had unleashed itself around the quartet, "Stalin didn't believe the Western Allies would hand over territory occupied by them in the post-war Soviet zone so he began the offensive on a broad front and moved rapidly to meet the Allies as far west as possible. Most of all, the prize for him was Berlin."

The men gritted their teeth. It was as though the newsreel had provided them with a camera and now they had painted the factual version on to it and it neither made for good viewing or reading. The previous wisdom that washed then coded their minds had deserted them.

Heinz Stegemann took up the reins, "In Munich a General called Gotthard Heinrici was appointed Commander in Chief of Army Group Vistula. A wonderful tactician, he arranged for engineers to turn the Oder's flood plain into a swamp by releasing water from an upstream reservoir then build three belts of defensive emplacements reaching back towards the outskirts of Berlin." Then he sighed, "It was only a matter of time because the Soviets had 2.5 million men, a thousand tanks, seven thousand aircraft and so much more artillery." As an afterthought he quietly remarked, "I'm surprised Berlin existed after the onslaught."

In Portsmouth, enquiries into the submariners' families had only just commenced so none knew of their fate and optimism was low, not helped when Joachim Reiz informed them that estimates of dead citizens in this battle alone had been put at 150,000. He added sombrely, "We know vengeful Soviet troops engaged in mass rape, pillage and murders while their high command did nothing."

Berlin had remained in the Western Allies and Russia's occupation for over forty years; West Germany and East Germany had been created and building of the Berlin Wall in 1961 has been designed to halt the mass immigration of those living in Russia occupied Germany to the West. All this had preoccupied the Berliners and had drawn them even closer in an understated way – they would look out for each other in their individual quests. None of them would ever feel alone, or so they hoped.

The priest celebrating mass in a small catholic church had a kindly expression which suggested he had never lost the sense of vocation that had caused his entry into the church almost fifty years earlier. Joachim Reiz was just another face in the crowd. His rosary beads moved around his fingers as he eyed the Stations of the Cross meticulously carved onto flat wood and symmetrically positioned along both walls.

The service finished with a hymn that accompanied the slow-moving priest and his altar boy leaving for the side door, curtained off. As his congregation of mainly older people shuffled out of their pews and shouldered their way along the aisles, the naval man sat down and pictures of his life raced through his eyes and brought a rich concoction of joy.

The sun piercing the stain glass window to his side, warmed half his body and face and he remained still until he saw the altar boy emerge from the sacristy and quickly walk towards the front entrance.

Unknown to the submariner at that point in time, most of his crew mates would visit all the places they and their family had been together, losing themselves in languorous ghosts and having to contend with the memories, the yearnings and the nostalgia still ripe in their minds.

Reiz put his rosary beads away, walked down the centre aisle, genuflected in front of the altar then made back for the sacristy where the door was half-open. He could see the back of the elderly priest painstakingly disrobing and placing, carefully, his attire on the table in front of him. He knocked twice on the door, slightly then forcefully. The priest remained, with his back to him.

"Come in… I'll be there shortly." When he turned round the impact of seeing his younger brother sent ripples through his body – his legs nearly buckled and his eyes filled up with tears. Neither man spoke and Jesus Christ looked down on them from a crucifix and he didn't speak, for words were irrelevant. Finally they embraced and didn't let go of each other for what seemed an eternity.

Three hours was insufficient time for the brothers to fill in the missing years yet their conversation was as smooth as a mill pond despite being effusive; and they held hands in that peculiar masculine manner that never encourages derision from other men. Though Reiz was booked into a low grade hotel it was decided he would spend the next few days accompanied by the priest who would introduce him to surviving members, which excluded their parents, of the family as well as some parishioners. Father Reiz knew he was going to be busy on the telephones and before their initial reunion was over he insisted his brother dine with him in his small flat overlooking the church garden at the rear. He boasted that his Italian housekeeper was better than any Michelin five star chef, then had to explain what that was, much to their amusement; and their smiles remained as wintry as the wind and conversation continued in overdrive.

It was settled and a flat-footed submariner left the sacristy salivating at the prospect of Antipasto, pasta, pesce, prosciutto, frutta, formagio and wine brought up from the vaults. Before walking into a municipal park he bought a national newspaper and splashed across the front page was a picture of Hans Fiebig with his wife Angelica in 1942. Above was the caption – *'Help me find my wife'*. The article revealed details of their life together prior to U-boat 116's last departure from St Nazaire.

It gave Reiz a ghostly pause for thought as well as taking the wind out of his sails. He hoped none of his crew mates would be left floundering in the dark.

CHAPTER 37

The authorities in Hamburg had been quick to exploit the presence of a U-boat, still revered in Germany, nestling in their harbour. Two ex-submariners still alert despite advancing years had been employed to guide parties of current servicemen through 116. This they carried out with enthusiasm and pride, offering occasionally near-truth cunningly fabricated tales and a little scorn towards 'today's servicemen' whom they had believed had an easy life.

It was a Thursday morning when a group assembled on deck and were escorted below to look around the control room and the conversation had been interesting.

"It's so cramped, didn't everyone go mad from time to time?"

"Son," the old sea wolf suddenly noticed the young man's carefully groomed hair, "That would have been like pitch wire before you were out of sight of the quay and that fancy uniform would have been covered in mildew." The ex-submariner knew he had their undivided attention and puffed his chest out in a defiant welcome to my world manner.

He continued again with a rasping voice, "You would have felt at times so hot and others so damp from the condensation caused by leakage through the hatch of the conning tower and that before you began to breathe."

He grinned at the men who weren't sure how to respond so he continued with pride, "Your bed was mouldy and everything – papers, charts seemed to rot. You boys ever seen a sausage sprout mould overnight?"

Again the party remained mute.

"That was our staple diet. Could a man go mad?" He deliberately paused, "Bleckholler, we called it Bleckholler. But we were an elite. Hardship and deprivation that was what welded us all. Camaraderie and that true sense of unity while the threat of death is all around. It is impossible to understand, only a sea wolf knows."

He looked around at the men, locked in their own thoughts, doubts about whether they could have coped. The ex-submariner now had a twinkle in his eye.

"Come, I will show you the torpedo store." They hustled their way forward and were invited to sit. The old man waited for the inevitable question and it duly arrived.

"Tell me, what was it like when you attacked a convoy?"

The ex-submariner suddenly looked younger and spoke in a subdued tone, "Once we had been directed onto a convoy and given permission to attack, tactics were left to individual Commanders. Sometimes we would penetrate a convoy at night." He began gesturing with his hands, "We would shadow the convoy at a good distance while the Kapitän decided estimates and the line of attack."

The dozen or so audience were transfixed, almost living the part and holding their breath.

"We had to avoid contact with the escorting ship. If the convoy was large we would attack ahead or astern of a column on one of the wings. From this position we could ensure a torpedo making contact."

All eyes went to the torpedoes and again there was another unrehearsed pause.

"A periscope was only raised when the Kapitän needed to re-estimate the approach course and speed of our prey. When that ship crossed the periscope wires the Kapitän would give the order 'FIRE'."

The word echoed through each young man before travelling along the galley and the guide detected heavier breathing in the young men. His eyes moved about the cramped area before he continued. "The number of torpedoes fired depended on the importance of the convoy and how many we had left. There would not be room for us in here when it was full of torpedoes."

The youngest looking sailor, handsome, charming, sweet and silly asked nervously what happened next and the veteran smiled, "Ah, once we had fired a torpedo our presence was known. The Kapitän would never wait and see the result – instead we would go deep at once, on another course. When the counter attack came that was when the real game of chess began. Have you heard of Pillenwerfer?" he asked in a strong, salty and emphatic tone.

A collective shaking of the heads encouraged the submariner to explain.

"This came half way through the war. These were chemical pills ejected from the submarine. Once in contact with sea water they created a disturbance which gave an echo to Asdic transmission and so created a disturbance which then created a false target."

One of the more thoughtful looking sailors responded, "But didn't this create a target just above you?"

The question was both sensible and serious and the old man acknowledged it nevertheless he smiled in an impish manner, "No, you see the pill didn't operate until two or three minutes after ejection and then this disturbance would last for five minutes or more, in which time we would escape." His face dropped, "but in time the British became aware. Often we gave away our position by reporting to headquarters on long-wave wireless transmission. It was as though we couldn't wait to report our successes." This sentence invoked a degree of melancholy for this veteran had always struggled to handle the common clay of mankind.

Everyone digested the recollection and it prompted another seaman to enquire whether this was why there were so many casualties among U-boat crews. His enquiry was followed up by another whose eyes met the submariner's.

"What was the casualty rate?"

The question was tinged with sadness and the former Engine Room Artificer looked dull and vacant as he answered it, "75% of crew didn't survive."

The sailors were aghast.

"Expectation of life was no more than four cruises." He shrugged his shoulders and then continued, "Each 70-80 days at sea. As the losses mounted, Commanders of U-boats were under orders not to reveal this information to the crew, the high command believing that morale would fall. But there would never have been a shortage of volunteers."

The naval men stood up and shook their guide's hand. One was prompted to suggest that he was a very fortunate man to have survived then, "Yes, I know that," he croaked in a whisper.

The party climbed up through the hatch onto the deck and everyone inhaled deeply which amused the guide. Before they climbed onto the launch ready to take them back to the jetty one of the young men put his hand on the veteran's forearm, "Tell me, is it true that there was a superstition that if a boat was sunk all those who had been awarded the Iron Cross 1st class would drown?"

The old man's smile neither confirmed nor denied the superstition and the young men were happy with that as they were the sun beginning to pierce the less strong cumulus nimbus clouds draped over the port.

Back on dry land the old man berated himself for not talking about religion for he had wanted to tell the young seamen that his generation had had to evolve their own morality and there was no such thing as an atheist in a submarine being depth charged for hours on end. He was pleased he still had an uninhibited voice free of the cool restraint, the boring rectitude of public figures despite carrying the weight of anxiety that afflicted most U-boat submariners who'd survived mission after mission and now spent much of their lives, especially nights, wrestling with the gods.

CHAPTER 38

Wolfgang Emmerich's time back in Cologne was a trial of strength. He marvelled at the sleekness of the train as it raced him to the city; the interior was noiseless and he only got an impression of speed as images rushed by when he gazed out the window. The train slowed a couple of times in the countryside as it approached crossings and the Seaman Officer was warmed by the sight of a small stream running behind a green hollow guarded by flowerless stalks of foxgloves and the tangle of honeysuckle. "What it must look like in summer," he whispered to himself and he was aware that a couple of passengers in the same carriage might be aware of who he was, nevertheless, he remained unselfconscious.

The memory of the allies' first bombing raid in May 1940 was fresh in his mind as was the utter destruction of Cologne's centre following the first 1,000 bomber raid at the end of May 1942. Shortly after that he had visited his family and was relieved to know that they were safe despite the destruction continuing into the suburbs. He remembered his time in Portsmouth library researching it when a cold shiver shot through him having found out that RAF Bomber Command Head Sir Arthur Harris's first choice had been Hamburg but he had been advised that for the purpose of accuracy using the radio navigation system known as GEE, Cologne provided a 'better fix'. The result had been so many incalculable griefs to heal, sorrow and broken dreams exactly what Bomber Command sought – a complete sapping of civilian morale. The images of Cologne burning and her fire brigades overwhelmed, while 150,000 of the city's 700,000 population fled death, ran around inside the Seaman Officer's head.

The smooth running of the high-speed train jolted as it gained rapid speed and Wolfgang Emmerich suddenly smiled at the recollection that, incredibly, with destruction all around the cathedral and despite several hits it still stood. He recalled his father taking him one winter's night, when he was a young boy, to the city and he'd watched the moon sail serenely in the sky beyond layers of still roof tops before appearing between the twin spires. His father, one of nature's gentlemen, had insisted it was magic.

It had taken ten years post-war to complete repairs but uppermost in the submariner's mind was his recollection of the majesty of the main entrance with the 19th century decoration and the nave looking east. This he thought had similarities, but on a much grander scale, of the interior shape of U-boats – the length far outstripping the width. His memories were alert and that was because they were less than a year old not forty-six years old.

Departure from the Cologne railway station was rapid and orderly and Wolfgang refused to be disorientated when outside the complex recognition was barely nil. A taxi driver offered his services, a rotund middle-aged man with hazel eyes, black hair and a good tenor voice. It was a quick journey to the cathedral.

Emmerich entered and was comforted by the familiarity of shape and height and he sat in a pew close to the altar looking at the photocopied street map, drawn up in 1940, which he'd been provided with following a request in England.

A cleric, slightly stooped and the same chronological age as the young man sitting motionless brought two glass vases of fresh flowers which he placed on the altar genuflecting twice – once on arrival and then when he left.

The usual suspects: a disparate collection of elderly women, a feature in any church, mumbled the rosary – some leading the 'Hail Mary' others responding with the 'Holy Mary' all pitch perfect and none frightened of journeying into the next world, even those with a lifetime's despair of doing nothing well.

When Emmerich knelt down to say a prayer for his family he moved with a slow tearing sound and suddenly felt pins and needles unaware a moth was resting on the collar of his dark blue overcoat. He didn't stay much longer for he knew it was early afternoon and in November once sky and country hedgerows faded, blurred with the uncertain edges of early evening, darkness quickly rushed in.

Fortunately his second taxi driver, this time a younger cocky man still some years off a decent baritone voice, knew the exact location his fare requested; it was a short drive and the obvious short cuts he took impressed the passenger who gave him a reasonable tip.

Emmerich walked along a residential street, map in hand, turned a corner and paused, scratching his head. He'd found himself outside an industrial complex and marked with an 'X' on his 1940s map. The realisation hit him that not only did the home he was born in no longer exist neither did the street. "An industrial complex," he said aloud.

He felt a door had been shut in his face, maybe even the Kingdom of Heaven and was understandably forlorn as images of his childhood friends, his neighbours entered his consciousness.

The twenty-eight year old put his map away and looked about; his eventual gaze noticed an elderly couple shuffling along on the opposite side of the road. He approached them and was warmed by their smile.

"Excuse me, but can you tell me when this," he pointed to the complex, "was built?" The couple looked at each other and then at Emmerich before shaking their heads and ambling away. The thought occurred to him that drink might ease his pain, might distract his mind but never revive his spirits so he gathered himself together.

Minutes passed before someone else came into view, a tall middle-aged man with sallow cheeks and a bulbous nose.

"Excuse me, I am trying to trace someone but I need to know when this complex was built?" He tried not to sound desperate.

"This was built around 1972." The man waited for another question and it came.

"I see, can you tell me what was here before?"

"Yes, it was just waste-land. For as many years as I can remember." He tilted his head, "Who are you trying to find?"

Emmerich inhaled then spoke, "Well, I don't think you would understand but fifty years ago this was all rows of houses in tiny streets."

Before he could elaborate the middle aged man chuckled, "God, you are going back, I've been in this area thirty years and I can never remember rows of houses here."

Emmerich smiled, "There were, believe me."

The other man pondered as though waiting for an obvious idea, "Have you been to the Public Records Office, Surveyors Department? They will have town and city planning going back donkey's years, unless it was destroyed during the war."

"I know Cologne was bombed badly." The younger man didn't elaborate, deliberately, because he wanted the stranger to provide any scraps of information that would help him in his quest.

"That's right. Most of the centre was pulled down and the surrounding area, it was all rebuilt. Funny that the Cathedral wasn't completely blitzed."

"Thank you," was the response and both men walked in different directions and it was fortuitous for Wolfgang Emmerich that a taxi appeared out of nowhere minutes later.

His obvious destination was the reference library. Inside the Mercedes he glanced at his watch and was buoyed by the knowledge that there were still a couple of hours or so left of daylight. No conversation passed between driver and passenger and neither seemed to mind. In the sky, the warm sun continued its descent.

CHAPTER 39

The interior of the library building seemed spacious and flooded with natural light, the people studying there appeared the complete antithesis of the dull, dusty academics Wolfgang Emmerich thought would be sat at every table. The librarian had a natural smile which brought faint creases around her eyes and as the submariner looked up at a window above head height he could see the branches of winter trees drawn against the fading sky. He recalled the raptures of his boyhood when he was allowed outside into the gusty twilight, to run errands for his parents for outside the darkness was alive with scents far different to those of oil lamps in the home.

In this milieu he sensed freedom not confinement. Then he smiled to himself because he had trained to be a submariner and trying to explain the freedom of the ocean to civilians, albeit in a metal tube, was frustrating.

He carried two boxes of microfilm and having taken one out quickly wound it on to the spools. He was alone at the table. He read accounts by German newspapers about the destruction of Cologne and looked carefully, almost forensically, at every photograph showing streets and desperate looking citizens bombed out of their homes. He knew it was a long shot that he would see his parents and sisters and once he'd accounted for six reels he looked tired but remained as solid as wooden pegs cut for a tent.

His eye did catch a story about Jews being rounded up and herded off to camps by train and in the copy there was a warning to Germans with Jewish sympathies. Again he retreated to his memories of childhood holidays – sun, smiling seas, constant winds when days passed noiselessly from bright mornings through to amber skies and eventual blossoming of silver stars individually and collectively following the law of the universe. Both his parents had worked overtime to provide this treat, each year, for their children. Understandably, his eyes moistened so he closed them and was about to doze off when a scholarly librarian with just the right amount of make-up to catch a man's interest appeared at his table.

"Excuse me, Sir, but we are closing in fifteen minutes." Her smile was angelic, like his mother's and it momentarily unbalanced the submariner who took a few seconds to respond.

"Oh sorry, yes, I was nearly asleep." He smiled and the librarian looked at the screen. "Did you find what you were looking for?"

He answered in a matter of fact manner, "No, not yet," and he was surprised by the young woman's response.

"Can I be of assistance?"

Again the smile threatened to melt him and he stiffened, "I don't know, you see I am trying to trace my family of fifty years ago."

The look on her face told Emmerich she'd recognised him, "I know you are one of the crew from…"

Before she could finish he interrupted her with a smile, "Yes that's right."

While most in the library began to put books back on shelves and navigated their way towards the front desk and the exit, the librarian sat down, her expression full of sober enthusiasm.

"I thought I recognised you earlier on but couldn't be sure. Look," she quickly glanced at the fast emptying tables, "when we close perhaps you would like to talk with Herr Schmidt, he's the senior librarian here and there's not much he can't tell you about Cologne and its people."

The Seaman Officer could feel a spark of hope suddenly ignite and he waited for her to continue.

"He's lived here all his life, his passion in life is local history so perhaps…" the sentence was deliberately left dangling and Emmerich responded.

"Yes, anything, I feel as though I am going around in circles."

A male voice was heard inviting those still in the library to return to reception as the time was approaching 5.30pm. The librarian instantly recognised the voice and turned towards reception.

"There he is. I will see him straight away." She walked briskly and Emmerich watched as they spoke before both glanced in his direction. He stood up as the woman returned, again smiling.

"He says if you would like to go to his office in ten minutes, he just wants to finish off the cataloguing for the new books."

Emmerich words of thanks registered hope and these pleased the librarian.

"Good I will tell him. His office is along that corridor," she pointed with her dainty hand, "and you'll see his name on it."

The submariner thanked her again then sat down, aware that he was the only person still at a table.

Schmidt's office was cramped with books and files taking up most of the area, nevertheless it had two chairs either side of his oak desk.

"You are trying to find out what happened to your family?" His words were calm and the stillness in his face betrayed him as an academic and Emmerich was pleased; in fact he wouldn't have cared less if it had been a monkey sat opposite him as long as he had vital information.

He was able to speak from the heart without restriction or reservation, "Yes, unfortunately the assistance I have been given hasn't got me any further than the road, you see there doesn't appear to be any records about its inhabitants. For all I know my mother, father and sisters could have died in the war." He looked at the gentle man sat opposite who indicated for him to continue.

"No one came forward following the story in the press and all the publicity has thrown up nothing." There was a degree of pleading in what he said next, "It is important, obviously, that I find out what happened to them."

As was expected, Schmidt digested everything quickly then responded, "Of course, I understand. Unfortunately Cologne was badly bombed, as you know, and many communities were broken up, horrendous. After the war it was as if a whole new population moved to the city. Those that left seldom returned, why should they? There must have been generations of families brought up in one house in a particular street and," he offered a reluctant gesture turning both hands flat, "when that went up Germany was a defeated country. Poverty and hunger like we'd never experienced before. People moved to wherever they could find shelter, food."

He paused for he knew Emmerich was creating images in his mind.

"Work was a luxury immediately post-war apart from construction. You say your father was a hairdresser and your mother?"

Both men adjusted body positions to get more comfortable in their respective chairs before any response was heard.

"She was a housewife, she was a ladies' stylist but after my eldest sister was born she never went back to work."

Schmidt's face lit up, "Ah, sisters too, interesting."

Emmerich looked quizzical and the senior librarian said, "Four are easier to find than one or two. I don't mean to be flippant." He smiled loosely and Emmerich spoke.

"That's OK. Any help you can give, anything is like a tiny piece of hope."

"Did your family live above the business premises or did you have a shop?" asked Schmidt.

"My father had a shop and when he had saved he bought a bigger house and turned the downstairs into his business premises. He was very handy like that."

Schmidt continued to write notes on library headed paper then looked up.

"That area I know was well-populated before the war, so he must have had good business, regular clientele and would be well-known in the community."

The submariner ignored the discomfort in his back, "Yes, he must have been. He encouraged his children to be courteous and sociable with all who came into the shop. That is what made him so popular. He wasn't the type to discriminate. He gave you a good haircut and probably good conversation at the same time." Both men smiled in unison.

"He wasn't a big man, physically, but his heart was."

"Forgive me for asking but did he have any political affiliation, did he belong to any party?"

The response was blunt, "No, not as far as I know. I don't think he liked the new Germany, the way it was developing. He longed for, as did my mother, the old days. He was a patriot; don't get me wrong – he was more proud than anyone when I left Naval College, a submariner. He was proud to think of his son as a sea wolf serving the fatherland."

Schmidt thought for a few seconds; he wasn't tongue tied merely building up a composite in his mind, "How often did you see him after 1939?"

The Seaman Officer replied immediately, "When I came home on leave twice in 1939, three times in 1940. In 1941 the Atlantic war was reaching a peak and we were given leave to Dönitz's holiday camps as they were called. I last saw him in March 1942 for two days, that's all."

"Think carefully, Herr Emmerich, about the last time you saw him."

The latter opened his eyes wide recalling the event, "He was happy to see me as were my mother and sisters but as far as I can remember he didn't want to talk about the war. He was very uneasy with what had been happening in the area."

"Uneasy?"

Again both men looked directly at each other.

"Yes, he didn't like the idea of the supreme race; he once said that during the First World War Germans fought side by side despite religious differences – that kind of thing."

Schmidt nodded his head affirmatively, "He was an astute man, your father."

"How do you mean?" asked Emmerich.

"Most Germans were afraid to say anything against National Socialism when Germany seemed to be winning the war. It was easier to get on the bandwagon."

Emmerich had listened to the other man with an inexpressive face most of the time, but now he suddenly tilted his head backwards, "What are you getting at Herr Schmidt?"

The librarian's face flushed slightly, "Please, Herr Emmerich, I am not getting at anything. I know how much you must feel but if your father had the courage to speak out against certain things that were going on in Germany…"

He was interrupted, "You mean treatment of the Jews?"

Schmidt's response was measured and the tone in his voice remained constant, this side of dull, "Not necessarily that – but yes, things that went against the grain."

Emmerich's expression remained non-committal.

"I will find out, make some enquiries and see if there are any former customers, after all they can't all be dead." If that was a joke in bad taste the librarian remained blissfully unaware and Emmerich knew it.

"I know someone who has access to material that helps locate missing persons that kind of thing but more detailed than what the police offer. Who knows what might turn up in the next couple of days?"

They stood up, gingerly, stretching their frames and walked to the door careful not to knock over books piled up, like towers, on the polished wooden floor.

"I appreciate what you are trying to do for me, Herr Schmidt," and with that statement both shook hands.

As an afterthought the older man spoke, "Think nothing of it, I am as intrigued as you. I understand how restless you will be until you've found out."

In modern Cologne a stranger could get lost, thought Wolfgang Emmerich and he found it difficult to reconcile the fact that merely six weeks ago, he knew the city and its landmarks like the back of his hand, yet his face remained full of kindness and he took his pride out of his pocket when he thought again of the city's world famous landmark – the cathedral. Despite being hit a dozen times by Allied bombs it survived. From nowhere came his recitation of words spoken to his class by a forbidding clergyman, "The Devil has to have an exceptionally strong hold on a soul before its likeness to God is removed... as long as even a trace of that likeness remains, a soul can be frightening." Then he asked himself in an opulent telephone voice, "Why? Any war, why?" The first or last lesson of life: to belong to the victors. Maybe this was true, he thought.

In 1988 he felt an alien. The change was overwhelming: foreign labels on half the luggage – marble-topped tables and cream leather upholstering in discreet gay bars. Ladies under-dressed often speaking in an exquisite chorus of taste and opulence in outlets for the rich. Music catering for all tastes and muzak catering for none in apartment stores and, of course, the mélange of talk and laughter swaying as though on a branch, to the beak of a robber jay.

The current scene might well be described as cosmopolitan but the Seaman Officer preferred it as it was, because then it had heart despite the poverty. His meditations in a relatively quiet café were interrupted by noise and conflict in another area where waiters were ushering two belligerent customers out of the premises following a dispute over their bill.

Only in the city parks did he find refuge of sorts and he didn't mind they weren't green with new leaves. "At least no one will get hay fever," he chuckled to himself, sat alone on a bench with barely a handful of people in sight. In the three days since he'd arrived in the city, the submariner had welcomed two heavy downpours as they directly connected him with his past, even if on the first occasion he'd returned to his modest hotel looking like a drowned rat.

He smiled at the memory as rain lashed the exterior of the city centre buildings while he sat comfortably in the hotel lounge with a glass of brandy in his hand gazing at the smoking flames being drawn up the chimney breast of the open fire which was a feature of this three star establishment. He looked tired but following his meeting earlier felt relaxed because he'd had an injection of hope.

A smartly dressed waiter who'd taken time over pressing his uniform approached him with a gleaming silver tray held parallel to his right leg.

"Sir, may I get you another brandy?" The question was asked in a roguish manner which appealed to Emmerich and he smiled.

"Yes please, Room 48, put it on the bill." And he laughed politely as another waiter, much older, attended to another guest for he had a paunch which gave the impression that it walked ahead of him! Not all was downcast.

He occupied the next two days using the multi-gym and swimming pool the hotel was affiliated to, ridiculously on favourable rates as well as reading voraciously about post-war Germany in the city's prestigious library and of course he walked in the park suitably wrapped up; he'd bought some woollen gloves and a scarf but couldn't bring himself to purchase a bobble-hat – his head would endure the cold and other young men could work fiercely and fastidiously at looking fashionable.

A phone message was delivered to him by reception, before he went into the dining room at 7.30pm, Schmidt wanted to see him the following morning. Understandably, Emmerich only slept fitfully and when he did wake was grateful that he had enjoyed limited alcohol the previous evening as well as a glass of house wine with his meal.

CHAPTER 40

Herr Schmidt, wearing a dark grey three-piece suit with the bottom button of the waistcoat undone, checked his watch and reclined in his chair reminding himself, as he often did, to get a more comfortable one. He groaned when he stood up and his right hand went to his lower back. "Four, five and six," his physiotherapist had told him repeatedly and no amount of pain killers, swimming and massage had rid him completely of pain yet he remained stoical and put a smile on his face as he heard footsteps outside and approached the office door.

Wolfgang Emmerich was about to knock when the door was opened.

"Come in," said the librarian in a flat voice.

"I got your phone message, Herr Schmidt," said the younger man who took a seat following Schmidt's gesturing.

"Good, would you like some coffee? I'm about to have mine."

Emmerich smiled, "Yes, please."

The obligatory phone call was made.

"Shouldn't be long," Schmidt adjusted some pages on his desk then looked at the Seaman Officer in a relaxed manner, "Good, now I have made some enquiries in the last couple of days and it's quite surprising what's been turned up."

He paused and Emmerich said nothing.

"Unfortunately, the relief organisation I told you about, the one that finds lost persons, were unable to find any customers of your father but who knows?" he didn't want the seaman to look dismayed so didn't pause, "What I have been able to find out is your street was badly hit in air raids during 1944."

The other man's face dropped but the librarian smiled.

"The list of casualties which were kept by the local police station showed that none of your family was amongst them. So we must assume that either your parents moved away from that street after the raid as it was raised to rubble or had moved away some time before."

Emmerich could hear his heart beating but was well practised in the art of remaining calm, "If they moved after the air raid how can they possibly be traced?"

Herr Schmidt spoke with re-assurance, "Don't despair. I am investigating that and have found out that a register was kept of all the people who declared themselves homeless, maybe this was part of a proposed compensation scheme, I don't know."

The submariner was quick in his response, "Germany was losing the war in 1944, so surely any compensation scheme must have been organised nearer the beginning when victory seemed a possibility?"

Herr Schmidt was fingering the four buttons on the left cuff of his bespoke jacket.

"You're right, Herr Emmerich, but there is no trace of your parents registering before 1944 and anyway your street was still standing. The difficulty is that morale being sapped up by increased air raids and with little prospect of Germany gaining victory, people registering as homeless after 1944, decreased. They must have thought, how can a broken country pay compensation to its people when everything has been spent towards victory?"

Emmerich tried not to sound reluctant, "You mean people just moved out, following bombing, and found shelter with relatives, friends, whoever."

Schmidt looked earnest, "Yes, you see by early 1945 Germany was like a country of refugees, people were moving around aimlessly, food was in short supply. It was a hard time, perhaps your mother and father were part of the countless thousands."

The knock on the office door was timely. A young woman, scholarly looking but not unattractive, carried a tray laden with coffee pot, cups, saucers and a biscuit barrel. She placed it on the table and both men were conscious of the sweet scent her perfume provided before thanking her in unison.

Schmidt poured the coffee and the aroma was heady. Extremely welcome in the circumstances.

"Have you found any other leads to follow?" asked Emmerich trying to submerge any hint of desperation.

What he heard informed him that the senior librarian had worked tirelessly.

"Yes, a colleague, Herr Mauser, has been able to trace one of the clergy who served the area during that part of the war. You told me that your parents were not devout in their religion but they did attend church, particularly the festivals."

The response was quick, "Yes, my mother adored the pageantry. Has this Herr Mauser spoken with the cleric?"

"No, you must appreciate the extensiveness of our enquiries, we are following chance leads you know."

Emmerich suddenly felt self-conscious, "Yes, it is I suppose impatience on my part, the waiting, the wondering."

Schmidt sought to put him at ease, again, "I hope that Herr Mauser will contact me tonight. Remember the cleric is a very old man now, whose memory may not be what it once was, but we shall see."

As an afterthought the senior librarian asked the naval man, had he been sightseeing?

Emmerich smiled. "I have wandered about the city, it seems very strange. Only the cathedral brings back strong memories of pre-war. Most of the time I have been preoccupied… the parks offer some solace."

Instinctively both men knew they would have to go to the bottom of the well to find the truth as Herr Schmidt wouldn't let pessimism take root. "Try not to worry – if we draw a blank with this one, we will begin somewhere else."

He took another mouthful of coffee and smacked his lips and he admired the grace and humility of the man sat opposite him.

"You're very understanding, Herr Schmidt. Please convey my gratitude to those who are helping to try and find my family."

The men stood up and stretched their torsos and suddenly Emmerich had the magnetic look and presence of a hunted animal driven from his lair. Admirable, frightening, absorbing, consuming. Magnificent.

"I will," said the librarian, "now I have some work of my own. Will you call me tomorrow about 11.00am, maybe I will have some good news eh? What have you planned for the rest of the day?"

The visitor opened his face, "This evening I have been invited to an ex-submariner's club. I think they want me to speak. About what, God only knows." He shrugged his broad shoulders, "They saw the whole war, not me! Perhaps, though, there may be someone who has lived here all his life who might be able to turn a few stones over."

Both moved to the office door, shook hands and Emmerich departed. Schmidt called to him and he turned round.

"Enjoy yourself tonight and don't dwell... I know that these ex-submariners' gatherings are quite jolly affairs. Don't get too drunk!"

Both laughed.

"Tomorrow then 11.00am" The last words were the submariner's.

Wolfgang Emmerich wanted to walk in the central park and gather his thoughts, just another devotee to the hour of solace and relaxation. He thought about the crew of U116; they were never far from his conscious mind and he replayed the stories: dolphins and flying fish leaping bright waves – men scouring decks with holystone and buckets of sea water until it shone and the clumsiness of sailors threading a needle before darning their woollen socks. All this brought a smile to his face and when he left at the West entrance he passed a small chapel with its door open to the outside world. He went in and immediately noticed the interior was as cool and swept as a sea cave and that the silence was only broken by shoes scuffing the stone floor.

The submariner sat in a pew at the back and looked at the half dozen elderly ladies parked on separate benches. All, no doubt, had an outstanding knowledge of the bible he thought and all might have searched for and found love and truth in the cavern which filled up with sunshine at a particular hour depending on the time of year when spirit met spirit. His attention was taken by the still flames burning their way down three candles and it prompted him to light one and put a donation in the metal box underneath the rack, before leaving. Cologne's unique hustle and bustle was waiting to greet him the moment he left the church as was the day's last sun, quenched low in the blue sky.

Had he bothered to buy Cologne's largest circulation newspaper and turned to the middle page he would have been elated to read an article about Wolf Hechler, the Hydrophone Operator being united with his mother, father and sister. Underneath the picture was the headline *"Mother says – 'Wolf you haven't changed'."* The journalist covering the story made much of the comical remark before quoting the submariner as hoping to meet up with old friends and acquaintances that had survived. Also mentioned was the invitation to be guest of honour at an upcoming civic function. Most telling was the acknowledgement that, perhaps, of all U-boat 116's personnel he was the luckiest of all to have found his family, alive, being a son of Dresden.

Of course, in part of Wolf Hechler's mind this utter destruction hadn't happened... wouldn't happen for another two and a half years and no one would find out the timetable of events until after the war – a group of Lancaster bombers from 53 Squadron whose job it was after the 700 mile flight to find Dresden and drop magnesium parachute flares to light up the area. Having achieved their objective the next step was twin engine Mosquito marker planes having found the target areas, to drop 1,000 pound target indicators which then created a red glow for the bombers to aim at. They were called 'Plate Rack', a group of 254 Lancasters who dropped 500 tons of high explosives and 400 tons of incendiaries. A fire storm engulfed the city the likes of which had never been seen before.

However, the article devoted half the two columns to the bombing of Dresden, the capital of the German state of Saxony. All the statistics were quoted including the casualty rate and whether it could ever be justified given that the war was almost over and to destroy the city often known as 'Florence on the Elbe' was a cultural crime against humanity. Naturally no reference was made to the London blitz or the fact that the Nazi propaganda bureau deliberately exaggerated numbers of civilian deaths. The piece ended with a photograph of a memorial at the cemetery Heidefriedhof in Dresden and the inscription blown up to legible size *"How many died? Who knows the count? In your wounds one sees the ordeal; of the nameless who in here were conflagrated; in the hellfire made by hands of man."* In 1988 the debate, in Europe was still raging.

CHAPTER 41

The atmosphere was boisterous. Aged men smartly dressed, with faces like those carved on wood by 'old salts' in residential homes all wanted a piece of Wolfgang Emmerich. His eyes were shining and his cheeks pink as alcohol attacked his metabolism. When the entrance door was opened to let in air, the large outside light was festooned with leagues of moths having travelled miles to congregate. Swiftly it was shut again.

Pockets of choirs sang their songs and bunting festooned the walls with a distinct absence of any reminders of Nazism. It seemed a sailor without a pint mug was akin to a soldier without a rifle. The Seaman Officer felt a hand on his shoulder and he swivelled round.

"You took your time getting back to Port."

Everyone laughed including Emmerich.

"Yes, it's a long time to go without a woman," he said mischievously and the laughter rose a beat.

"Well," said a portly ex-serviceman with ribbons on his blazer, "You won't be short now, German women have a fascination for men in uniform. You put on your uniform and walk around Cologne… you'll see what I mean."

There was a pause before one of the group looked at his overweight friend, "Well, it didn't get you what you wanted!"

Laughter was followed by retaliation.

"You wouldn't know one end of a woman's arse from your old bald head."

The spontaneity of the caustic remark had Emmerich chortling and it wasn't over.

"You're still living in a dream. Every time you have a drink it's the same. I feel sorry for that long suffering wife of yours."

The laughter was muted and back came the response, "Well at least she didn't pitch me out like yours did."

He laughed heartily and the other sailor waited with a sly grin, "No, it was me who pitched her out!"

Everyone chuckled and as they did the small band struck up a tune familiar to all of them which resulted in friendships being enhanced and any hostilities diminished.

Emmerich declined a further drink, happy to pass out time with his pint mug still a quarter full. He was acutely aware that these lovable rogues were his contemporaries and felt quietly humble when strangers told him repeatedly during the evening they were happy to have him among their presence. They were so incredibly polite he wondered if he was being killed by angels.

The following morning Herr Schmidt was in his office taking calls; his eyes hardly moved in a face that registered concern and he wrote furiously on the open page of his note pad.

He spoke, "Yes, thank you very much. I will tell him, he should be here soon. Would you give me that again? I've already scribbled it down but just to be sure." There was a pause before he repeated what the caller was telling him, "Yes, yes, Usingen and that's near Frankfurt. Thank you, it's one further step down the track... anyway, thank you."

The connection, which had been difficult, began crackling as the librarian put the phone down.

Within an hour, Wolfgang Emmerich, having mastered his hangover, was sat in a train compartment. Occasionally he looked out the window watching pockets of countryside float past like a leaf on a stream. An old man in the same compartment smiled and looked at the Seaman Officer in the face with a strange, soft radiance in his eyes. The smile was returned.

"Where are you heading?" the old man asked quietly.

Emmerich looked at the crumpled paper in his hand, "Usingen, do you know it?"

A cheeriness attached itself to the other passenger's voice, "I've been there but I wouldn't say I know it all that well. Are you visiting someone?"

Emmerich replied in the affirmative and turned to look out the window. The old man did likewise.

"Looks like it's going to be a bright day. We could do with it before winter really settles in."

The younger man smiled then leaned into his seat and closed his eyes, wondering what he would find.

His expression turned to joy as he approached a small detached house having navigated his way from the station using Herr Schmidt's vague details; he looked at the torn off sheet he'd been given in the office.

He rang the doorbell and it was answered by a stout housekeeper with an engaging smile.

"Good day, my name is Wolfgang Emmerich. I believe you are expecting me. I've been trying to…"

He was interrupted.

"Come in, Herr Schmidt talked about you, yes we know."

He took his coat off, "Herr Schmidt has been very kind and helpful to me these last few days."

The housekeeper draped his coat over a hook on the stand then turned to him.

"Father Patzig has made a few enquiries of his own. It is so long ago, but not for you. Come, let me introduce you."

The submariner was ushered into a living room where the Priest was sat with a cup of coffee; immediately he stood up and put his cup back on the saucer. As the housekeeper spoke he walked towards them.

"Father this is Wolfgang Emmerich."

The men shook hands and the housekeeper quietly left them. They sat in well upholstered armchairs opposite each other and their knees almost touched as both men leant forward.

"Wolfgang, you have travelled considerably this last week, please be my guest tonight and dine with us. My housekeeper is priceless in that small kitchen of hers. Please stay the night."

The Seaman Officer was careful not to appear impatient when he spoke.

"Thank you, Father, but please what news?"

The cleric smiled and his face relaxed into a semblance of animation, "Patience, my son. I remember your father and mother and those dear sweet sisters of yours. I was away in Cologne for six months while you were away but despite being war-time the people in the parish were simple folk. Your father cut my hair a couple of times. I remember your older sister would bring him a drink towards the end of the day. He doted on her as you probably know."

Emmerich felt his inside churning up and nodded.

"Then I was moved, it was a sudden thing, just as I was getting to know everyone. Why, I never did find out but we never questioned our superiors."

Outside, the wind began to blow in several directions like a swordsman probing his next strike. The submariner tried to remain as calm as seamen do during a storm.

"So my family was alright when you moved. Can you remember the exact date… think, Father."

He smiled sunnily, "That's no problem, it was my birthday August 15th. I left that part of Cologne. I never went back until after the war but that was a nightmare, the city was in a mess and what stood was barely recognisable. Some of my old parishioners were still living in the same area but it hurt me to see what had been a law-abiding gentle community torn about and extinguished and for what?"

His eyes moistened then he regained composure, "The pursuit of some Nazi ideal which many Germans didn't much care about but were powerless to go against those criminals."

Emmerich reclined into the seat and thoughts raced inside his head. Maybe his destiny had been worked out, "It seems I've come a long way and no nearer finding them."

He suddenly looked tired and that wasn't lost on the Priest who leaned forward, once again, in his chair.

"Please don't give in, stay the night, you look exhausted, already." And he was right for this son of Cologne was more weary than a man who obeys a sudden impulse to sit out winter and count down the days to Spring.

"OK, Father."

The housekeeper's entrance was timely and the aroma from the coffee jug she carried on a tray was hypnotic and both men's eyes lit up when they gleaned home-made fruit cake. She left as smoothly as she'd arrived and no conversation passed between the duo until they'd relaxed and were drinking a steaming cup of coffee; only half the cake remained. Outside, the sky had dipped, weighed down by hastily assembled rain clouds and this prompted Father Patzig to switch the table light on. Try as they might it was difficult to be freed from the solemnity of the occasion and the priest felt he had a duty to recall events no matter how painful despite, for him, the customary passage of time.

"After I left, my successor was Father Raeder. I found out years later that he was killed during a bombing raid in 1945."

Emmerich suddenly looked sedated as if his final lead had shrivelled up and he closed his eyes as though resigned to living in a future world of stone and water, light's splintered exhalations and exhausted humanity. He recalled his Kapitän's fear that many of the crew would find that the time being whistled in the distance was not for them and the landscape they found themselves in might shrivel to a desert – dry, bleached and blackened by the hand of grief.

The saintly priest offered a smidgen of hope.

"You may be able to find out something more because this parish clergyman encouraged all the denominations to remember that they all served God and therefore were brothers. Father Raeder, I was told, would not discriminate ever against Jews which, as you know, was a punishable offence."

A brief discerning silence passed between them before Emmerich spoke, his voice now hoarse, "Father, how did people let it happen?"

"We must all bear the burden of guilt, especially the church," he nodded slowly before continuing. "We, more than most, had a responsibility which we neglected and will one day have to explain to our Creator."

Emmerich's eyes still glared consternation, "Forgive me if I've upset you. You have been generous with your time and hospitality."

His host nodded slowly once, twice with total comprehension before leaning forward and putting his hands on his guest's forearms.

"Tomorrow, I will give you an address in Cologne and a letter to give to Rabbi Stern... perhaps he can help. In what way I don't know, but because of their persecution they have helped their own people trace families. Maybe someone in his Jewish community knew of your father's business. It's a chance but better than nothing." His piety was sincere and far removed from the variety used at interviews and it was a much needed beacon for outside swathes of darkness fell from the sky.

The submariner adjusted his position in the armchair, cleared his throat and tried to speak in his usual virile, pleasant authoritative voice.

"I will follow it up, thank you Father but I don't think anything will come of it." He expected an interruption but there wasn't one, "We didn't know any Jews before the war. We weren't really aware of them; we knew they lived in ghettos but that was all. Occasionally parties of men wearing swastika insignia would beat up a group of Jews but we didn't concern ourselves."

He reluctantly shrugged his shoulder and Father Patzig responded.

"You see how it happened… before your very eyes."

Nothing more was said. Nothing needed to be said and the second intrusion by the housekeeper was a welcome relief for both men as was the new conversation about the evening meal and the bedroom already prepared for Herr Emmerich and sufficient hot water for him to have a bath before dining.

The hot water bottle in the guest's bed lulled him off to sleep and the faint aroma of fabric softener attached to the crisp cotton sheets was in marked contrast to the bed linen in Emmerich's hotel room. He rose early, washed, shaved then crept into the kitchen surprised to find the Priest and housekeeper immersed in their daily newspapers, as though they'd been up hours.

The usual pleasantries were exchanged before the men retired to another room, giving the woman sole access to her kitchen. After breakfast a taxi was summoned which arrived with indecent haste and hurrying along the goodbyes.

"Once again, Father, thank you. I will keep you informed."

An hour later Emmerich was boarding a train back to Cologne. In his carriage lay two national newspapers and he picked up *'Der Spiegel'*.

Had he picked up the other one he would have read a story with pictures of Bernhart Frantze, who was on his maiden voyage in U116, sat at a reunion with his family. The newspaper columnist described how the submariner was moved to tears listening to his brother's two grandchildren singing 'Guten aben Gut Nicht'.

CHAPTER 42

Seaman Officer Emmerich was sat alone in the lounge of his hotel with only a drink and the local newspaper for company. Gradually he dozed off only to be woken by a hand touching his shoulder and from nowhere an elegiac voice rolling out the words, "Pardon me for waking you."

Surprised the submariner looked up.

"Rabbi Stern, please sit down, can I get you anything?"

The years of suddenly being woken while serving in a submarine and regaining one's senses within a second were evident.

The Jew spoke with frankness and an almost secretive spurt of triumph and his smile caressed the naval man's heart, "No, I thought I would come to your hotel. Since you called yesterday I have been able to find someone who knew your family."

Emmerich's pupils visibly dilated as though they were suddenly staring at one last odyssey.

"This person survived Auschwitz and has lived for the past twenty-five years in Overath, it's only a train ride away."

The response was rapid. "Yes, I know it. But my father and mother…"

He was interrupted by the soft trumpet blast of statements.

"All I can tell you, I have told you. I don't know any more. This person will welcome you."

The Rabbi took out a sheet of paper crisply folded in half from his inside coat pocket.

"Here is the telephone number, address and his name."

It was accepted graciously, "I will call on him." Emmerich said with a smile but couldn't get the word Auschwitz out of his head.

Before leaving the Rabbi paused. "One thing."

"Yes, Rabbi."

"Remember what this person has been through, most of those who survived the holocaust are still affected by it. No one likes talking about it, you understand. It is too traumatic. Yet I think this man will help you, if he can."

Emmerich struggled for words, "Thank you, Rabbi. I just want to know the truth… to put my mind at rest."

The other man thought for a few seconds, "Yes, that is the wish of every man. Don't give up. Suffering and melancholy weaken any man's will to live."

Wolfgang Emmerich sat staring at the open fire; he had long relinquished the idea that he was a hero or a pioneer with a torch in his hand; and he was tired. The usual serenity attached to the room was broken by a boisterous group of young professionals, early thirties, well-dressed with expensive footwear but their loud conversation told the other couple of guests, besides Emmerich, sat near the fireplace that they were people with opinions but no breeding… and to analyse what went into making a hero would be beyond their comprehension. Disdainful. The Seaman Officer stood up and promptly left the room. He soaked longer than usual in the bath then climbed into bed repeating the affirmation "I must make the best of it." He slept for eight hours and in the morning the bedspread still hadn't moved a fraction as he stared at the ceiling contemplating whether this was finally the day, his quest would end and he knew he would have to steal himself for every and any eventuality.

Continental breakfast over, he left the hotel and made for the station via a taxi, purchased his return ticket and found an empty carriage which quickly filled up with commuters, most his age.

Outside Overath station he walked to the taxi rank and engaged a surly looking, unshaven driver slumped against the driver's side, in conversation.

"Will you take me to this address?"

The driver scanned it, "Yes, it's not far."

Inside the cab the Seaman Officer could feel his heart beating recalling the apprehensive voice on the other end of the phone line when he'd made initial contact before sitting down in the hotel restaurant for coffee and croissants.

The taxi pulled up slowly and the driver was paid. Emmerich stood upright checking the address again before approaching a small house a dozen yards to his left. As he walked up the garden path the front door opened and a small man enquired, "Who are you please?"

"Wolfgang Emmerich. Rabbi Stern sent me."

The tension in the first man's features underwent a sudden relaxation as though he felt a quickening of the sense of life, "Come in I have been expecting you, forgive me for my not too friendly welcome but I don't see so well these days."

The interior was modestly furnished and the visitor was quickly introduced to the old man's wife, a small kindly looking lady.

"Come, we will go into the small room." He looked at his wife, "Will you bring us something to drink?"

His wife smiled "Yes" and both men shuffled through the main living room to a side room.

No sooner had they made themselves comfortable, Emmerich detected a hint of aromatic foam of wild parsley possibly growing in the back garden, the wife appeared with a bottle of wine and two glasses on a wooden tray.

"Thank you, you are most kind," said Emmerich, standing up offering to put the tray on the table in front of him.

Once the men were alone the elderly man poured the red wine into both glasses.

"I didn't want to talk in front of my wife. She does not know the purpose of your visit – like me she is a survivor of the camps but any recollection or reminder, no matter how small and she breaks down."

Emmerich looked at his host's intelligent eyes, "I'm sorry," he said and suddenly felt his hand being held and an expressive face on the verge of revealing conversation he knew would be ultimately painful.

This probably accounted for the elderly Jew averting his eyes as though he was addressing an invisible audience at the other end of the room, "Sometimes the memories affect me but together we try to live each day as it comes. Rabbi Stern has told me of your search for your parents. I understand how you must feel."

Slowly he turned his gaze to look at the submariner, "Yes, I knew your father."

Anxiety leaped in Emmerich's stomach but he controlled any restlessness and waited for the old man to continue.

"He talked of you, how proud he was of his son who had joined the navy."

The men exchanged half-smiles.

"I met him early in 1942. Not looking overtly Jewish I suppose I could wander about free of the abuse we were being subjected to more and more. Anyway I visited the shop one day. As he cut my hair he told me how proud he was of his son fighting for the fatherland yet he despised the way Germans, who happened to be Jews, were being treated."

Suddenly his face looked fatigued, nevertheless he ploughed on.

"I remember one of the other customers warning him he'd better be careful who was listening. But he was brave, your father. He didn't take any notice."

The Seaman Officer's heart was raining and he craned his neck, he didn't know why.

"I went back to his shop a couple of times and he was even more vehement about the Nazis. I wanted to tell him not to be so foolish but I was scared."

Another blot of silence occurred as though the narrator of events was re-running a silent film in his head, he shivered and Emmerich squeezed the frail hand that had been holding his and indicated for him to continue with a nod of his head.

"Anyway, November I think it was, in 1942 they came, the secret police. They started breaking up his shop and when he objected they assaulted him."

Emmerich gritted his teeth and a fierceness enveloped him.

"Your mother came from upstairs and they flung her to the floor and went upstairs. They were like animals. Everyone had been cleared out of the shop but we just gathered and watched. I heard screaming coming from upstairs." His voice was very hoarse and he struggled to continue, "Your mother was pleading with the officer in charge begging him to stop but he just laughed."

Tears filled the old man's eyes, "And laughed and your sisters appeared in a state of shock when they came down the stairs."

The submariner looked crushed and tears rolled down his cheeks for he feared what was to come.

"Your father regained consciousness after the beating and seeing what had happened, wrestled with one of the soldiers. The officer took out his revolver and shot him through the head."

Emmerich's body slumped into the back of the chair; momentarily he was paralysed with shock; and even the sunlight coming in through the lounge window offered no warmth – he was rudderless in unchartered waters.

The old man spoke in a whisper yet his words were underpinned with compassion.

"I'm sorry to have to tell you this, you may think it is heartless the manner in which I have recounted it but your father's suffering was short. I saw so much it made me immune to feeling. It was a way to survive that has never deserted most of us."

His words were only half heard by Emmerich who regained sufficient composure to ask about his mother and sisters.

"They were taken away and I heard they were sent to one of the camps… not the same one as me."

A fog of torment filled up the room before settling in each man's face.

"I'm sorry," was the elderly Jew's final words.

The mood was distinctly different in a large department store in West Berlin, particularly in the toy department where a sales assistant was demonstrating the workings of a toy submarine to a group of enthusiastic boys. Also watching was Friedrich Schreiber who looked around in wonderment at the range of electronic software and computers on sale. He couldn't resist picking up some of the objects and scrutinising the workings of them.

He strolled about before his attention was taken by the model making section. He looked at the kits for Spitfires, Hurricanes, Stukas and Messerschmitts but his eye caught a larger box containing a U-boat. He smiled, loudly, and an assistant approached him.

"Can I be of any help, Sir?"

"That model…" said the Chief Engine Room Artificer.

He was interrupted by the sales assistant, a young man with carefully rehearsed sales patter, clean fingernails and an eye on middle management.

"Oh yes, that would make a very good Christmas present, thinking of buying it for your son or nephew? It will keep him occupied for hours. Many people have commented on the fine technical detail. It's hard to believe, though, that up to fifty men lived in one of those for months on end."

Friedrich, barely recognisable in a light grey suit, white shirt and maroon coloured tie smiled but said nothing. Instead he shifted his weight from one leg to the other as the patent leather black shoes he wore, he still conceded needed breaking in after several days wear.

The young assistant continued, "It's quite reasonably priced as well, don't you think?" He pointed to the tag attached to it but the submariner only half heard him.

"Sorry, oh yes… I will buy it please." He expected to give the money and walk off with the box.

"Would you like it gift wrapped, Sir?"

Schreiber looked perplexed, "Sorry?"

"Gift wrapped, ready to give your son or nephew."

"Oh, yes please."

He looked uncomfortable among the throng of shoppers filling West Berlin's city centre and clambered into the back of the first taxi that responded to his hand waving. He played with his 'toy' that afternoon and then dined, sat at a simple table in the corner of the hotel restaurant, before enjoying a couple of beers in the hotel bar.

Finally he retired to his room at 9.00pm for tomorrow was his big day and he thought about it until sleep overtook him and he dreamed of ice cold water in lakes under a full moon broken only by the ripples caused by a diving waterfall.

CHAPTER 43

The Russian sector of Berlin looked hostile even on a sunny day but in winter it evoked repression; few if any had a smile on their face for elegancy and grace of wealth had long evaporated and the promised advantages of socialism were yet to appear on the horizon. Blocks of apartments all concrete and glass, all uniform, dotted the landscape and the only vehicles which looked healthy were official government cars – black, all shining.

When one stopped outside such a block, residents sat by the windows quickly moved away. On the fifth floor washed, shaved, slightly underweight and wearing a shabby suit Gunter Schreiber sat waiting for the inevitable knock on his door.

Within two minutes he was escorted down stairs by a party member and climbed into the back seat of the waiting car with the official, wearer of a dishonest face, dark suit, black shoes in need of another polish who opened up conversation.

"You must be happy at the chance of seeing your brother after all these years?"

The response came in a voice which rang out clear and true and the words were sonorous, "Yes, I never thought…"

He was rudely interrupted, "Our friends in the West have arranged with me that you can spend two days with your brother in their sector. We have arranged, all the documentation there will be no problem."

The official revelled in his smugness and pomposity and Gunter Schreiber was quick to thank him for he was on the cusp of a journey of a life time and wanted no aberration, so he quickly forgot he often compensated for his sensitivity by adopting a shield of brutality.

The official's next words sounded more like a faintly disguised order than any light conversation.

"Tell them that everything they say about us, the way we treat our people is all lies, propaganda that discredits the West as much as it tries to discredit the East."

The passenger smiled and nodded his head but there was little conviction in his actions.

The car sped through a rather bleak area of Berlin, where the most robust dashed about in whispers before it approached Checkpoint Charlie and Gunter Schreiber could hear the butterflies playing in his stomach as the vehicle slowed to a halt. He was escorted by the man from the ministry to the official cross-over point and they were greeted by a tall athletically built American M.P. with perfect white teeth, "OK buddy, welcome aboard."

The German was escorted to the office while the black car turned and drove back. The M.P. watching the Russians' departure was tempted to say something but resisted.

Friedrich Schreiber, wearing his grey suit but with a pale blue shirt and submariner's official tie, was fidgety as he sat in his hotel lounge occasionally looking out of the window and at his Rolex watch. Every time a car drove towards reception his heart jumped; not even the morning newspaper he held offered any distraction.

His spirit lit up when a young receptionist with soft eyes and a feline figure approached him.

"Mr Schreiber, the border police have just phoned to say your brother is on his way."

Her smile melted the Chief Engine Room Artificer.

"Not long now."

"Thank you, thank you." He instinctively checked the knot in his tie, pulled his socks up and gently lowered the trouser legs back over his ankles. He began biting his lip in nervous fashion, more so when a limousine pulled up outside the main entrance.

The naval man stood up, pulled his shoulders back and his eyes never left the door to the lounge which was ajar. Suddenly Gunter Schreiber walked in boldly, caught sight of his brother and smiled; all fears were immediately assuaged and the brothers embraced and cried unashamedly; they might have been mistaken for God's madmen. Fortunately the only other resident in the lounge was an octogenarian who resembled a bag of bones enjoying another deep sleep.

The brothers stayed in the hotel, full of emotion, sensation, alcoholic beverages and haute cuisine; it was a revelation for the East German and both ventured out to explore the new Berlin and revisit those places that remained from the old pre-war Berlin; and they were dulled by love but in a pleasant way as forty-six years was condensed into those two precious days.

CHAPTER 44

Jubilation was the property of the few. The noises began, a heavy clanging of metal doors being slammed shut, shot through Wolfgang Emmerich's heart as finally the porter closed the last one, glanced up and down the platform of Cologne station and blew long and hard on his whistle – destination Hamburg.

In Southern Germany, also travelling on a train back to Hamburg sat Hans Fiebig. He had scoured Munich, cursing Hitler for having been born, for this city had been a hotbed of extremist politics in the 1920s among which Adolf Hitler and National Socialism rose to prominence.

Fiebig's home city had witnessed the Beer Hall Putsch in 1923 when the party had attempted to overthrow the Weimar Republic and seize power. It had failed, its leader arrested and it had temporarily crippled the Nazi party which was virtually unknown outside Munich. Fiebig remembered his father had rued the day ten years later when the National Socialists took power in Germany and created their first concentration camp, Dachau, ten miles north-west of the city. Because of its importance to the rise of National Socialism, Munich had become known as Hauptstadt der Bewegung (Capital of the Movement) and many of the 'Fuhrer-buildings' had survived into the 1980s.

Fiebig remembered, vividly, the city and its association with the culmination of the policy of appeasement employed by Britain and France who had assented to the annexation of Czechoslovakia's Sudetenland region with Greater Germany in the hope that would sate Hitler's desire for The Third Reich. He'd also found out, in England, of the damage caused by over seventy air raids and the rebuilding programme post-war following a meticulous thorough conservative plan which preserved its pre-war grid. Munich was now rated as enjoying a higher quality of life than most European cities.

However, none of these had ultimately helped the Seaman Officer. He looked broken, dispirited and scruffy sat in a second-class compartment. The quest to find his wife and daughters had ended in failure. He looked at a young married couple sat opposite him and remembered, then smiled. They returned it and the man asked him if he was going all the way to Hamburg. He said he was and he also knew it would be a long painful journey.

The train from Berlin to Hamburg thundered through the night and slumped in a compartment Franz Seilerman looked weary as he tried to sleep. When a middle-aged man drew back the sliding door it alarmed the submariner.

"Excuse me, I didn't mean to wake you." The voice was quietly apologetic and the submariner adjusted his head and shoulders.

"I wasn't asleep, just cat-napping," he said.

The other passenger started to read his newspaper having turned on the reading light but occasionally looked at Seilerman before enquiring, "Forgive me, I don't intend to be rude but I couldn't help recognising you when I entered the carriage. You are one of the men from U-boat 116?"

Seilerman hauled his frame upright, "You've read about it too?" he said in a flat tone.

"Why, everyone has read about it. Have you been able to find your family? Oh, I'm sorry, I shouldn't pry, forgive me."

Seilerman deliberately took his time before answering, "I found out what happened to them."

The older man didn't note that there was no emotion attached to what he'd just heard and looked eagerly.

"My wife and two sons were killed when the Russians invaded Berlin in April 1945."

The other passenger was visibly moved and slumped back in his seat, having put his newspaper down, "I am sorry, so very sorry, I…"

Seilerman, a naturally gallant man said quietly, "Yes, I am sorry too."

Both men retreated into silence and he felt the small tears of anger and pain and fatigue rolling down his face, unchecked and the older man turned off the reading light, and both felt an involuntary stiffening of their own body.

Outside, a pitch black sky threw out buckets of rain and the torrential downpour stretched as far west as Hanover where the streets were deserted. In the warmth of his city centre hotel room, Uve Stührmann sat at a small table, shirt sleeves rolled up, composing a letter. He wrote two drafts before he was satisfied; and then he wrote the final piece to his commanding officer.

Dear Kapitän

I hope this letter reaches you as I have requested your hotel in Hamburg to forward it to wherever you might, now, be staying. I write to tell you the good news that I have found my sister or more accurately she found me. My mother is dead but something that has given me great heart is that right to her dying day she never gave up hope that I was still alive and accordingly she instructed her solicitor to make such plans with her will. Despite the obvious age difference now between me and my sister, during the past week, we have enjoyed each other's company. Funny or is it strange I don't really take much notice of the gap in our ages. I have listened, fascinated for hours, as she has recounted her own life and that of people I knew. I do hope you were successful and that great colleagues and friends of mine have found some happiness these last couple of weeks. But I fear the worst for some. I am fortunate that I have been left something that will help me start afresh. I always remember, Kapitän, your telling us to see every day as a fresh challenge, never to let complacency set in. Now, that advice has never been more apt than now. The son of an old friend of mine has offered me a start in his company if I want it. Of course it is much more than just re-training, everything from scratch will have to be re-learnt. Please pass on my good wishes to my fellow men and I will look forward to meeting them and you at the reception in Hamburg next week.

Your Loyal Hydrophone Operator,
Uve Stührmann.

CHAPTER 45

Kapitän Peter Werner looked dashing in his double-breasted bespoke, navy blue suit. It had been crafted by a middle-aged tailor working from the same premises for over forty years; his father and uncle had also been tailors whose work ethic and attention to detail, both, had passed to him.

He had taken it upon himself to seek out the U-boat Kapitän, 'measure him up' in his hotel room and promised delivery 'within days'. Werner was surprised at this gesture and money was never discussed for the tailor had given him his business card with the proviso "If anyone asks please tell them it was me who cut and stitched following the traditional pattern only the best refer to – *The Tailor and Cutter* magazine from 1951." As an afterthought he'd added, "The plates have long gone."

Admiring glances from staff and guests came the Kapitän's way as he crossed the foyer with that unmistakable naval gait. Outside the entrance he signalled for a taxi; a minute later the driver leaned out the window.

"Where to?" He was given a card with the hospital details printed on it, "It will take half an hour, Sir."

Werner smiled when the Mercedes pulled up at the hospital entrance for it had taken exactly 30 minutes and he thought it merited a decent tip, besides there was still another couple of hours daylight left in the sky.

A kind of charming excitement was caught in his stomach as he walked boldly into hospital reception where he was greeted by a staff nurse relieved to be rescued from a preposterously rakish patient being discharged.

"Excuse me, I am Peter Werner, my brother Fritz was brought into casualty last week or so. I have already visited him three times but I will be returning to Hamburg shortly and wanted to see him again. I know it's not visiting hours but…"

On a bright day, the U-boat Kapitän's smile was enough to disarm any potential enemy and ironically he didn't know it was in his armoury! The young lady, in her starched uniform, blushed.

"Never mind, Kapitän Werner, of course you may see him. The doctors say he is making good progress and will be allowed home within a fortnight."

He looked at her with his formidable eyes and she thought his thick eyebrows shaped a natural frame to them and she was also aware of her heart beating.

Werner said, "That is good, I don't think he likes these places you know."

She responded in a mildly flirtatious manner, "I shouldn't think anyone likes these places, Kapitän."

He was enjoying the rapport, "Well, would you like to steal yourself away from here and take me to my brother?"

"Why not."

As they walked, the Staff Nurse looked at the box U116's Skipper carried.

"Are they for your brother?" she enquired.

"Yes, caramel toffees, he has a lifelong passion for them, or did have."

Both adults laughed and then continued as they passed other medical staff in the corridor.

"How long have you worked here?" asked Werner politely.

"Eight years now, I trained in Nuremberg, that is also where I began my nursing career."

He smiled, "I was there before the war."

She replied immediately, "That was before my time."

Werner stopped and looked at her, "I can see."

Both chuckled before breezing into a small ward. On seeing his brother, Fritz Werner tried to sit up prompting the Staff Nurse to instinctively help him, "Here, let me get you comfortable."

She propped him up placing the pillows in an upright position to give the patient maximum support.

"Thank you, Nurse."

"Right, I will leave you two together… I'm sure you've got much to talk about."

Seeing the brothers together, she could see the strong family resemblance despite the disparity in years. A warm smile full of compassion passed between nurse and visitor and then she was gone leaving Peter Werner to sit on his brother's bed.

"How are you today, Fritz?"

"Much better for seeing you. You know it's not visiting time." He looked from left to right as if the impromptu visit might suddenly be quashed and this elicited a chuckle in the younger brother.

"That kind Staff Nurse let me in."

His brother looked anxious, "Why, are you coming tomorrow? I thought that…"

He was immediately put at rest.

"Don't alarm yourself. Yes I will be coming tomorrow but the day after I am returning to Hamburg because the crew are meeting once more. I just thought I'd come and see you now. It's impulse."

Fritz gave a throaty laugh, "Remember when we were kids it was me who was the impulsive one. You always planned everything out, not a moment's recklessness. Even though I was older. I knew mother told you to keep an eye on me."

Werner loosened his tie and undid his shirt top button, "Yes, I was thinking the other day of the scraps we used to have with the brothers Wilhelm and Adolf Newmeister. You were forever getting into scrapes of one kind or another."

"And you had to bale me out."

The naval man paused, "I wonder what became of the boys?"

"God knows," replied his brother continuing to look at the box held in Peter's hand.

"Are those for me?"

"Yes, sorry I forgot, here." He waited for his brother to tear at the wrapping then saw his eyes light up as though a miracle had just occurred.

"My favourite."

"I thought as much."

"Tell me if you see a nurse," and with that he put two toffees in his mouth before offering one to his brother.

"No, they're for you."

"Come on take one for later," came the muffled response.

"OK then."

They waited until Fritz had chewed both toffees down to pulp before resuming their conversation.

"Have you heard from your crew at all, since last time?"

"Yes, several have written to me, though not always good news. At least eight have found no trace of their families or any relatives. It was inevitable I suppose."

There was no denying the sadness in the Kapitän's eyes even if he tried to disguise it.

He suddenly became upbeat, "Mind you some have been overjoyed with what they have discovered so it isn't all on the black side."

His brother adjusted his position, declining any offer of help, "What are you going to do?"

The younger sibling tried not to appear a stranger in a strange world, "I don't know yet, I haven't really thought about the future. Everything has been unreal, at times I still feel a strong sense of duty to my men…"

Now it was the older brother's turn to offer sagely advice, "Of course you will, you faced many dangers together. I bet they look up to you, rely on you for guidance."

Both held hands.

"I suppose they do Fritz."

"And you won't fail them, I know that brother." He summoned up a faint smile followed by a circus grin which revealed the spark of life was far from extinguished...

The appearance of a young registrar, dressed in bottle green corduroy trousers, white coat with stethoscope around his neck and a freshly laundered look about him and the air of a man who always follows routine, at the ward entrance, was the signal for Peter Werner to leave. Goodbyes were swift and suddenly he was walking out of the hospital grounds searching for a taxi and when one didn't materialise immediately he remained unconcerned for the sky was blue, the air crisp and winter in Munich, surely, couldn't always be as intoxicating as this he thought. And he was right. Elsewhere, Germans were enjoying the powerful winter sun.

Everyone marvelled at the forty metre high clock tower that was the main characteristic feature of Wiesbaden railway station; the whole complex was a prime example of Historicism dedicated in November 1906. It had been designed as a terminal station to avoid the noise of trains crossing the city and to show consideration for the spa guests who had no stairs to climb in the new station. As an appropriate reflection of the need for prestige the decision to use red sandstone as a building material had been taken and though the original imperial reception hall had been destroyed during the war it was reconstructed.

All this, of course, was of little concern to an increasingly agitated submariner constantly looking at his watch as each porter's whistle signalled the departure of a train, Peter Neister stood among the other commuters, suitcase in hand, looking left and right towards the entrance and exit. Slowly a train with extra carriages snaked its way across an intercepting railway track before coming to a standstill. Suddenly doors were flung open and passengers alighted, thronging the packed platform.

A multitude of signals lit up as the train left the station. Neister thought he heard his name being shouted above the din and looked in all directions before standing on a bench to give himself an elevated view. Immediately he saw the cook, Ernst Bortfeld also carrying a new suitcase running in his direction face glowing, perspiration dripping and obviously delighted at seeing one of his fellow seamen again.

Neister smiled, shook his head and waited for the cook to regain his breath before stepping down and pointing at his watch, though if asked he would probably have said Ernst Bortfeld had outshone every other passenger waiting by the sheer flamboyance of his arrival!

Bortfeld had regained his breath but looked tired yet he spoke in that light-hearted, slightly mocking voice for which he was famed and with a grin that implied – so what if others' approach to life is opposite mine!

"I know, I thought I was going to miss it. My taxi arrived late. I thought I would have to pick up another train at Glesson." He loosened his tie and looked, admiringly, at his colleague's winter wardrobe noting that they both wore almost identical shoes but in different sizes.

"Well friend, any news?"

Neister shrugged his shoulders, "No, I'm afraid there were only a handful of people who remembered me and of course I didn't recognise them. Time fades memory so it seems."

The Steward wanted to avoid melancholy for he had endured a shed load and like some of the others, formerly of U-boat 116, his eyes registered suffering. Behind the jovial persona Ernst Bortfeld was no fool and shrewd as well as courteous when the situation demanded it; his eyes were quick and knowing when he spoke.

"But what about your father and mother… was anybody able to tell you what happened to them?"

The answer came in a tone of resignation, "It is doubtful that either survived the war. They are not listed as buried in any cemetery. I know we suffered heavy bombing. It seems after the war most of the country was on the move, somewhere or other. I know my mother, she would not have wanted to go far away. She was born and bred here apart from the two years my parents lived in Dusseldorf... My father's mother resided there. Unfortunately, neither of my parents came from large families."

He paused and what he said next had an element, a very fine element, of hope attached to it, "I'm sure they would have contacted me had they still been alive."

The cook spoke kindly, "Of course they would have... Did you contact the radio stations?"

"Yes that was the first thing the newspaper running the story did. Not one single person came forward. I must assume that they are dead."

There was a chilling finality about those words.

A gust of wind blew up between the men as the cook shook his head, his eyebrows raised questioningly, "I'm sorry for you, Peter. Your task is not much different from mine. I hope some of the others have made out better than us."

Peter Niester inhaled deeply. "Yes, it will be good to see the Kapitän again."

Ernst Bortfeld added, "And the crew. Things won't be the same though." He paused and could see his crew member agree with him, "We all knew that though didn't we?"

The wind suddenly died down and Peter Niester replied to the question with a single word, "Yes."

Over the tannoy came a booming voice as though the announcer might have been drinking, "Train about to pull into platform five." The submariners looked at the signals and lights changing in all manner of frenzy at the very end of the platform. Then they were still.

"Ah, here she comes," said the cook and both absorbed the heady aroma associated with trains coming into stations everywhere in the world. Passengers were quick to alight while those waiting to board stood back, patiently. The submariners' offer to help an old man, his face white and beaded with sweat, were warded off with a weary gesture as he struggled onto the platform accompanied by a heavy suitcase.

"Come on," said Ernst looking at the steward and picking up his own suitcase before climbing into the carriage. Both put their luggage in the rack overhead and made for the corridor where they wound down the window and leaned out as the train slowly pulled out.

Peter Neister felt a short gasp of pain as he said quietly to himself, "Goodbye Wiesbaden." He recalled that magical day when his father took him to admire the ducal palace and the sheer majesty of the Schlorsplatz and because his father loved church architecture they had spent an hour inside St Bonifatius church admiring its interior and despite his age he wasn't the least bit bored.

Ernst Bortfeld tried to lift his friend's mood, "Goodbye Wiesbaden, see you again." He blew a kiss but felt nothing of emotion and little sensation. There wasn't a cloud in the sky above them; in front of them lay a long train journey which would make inroads into their emotional state…

U-boat 116's crew were gradually on their way, making preparations to travel or were actually back in Hamburg though the official reunion date wasn't for another week. As befitting his rank, Kapitän Peter Werner was billeted in one of Hamburg's superior hotels whilst the crew were staying in less salubrious surroundings but they didn't care a jot for it was the government footing the bill.

Rain had returned to Hamburg with a vengeance and the commander was relieved to be back in his room having spent much of the morning sightseeing before retiring to the municipal park to read his newspaper, suck in the fresh air and admire the shapes of skeleton trees shorn of their foliage. Most visitors walked at leisurely paces depending on age and this amused Peter Werner who cut a figure of youthful elegance in his expensive looking black overcoat made of pure wool and elegantly lined.

Half an hour passed before he could feel the chill, by which time he had read the sports pages aghast at the earnings and transfer fees concerning professional footballers that two columns were devoted to. He walked purposefully towards the exit gate passing three teenage girls who looked at him with teasing and sincere eyes before huddling one another and giggling. It elicited a smile and that remained when he thought that he was entertaining his First Lieutenant that afternoon. He looked at his watch and nodded, approvingly.

CHAPTER 46

The Kapitän sent down for coffee and biscuits and within three minutes a waiter was knocking on his door. He relieved the hotel trainee of the tray and moments later he heard a brisk knock on his door. He smiled and welcomed Dieter Hoffman, "You must have been tired if you've slept right through?" he asked enquiringly.

The First Lieutenant smiled. "I've been up a couple of hours Kapitän. That bed, I've never known anything so soft."

Werner gritted his teeth, a gesture Hoffman had witnessed many times.

"Ach, mine contributes to my bad back... half way through the night I'm dreaming I'm on a rack."

Both men laughed but it was of the conservative variety.

"Anyway, Dieter, today's the day." He began pouring coffee into two cups and indicated for his officer to help himself to the biscuits.

"Yes, Kapitän."

"I would have thought your son would have been one of the first on the quayside to welcome us home." He looked at Dieter Hoffman who looked reflective when he responded.

"He was at the quay but last night he spoke on the phone to me and said he was overcome with emotion when he thought he recognised me. Funny you know." Silence entered the room and it was a warm silence. "He says as we drew up and came on deck he looked for someone who looked like he did twenty odd years ago."

Peter Werner smiled and relaxed his broad shoulders as he waited for the continuation.

"He said as soon as he clamped eyes on me, he knew. I suppose he was as confused as we are."

"You haven't seen him yet?" It was as much a statement as a question and the First Lieutenant widened his brown eyes.

"We are meeting in town tonight. I thought it would be a good idea if we met first and then, perhaps, I meet his own family."

The submariners drank their coffee and while Kapitän Werner replenished the cups he enquired, "And Marlene and the girls?"

Again Hoffman offered an eager smiling charm enhanced by a crest of luxuriant black hair which caused women to find him dashing even though he remained blissfully unaware.

"Dieter says she was there last week, his own children are very fond of her. She is a frail lady now." He paused, "Gabi is no longer with us, she died of cancer in 1961. Fortunately she never married. My other daughter married a Spaniard but Dieter says she hasn't been in touch, they haven't seen or heard of her for five, maybe six years."

Hoffman smiled to himself. "I always thought that one was independent, nay strong minded when she was tiny."

Darkness was falling from the sky, the rainfall increased and suddenly lightning lanced the air but it was minimal to what both naval officers had experienced when on duty, in the conning tower, on a filthy evening.

Werner drew the curtains before the conversation continued.

"Did you ask him if Marlene had spoken of you, since?"

The Lieutenant looked bashful, "For some reason I just skirted round the issue, Kapitän. I can't take it in that my son is nearer in age to me." He paused, "Marlene," he struggled for words, "I'm still a young man, Marlene is seventy-eight years old."

The Kapitän tapped his lips with his index finger thinking about their conversation.

"You will have to face it, Dieter, your son is a shrewd man, he has the same understanding as his father."

It was the conversation Dieter Hoffman had wanted to have, needed to have with his Commanding Officer whom he had always regarded as astute.

"Thank you, Kapitän."

Werner was quick to respond, "No, I mean it. You have been one of the mainstays of the crew, Dieter, the men recognise you, I know it. Enjoy yourself tonight. It is not a trial or an order, only if you look upon it as such. Remember your son has not seen you for over forty years. He is a mature man now. It will be good for both of you, I know it. A few drinks and I bet the roles will be what they were, despite the ages being the wrong way round."

Both officers chuckled and the Lieutenant felt as if a gnawing weight had been removed from his mind.

"Kapitän, you always seem to know what to say… I feel better."

"What time are you meeting him?"

"7pm outside the station where the taxis are parked. We shall probably go for a drink. I'm sure we will both need one."

Any brooding silences had dissipated before they might have been planted and Dieter Hoffman was now aware that his voice was expressing nothing more or less than simple pride and satisfaction in his quest.

"Then I don't know, perhaps a meal, there is so much to talk about, his family, children, home. I don't know what work he does, he may have told me last night but it's still a blur."

Werner gave his fellow officer more assurance, "He will want to know about his father, remember he grew up without one. That's not a good thing to happen to a boy."

Hoffman agreed, "You're right. He has two girls, both in their teens."

The U-boat Kapitän stood up and looked at his watch; his composure was always admirable, "If I were you, Dieter, I would go back to your room and have a nice long soak in the bath, put the radio on and listen to some music and take your time about getting ready."

Hoffman had risen to his feet while listening and was stretching his upper body arching his back a couple of times, "Yes, Kapitän, that seems like a good idea."

Both walked to the door and the last words belonged to Peter Werner offering yet more encouragement, "Dieter, don't worry, everything will be fine, trust yourself."

Then he patted him on the shoulder and Lieutenant Hoffman shouldered his way back to his own room on the floor below, like a thoroughbred. Before he left the hotel for his rendezvous he asked himself how many men would ever experience what he was about to and he felt elated.

An hour later, stood outside Hamburg railway station, that unique sense of occasion hadn't deserted him, despite the perishing cold. Hoffman (Senior) shuffled on either foot to keep himself warm while scanning everything around him, as he'd done so many times before when it was his watch.

Unknown to him, his son had spotted his father, smiled gently, then walked at a slow pace knowing in less than a minute they would be looking at each other.

The shuffling slowed to a halt when the Lieutenant realised the man approaching him was the son he had not seen for forty-six years; and he had to pinch himself that it was not some drunken dream. The embrace was un-showy but it was shot through with love and wonderment and, of course, tears of joy.

Father and son, struggling to find words, hastened to a licensed café, which was well patronised at this time of day, as the sky's awning began to usher in even more winter darkness. A bottle of Schnapps and two glasses were quickly ordered and the men entered a state of suspension – the past was done, the future postponed – all that mattered was the present and the array of photographs the submariner's son had laid out on the table.

"That was me two years ago in Spain. We stayed at a place called Malgrat. The girls loved it and Heidi thought it was marvellous that I did all the cooking."

More photos were picked up for consumption.

"That's me at the barbecue… look at those steaks."

His father could feel his heart hammering against his chest, "Son, I think I could eat one of those right now."

It was the word 'son' that vibrated through Hoffman (Junior) and now his heart hammered, though in his throat and finally his emotional barrier cracked apart like a scalded chestnut and his father comforted him; it was reminiscent of the time Dieter Hoffman climbed into his father's bed because he was frightened of the dark having woken once in the early hours. Fortunately none of the guests took much notice and within minutes the son had regained his composure.

"I know of a restaurant, highly recommended, we can go to but I'm enjoying the time here, just being with you."

"Me too, even if the drink is beginning to go to my head."

More photographs were produced.

"Here, this is Heidi and Gabi when she was eight. That's the Rhineland in the background."

The naval officer scrutinised these pictures as he'd done the rest, "She's a lovely looking girl."

Both looked at a customer who'd sat down at a table adjacent to the window; he looked a tired man, drained and dry, even of blood and Dieter Hoffman worked out that he was of similar age to what he would have been but for the extraordinary event. It only increased his impatience to hear from his son about Marlene and of course look at her photograph but he didn't want the carnival atmosphere between them to alter one iota so he bided his time. When a middle-aged man with his elderly mother walked into the café both father and son watched her being helped into a seat then looked at each other.

The son spoke, "I want you," he hesitated, "father, to stay with us for a few days, meet my family they are very excited, the girls, even if they don't quite understand."

Again he hesitated and breathed in slowly, "Tomorrow evening I will take you to see mother and leave you with her."

Utter relief flooded through the naval officer, "Thank you. I know it's difficult. It's the same for me to talk about your mother." He smiled and poured another drink, "Let us see what tomorrow brings."

The atmosphere was beginning to get rowdy as the café began filling up with the uncertain edges of the evening patrons.

"Let's not bother to eat out, let's go home. I'm sure we can find something to eat. It won't take Heidi long to cook." His words sounded like statements rather than conversational sentences and his father acquiesced.

"OK. I feel as though I could eat an elephant. It's been a long old day."

They chuckled and rose to their feet both in good spirits and firmly part of the cafe's early evening success.

"You can relax much more at home."

And with that they emptied their glasses and left. The cold air hit them and both laughed in unison and the Lieutenant, especially, felt good and mused that his Commanding Officer had been right, as he so often was.

Peter Werner was in his room seated at a table writing a letter under the gaze of a table light; he had deliberately turned the main light off for it disturbed his concentration when he settled down to read or write.

Dear Captain Shaw

We made it back home as you no doubt know!! It is over two weeks since we arrived in Hamburg. I have been to see my brother, who is recovering from a heart attack, in Munich hospital. We spent what time we could rambling on about every topic under the sun. I'm grateful that he is going to be OK. How many more years has he left is anyone's guess. Some of my crew have written to me. I have been overjoyed by those who have found something to help them in this modern world of yours! Alas, most have not been so fortunate. One described the part of East Germany he found himself in as desolate, tall giant buildings, dusty and echoing and people outside, without smiling faces. Utter despair! I don't want to go into too much detail as I know my men value their confidentiality but here is an example of what I have received. You remember Klaus Bonner – he's the one that spent an hour questioning you about the space race. He told me the subject had been a hobby of his since he was a boy. He was married and his wife was pregnant when we left St Nazaire. They lived in Dresden and their home was bombed out, his daughter didn't survive and his wife suffered terrible burns to the side of her body. She is still alive living in East Germany but Klaus found it a shattering experience when he saw her. He said he broke down and blamed himself for the life she had lived. He said she had never really recovered from the loss of their daughter and had gradually veered towards senility. I don't wish to depress you captain, but you will understand the dilemma fast approaching me. In a week's time the crew meet up again. I am at a loss...

Peter Werner rose from the table and poured himself a cold beer, having retrieved a couple of bottles from the fridge. He intended to finish the letter the following day and, having made himself comfortable in the leather armchair, thought about the English officers and the ratings who had all been unfailingly polite and hospitable and not for the first time wondered why their countries had gone to war twice in the first half of the 20th century. He cursed the ruling elite for allowing what happened to happen and the dysfunctional apathy of citizens, of which he included himself. "Duplicity," he said quietly to himself before taking a large mouthful of beer.

The rattle on his window informed the Kapitän that the wind outside had changed direction from the south and the panoramic view with colourful lighting he enjoyed over part of the city centre, suggested that retail empires were gearing up for the onslaught of Christmas; and he thought of those men whose only gift would be to endure. His scalp prickled, his brain fluttered and he felt restless so he opened another bottle of beer and dispensed, this time, with the glass. He also thought, suddenly, optimistically about his First Lieutenant.

The Hoffmans reunion was more like a get together between mother and son rather than husband and wife. They sat holding hands, smiling having looked through albums of photographs, paying particular attention to those crisp black and white images that captured their courtship and early married life. Memories were relayed like messages from the spirit world and it was obvious and not a small relief to the whole family that Dieter and Marlene Hoffman had come to terms with the extraordinary event and that there was no measuring the joy that both were alive. That, after all, was all that mattered; what tears had fallen had come from a well of happiness; and Marlene Hoffman was grace personified as naturally as a Hawk flies and as clearly as a lake reflects... This wasn't the case with Conrad Meiner.

CHAPTER 47

In his hotel room near Hamburg's main railway station, the submariner looked pensively at the registered envelope addressed to him. The handwriting was recognisable, just, and he hesitated before opening it and taking out a large single sheet. Before reading the contents he turned it over and saw the signature before whispering "Elsa".

He drank the large measure of whisky he'd poured for himself in one go and let it run into his metabolism repeating the opening line "Dear Conrad". He said it several times then poured himself a second glass. Outside the noise of traffic was sufficiently dulled by the double glazing all windows in the front rooms enjoyed. His concentration didn't waver as he laid the letter flat and pulled his chair closer to the table. He tilted his head forward and the scent touched his heart immediately.

Dear Conrad

I am filled with a mixture of joy and sadness as I settle down to write to you after all these years. Joy, that you are alive. I am overwhelmed with such joy – but sadness that we never lived our lives together. The pain of losing you all those years ago was intense but time is a great healer and I have been very fortunate in my life that I have known two very fine men. I have been married for forty years to a good man and we have both been very happy. It probably would have been the same with you, so you see why I have been lucky.

None of us can predict what will happen in our life, of course we can guess but how many really guess right? I have learnt one thing in this life, that one has to go forward somehow or one gets stuck and eventually goes under. This goes particularly when one has experienced short or lengthy traumas.

I don't want to depress you but I am a wise old woman and you are a young man with your life ahead of you.

Dear Conrad, this is advice from the heart. How has my life endured over the last half of the century – well, the world has changed as we knew it, so much advancement in science, medicine but with it has come the threat of a war too terrible to contemplate. People go hungry as they always have.

As you will see from the address, my home is in Stuttgart and my husband, though officially retired, still works on a consulting basis for an engineering firm. He is fortunate that he loves his work and this has helped him in retirement. Oh yes, I am a grandmother, my son is married with a family and all things being equal we are comfortable and contented which is more than I can say for many in the world today.

Helmut, my husband, is sometimes away at weekends which allows me time to spend with girlfriends; being apart from time to time has kept everything quite fresh over the years. I shouldn't really say this but I have wondered if he had a girlfriend somewhere but when I look at him and see how much he loves his work…

Well… you will hardly have had time to gather your feet and will want to trace your family. If you would like to see me, that is alright. Perhaps you would phone me one evening and we can talk. I haven't said anything to my husband, the circumstances surrounding our meeting and getting married so long ago, although I know in your case is so recent. Unfortunately I can neither do anything about that nor how you feel.

Probably the best time to meet once again and talk would be when Helmut is away. I know I must sound very secretive but this is the right way. Conrad, don't judge me as being harsh, we were victims of circumstances not of our own

*making. I am beginning to feel tired now and wouldn't it be
so easy to become sentimental but that would only hurt you.
I haven't forgotten everything, so I will close –*

*Affectionately,
Elsa.*

The young seaman choked back the tears but they kept
falling and he slumped into the back of the chair and stared at
the ceiling in one of those natural reflective silences all men
experience at the point of death.

However, this silence was broken by a sharp knock on his
door and when Conrad Meiner opened it he was greeted by
an older waiter, a little wizened man with a lined face, smiling
and carrying a tray of sandwiches and a pot of coffee which
the guest had forgotten he'd ordered earlier in the day. The
waiter put the tray on the table and left while the submariner
stood at the door, revealing nothing.

Hours passed and Meiner, pale faced, paced about his
room speaking to himself – choppy and disconnected
fragments, aware of a pain as sharp as a tooth, reef of rocks.
He shot lusty glances at the letter lying flat on the table. He
felt meek and the idea that he should have taken such a
disappointment more manfully was utterly irrelevant.

He couldn't remember getting undressed and climbing
into bed, an act which psychologically, might have been
prompted by the need for some sort of protection. The distant
church bell ringing as it did on the hour interrupted his
reminisces, three times after midnight…

Morning broke with a burst of sunshine before clouds
moving from the east coated Hamburg with greyness. Pockets
of rain fell during the afternoon but when the evening set in
so did the cold air travelling rapidly from Siberia and those
workers who liked a drink after work, before returning home,
were quick to shut the door of any bar they frequented.

Elsa, formerly Elsa Meiner, sat in her armchair close to the crackling coal fire, seemingly absorbed in her knitting. A pleasant sound coming from the clock on her mantelpiece registered nine o'clock. A minute later her telephone rang and she responded like a startled cat hit by a stab of panic, before calmly leaving her chair and walking over to a small table adjacent to the door on which her telephone rested. She felt a pang of anxiety when she lifted the receiver up.

"Hello," she said in a soft voice and her whole body relaxed when she recognised her caller. "Yes, Freda, three weeks today – that's right. I hope Helmut hasn't left anything to chance. You know some of his best laid plans often don't go accordingly…" she laughed again but not as energetically. "Yes, OK. Goodnight. Bye."

Another hour passed and the fire began to flag but the room was sufficiently warm enough so Elsa dispensed with the idea of putting any more coal on. When the phone rang again, the tone seemed much quieter and Elsa sighed before putting her knitting down and approaching the table in relaxed fashion.

"Hello, hello… hello… can you hear me?"

Now, she needed her courage because she suddenly realised the person at the other end of the line was the man she was in love with forty-six years ago. Instinct had told her and that same quality had also informed her, that it would have taken a ferocious effort by a brave man to make this telephone call.

"Conrad… please say something." Her voice trembled with emotion, "How are you?"

The submariner instantly recognised those three words for it had been a long-standing joke between them during their courtship and early marriage that no matter what the occasion Elsa would ask the question and now four decades later, it paralysed both of them.

High above, the wind stared down glassily from a black sky and any conversation between husband and wife would commence, firstly, in the mime of silence; and the next day would offer Conrad Meiner a cold sunrise, that hardest moment for courage in the world of fear. There would never be lies that leave scars, to tell, ever again...

CHAPTER 48

The hustle and bustle and people swarming like flies through the ticket barriers before quickening their pace to respective platforms was a feature of morning rush hour at Hamburg station. Finally, Conrad Meiner had his ticket punched and was informed, although he already knew, his train was departing from platform seven. "Thank you," was his polite response.

His train departed on time and after an hour of looking out of the window he left the carriage for the restaurant car, where he sat at an empty table and ordered a continental breakfast. He flipped through a magazine left on the seat next to his and put it away as soon as the Slavic looking waiter in a starched white jacket began pouring piping hot coffee from a silver pot, with the cup already laid on the table. Courtesies were exchanged before the submariner sipped his first hot drink of the day. Short work was made of the croissant before he finished the coffee and leaned back in his chair for a doze.

In this mild slumber he heard the crew of U-boat 116 singing some of their favourite songs followed by conversation of a comic nature about the quality of Ernst Bortfeld's cooking and then he smiled when he recalled Horst Kruger saying he couldn't play cards as he had to check the battery levels for the Chief Engine Room Artificer "for the 15th time."

He was roused by the same waiter leaving him his bill, which he promptly paid then returned to his carriage. Two ladies, both portly, were now ensconced in seats opposite each other by the sliding doors and though both read magazines there continued a steady flow of conversation about their work.

Conrad took out his wallet from his inside jacket pocket and looked at the contents – receipts, business cards before extracting a picture of Elsa and running his thumbs slowly over it. The calm was interrupted by a busy ticket collector who tore the sliding doors open and asked for tickets. He closed the door in the same brusque manner which impressed none of the three passengers in the compartment. The submariner looked out of the window and looked at his watch and repeated this drill again and again until Stuttgart approached.

Before the train came to a halt the two ladies had powdered their faces and stood up, straightening out the creases in their suits. The naval man helped lift their cases down from the rack before sitting back down for he had decided to leave after the inevitable rush to clear the platform and ticket barrier.

Eventually he strolled down the platform feeling the stiffness in his cramped body melting away in the sunshine. The air had a crisp freshness which helped relieve his apprehension.

The hissing of trains arriving and departing could be heard over passengers' conversations as could the impersonal booming voice, announcing the arrival and imminent departure of trains, through the public address system. He saw a serviceman embrace his sweetheart and he stood still reminiscing before his attention was taken by an elderly lady sitting alone on a seat outside the waiting room.

Conrad Meiner could see the warmth and serenity radiated in her smile and he knew it was Elsa. He approached, slowly, but she didn't notice him and somehow probably instinct he knew everything was going to be alright. He felt elated.

Less than fifteen yards away she stood up; her overcoat looked expensive and she smiled, "Hello Conrad." Her voice was subdued.

"Hello Elsa."

They embraced and passing commuters might have thought how touching it was to see a mother and son embrace in a public place.

The rest of the day was spent in conversation, examining the garden and doing crossword puzzles – an activity both had enjoyed over four decades earlier. Despite the age gap both still enjoyed each other's company and, as was pre-arranged, he stayed overnight and slept soundly, which surprised him.

Over breakfast the mood was slightly subdued because Conrad was leaving. Elsa wore a fetching skirt and jumper as she poured coffee; her shoes were highly polished and looked expensive.

"What time did you say the train…" she was interrupted.

"10.35am."

Elsa nodded, "I'll call a taxi for 9.50am so you should be there for ten past at the latest."

Conrad smiled, "Thank you, I don't want to be rushing to the platform trying to find a seat. It's a long journey," he smiled, "but it's been worth it."

The former lovers looked at each other and he cleared his throat.

"I would have liked to have met your husband, he seems a good man. I enjoyed looking at your photographs, last night."

Elsa picked up the threads, "Yes, Helmut is a keen photographer. To me, you just point the camera in the right direction, look through the eye hole and press the button."

Her guest took another drink of coffee, "When does Helmut get back?"

"I should receive a phone call tonight and presumably some time tomorrow. He had arranged to meet my son as he often travels for business. Sometimes they work out the schedules so they can meet up for a day or so."

Conrad looked approvingly, "That must be nice for them. Father and son should be good friends besides just flesh and blood," he paused, "agree?"

Elsa looked slightly embarrassed and responded quickly, "Yes, I suppose so," and with that she stood up and took hold of the coffee pot.

"Let me make some more coffee."

Conrad hadn't noticed the change of colour in her face, "Don't make it just for me, you are going to have some?"

"Oh yes," she said with her back to him. "I think, sometimes, I'm addicted to the stuff."

Conrad grinned, "Well, it certainly tastes good."

The clock on the kitchen wall revealed 9.20 and Elsa left the coffee percolating.

"I'll call the taxi."

Conrad leapt to his feet, "I can do that, you continue with the coffee."

"No, I'll do it, it's a family firm and they know me so there won't be any hitches. Nothing is worse than a taxi arriving late when you've a train or coach to catch, worse an aeroplane."

Conrad acquiesced and sat back down.

As Elsa made for the phone the doorbell rang.

"Conrad will you answer that for me?"

Elsa had her back to the door when Conrad opened it.

"Hello," said the middle aged man with a warm smirk. Immediately recognising the voice, Elsa put the phone back down on the receiver and turned round as Conrad Meiner introduced himself.

The men shook hands while Elsa looked perplexed, "Hello darling, I thought you were with your father?"

Her son stepped into the hallway, "I was but the office called me and asked if I could get back a day earlier as important clients from Belgium are arriving tomorrow and they want someone to look after them – do the usual public relations job about the family."

He raised his eyes upwards.

His mother looked tense, "Couldn't they have got someone else. I mean calling you back…"

Her son looked exasperated, "Mother, you're like Renata, you don't appreciate there's no sentiment in business." He turned to the submariner, "You understand?"

Both men smiled and Elsa gathered herself, "Oh, I'm sorry Conrad, this is Conrad Meiner – Conrad my son."

The latter looked at the submariner, "I recognise you from somewhere."

His mother interrupted, "Conrad is one of the submariners from U116."

"Yes, that's it," said her son.

His mother continued, "Conrad was one of the crew that I knew all those years ago."

Her son became animated, "That's amazing."

"Yes, it sure is," stated Elsa's guest.

Her son, taking off his coat, continued, "Have you been meeting your family… do you come from this area?"

"No, I don't come from Stuttgart," he said firmly, "but I wanted to visit and thought I would like the opportunity of seeing your mother again."

Elsa appeared slightly self-conscious, "Conrad stayed and we have had a laugh talking about the old times."

Her son remained intrigued, "I wish I had known, you should have told me, mother. I would have loved you to have met my family and to have entertained you."

His words sounded more than sincere, "You know you and your crew are something of heroes round these parts."

Conrad Snr deliberately appeared nonchalant, "I didn't know I was coming here myself until late – besides I wasn't sure."

Conrad Jnr was still bursting with enthusiasm, "You must come again. I would be intrigued to know what life was like in those 'stove-pipes', especially as it is still so fresh in your mind."

"Perhaps," was the former's response.

Elsa's son continued, "My father is very vague about the war. I suppose for some people they bring back memories they would rather forget."

Elsa spoke, "That is correct Conrad. Just thank yourself that you didn't live during those years."

She glanced at her guest who looked at his watch which prompted Elsa to pick up the phone again. Her son enquired what the taxi was for.

"I have a train to catch," said the submariner.

"Please, let me drive you to the station." He turned to his mother, "Mother, don't call a taxi, it's stupid."

His mother put the receiver down and her son clapped his hands together, "Ah, I can smell coffee."

"Help yourself, Conrad, it's just been percolated."

While he breezed into the kitchen Elsa and Conrad realised they had precious moments to say their goodbyes before the son undoubtedly came back into the hall. Both were lost for words, not dissimilar to when they said their goodbyes in October 1942, and for a fleeting second the wretched news of that moment spilled over into the present. Both had the same tear in their eye when her son bounded back into the hall.

"What time does your train leave?"

Composing himself, Conrad Snr replied, "10.15am." He looked at his watch, finished his coffee then opened the front door, "Shall we?"

Elsa's son appeared to have no inkling of the delicacy of the situation he had unwittingly contrived. Both men walked down the pathway and as the middle-aged man unlocked his car door, Conrad Meiner stole a moment to look back at Elsa, stood in the doorway. It was enough... The car pulled away and both men stared straight ahead. Elsa remained standing until the car was out of sight.

Having found a parking space immediately outside the station and because Elsa's son had time on his hands, he accompanied Meiner onto the platform, having purchased a ticket. Their conversation was light-hearted and mainly about the observations they made about other passengers. The sky was sheer blue and therefore uninteresting, unlike the sleek train gliding into the station alongside platform seven.

Both men walked to the top of the platform; trains were less crowded at the front because commuters seldom gathered far away from the middle of the platform having entered there.

The submariner quickly found a seat and placed his case in the roof rack above before returning to the carriage door where Conrad Jnr stood. He descended to the platform and they shook hands as a loud blast was heard from the rear of the train.

It moved and quickly picked up pace and Conrad Meiner noticed the adjacent platforms seemed to swim in a blur of faces. Elsa's son remained on the platform watching and before the train disappeared he waved then shouldered his way back to the ticket barrier and then out of the station.

He noticed a couple of pigeons resting high on the edifice being found by others, all squawking. He smiled then got into his car and leaned back in the driver's seat, deep in thought. Perhaps he had played out a charade for the benefit of his mother and father. Other submariners, too, were on the move.

CHAPTER 49

Despite the time of day, mid-afternoon, Hamburg station was almost saturated with passengers arriving and leaving. No sooner had a train slowed to a halt at platform three, the doors opened and people, seemingly, tumbled out as though they had spent their whole journey pressed up against the carriage doors.

Once the initial rush had subsided Karl Boeck, Wolf Hechler and four other crew members appeared on the platform; though they were dressed in fashionable leisure wear for the late eighties all carried with them an air of self-consciousness and all kept together in a tight unit making themselves even more conspicuous. When they approached the ticket barrier they moved into single file with sublime ease and it was this simple action which aroused the interest of other passengers who nudged one another and pointed at them. This only added to the men's discomfort.

They were relieved to get through the station and out into the hustle and bustle of the city. On the train journey they had shared their stories, their heartbreaks and their expressions had altered subtly; each had seen some reflection of their own pain in their colleagues. Within fifteen minutes they were drinking coffee in a quiet bar and talking about U116's reunion, in a private suite, later in Kapitän Werner's hotel. Fortunately all were staying in the same hotel close to their Kapitän's and within walking distance. First though was a long hot bath and change of clothes – something more formal but not uniform.

Peter Werner stood at the entrance to the suite and many saluted when they made eye contact, he shook each man's hand

and pointed to the bottles of beer, spirits and accompanying glasses on one table and a generous buffet laid out on a larger table.

U-boat 116's proud Kapitän could see a current of animal warmth flowing freely between the men as the arrivals increased. Magnificent. He also knew, shortly, that long shadows would appear. He turned over in his mind the content of some of the crushing honesty in the letters from his crew – *"she had always been romantic with brutal eyes and a magnificent body made to torment me I'm sure… now I see torment in her face and a body wracked with arthritic pain"* – *"once she was the embodiment of lavender, sensual aroma and expensive lace now unrecognisable physically, mentally"* – *"I thought I was prepared but I wasn't…"*. It took an effort of will to re-engage completely with the exact 'here and now'.

The party was distinctively divided into two groups, as was to be expected despite everyone being eager to see each crew member again. For those who found only sorrow it was a difficult occasion, but they bore no grudge towards those who eagerly talked about their family reunion. The latter were in the minority. All had turned up out of sheer loyalty to their Commanding Officer.

First Lieutenant Dieter Hoffman poured himself and a forlorn looking Hans Fiebig a large beer, knowing that the Seaman Officer's attempts to trace his family had failed. When he gave the drink he put his arm around his fellow officer's shoulder, "Here, Hans, drink this, it will help."

"Thank you," he croaked. In a louder tone he spoke and threw his shoulders back, "How was your family Dieter? What was it like to see them all again?"

Hoffman smiled, careful not to appear triumphant, "It was wonderful." He looked Hans Fiebig in the eye, "I'm sure you'll feel just the same."

He dismissed the man's maudlin expression and spoke with conviction, "Give it time, don't give up, we've only been back…" he paused deliberately, "a month, not even that. I know how you must feel perhaps…"

He was interrupted by Hans Fiebig changing the subject, "Wolfgang says the Kapitän had to be at his most persuasiveness to get the Navy to consent to U116 going out to sea again."

"Yes," Hoffman responded crisply. "She's still sea-worthy."

Fiebig smiled though this time it was with his piercing blue eyes, "Of course, she'll go for ever more. No, someone was worried that old wounds would be opened up if U116 was permitted to leave Hamburg." He sighed and then continued, "I suppose with all the fuss last time."

The First Lieutenant swallowed some more beer, "Kapitän Werner is a sentimental man."

Both officers nodded and looked about the room but their Commanding Officer wasn't there. He had retired to his room where he poured two glasses of brandy before carrying them over to the window where Gunter Kessler stood looking out at the darkening sky. He looked nervous and his Kapitän put him at ease.

"Ready then?"

Kessler braced himself, "Yes, Kapitän."

Both drank the large measures in one gulp.

"It will be alright, you'll see." As usual, Peter Werner's voice had the stamp of conviction.

Dieter Hoffman walked to the suite entrance and opened the door to let the fug of smoke out and as he did he saw the Kapitän walking along the corridor with his guest. Quickly, he announced to the men that their Kapitän was returning and conversations died down. This show of reverence Werner found slightly embarrassing, yet he looked around and smiled.

"I've brought an old friend of ours along."

Murmuring was heard until one of the crew called out, "Gunter!" then another did likewise. The crew moved en masse circling both men and jostling to shake hands with their former crew member, both men were deeply moved by this spontaneity and Peter Werner couldn't help noticing a large framed photograph of U116 and crew, taken at St Nazaire, hanging in the recess of the room's top wall.

The Kapitän took the opportunity, while the crew were around him, and announced, "I want to speak to you all, individually, during the course of the evening and before you get too drunk."

A cheer went up even from those with downcast faces at the mortal end of hope; and all the officers, despite looking bashful, joined in. That night Werner finally retired on the stroke of 12.00pm. He had much to dream about.

CHAPTER 50

The following evening Peter Werner had an audience with Father Reiz, in a small room on the hotel's first floor with two brown leather armchairs, an oak table, a standard lamp and one large radiator working at full blast filled up the room; nevertheless it was cosy. Both men looked tired.

"I cannot condone what you are going to do, Kapitän," the priest said without a sliver of judgement.

"I know that, Father."

"It goes against all God's teaching." The words were said in a sympathetic tone and Werner adjusted his upper body position.

"Then, perhaps, God and God alone will be our judge."

Father Reiz looked the other man in the eye, "God does not judge in the way that we do."

"Then what way does…"

"We fully cannot apprehend His ways but judgement is man-made. It provides us with a means of shifting our own guilt."

The Kapitän thought before responding, "I am not sure that this is the way but I don't feel any guilt. Many of the clergy talk about love. I remember being taught that love is the greatest gift we have and the way we distribute it shows our worth. Do you think it is wrong for a Kapitän to love his men?"

His question was answered immediately.

"If every man loved his fellow man like you do your crew, this world would be a harmonious place to live in."

Peter Werner spoke in a monologue, occasionally broken by a sigh and a slow headshake as though his life might have been similar to a regrettable statement of expenditure. He told Father

Reiz he seldom came up to scratch "a serial disappointer" he called himself. He asked the cleric if "God had ruined his life" for having given him, ostensibly, every advantage and set of good examples, he had tried to be good, still did but the path was thorny.

"From an early age these I was taught were virtuous and to have respect for I saw as untruthful, unkind."

The priest listened intently, as he confided in him about God imploring him not to be led into temptation then putting temptation in his way and the punishment as ever for all men, was for their own good.

"My Mother told me He loved me, but I soon worked out that He loved me too much to grant mercy." He told Father Reiz of his childhood confusion and why he'd stopped short of asking his Mother if Jesus put in a kind word for Peter Werner, the God would approve. When the cleric asked "why?" the submariner replied with an honest sincerity, he said,

"I didn't feel enough confidence in Him because he had his biggest failure with God which was to scuttle the whole crucifixion episode."

There was a pause, but it was relaxed, and Werner spoke.

"Have you spoken to your brother, Father?"

It was an obvious question and the priest answered it.

"We have spoken almost non-stop since we met. He knows my feelings but I respect his need to do what he thinks is right for him. Because we disagree doesn't make me love him less. A priest can only interpret the Lord's teaching the same as any man. Because he has ecclesiastical training does not give him impunity or infallibility. In fact he is more fallible before God because of his training. When you wrote back to Joachim and asked that I say a special mass for your crew, you didn't say whether you were a religious man or if in fact any of your crew had been christened into Catholicism. Am I wrong to offer up Mass for men who might not believe in God, my God. People will judge but not God."

Peter Werner had listened carefully, "And what of the day of reckoning Father? Doesn't God decide who is fit for His Kingdom and who is not?"

Father Reiz smiled, "That is what is assumed, wrongly, I hope. None of us can return to give the answer – this is the true rock upon which we base our faith."

The Kapitän had been impressed by the clergyman, "Father you are a caring gentleman and unassuming like no other religious person I have known. I think it is fitting that you are saying Mass for us. I've enjoyed our conversation. I think you should get some rest... in more than a few hours we shall be gone."

Outside the wind was whipping itself into a frenzy...

The previous evening Willie Schultz and Franz Overath had met in a bar to escape the same frenzy and the torrential downpour that reduced visibility to a dozen yards. Both remarked on the size of the raindrops that bounced off the pavement.

"The last time I saw these was in the conning tower which was dripping," said the Officer. He raised a chuckle, "Of course then it churned the olive green sea into white lather."

The Artificer had forced a smile but it didn't last for he had lost his mother, father and younger sister during an air raid and had confided in the bachelor, desperately holding back the tears.

It had taken the submariner from Leipzig less than a day to find out that his parents had survived the war but died from cancer two years apart in 1984 and 1986. The only other surviving Overath was an uncle, also a confirmed bachelor still living in Leipzig with whom the submariner had spent a day before revisiting his old school. Willie Schultz had feverish eyes and a hard hurting cough which died down after a few glasses of Schnapps; Franz Overath was content to stay on the beer before a taxi raced them to a recommended restaurant.

CHAPTER 51

U-boat 116's crew, in uniform, assembled in a basement room of the officers' hotel which had been converted for the celebration of Mass.

The submariners had left their hotels and met in reception at 5.00am where they enjoyed very hot, very strong coffee before descending the tradesman steps, hidden behind the hotel's cloakroom. Most shook off the cold though their eyes were rimmed with tiredness which they discounted for these men took pride in the acknowledgement they were imbued with the endurance of prize fighters. Nothing could stop them. For a couple though, caterpillars they were but as the waiting became intolerable they became butterflies gnawing at the lining of their respective stomachs; it didn't happen during the war but this was peace-time. The signal was a relief.

They filed in orderly and were greeted with the sight of a table covered with a crisp white cloth upon which a chalice, a prayer book, a hymn book and two vessels containing holy water and Eucharists. Collapsible chairs had been carried in and the room was cramped under a dim light – an environment familiar to all. The respect displayed to Father Reiz and his religious conviction was obvious despite the fact that many in the congregation had little Faith. Joachim Reiz had offered to act as server following the earlier conversation with his brother.

The service began with the priest dipping the aspergillum into the aspersory holding Holy water and sprinkling the crew with robust right arm throws.

"Lord God Almighty, Creator of all life of body and soul, we ask you to bless the water as we use it in faith, forgive our sins and save us from all illness and the power of evil. Lord, in your mercy give us living water always springing up as a fountain of salvation, free us body and soul from every danger and admit us to your preserve in purity of heart."

Droplets ran down some of the congregation's faces as Father Reiz repeated his action. Peter Werner stood in the middle of his men and when he felt a droplet on his lip he immediately moved his tongue to absorb it and it never occurred to him that might be a symbolic gesture. His officers flanked both ends on alternate rows and everyone could sense the clergyman's turmoil about the crew's impending departure.

"In the name of the Father and the Son and the Holy Ghost." The crew responded, "Amen."

The priest continued, "The grace of our Lord Jesus Christ and the love of God and the fellowship of the Holy Spirit be with you." The response was resolute, "And also with you."

The big animal of a city that was Hamburg in the 1980s was still asleep – the buildings, the factories, the trains, the houses, everything had not stirred from its slumbers, en masse. There were pockets of activity like a faulty streetlight flickering and raucous alley cats fighting over discarded take-away food. Inside the basement room solemnity had met serenity.

"My brothers, to prepare ourselves to celebrate the sacred mysteries let us call to mind our sins." The crew referred to the hastily copied sheets Father Reiz had made the previous evening.

"I confess to Almighty God that I have sinned against you in my thoughts and in my words and in what I have done and in what I have failed to do and I ask the Blessed Mary, ever virgin, angels and saints, to pray for me."

The priest again took the lead, "Lord, we have sinned against you." The crew responded, "Lord have mercy."

"Lord show us your mercy and love."

"And grant us your salvation."

"May Almighty God have mercy on us, forgive us our sins and bring us to everlasting life."

"Amen."

Silence entered the basement room after the priest had asked each man to pray.

Almost all closed their eyes and Dieter Hoffman watched those in front of him, with absorbed attention, speculating whether some had found inner peace and glad to be quit of their burden. The crew then recited the Creed. "He suffered death and was buried. On the third day He rose again in accordance with the scriptures. He ascended into Heaven and is seated at the right hand of the Father. He will come again in glory to judge the living and the dead and His Kingdom will have no end."

Outside the hotel entrance a mail van pulled up; its young lively driver emerged from the driver's seat, whistling a tune and carrying a registered letter. He approached the even younger receptionist sat behind two small computer screens.

"Good morning."

"Good morning."

Both swapped simple smiles and the receptionist's eyes went to the envelope. This prompted the postman.

"I have a registered recorded letter for Herr Fiebig."

The receptionist stretched her hand over to take possession but the letter was withdrawn.

"I will sign for that," she said.

The young man opposite her hesitated, "I am sorry but my supervisor has told me that Herr Fiebig must sign personally… it must be of the utmost importance."

Despite her youth the receptionist was quite authoritative, "Do you want me to interrupt the service?"

The postman looked vacant and she continued, "They are having Mass said especially for them in the basement."

The postman was in a quandary, he didn't want an avalanche of belligerence for which his supervisor was well-known, coming his way, "My supervisor was explicit."

The receptionist had learnt guile in her two years from the older more worldly girls.

"Look," she smiled radiantly, "leave the letter here and the receipt book and as soon as Mass is finished, the crew will have to come up through reception and I will make sure Herr Fiebig signs before handing him the letter."

He looked thoughtful and she continued.

"Then when you've finished your round, call back here and I will have the receipt book for you to collect." Her next smile relaxed the young postman.

"OK then, but be sure."

"Don't worry."

Downstairs the service was nearing Communion. Father Reiz held the chalice up.

"Let us pray to the Father in the words our Saviour gave us."

The crew responded, "Our Father who art in Heaven. Hallowed be Thy name. Thy Kingdom come. Thy will be done on earth as it is in Heaven. Give us this day our daily bread. Forgive us our trespasses as we forgive those that trespass against us. And lead us not into temptation but deliver us from evil. For Thine is the Kingdom, the Power and the Glory, for ever and ever."

Father Reiz gave communion to the men who filed up row after row before offering a final blessing, "May Almighty God bless you, the Father, the Son and the Holy Ghost."

The crew responded, "Amen."

Another silence settled on the room broken only by the Catholic priest who for the first time bent his ear towards the congregation with the air of a magistrate prepared to grant a deferential hearing, "Go in the peace of Christ."

The final order of service was the singing of 'The Lord is my Shepherd' and because U-boat 116's Kapitän sang the opening line with gusto, his crew followed suit.

In reception, the thirty year old ambitious and clean cut assistant manager arrived to relieve the receptionist, encouraging her to enjoy a break in the kitchen. She was about to instruct her senior about the earlier arrival of the post but his attention was suddenly taken by a large bombastic guest with a face full of war paint rather than make-up haranguing a skinny porter struggling with her three suitcases – a scene familiar to all hotel employees and one which required intervention with the left leg leaning forward tactfully. The assistant manager moved swiftly into role play while the receptionist looked at her watch, pondered then put the registered letter and book in a drawer with the intention of putting it in Hans Fiebig's pigeon hole when she returned. She smiled as she passed the guest with too much feminine apparatus, the porter with too little aggression and her immediate boss with far too much lugubrious charm and all to the just audible line of, "He guides me through life." She smiled, again, because 'The Lord is my Shepherd' had been her grandmother's favourite hymn. What she remained blissfully unaware of was the invisible banners of defiance and pride hung out by this choir.

Three minutes elapsed before the submariners filed out, each man shaking Father Reiz's hand and thanking him. Strangely some felt an inner peace as though they had been reborn, again, but it wasn't for discussion – what occupied them was what lay ahead in the last couple of hours of morning darkness.

In reception, the officers looked in empty pigeon holes. Seaman Officer Fiebig was accompanied by Gunter Kessler. They had stood and sat together during the service and the previous day before the official party their Kapitän had brought them together to have a private conversation as much to assuage his officer's melancholy as steady the older man's nerves. They had hit it off immediately, shared Schnapps in the Kapitän's room while he took a deliberately long bath with a magazine and a cigar for company.

Hans Fiebig was intrigued with the intervening years which his crew mate talked about as careful as he could so not to

319

invoke the maudlin and maniacal tenderness of unconfessed, uncompromising cruelty. Fiebig quickly realised the man's life had been a compendium of sentimental horror, hellish altercation and a relationship with mental torture. He also marvelled at his bravery to have endured it but said nothing too much of his own present anguish for by comparison it might seem an example of self-pity and as Peter Werner, who could occasionally be heard bawling out a verse from a submariner's song, had said quickly to his Seaman Officer on his immediate return from Munich, "Don't disbelieve in Hope."

Despite the presence of U-boat 116's crew in reception the atmosphere was bare and sober; it was the no fuss servicemen of all ranks mostly enjoyed and one which the assistant manager had the nous not to interfere with; he merely passed a general smile as he took up position behind the large reception desk.

As previously arranged the crew departed in pairs and trios and because despite the early hour, they didn't want to attract any attention, walked to different taxi ranks adjacent to the city centre hotel. Their only destination was the quayside. It was bitterly cold but already some venders had set up their stalls and Dieter Hoffman bought a large bunch of different flowers, double wrapped on his insistence and he tipped the old woman, scruffily dressed, handsomely. His co-passengers on the day were Siggi Maier the Radio Operator and Max Fromer the Planesman who was from Hamburg. In the car the First Lieutenant announced, "Flowers are for happiness." The men's smiles were subdued for they knew they were also for other occasions.

The loose arrangement had been to assemble on the quayside between 7.00am and 7.30am and as the journey was comparatively a short one it was a time for reflection. The driver of Emmerich's cab, having taken instruction, said nothing throughout the drive; he was a wistful type. Within minutes the flowers' scent was everywhere and it sat perfectly with the First Lieutenant's thoughts about the faces sat next to him and of the faces in other taxis – all the human dignity, all the courage, and endurance and loyalty that was still unspoiled and he desperately wanted to vindicate it, to preserve it.

He wasn't alone in overhauling the last, miraculous, two months; all the submariners had done that, some with insight and a few with philosophical understanding which included Kapitän Peter Werner, who at 4.00am on the morning of departures had written a final letter to Captain Shaw before snatching an hour's sleep. He talked of battering himself against the limits of his personality, of having lied to himself and God now that he sought truth from inside a "last cage I didn't ask for."

His quest for personal freedom he believed could only come at the cost that made life worthwhile, *"Absolute freedom, Captain Shaw, demands absolute courage, absolute selfishness, rare egotism."* He wrote that any man's personal freedom is limited by his ability to soar above and beyond his fears. Once again he thanked Shaw for his hospitality and enlightened conversations he'd enjoyed with him and his officers before swinging the final paragraph back to his own philosophy, *"A man alone that is the true meaning to be free, an egotist without a God who never loses the essence of his humanity?"*

His final sentence informed the British Captain that he had taken a strip of mahogany wood to a recommended carpenter in Hamburg and had asked the skilled craftsman to "plane down and then burn on an inscription into it before lightly varnishing the finished article." This he said he intended to hang in the engine room. He had signed the letter and underneath had written, using a calligraphy pen – *"Truth is the secret of eloquence and of virtue; the basis of moral authority; it is the highest summit of art and life."*

AMIEL

When the British Captain received the registered, express delivery letter two days later he instinctively knew and summoned his Commander to inform the officers that he wanted them in full dress, in the mess that evening at 7.00pm sharp. And when they had arrived, each man with a large measure of Schnapps in ultra-polished glasses, listened to their Skipper pronounce a toast, "To Kapitän Werner and his crew who have dipped soundlessly beneath the sea and touched the bottom countless fathoms below."

The officers drank as one and then sat down waiting for their Commanding Officer to address them...

CHAPTER 52

The quayside at such an early hour had a haunting elegance and the rhythmic footsteps of the crew was dramatic as led by their officers they approached officials who were acting as 'guardians' of U116. Peter Werner was escorted into an office and he saw a stern looking man with a square jaw and he immediately thought he might be submarine material; that was until he heard his voice (slightly high-pitched).

"Kapitän Werner, it is a sentimental occasion for you and your men."

Werner smiled and it melted the cold atmosphere in the room.

"This must have been like it was during the war. Slipping out under cover of darkness, going in search of the enemy?"

Again Werner smiled and the second official, also dressed in a black cumbersome overcoat, caught the Kapitän's eye.

"Kapitän I've heard it said that the Atlantic was seen as a chessboard upon which a harsh but noble game was played to the very end?"

For the third time Werner smiled for he knew neither man would ever experience the smell of death that was the price of sea power, often a squalid currency.

He remained nonchalant when he spoke, "Has everything I requested been…?"

He was interrupted by the first official who looked disappointed, as though he hoped the U-boat Skipper might have responded to their questions, with gung-ho propaganda about both enemies slugging away at each other and extracting maximum enjoyment.

"Everything Kapitän… even the press has been kept in the dark so no one, apart from yourselves and the Minister know of the voyage. Perhaps it's just as swell, most of the people don't understand sentiment, eh Kapitän?" He desperately wanted approbation and Werner obliged him.

"You're probably right," he said with his fourth and final smile.

The second official asked a question, "Kapitän, you will be back tomorrow or…"

He was interrupted, politely, "We have not plotted our course, that will be done once we are outside the sea straits."

The formalities were almost over and Werner felt he was signing for the keys to some flat. Once again the senior official spoke, "But when will you be back? You know the press will get wind, obviously with the submarine gone, and will be looking for a story. You know the sort of thing?"

Now it was the junior official's turn, "Some of them are like leeches these days, but never mind, enjoy yourself Kapitän and your crew."

Werner nodded.

"It will be a sad day when that old tub returns for scrapping."

The Kapitän remained cordial even though he felt he was being pecked to death by a couple of birds and his final remark flew over the heads of both officials, maybe because it was said in a quiet tone, "Yes, that would be sad."

The three men emerged from the office where the submariners immediately stood to attention, surprising the officials. There was no necessity for further pleasantries and U-boat 116's crew walked purposely, as a unit, to the two transport motorboats manned by a quartet of dockworkers waiting to carry them. For Gunter Kessler, especially, this was an electrically charged occasion and he wasn't sure if he would survive, his knees buckling, nevertheless he braced himself not dissimilar to the stance some convicts standing on the scaffold adopt.

Peter Werner looked across at U116 and then at his crew and everyone could see the wicked glint in his eyes, "Shall we take her out?" he asked boldly and nearly all the crew were unanimous.

"Yes, Kapitän."

He looked back in the direction of the office and because no light was on, he assumed the officials had departed, and heavy wisps of fog he knew would have prevented anyone left from having a clear picture of the men.

Without instruction the majority moved back allowing the Commander of U-boat 116 to look at Krantz, Uve, Horst, Conrad Meiner, Dieter Hoffman and three others who had decided not to make this patrol, move to the front; everyone had respected everyone's decision without rancorous question or a modicum of dissent and now for the final time the full complement of this submarine stood together – a composition of tenderness and almost forgotten confidence. All were of the same stamp: Seamen first, decent human beings second.

Kapitän Werner looked at his watch in a swift movement before his First Lieutenant gave him the flowers; tears tried to swim in both men's eyes; and they remained resolute in a reflective silence until the Kapitän broke it.

"Good luck, Dieter, I hope you find lasting happiness."

The response was low key, "I will never forget you."

Werner looked at those stood around the officer, "I will never forget you, any of you."

Uve Stührmann choked back his tears, "Kapitän, we will make something of ourselves, I promise you. We shall preserve the memory of our tub and her family forever."

His response was barely audible, "Thank you… thank you."

All the submariners stubbed out their cigarettes and they climbed into the motor launches having shook hands with those who would remain. Hans Feibig gave his fellow officer a badge off his jacket and Hoffman received it without saying anything.

Suddenly the engines turned over and foam bubbles rose up from under the propeller and then they were gone, watched by the square shouldered submariners, motionless, on the quay. In the distance a church bell broke the blot of silence with a very brief solemn toll, ushering in what was already a difficult day. This was followed by thunder breaking and a sprinkle of raindrops fell, then some more and finally a deluge. The submariners remained still.

Slowly, U116 glided out of Hamburg's port. Alone in the conning tower, Kapitän Werner could still see some of his crew standing as the mist momentarily cleared. "Farewell," and he saluted hoping they would see this. They did and in unison returned the salute until the submarine was lost into the mist. Even though she had disappeared they remained rooted to the spot and Dieter Hoffman permitted a warm smile to descend over his face as he watched a couple of seagulls fly overhead, chirping.

CHAPTER 53

Hans Fiebig was in charge in the control room and the crew looked relaxed, back in familiar surroundings. Gunther Kessler found his Kapitän in the conning tower and they spoke freely. The Kapitän revealed that 'upstairs' the distillation of fear: the twitching of shoulders, the facial expression, the shining sweat on the brow, the movement of feet and hands could be detected. His revelation surprised the old man.

"But, Kapitän, you never showed any fear that was why the men admired you so much."

Werner smiled, "I stored it up until I climbed into the conning tower then it could be manifested, released into the sea." He spoke in a dry strained voice, "It was about duty, Gunter."

Both men smiled and turned instinctively to the black expanse of water washing and swirling over the deck.

"I finally feel at home Kapitän," said Kessler with a smile and seemingly shedding forty years in saying it. Then his smile turned into a cheerful grin and Peter Werner joined in.

In the afternoon U116 carried out manoeuvres to everyone's satisfaction and that evening the crew dined like kings and drank quality wine and because the Atlantic was exceptionally calm the Kapitän allowed his men on deck to smoke their Havana cigars and sing the songs to the accompaniment of their repaired, renovated accordion which had been included in the submarine's inventory following delivery to St Nazaire.

The three officers roared their delight when Ernst Bortfeld danced a jig with Max Frommer especially when the Cook, obviously intoxicated, nearly spilled off the deck into the ocean

327

taking the Planesman with him. A show of hands quickly revealed the intention to throw the Cook overboard and the biggest roar of the night happened when the Kapitän suggested that the world was a better place when democracy reigned. For a few seconds Ernst Bortfeld looked distinctly worried!

The watch was set for the night and the crew slept peacefully, intoxicated as much by the North Sea air as anything else. At 8.00am breakfast was served, a hearty affair with copious amounts of fresh coffee devoured. Not one single submariner shaved.

In his quarters the Kapitän and his Seaman Officer plotted a new course, different to that they had submitted to their government who expected them to return before midnight on their second day at sea.

Throughout the submarine there was a cheerful buzz of conversation as each submariner applied himself to each task as U116 moved further into the vastness of the sea.

Lunch was an orderly affair and an hour later Kapitän Peter Werner summoned the crew to the control room; though not everyone could fit in, he stood on a box so his words could be heard by everyone. In the dim light he appeared physically larger and what he told the crew was unrehearsed for he'd always possessed that canny knack of knowing what and more important what not to say on a particular occasion and today was no different. He wanted the engines left running because it provided an essential backdrop to what he had to say. The acrid fumes now beginning to build up slowly in U116 had the feeling and quality of war which the men immediately recognised.

The crew looked optimistic as their Commander thanked them for all the sterling service and especially loyalty to him. He talked of servicemen and medals being out of favour in this part of the 20th century and told them this was the moment they could abandon the mystery that had befallen them and caused so many to stumble into an abyss.

He confirmed what they all knew. Just before complete darkness descended he would be with the Chief Engine Room Artificer and those crew already assigned, "Then we will dive." His words were strong and he felt the comforting elation in his crew. He paused and smiled, "U-boat 116 will, forever, be on patrol."

A raucous cheer and stamping of feet reverberated throughout the submarine, and it lasted seven minutes… Now he sought one final time, alone in the conning tower, while his crew enjoyed a session holding glasses spilling over with Schnapps accompanied by favourite songs and all insisted "our revered Cook" lead the choir. The word scuttle had meticulously been avoided in conversation just as the word death is never mentioned when family finally gather round the bed of an elderly matriarch and wait…

Kapitän Peter Werner stood rigid, marvelling at the sight he'd so often seen before for each time was special, individual and he relished every second. His face was neither solemn nor blasphemous; not for him a Judas Iscariot character stealing somebody's identity, post betrayal. The treasures of the Ocean was all he wanted and he thought of his mother and he felt contented and then he went below.

The submariners who'd returned to their respective hotels from the port went to bed to replenish their spirits. They dined as a group that evening, as their Commanding Officer had asked them to do, in the knowledge that all the submariners' complement would be eating at the same time. Peter Werner had insisted that no melancholy should prevail only the "absurd for there were many and happy occasions, were recalled."

Dieter Hoffman had instructed, during the course of the evening, that they were to gather in his room "in full uniform, meticulous" mid-afternoon the following day to drink their final toast and "pay our respects to our shipmates knowing they are on patrol."

Alone in his room that night he took the registered letter he'd signed for on behalf of Hans Fiebig and put the official signing-in book back on reception; he'd only returned it before booking a taxi for an established restaurant in the city centre. He agonised before opening it for he felt raw because he knew once U-boat 116 was out in the open sea his Kapitän, Peter Werner, despite orders to the contrary would never break radio silence. Never.

The First Lieutenant began pulling at the envelope but couldn't bring himself to do it, so put it back under his pillow.

Before the men arrived he tried to open it again but needed a tranquiliser size measure of Schnapps before doing so. He looked at his watch; he knew Conrad Meiner would be the most punctual and soon a bold knock on his door would be heard in fifteen minutes.

Outside the sky which had been gloriously blue all day was losing its lustre as the winter sun began to slide down the back of Hamburg's tallest buildings, its vivid red was reminiscent of an open sore, weeping copiously.

Dieter Hoffman opened completely the envelope flap, took out the letter, read it and then read it again. Then he heard a knock on the door and fumbled the letter into his uniform pocket.

"Ready to proceed Kapitän." Tension was binding them all in the engine room as U-boat 116 began its dive; a sliding movement that was felt by everyone who knew what the next sound would be. The final words belonged to the Chief Engine Room Artificer Friedrich Schreiber, as professional as ever, "Nothing to report, Kapitän."

Above the waves, the only sound was a bleak mourning wind, offering a whole realm of death.

The End

HISTORICAL FACTS

German submarine U-116 was a U-boat of Nazi Germany's Kriegsmarine during World War II. On her fourth patrol, she sailed under the command of Wilhelm Grimme. Leaving Lorient on 22nd September 1942, she sent her last radio message on 6th October whilst in the North Atlantic at position 45°00′N 31°30′W, and was never heard from again. 56 men were lost with her.

BY THE SAME AUTHOR

The Bridge – ISBN 978-1-85858-486-7
For the Glory of Stevenson – ISBN 978-1-85858-496-6
A Village Tale – ISBN 978-1-85858-535-2
9/12 Another Day – ISBN 978-1-85858-550-5

All available to purchase from www.brewinbooks.com